VENOM REEF

WILD CRIMES MYSTERIES
BOOK TWO

BELINDA POLLARD

SMALL BLUE DOG
PUBLISHING

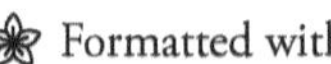 Formatted with Vellum

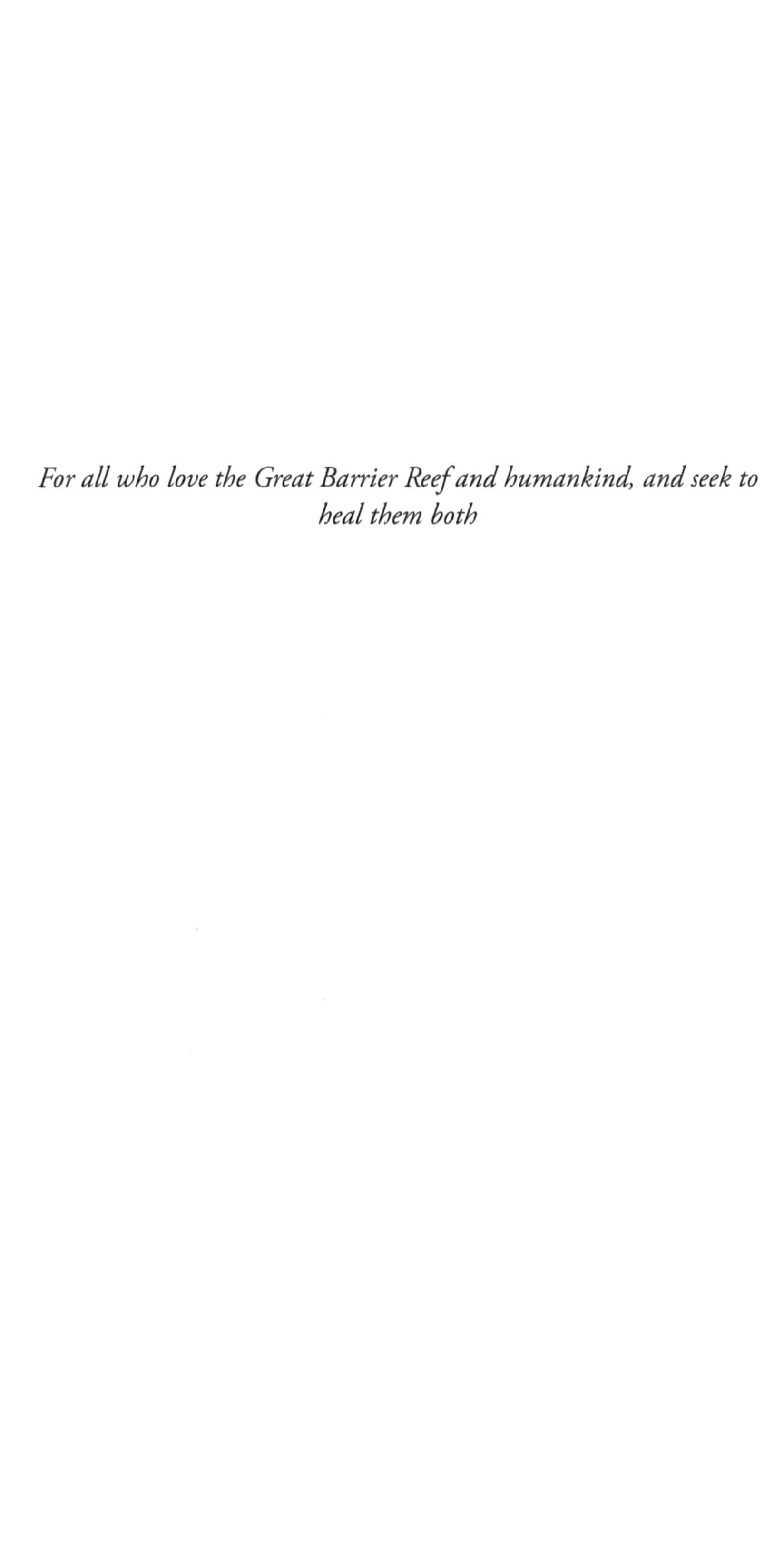

For all who love the Great Barrier Reef and humankind, and seek to heal them both

AUTHOR'S NOTE

Welcome to a book by an Australian author! Some of the spelling and punctuation may be unfamiliar but is nevertheless correct. Keep your eyes peeled for uniquely Australian terms, and some others that are relevant to coral reefs—here's a taster.

BOMMIE. A submerged coral outcrop, often rising in a column.

CHIPS. In Australia, this typically refers to deep-fried white potato. Packaged chips are thin and crunchy, sometimes known as crisps. Hot chips are similar to French fries but usually thicker.

CYCLONE. A huge rotating tropical storm, known as a hurricane or typhoon in other parts of the world, which begins at sea and usually loses power once it crosses the coastline. Category 5 is the strongest on the scale. The largest to date in Queensland was Severe Tropical Cyclone Yasi in 2011. The core was 500 kilometres (310 miles) across, its associated activity stretched more than 2,000 kilometres (1200 miles), and it endured for well over a week.

DAGGY (adjective), DAG (noun). Australian slang for something or someone unfashionable or uncool. Can be insulting or affectionate in tone.

LOLLY, LOLLIES. Australian term for a piece of candy, a sweet, confectionery. Not to be confused with the British usage where it is usually an iced treat or money.

THE NUTBUSH. A line dance to Tina Turner's *Nutbush City Limits* that has become a long-running tradition in Australia. The world record at the time of writing is 5,838 people doing the Nutbush on the red plains at the edge of the Simpson Desert. Inexplicable, yet fun.

SOOK (noun, rhymes with look), SOOKY (adjective). Australian slang for a cry-baby, usually insulting, sometimes self-deprecating.

SUB JUDICE. Before a judge or court of law. Once someone is charged with a crime, journalists cannot report details that might prejudice a trial.

WHINGE, WHINGING, WHINGER. British and Australian slang for complaining. Usually insulting.

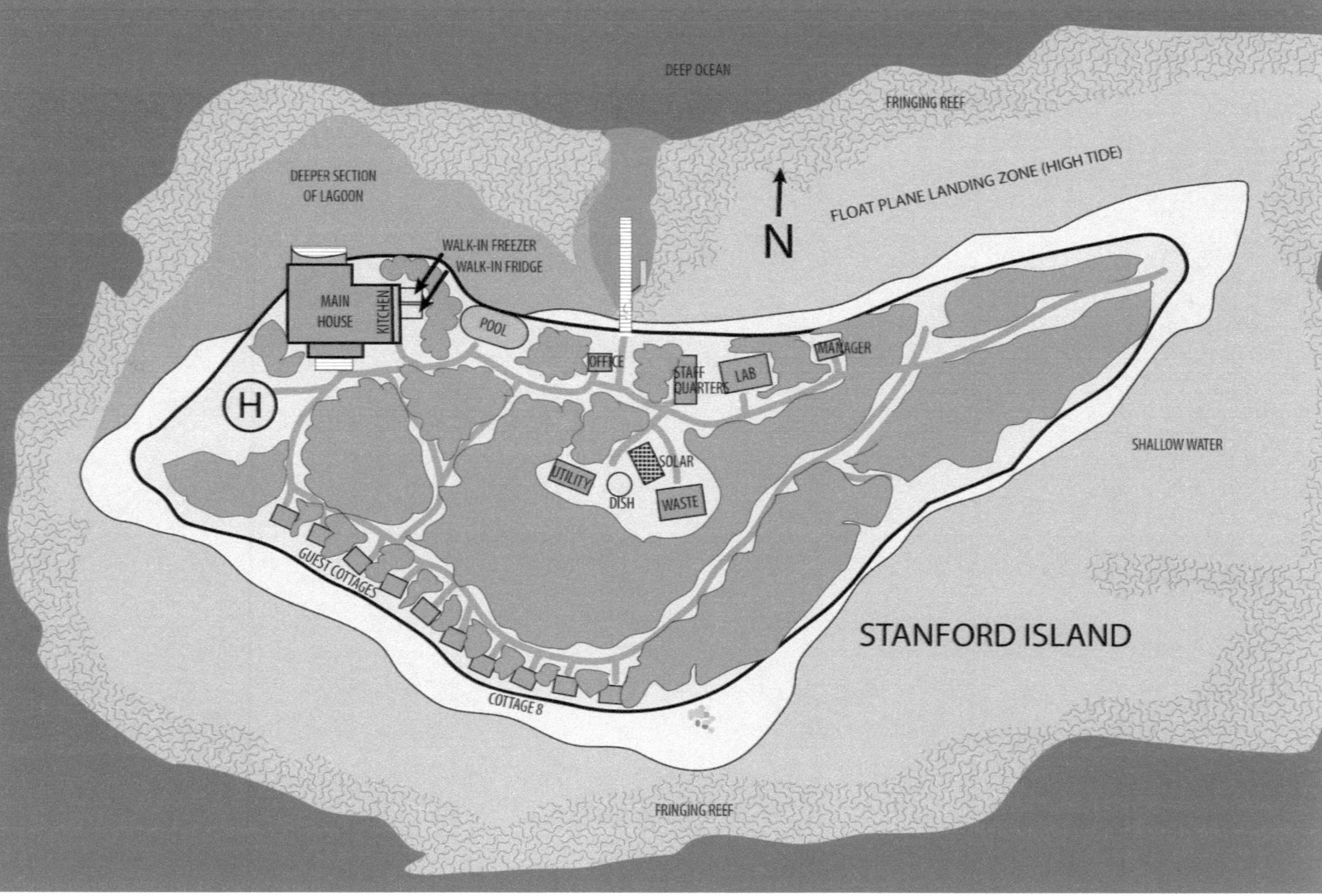

DEEP OCEAN
FRINGING REEF
FLOAT PLANE LANDING ZONE (HIGH TIDE)
N
SHALLOW WATER
STANFORD ISLAND
MANAGER
LAB
STAFF QUARTERS
OFFICE
SOLAR
DISH
WASTE
UTILITY
DEEPER SECTION OF LAGOON
WALK-IN FREEZER
WALK-IN FRIDGE
POOL
KITCHEN
MAIN HOUSE
H
GUEST COTTAGES
COTTAGE 8
FRINGING REEF

1

A glimmer of silent moonlight followed a dinghy into the lagoon of a tiny island ninety kilometres off the Australian coast. The two rowers wore dark wetsuits despite the fragrant warmth of the tropical night. One stifled a gasp as a large plastic tub full of water—and something else—shifted.

A long, tall jetty speared into the belly of the island. They eased their vessel beneath its timber decking and hooked a rope firmly to a pylon. Then they waited and watched. Apart from the soft glow of a solar-powered security light at the head of the jetty, not a single artificial light was visible. After midnight, guests and staff of this opulent eco-resort should be tucked up beneath crisp white sheets, but they had to be sure.

The birds were not asleep—they never seemed to sleep. The cries of thousands upon thousands of flapping, whistling, chattering, shrieking, moaning birds fluttered across the lagoon.

Its own personal, protective coral reef encircled Stanford Island. Beyond that, a satin sea rose and fell as subtly as the chest of a sleeping child. Sixty kilometres to the nearest substantial settlement on Eden Island, and twenty to the edge of the continental shelf. The ocean appeared empty—until one looked closer and realised the horizon was not entirely flat.

The waxing moon had pulled the tide to the other side of the Pacific, causing reef after reef after reef to break the surface. Three thousand individual reefs covering two thousand kilometres, forming one of the seven wonders of the natural world, sailing like a massive armada all the way to the tip of Queensland.

"Okay," murmured one of the rowers. They braced themselves, gripped the plastic tub, wrestled its shifting weight, lowered it till it balanced on the lagoon surface.

"Go," whispered the other and carefully, carefully they tilted until it spilled, wobbled, and emptied.

They waited and watched again then rowed back out—oars hissing in well-oiled rowlocks—along a channel blasted decades ago through a vibrant coral civilisation. They rowed onwards into the deep dark—probably being over-cautious but determined to resist starting the outboard until the island was no more than a smudge against the horizon.

The rowers finally shipped their oars and the taller one reached for the engine. A stingray rose toward them from the depths then swooped away with a shiver of its barbed tail.

———

Ninety kilometres to the west, in a budget motel in a small coastal town, television journalist Callie Brown lay sprawled in a not-dark-enough room, scrolling on her phone, fighting not to be swallowed whole by the aging mattress. She had cast aside the sweaty microfibre sheets hours ago and propped her lumpy pillow against a seventies-style exposed-brick wall behind her, hoping the particularly gaudy art print of seashells wouldn't fall on her head in the night.

She should be sleeping, not reading a wildly uncivil social-media debate about whether it was dangerous to wear socks to bed. Started by someone in the northern hemisphere, clearly; February in North Queensland did not evoke thoughts of bedsocks.

She peeled another errant strand of long red hair from her

clammy neck and shoved it among the tangled knot on her pillow. In Sydney this morning she'd laboriously blow-dried her crowning glory silky-straight. A few short hours in the tropics and it looked like she was wearing an orange sheep on her head.

She'd been trying too hard as usual, even putting on makeup before she boarded the plane to meet Jack though he never seemed to notice cosmetics and always just looked her straight in the eye.

Jack the Unkisser. Not very tall, not very good looking, not very anything, and yet somehow stuck in her soul like a splinter.

She'd been hoping a week together on a desert island would bring progress to their confusing long-distance relationship, or at least clarity.

He'd landed from Brisbane an hour ahead of her and had been waiting, hands in the pockets of his chinos, when she stepped into the shed that passed for a regional Arrivals lounge. He'd grinned the moment he saw her, eyes alight with unmistakeable delight… but then given her a brief platonic hug. As recently as Christmas, something rather wonderful seemed to be happening. Where had it gone? It wasn't like Jack to be subtle—why hadn't he told her what was wrong?

And… why couldn't she just ask.

She sighed and dumped her phone on the bedside table. Yellow security light poured through an inadequate blind from the walkway outside, creating leaping shadows in partnership with a wobbly ceiling fan that mostly just rearranged the humidity. Its loud syncopated clicking was irritatingly out of time with the rattling wheeze of an elderly window-box air-conditioner currently delivering a chill draft to her left foot but achieving little else.

Only a very charitable person would describe any of this as "white noise" but it did slightly mask the raucous hotel across the road. What sort of pub discoed into the small hours on a Sunday night? Didn't anyone work in this town?

They'd dined there earlier, she and Jack—darting across the highway in the dusk (definitely not holding hands) to eat chicken parmigiana with beer-battered chips while their conversational elephant stood embarrassed in the corner and Callie drank her house chardonnay and Jack his lemon squash.

Work-talk had saved the day. A little light planning for Stanford Island, waiting for them out there on the Great Barrier Reef all remote and exclusive and alluring. Jack had outlined the extraordinary medical research taking place there, using compounds developed from nature. They'd discussed which scientists they might interview first. The types of overlay vision they'd record. The practicalities of beginning to pull together a rough script for this, their second documentary together.

If the website told the truth it was a fabulous island, abounding in wildlife and glorious views, nestled in a coral-fringed lagoon the colour of window cleaner, and tastefully and sparsely populated by rich tourists in floaty white clothes. Jack had made all the arrangements and warned her they'd be sleeping not in the luxurious beachfront guest cottages but in simple dorms with the staff.

Dorms were okay, all things considered. Less complicated.

In three hours, her alarm would detonate and she would absolutely have to get up. The floatplane could only land on the island's lagoon at high tide—6.00 am. They must be at the airport by four-thirty.

Headlights swept across her room as yet another semi-trailer thundered by outside, and then over the clamour of her not-cooling appliances Callie caught a distinctive synthesiser wail from the pub. Surely that was *Nutbush*? Could the traditional Australian line dance be the last one of the night? Please?

Voices shouted "Nutbush city limits" again and again, punctuated by screams and whoops, culminating in thunderous applause and the stamping of feet, and then… blessed silence.

Well, except for the air-conditioner and the fan. And another truck.

Callie sighed—a long slow exhale—and resolutely closed her eyes.

Jack Metcalf stood in front of Room 5, took a deep breath, and delivered three quick raps on the door. Not too loud, though; people were sleeping.

The door swung open almost immediately and there stood Callie, tall and magnificent.

Her eyes looked a little strained, probably tired, but he grinned like an idiot as usual. "Taxi's here."

The eastern sky was turning navy blue behind the pub over the road as they climbed into the back of a stale-smelling sedan. While Jack was still pulling his door closed the driver took off, accelerating over the lumpy driveway. The taxi pulled out onto the highway with a squeal of tyres, across the path of a lumbering road train that flashed its headlights.

Jack eased his foot off an imaginary brake pedal under his right foot. "How'd you sleep?"

"Sleep no more," she intoned, "the pub hath murdered sleep."

"What?"

"Please tell me you heard the disco."

"Oh. Maybe? But not after I went to sleep."

He hadn't meant it to be sarcastic but she rolled her eyes and leaned forward to address the speeding driver. "Anywhere open for a coffee at this hour?"

The man grumbled, "Yer not in Sydney, love."

They didn't really have time, but a caffeinated Callie was better than the alternative so Jack said, "What about that roadhouse?" as they flew past a frankly unmissable 24-hour service station lit up in glaring neon. The driver huffed and pulled over abruptly to do a U-turn, getting headlight flashes from another road train.

Only a couple more near-death experiences and the taxi was zooming past two refuelling semi-trailers towards the service centre door while Callie murmured somewhat cryptically, "Oh good. More trucks."

Seven long minutes later according to Jack's diver's watch they were back on the road, Callie's nose wrinkling as she sipped from a takeaway cup.

"Not much good?" Jack asked. He had risen early enough to have a perfectly adequate free cup of tea in his room before they left the motel.

She cut him a sideways glance. "Yer not in Sydney, love."

She drank it anyway and it must have helped because she looked markedly less haggard twenty-five minutes later when a grinning pilot, having weighed them and all their gear, was handing her into the front passenger seat of a tiny single-engine amphibious float-plane. The man seemed content to let Jack find his way into the back seat unassisted.

Their luggage was jammed into a compartment behind Jack. His digital SLR rested on his lap, ready for action. Tough camera in his pocket. The window beside him was small and not exactly clear, and the wing would block part of the view, but he'd give it a go. The plane lifted steeply into a cloudless sky—now lightening through shades of royal blue towards cobalt—as rectangular fields in dimly-visible browns and greens unfolded beneath them. They banked east and there was the ocean, ruffled silver, spilling all the way to a horizon beginning to gleam pale yellow.

Jack recorded some footage of Callie and the pilot laughing and chatting together, silhouetted against the dawn sky through the windscreen. Not enough light yet to capture the broad and endless chain of reefs erupting from deep ocean beneath them, so he concentrated on atmospheric shots. A shame high tide was so early today, or he could have asked for some flyovers of various reefs.

As they descended towards the tiny dark blob that was Stanford Island, a round golden sun popped up straight ahead. Jack stuck his tough cam in the head strap for this, so he could get the wide angle view. As they hit the glassy surface of the lagoon, water sprayed up either side and Callie glanced back at him over her shoulder, her face luminous with delight.

Callie stepped out onto the float and grabbed a strut as the plane wobbled. "Um," she said, but no one was listening.

She'd expected they'd tie up at a floating dock or something, not just park a couple of metres off the beach and toss an anchor out.

The pilot was occupied carting some of their luggage ashore and Jack, also laden with various things, was wading right behind him. In reef shoes. Always prepared, Jack. But not apparently prepared enough to have warned her to wear hers—which were in her duffle bag on Jack's shoulder.

It looked sandy here. Maybe she could just go barefoot. Then again, not a good idea to cut her foot this early in the trip.

She frowned at her new sandals, hitched up the skirt of her sarong, and plunged in.

"You've arrived." A tanned and compact brunette was approaching Jack, arms wide. She wore a figure-hugging resort uniform of turquoise polo shirt and white shorts.

"Laura!" said Jack, and placed his gear on the sand in time to enfold the woman in a bear hug.

As they moved apart, Laura said, "Welcome to my place," still holding onto him and making thorough eye contact.

He grinned while returning the eye contact with interest, and thanked her before half-turning to indicate Callie. "My colleague," he said.

Callie's foot snagged on the hem of her sarong but she caught herself with only a slight lurch, smiled serenely and extended a hand to the glowing athlete before her. "Callie Brown."

"Laura Jensen." The woman's smile had apparently undergone refrigeration since she'd received it back from Jack.

"Laura is the deputy manager here," Jack said, looking pleased with himself. "And a marine biologist. She gave us the tip about this story and she'll be helping us this week."

"Come. I've a trolley for your gear." Laura scooped up one of their bags in one hand, hooked the other through Jack's elbow, and turned towards a path through the trees.

Ten minutes later, they stood outside a compact timber building on the other side of the island as Laura unlocked the door.

"Is this…?" Jack said. "This doesn't look like a dorm…"

"Surprise!" Laura popped up on her toes in a funny little bob. "We had a cancellation." She helped carry their gear inside then checked her watch and pressed her hands together in front of her chest, elbows out, like a cartoon princess. "Things to do. I'll see you in the main house for breakfast in half an hour." She flashed a bright smile and dashed off.

There were two bedrooms and Jack offered Callie first choice. She shrugged, went into the left-hand one and threw her bag on the bed. Thirty seconds later she was tossing the empty bag on the floor, having stuffed its contents into one big drawer. Usually, she didn't bother to unpack at all when she was on location—just rummaged for things as she needed them. But that was with a big suitcase that opened wide; this was an awkward duffle bag squashy enough to fit better into a tiny plane. And they'd be here a whole week. It was worth unpacking for a whole week.

She grabbed a notebook and pen and her skin cancer forcefield: wide-brimmed sunhat and loose, long-sleeved overshirt. Jack was still thumping and bumping next door, probably arranging his clothes alphabetically.

Callie explored what would be their home for the next seven days. Along one wall stood two cheap desks with office chairs, no doubt moved here specially for them. An elegant teak cabinet concealed a bar fridge and tea and coffee station—with chocolates! A shared bathroom opened off the tiled entryway at the front door.

No television. Not that kind of island, clearly. She was slightly surprised to see a wall clock nestling among an arrangement of pale, abstract paintings, since people surely came here to *avoid* clock-watching? But then, they probably wanted to know when to eat. And it was a very calm and subtle timepiece, an off-white timber disc almost disappearing into the off-white wall, whispering the hours via pale blue markings.

The simple but expensive furniture and fittings were all in muted neutrals—soft browns and off-whites—with occasional touches of pale blue in a cushion or drink coaster.

The decor formed an understated frame for the work of art outside, allowing the stunning lagoon to take the spotlight, its crystal water various shades of aqua under an electric-blue sky. It looked shallow out front, so that she would probably be able to wade out to the natural coral barrier that contained it. To the left, the...

south? the lagoon narrowed toward a small rocky prominence. To the right, north-west-ish, the colour intensified as the water deepened, passing other beachfront cottages hiding in the trees, and curving towards the highest point of the island where they'd been told something called the Main House awaited. Somewhere out there beyond the flat western horizon was the mainland they'd just come from.

A huge sliding-glass door notionally separated the indoors from the floorboards of the covered verandah, but no doubt it would be open all week. On an island so remote and with such a small population, crime was surely not a risk.

Callie ambled onto the verandah, dropped into a teak outdoor armchair and removed her wet sandals. She stood, put on her sun protection, and wriggled her bare toes on the smooth timber.

She glanced inside. The clock hinted discreetly that it was nearly seven o'clock. On a Monday morning. She should be running late for work right now—but the salt and vinegar of Sydney newsroom politics was two thousand glorious kilometres away.

And that's when the screaming started.

2

Callie turned right, towards the noise. Kids skylarking? No, too throaty. She launched off the verandah and ran, journalist-instincts firing. A shark? The scream kept coming so she kept running along the sandy curve of the beach, wanting to help, wanting to know.

She rounded a cluster of palm trees and the main house came into view up on a promontory. On the beach below it, a young woman in a hot-pink bikini was staggering out of the water, snorkel and goggles askew. She pulled at her thigh and screamed, high-pitched but hoarse. Lime green flippers confounded every stumbling step.

She slumped to the hot sand just as Callie reached her. "What's wrong? What happened?" No visible bleeding. A spiderweb of pinky-brown welts was rising on the girl's leg, curling over one hip, becoming more prominent even as Callie watched. Something adhered to the woman's skin—pale and textured, like translucent fettuccine. A stinging seaweed, maybe?

Callie knelt awkwardly, puffing from exertion and adrenalin, and was reaching to pull the tendrils away just as Jack arrived and yelled, "No!" He slapped her hand away, hard, their wrist bones connecting like bricks. She gasped in pain and shot him a glare but he was now looking at Laura, coming towards them at a full run, a large plastic bottle of clear fluid in her hand.

Laura uncapped the bottle—cheap vinegar with a plain black and white label—and poured it over the woman's injuries. She said, "Hold her down, Jack."

Pounding footsteps and a spray of sand. A harsh, deep voice: "I called the rescue helicopter." Callie squinted up into piercing sun for an impression of straggling blond hair and those wraparound reflector sunglasses that look like a fly.

Laura said, "Thanks, Baz. Stick around in case she needs CPR—we can tag-team." And then to Jack, "Don't let her rub the tentacles. Releases more venom."

"Tentacles?" Callie had to raise her voice over the eternal screaming.

"Box jellyfish." Laura shook her head. "Don't ask me what it's doing ninety kilometres offshore."

Callie's eyes widened at Jack, who glanced at her and half-shrugged.

She had specifically asked him: would it be safe to swim at this time of year. "Stingers don't inhabit the outer reef," he'd said in his deep, trust-me voice. "They breed in rivers on the mainland," he'd said. "These scientists travel for hours just to get new specimens," he'd said.

She'd been looking forward to her very first box jellyfish in the flesh—but later, in the lab. The slow-motion murder unfolding in front of her was a childhood ghost story come to life. Growing up in the south of the state, safely distant from the creatures' normal range, the stories had been thrilling.

This was not thrilling.

Laura flicked tentacles off with a fingernail as the vinegar washed them loose. She gasped as her fingertip made accidental contact, shook her hand violently, poured vinegar over the finger, then continued her task, puffing a little, her eyes watering.

The welts were turning red. The woman's breath now came in ragged gasps between screams.

A wooden deck extended over the lagoon along one edge of the main house, and several staff prowled along it. One held a long-handled fishing net and a bucket.

A man emerged from the sea. He cast off flippers, snorkel and goggles in a trail behind him as he ran towards them.

Not another one! Callie thought.

"Honey! What happened? Honey?" A particularly shiny gold band glinted on one finger.

The screaming stopped. Callie exhaled in relief, then realised the eyelids that had been fluttering in agony had stilled, half-open. She time-travelled to a snowy New Zealand mountain when an old friend's eyes had looked almost exactly like that.

Laura felt under the girl's chin. "I can't find a pulse. Jack, you do compressions."

Within moments they had positioned themselves and begun. Laura blew air into the young woman's silent lungs and Jack compressed, one hand atop the other, fingers interlocked, the heel of the lower hand landing on the woman's sternum.

Callie wished she'd learned CPR. After New Zealand, she and Jack had talked about learning CPR. Learning it urgently.

The husband turned to Callie, eyes empty. "Will she be okay? What's wrong with her?"

Callie put an arm around his damp shoulders and used her calm voice. "She's been stung by a jellyfish. The rescue helicopter is coming. Hold her hand—so she knows you're there." Was that even true? Maybe.

Jack and Laura switched tasks. Minute followed minute and they switched again. The man's skin felt vaguely slimy under Callie's forearm where her sleeve had pulled back. Sunscreen, probably.

She heard a crack and muttered to Jack, "Are you doing it too hard?"

"My instructor... told us," Jack said, puffing, "if you're not... breaking ribs... you're probably... not doing it... right."

A man spoke from behind Callie. "I also am trained," he said. "Let me rest you."

"Thank you, Silas." Laura signalled to the newcomer to relieve her while Baz took over from Jack.

Silas looked fifty-ish. Athletic and wiry. He'd spoken precisely, with a guttural edge and flattened vowels. German? Dutch? Somewhere down the bottom of Africa?

The husband trembled, a steady vibration. Callie's wrist ached from Jack's protective slap. The sand beneath her knees was surprisingly gritty. Like a thousand tiny stab wounds, even through the silky fabric of her sarong. *Must be the way coral breaks down. What is other sand made of?* The tropical sun fried her face, straight through the sunscreen applied an hour earlier. She looked back up the beach to her hat where it had blown off as she ran. *Would it be rude to leave for a moment?* From where he stood, absent-mindedly massaging his lower back, Jack must have seen her looking. He retrieved the hat and set it on her head, where it perched a little too high. She adjusted it with her free hand and smiled her thanks.

A sinuous tattoo of a shark, serrated mouth gaping, swirled around Baz's muscular forearm. Its tail fin flicked with each pump.

"Okay, switch!" Laura said. The second team moved aside for Laura and Jack.

Please, God, if you're up there. She's so young.

Guests and staff hovered at a respectful distance. A couple of people had their mobile phone cameras out. No signal on the island so they wouldn't be internet-famous—at least, not today. But the footage might be handy… Callie's gaze roamed the faces then locked on to a young woman with long, straight, jet black hair who was steadying her hands on a post.

The small crowd parted and another man strode through. Similar age to Silas and equally sun-weathered, but taller, heavier, messier. Silas had impeccable grooming and the too-tanned look of the professional tourist. The newcomer had chaotic hair—what was left of it—and the telltale facial scars of sunspot removal, one of them red and recent.

He wore a loud floral shirt and carried a small black plastic hardshell case with a handle.

He squatted heavily opposite the bikini girl's husband and addressed him directly as the CPR team continued.

"Mate, we've got a new antivenom we've been working on." No

mysterious foreign accents here. "It hasn't been tested on humans yet. I could try it on your missus if you give me permission."

Laura stopped resuscitation a moment and stared at him. "Kevin!" was all she said.

Kevin ignored her. "The venom has stopped her heart. We'll continue CPR till the rescue helicopter arrives, because that's the protocol. But I'll be straight with you, that's a very big sting." He withdrew a vial of cloudy liquid from a foam bed within the case and displayed it. "This could save her life. It's had incredible results in our lab, for animals in cardiac arrest from chironex venom."

"Do whatever you need to," the husband said in a small voice. He looked at Callie, his face oddly devoid of emotion. "We got married on Saturday. There were lots of ferns. And orchids. Pink orchids. She loves pink."

Kevin donned gloves, whipped out a syringe and filled it from the vial, then tore the foil wrapping on an antiseptic swab. His thick fingers proved unexpectedly deft.

Jack paused CPR. "Do we keep going?"

"Yeah, mate. Her blood has to move."

Kevin located a vein, swabbed it, and began to inject. He depressed the plunger a minuscule amount, paused and watched the woman's face. Then a tiny amount more. By slow increments, he emptied the syringe into her body.

The CPR team swapped again. The husband let out a sound that was part sob, part groan, and squeezed his bride's limp hand. Since Callie last looked, his face had somehow become shiny with tears, his upper lip a mess of mucus. *Should I offer him my sleeve? How would he get it to his nose?*

Kevin filled the syringe a second time and continued the process, oh-so-slowly.

The husband said, his voice thick and wheezy, "Her finger moved!"

Laura said, "Are you sure?"

His Adam's apple slid up and down. A pause. "No..."

"Stop compressions." Laura felt under the woman's chin. "I've got a pulse!" She frowned. "It's gone again."

"Resume CPR." Kevin continued injecting and watching.

This time, Callie saw the woman's hand twitch. "She definitely moved!" The eyelids twitched too, though they stayed half-closed.

"Stop again," Laura said. "Yes, there's a pulse." She directed an open-mouthed smile at Kevin, eyebrows raised, her face alight. "It's working!"

From the direction of the mainland came the deep thock-thock-thock of a helicopter.

3

Once the chopper left, the CPR team moved as one to get out of the hot sun and into a cold drink. Inside, the barman was ready for them with tall fancy glasses with ridiculous paper umbrellas hanging over the side. A variety of tropical fruits, freshly pressed and full of ice. Jack could taste mango, and pineapple, and… something else. Lychees?

He thought about massaging his back, but the drink had to come first. CPR was a marathon.

His lower back ached where it had hinged up and down. His hands felt bruised. The CPR trainer had said, "When the real thing happens you'll need plenty of stamina, and you'll be scared as well." It had seemed so straightforward as Jack thumped on the mannequin, breathed into its mouth and waited for the tick-tick-tick as its plastic lungs expanded and contracted. A maths equation. A science project. He hadn't planned to actually do it for real.

The bride and groom would be halfway to the mainland by now in the rescue helicopter. She hadn't looked terrific when they'd departed, but she'd been breathing.

Soon, he'd have to face the wrath of Callie. Had he been a bit of a smart-aleck about how safe this trip would be? Hadn't meant to be. Just wanted to reassure her after the disaster in New Zealand. Well, mostly he'd wanted her not to say no. For now, she seemed content to gaze at the view in silence, so he kept a low profile.

A big-bladed fan whirred lazily overhead, and a soft breeze off the ocean brushed across his overheated skin. The group—minus the man named Baz, who'd disappeared as soon as they left the beach—sprawled in lush rattan armchairs with high backs and gleaming curved armrests, like something from the Singapore of colonial days, sumptuously padded in bright colours and arranged in a semi-circle on gleaming dark-timber floorboards. The building resembled a good old-fashioned Queenslander, with high ceilings, tongue-and-groove interior timber walls painted white, and big verandahs. He'd expected something with a Hawaiian or Balinese feel, like most of the island resorts. But this felt like the big homestead you might have found at the edge of a North Queensland sugar cane field in 1950, only a lot more posh. The guest cottages complemented it, giving the impression of simple beach shacks, their luxurious fittings understated. This was a resort for the type of people so rich they didn't need to look rich.

Concertina glass doors framed in dark wood had been pushed right back, allowing the room to flow out onto a broad verandah that hung suspended over a turquoise lagoon deep enough for snorkelling. Resort guests reclined out there on sun loungers, napping or reading books. A wide timber staircase descended from the verandah's edge to skim the water surface—a perfect entry point for swimmers.

The coral that had formed this cay over millennia lived and breathed around them. Stanford Island was completely enclosed by a reef that spread in weird shapes in all directions, an enormous organism that must be at least twice the length of the island. At the eastern end where their floatplane had landed this morning, the water within the fringing reef was pale aqua, shallow, only wading depth. At the western end, here, near the main house, parts of it were much deeper. Gazing north from his armchair, Jack beheld a huge natural swimming pool of vivid turquoise, then a line of fringe reef in soft, mottled browns and greys and, where that ended, an ocean suddenly so deep it looked black by comparison. Just a trick of eyesight—he knew that really it was a dark greenish-blue. The flat and empty horizon announced how far they were from any other land, or any other human settlement.

Kilometres away, the top sliver of horizon glowed, signalling another reef, this one without an island. It would be beginning to break the surface as the tide dropped, only to submerge completely again, twelve hours later.

Callie broke the silence. "Will she be okay?" She was looking towards Kevin Harris, leader of the research project and also manager of the resort.

"It's hard to tell, but the signs are good," Kevin said. "We'll contact the hospital for an update later."

"If the new antivenom is untested," Callie said, her tone curious rather than challenging, "why didn't you wait for the helicopter?"

There was a funny little pause. The answer came not from Kevin but from Laura. "There's debate about the efficacy of the existing antivenom. But you must do something, particularly with such a large sting."

Callie said, "Jack told me it was heart research you were doing here." She flicked him a glance that didn't seem entirely friendly and he studied the little wooden spokes on his drink umbrella.

"We're researching various types of reef venom," Laura said. "We came across the antivenom by accident. Our flagship project with the box jellies is heart research, and Silas Delport"—she smiled in the direction of the third man—"is our major investor."

Kevin added, "We found Silas back in September. And he could pitch-in straight away. It's made a huge difference to our progress over the summer."

Callie made a vague hand-gesture. "What's that accent of yours, Silas? I couldn't decide."

"I have lived many places." Silas beamed, extending his hands in an expansive movement. "I am a citizen of Earth."

Jack said, "We'd love to interview you as well, Silas."

The corners of his eyes crinkled. "It would be my pleasure."

Kevin remained slouched in his chair but his shoulders looked tense. "We shouldn't have to chase private investors, but the government couldn't find the possibilities if we drew them a flaming map."

Jack suspected he might have used an adjective other than "flaming" if resort guests hadn't been nearby.

"When can we see the lab?" Jack said.

Kevin said, "I'll get Laura to give you the grand tour so you know where everything is."

Laura stood. "I might pop home for a change of clothes first, though. I'm all-over sand and vinegar." She looked at Jack, then Callie. "And you've missed breakfast so I'll bring something to your cottage."

The gorgeous lagoon called to Jack and he wished he could dive into it straight from the deck, fully clothed, and feel the sweat and stress of the past hour slide off his skin. But the stinger might have brought friends, so he turned his back on that view and headed for a quick shower instead.

4

Callie really just wanted a nice long nap to recover from the terrors of the morning, not the least of which had been getting out of bed at 4.00 am. She trudged behind Laura down yet another sandy track through trees, uncharacteristically compliant. The heat must be making her weak.

From the air, Stanford Island had been a tiny dark-green blot among the dollops of turquoise reef stretching north-south, but it packed a lot into a small space.

A small space full of trees. Trees full of birds. Birds full of noise. And horrendous smells. When she'd first stepped ashore, Callie had assumed the island had a fancy eco-toilet system and it was on the blink. Eventually she realised the odour was everywhere the birds were. The whole island was a bird-toilet.

Their favourite hangout was a tree that Laura deemed ecologically important, three or four storeys high with long glossy-green leaves adorned with white streaks and a ceaseless flutter of birds. Some sang a high-pitched whistle rising on the end, melodic as fingernails on a chalkboard. Others sounded like crows trying to clear their throats. Shy speckled brown birds—yet another species— ran from their feet. Callie gave up on Laura's descriptions, identifications and definitions. Jack was taking notes, so she pasted on her "interested" face, and trudged.

"Life on a desert island is not as romantic as I expected," Callie said, then ducked abruptly to one side, narrowly avoiding a collision with a bird that corkscrewed down the path at eye level like a fighter jet under enemy fire.

Laura gave her a half-smile. "They're more graceful at sea." She strode ever onward on sleek, tanned legs. The woman showed no sign of her CPR exertions. Jack on the other hand was absent-mindedly massaging his shoulder, the one he injured in New Zealand.

Sand invaded Callie's sandals and eroded the skin between her toes. She wasn't sure if the heat was coming at her from the environment or emanating from her own skin. Tall vegetation stood like a row of riot police between her and the ocean breeze. A couple of months ago, she'd hiked Fiordland's steepest mountains without puffing. A few weekends of video marathons and she was a pudding on legs again.

They inspected the huge array of solar panels that provided electricity, and the backup generator. Nodded sagely over the desalination plant and the backup water tanks, all while Callie snapped photos on her phone as memory aids. They kept a respectful distance from the processing plant that pumped out recycled wastewater to flush toilets and water gardens.

"You seem so self-sufficient in some ways, but then you have things like this." Callie indicated a huge package labelled "night soil" that awaited not a horse and cart but the weekly barge.

"A couple of people could probably live out here without services from the mainland," Laura said, "but not forty people."

"Forty?" Callie mentally reviewed the small number of cottages.

"Twenty guests, twenty staff and researchers. Sometimes a few more."

Callie said, "How long have you lived here?"

"Three years."

Jack said, "Do you get home much?"

"Staff work ten days on, four off, but I don't always go off-island on my breaks anymore. I've rented out my house on the mainland.

This is my address now." She smiled, as much to herself as to them. "This is home."

Callie tilted her head. "Is it an adventure, or a career?"

Laura considered. "I came for the adventure, but I stayed for the career. And now it's my life."

They passed a building where domestic staff and researchers slept —concrete block construction with simple bunk beds glimpsed through glass louvres, about the standard of a pleasant youth hostel. Jack said to Callie, "We'd have been sleeping in there if not for the cancellation. We've only paid the researcher rate."

"Kevin has even invited you to eat with the guests," Laura said with a smile at Jack.

A radio mast, the tallest structure, kept bobbing into view above the trees. Signs pointed to the main resort facilities but not the other buildings, so Callie started testing whether she could get her bearings from the tower as they followed twisting, interlocking paths. The internet connection beaming into the mast's big dish was invisible to the electronic devices of resort guests—as Callie had discovered when she checked her phone on arrival. Splendid isolation, or at least the illusion of it, was what people paid thousands of dollars a night for.

But she and Jack weren't here for the splendid isolation. Laura said, "I'll give you a sheet with login instructions when you sign off on your site induction."

Callie caught a glimpse of aqua sea through a gap in the trees, and a reviving breeze tickled her neck. Where they stood seemed no more than two or three metres above sea level and she said, "How would you cope in a tsunami?"

"We'd drown."

Callie had an instant vision of waves swirling through the resort, sweeping clouds of deadly jellyfish across the skin of people whose mouths opened in agonised screams one by one, like pop-ups of Edvard Munch's famous painting.

"And here is the lab," Laura said. "Most of the research stations on the reef are university-based. We're privately-owned. It gives us less options in some ways, but more in others."

A utilitarian building, windowless, built from a combination of concrete blocks and powder-coated steel, and liberally festooned with bird droppings.

Laura glared at Callie's sandals. "Closed shoes are required for the lab."

"Oh, sorry." She'd been told. She'd forgotten.

<hr>

WOULD IT HAVE KILLED LAURA TO NOTICE HER FOOTWEAR *before* they began the tour? Just as Callie finally found her way back to the lab, she received a clear mental picture of her phone, as though it was transmitting images directly to her brain… from her bed. That thing was her mobile multi-media studio—and her time-piece. So she power-walked back to the cottage, wishing she'd taken an extra thirty seconds to thoroughly de-grit her feet before entombing them in sneakers.

Reunited with her phone and in search of the lab once more, she rounded a blind corner and collided heavily with something angular —right across the solar plexus.

"Oi! Look where you're going!" a sharp voice said.

In the process of folding forward in agony, thoroughly winded, Callie glimpsed the angry face of a woman toting a large, square, plastic storage tub full of ropes. "Oh!—so sorry—didn't—see you—"

"Cornering too fast, that's your problem." The woman's anger seemed to be dissipating. She plonked the tub on the path and rubbed her own mid-section as she bent to retrieve a cotton sunhat.

"Sorry—hope I—didn't—hurt you?" Callie gasped.

The woman jammed the hat firmly over her short, spiky, blonde hair and said, "Not to worry, you gave me a fright is all." She looked mid-thirties and had a British accent. Not one of the plummy ones, one of the regional ones. Cornwall? Devon? The sour tang of sunscreen emanated from the woman's reddened arms.

Callie smiled. "You and me both." She forced in another breath and pressed on her offended diaphragm. "Can you tell me where the lab is?" They stood amid thick tree cover at the intersection of three identical, unsigned paths.

The woman swivelled and looked around. "Might as well be in the jungle once you lose sight of the water."

"You're not on staff?"

"Not likely!" Her face brightened to smug. "I'm sailing the Great Barrier Reef. Solo."

"Really? I've always wanted to do that. I'd love to see your yacht."

"Always happy for a chinwag. I'm moored at the jetty, which is," she gesticulated in a slow, vague circle, then chose one of the paths to point towards, "thataway."

"Thank you!" Callie said. "I've got to work this morning. How long are you here?"

"Just overnight, probably. And I'll eat in the restaurant if I can twist the right arm." She rolled her eyes. "Or if I can afford it."

Callie laughed. "I'm Callie, by the way." She extended her hand and received a firm handshake in response.

"Mary." The woman hefted her storage tub. "Might see you later on."

She strode off. Callie took a chance at path number 3 and won. Finally back at the lab, still a little out of breath, she was confronted by a steel door fastened with a combination-lock keypad. The door bore a large vinyl sticker proclaiming in bold red letters "Strictly No Admittance" and there was no sign of Jack or Laura or anyone else. Callie knocked tentatively and waited. She knocked more firmly. She was just reaching forward to knock a third time when the door swung outwards, fast. She dodged it like Keanu in *The Matrix* avoiding a bullet, but her heel slipped off the edge of the concrete path. She flung out an arm, grabbed the nearest tree, and startled a squadron of birds. Their rough, warm feathers smelled of yeast as they scraped her face and arms. Instead of a sturdy branch she had gripped a swaying fistful of shiny leaves and performed a full-body undulation.

"Oh, there you are at last," Laura said, making no sign that she'd seen Callie's impromptu performance. "Come in. You're permitted to enter the lab while you're on the island so long as you don't touch anything. This week's code is C4568."

Callie followed her inside and felt the welcome blast of air-conditioning chill the sheen of sweat on her skin. She got a faceful of white—ceilings, walls and benches. But the benches were crammed: microscopes, electronic gadgets made of metal and glass and coloured lights, jars and beakers and boxes, and a clutter of paperwork. She had expected tidiness and order, like the bridge of a spaceship, but instead it reminded her of a white version of her kitchen at home. Stainless steel sinks shone in the fluorescent light, and harshly-worded signs declared what could and could not be washed down them. To her left, in front of a wall of windows, two women wearing white lab coats over shorts and sneakers pored over a microscope.

At the far end of the room she spied Jack, slouched against a bench talking to Kevin. She strolled towards them in Laura's wake, keeping one hand behind her back while she tried to shake off a feather that was adhering to her fingers with… something? When it struck her what the adhesive compound might be, her eyebrows rose a few millimetres before she could get them under control. It seemed too late to ask Laura for help or handwipes, so she rubbed her hand on her skirt as discreetly as she could and launched straight in with her confident-and-relaxed voice. "Sorry to hold everyone up. Forgot my safety footwear. Blame the birds. It's like being in a Hitchcock movie."

Kevin released a short bark of laughter. "Wait till tonight when the mutton birds come ashore. You'll love 'em. They sing romantic songs to each other all night long. Sounds like someone strangling a sheep—"

Laura spoke over the top of him. "We've already shown Jack around the dry lab. He can tell you about it later. Let's take a look at the sea tables on the aquaria deck. Through here." She led the way. Kevin held out a hand to invite Callie to go ahead of him. She thanked him gracefully while hoping the feather was not still stuck to her backside.

They sidled past the women at the microscope, out a glass door, back into the heat. Huge shallow rectangular tubs squatted on tables on a timber deck while a framework of hoses formed a network over their heads. These were nothing like the glass aquarium Callie's dad cosseted; these were solid constructions, made of some sort of grey material—fibreglass maybe?—coloured light aqua on the inside.

"We have a continual flow of saltwater coming in from the ocean," Laura said. "It goes back out to the ocean as well, so we have to ensure nothing goes out with it that would harm the reef or its creatures."

Jack asked how the seawater came in and a boring technical discussion ensued. Callie felt strangely claustrophobic. The deck was open to the sky yet surrounded by high, solid walls. When the explanation finished, she muttered, "It's like Fort Knox with no roof." The other three stared at her.

"We work with dangerous animals," said Laura. "We must ensure resort guests are safe from their own curiosity."

Jack said, with the air of a kid in a lolly shop, "What sort of dangerous animals?"

Kevin led them to an enormous oval tank in one corner. Unlike the others, it was deep, extending right through a hole cut through the timber decking, no doubt resting on the ground beneath. "Things like this."

The tank seemed empty at first glance. Callie stared into the swirling aqua water, and initially discerned not the creatures but the shadows they cast.

Kevin leant towards her conspiratorially. "Don't stick ya hand in there." He immediately darted his own hand in there and plucked out a huge transparent jellyfish, holding it gently by the bell as its tentacles draped down into the water and quite a bit beyond, longer than a broomstick.

"Is that what I think it is?" Jack's eyes were a little wider than normal.

"Scariest thing on the reef." Kevin was still holding it. "*Chironex fleckeri*. Box jellyfish."

Jack crossed his arms and rocked back on his feet. "As we saw demonstrated this morning."

Laura added, with what sounded very much like pride: "Some scientists regard it as the most venomous animal in the world."

Callie felt winded all over again. "How can you hold it?"

"No venom in the bell. It's the tentacles ya gotta watch. You get good at picking them up." Kevin winked. "Or ya don't."

Laura said sharply, "I wish you wouldn't handle the animals when it's not necessary."

Kevin grinned. "It's not me she cares about." He lowered his hand to the water and gently released the creature.

Laura huffed. "He's got skin like leather. But the jellyfish are extremely fragile. We keep them in this special tank with no corners so they don't get injured. We try to handle them as little as possible."

"Could the one that stung the woman this morning have come from this tank…"—Jack paused and raised his shoulders in an elaborate shrug—"somehow?"

"No." Laura shook her head emphatically. "They cannot get out the pipes. Not so much as a stray tentacle."

Jack nodded. "I guess you'd have to be pretty careful about that."

"And anyway, all our animals are accounted for."

Callie said, "Aren't they supposed to live close to the mainland?"

"Yep, they breed around the river mouths—warm, shallow water." Kevin shook his head slowly. "Never seen one this far out."

"Could it have been dragged accidentally by a boat—in a fishing net, say?" Jack said.

Laura frowned. "I don't expect so. A jellyfish wouldn't survive that sort of treatment."

"Can they still sting when they're dead?" he said.

"Yes, but the specimen that stung our guest is quite healthy. It's in this tank now, in fact."

Callie gazed into the watery shadows. "Why is the venom so deadly? It seems like overkill."

"So to speak." Jack gave her a half-smile. The other two stared at *him* now.

"They use it to immobilise their prey." Laura acted as though this was a full and reasonable answer.

"Have you ever been stung?" Jack was getting that lolly-shop look again.

"She was stung this morning," Callie said.

Laura looked at her red, slightly swollen fingertip. "Just a sore finger. I didn't get much venom into my system."

"We all experiment on ourselves a little bit." Kevin grinned when Callie's eyebrows went up. "A small sting hurts like hell, but it won't kill you."

Laura rolled her eyes. "*Some* of us experiment on ourselves. And *usually* it won't kill you."

Kevin thrust out his forearm for examination, displaying a faded red scar the size of a large coin and shaped like a coiled snake. "There's one of mine from a time I went just a little bit too far."

Jack leant forward for a closer look. "What does it feel like?"

"Being boiled in acid."

Though Callie had been looking forward to seeing these creatures, her skin started trying to crawl right off her body. She wasn't sorry to climb back into it and reverse it away from that tank. They had a quick view of a second indoor lab opening off the deck—this one full of tanks under bright lamps.

"We'll tell you more about this project when the researchers get back. They're out on the reef today."

At the side of this lab Callie saw another door, again with a combination-code lock. "What's in there?"

Laura didn't even look at her. "Storage."

"How do you find investors?" Jack said.

"Lots of ways." Kevin waved a hand vaguely. "In the case of Silas, I was sifting through the archives and found out his dad had a connection to the island back in the eighties. Then we used the mysteries of the internet"—he twiddled his fingers in a "spooky" gesture—"to track him down."

"How did you get involved in this research, Kevin?" Callie said.

"Ah, now, that's a long story. Let me show you something." He led them past the big scary tank and back into the first room, the dry lab with the white walls and computers, where he paused beside a framed black and white photo. It showed a big man in old-style swimming trunks, grinning and relaxed, standing in knee-deep water, with a snorkel and mask dangling from one hand. He could almost have been a younger Kevin with more hair. Beside him, a curly-haired woman in a vintage bikini had her head thrown back in laughter. "My parents."

Callie took a quick photo of it with her phone, then switched to the voice recorder function. "Mind if I record this? Saves me taking copious notes."

He shrugged. "Sure."

She put her phone on the bench near Kevin while she rummaged in her capacious soft shoulder bag for a notebook and pen.

"My dad won this island in a game of cards, if you can believe it." He grinned and maybe even preened a little.

"A card game?" Jack frowned, his chin forward.

"Yeah. Back in the fifties. Nobody else wanted it. Too much trouble, this far out. Dad set up a holiday resort with research station. Tents and a camp kitchen, basically. A few microscopes and fish tanks in a hut. And people who loved the reef spent six gut-churning hours getting out here on an old launch—none of your high speed catamarans back then. Or if they had the moolah, they'd hire a crazy pilot and one of the amphibious planes leftover from the war. I used to run out on the jetty to watch them land on their belly at high tide, the water spraying up all around them—the lagoon was *nearly* long enough for them to stop in time." He grinned. "People would stay for weeks or months. Learn to love the reef. Understand it. Want to protect it. My mum was one of the people who came. She met my dad here. I was born here, accidentally, when I came two weeks early, just up the top of that hill"—he pointed toward the east, where the main house now stood—"but our house is gone now." His face clouded. Closed. "Then Mum died, and, well, Dad never really got over it. We're fighting the disease that took her. And we're using the reef he loved to do it."

Jack said, "I thought these islands were lease-hold, not freehold."

Probably not the question top of Callie's mind. Was he still stuck on the card game?

"Most of them are," Kevin said.

Callie's eyes widened. "Do you own the island?"

"No, I don't. Things… changed." He shrugged. "But it would be good if we could get back to basics. If people could come here not just for a nice holiday but because they love the reef, and want to save it, and use it to help people."

"An inspiring goal." A hundred questions were queuing up on

Callie's tongue to be next, but the walkie-talkie on Kevin's hip burbled.

"Chief, can you come to the jetty? You need to see this."

Kevin shrugged apologetically. "Duty calls. We'll talk again later."

As Laura turned to lead them outside, Callie indicated another combination-locked door beside the photo of Kevin's parents. "What's that one?"

Laura glanced at it. "Nothing much. You've seen the important parts of the research. When Aaron comes back in off the reef, I'll get him to tell you about his cone snail project. Lunch is in the main house at noon."

As Callie and Jack ambled back to their cottage alone, Callie said thoughtfully, "There's a big story living under that man's skin."

"Yeah," said Jack. "Reckon he wants to tell it?"

"Probably not the best bits." She shot him a side-glance.

He raised his eyebrows. "And what kind of card games was his father involved in if they were playing for islands?"

5

An hour later, Callie miraculously remembered the combination and nudged open the lab door. "Hello?" No one answered. She'd be late for lunch, but she had to get her phone. She could see it over there, right where she'd left it, on the bench against the back wall under the photo of Kevin's parents. As she walked towards it, she noticed the door beside it temptingly ajar. She glanced over her shoulder to check she really was alone, eager for just a quick peek inside Laura's "nothing much" room.

But there was already someone in there. Two someones. They seemed to be having a disagreement—a series of shouted whispers. She edged closer.

"…dangerous to use it when we haven't finished testing it!" That might be Laura.

"It was a golden opportunity, right there in front of our faces." That was definitely Kevin. "And it worked, so what are you carrying on about? Stop being stupid."

"Don't you dare patronise me. You can talk it up in front of Silas Delport if you want, but she's not out of the woods yet, and as for potential side effects—"

"Did you seriously think we wouldn't need to test it on humans one day?" Kevin huffed in frustration or maybe contempt. Callie could imagine him crossing his meaty arms and leaning back. "How naïve *are* you?"

Silence. Then a muffled noise.

"Yes… I know… but it's just that… it was *horrible*. You weren't the one doing CPR. I thought she'd die and it would be my fault. And they were so *happy*, hanging all over each other…"

More sounds of movement. "We knew it would be hard." His voice was much gentler. Callie had to lean a little closer. "We can't give up now. Think how many lives this could change."

"Can I help you?"

Callie's phone clattered back onto the bench and she spun round to see a man wearing the staff uniform. He had curly black hair, classic features worth carving from marble, and unexpectedly-blue eyes that currently held a steely look. He was even taller than she was and wore every inch of it with a magnetic kind of certainty.

"I left my phone behind and came to get it." She tried to look like a person who never eavesdropped. It didn't seem to be working; his lips remained set.

"I doubt you'll find it in there." He angled his head toward the "nothing much" door, which swung open to emit Kevin. He closed the door carefully behind him, but not before she caught a glimpse downstairs into another lab—with a cave-like feel, more glimmering tanks under bright lights, and a flustered-looking Laura turning away.

"Everything okay out here?" Kevin said.

Callie smiled. "I left my phone behind earlier, but here it is."

"Right-o." He looked relaxed, although Callie thought she detected a swift, significant look pass between him and the other man. "While you're here, let me introduce you to Aaron Ferraro. He's one of our most gifted PhD students."

Callie showed a civil amount of interest in Aaron's work in diabetes research, made an appointment to interview him this after-noon, really quite enjoyed shaking his beautifully-sculpted hand, and then excused herself and left. Pretending not to be embarrassed wasn't something she could do all day.

Jack surveyed the feast spread out on the huge antique silky-oak dresser that held the buffet and heard his stomach gurgle loudly enough that it had to be audible over the murmur of conversation. Platters of cold roast meats carved into thick slabs, several kinds of seafood, lush salads, aromatic vegan patties full of lentils and chickpeas, slices of bright tropical fruits, crusty grain-smattered bread rolls with curls of butter, all suspended over trays of ice. It was already 12.15 and the resort guests were well involved in their lunch.

Nearby, Silas indicated an empty chair beside him. "Would you like this seat?"

"Thanks, but I thought I'd wait for Callie." Only Callie Brown could run late on an island the size of a bathtub.

"How long do you stay on Stanford Island?"

"A week."

"I plan a helicopter journey to Eden Island and the outer reef, to the north, this afternoon. For photography. You are welcome also."

"Really? That'd be incredible."

"It is a photography helicopter. No doors, so we have the clear view."

Jack tried to loosen the smile that had seized on his face. "What time should we be ready?"

"I will confirm with my pilot after lunch."

Callie breezed in with her phone held high. "Got it!"

"I think I'll have to put that thing on a lanyard around your neck. And tie it really, *really* tight."

She poked her tongue out at him. He told her about the helicopter invitation. "Ooh!" She beamed at Silas. "Thank you so much." As Jack passed her a dinner plate from a stack, she cut him a sideways glance. "Will you be okay? I mean, I noticed you gave me the front seat on the plane this morning."

He said, each word distinct, "I was being kind."

She narrowed her eyes as she poked through a bowl of lettuce with a pair of tongs and seized an olive. "You sure that's all it was?"

He ignored her and reached for another chicken drumstick.

They were seated in front of piled-high plates when Kevin and Laura appeared and pulled out the chairs opposite.

"How do you like our restaurant?" Kevin indicated the long

table stretching forward to the ocean deck with guests seated each side, smiling and chatting to one another. Crystal wine glasses sparkled and crisp white tableware contrasted with the gleaming dark timber of the table and floor. The big space was open to the air on three sides where the glass doors folded back. Cool breezes swirled through off the ocean.

Callie nodded. "It's fabulous."

"How did you get such a long table out here?" Jack was trying to imagine a vessel with a clear space long enough.

"It was built here. The whole thing was based on my dad's idea. He wanted people to feel like they were joining a big, friendly house-party, not sitting in their own little puddle of silence in some posh restaurant." He half-shrugged. "At full capacity we only have about twenty guests—and the occasional yachtie dropping in for a feed or supplies—so it seems to work. People can order a meal to their cottage if they really want privacy, but hardly anybody seems to take us up on that, even the honeymooners."

Callie peeled a prawn the size of a small banana. "What was it like when you were a kid, Kevin?"

"The kitchen and dining room were exactly here on this abutment, but it was just long trestle tables and folding chairs in a tin shed. Stinking hot in summer, but some great tucker and great friendships."

Jack said, "Any other kids?"

"No, just me. My mother taught me. We used to sign in to the School of the Air over the shortwave radio. All these kids out on remote cattle stations in the outback riding camels and kangaroos, and then little Kevvy Harris chimes in from the reef." He laughed, but then became more serious. "Mum did a good job—good enough to get me into marine biology at Queensland Uni." He licked a splodge of salad dressing off his thumb.

Callie said, "Had you ever lived on the mainland before you started uni?"

He shook his head, then devoted his attention to the thick sandwich he was assembling and took a large bite.

Jack broke the silence. "Where do the staff eat?" He caught a swift glare from Callie and wondered what he'd done wrong.

Laura answered him. "Kevin and I generally dine with the guests in the role of house-party hosts, and the other researchers rotate through, as well—guests find their work quite interesting. The rest of the staff eat at a table in the kitchen. They lunch an hour later on a simpler menu, plus whatever is left over from here. We can't afford to waste anything."

Kevin leant forward conspiratorially. "Guests think they're castaways in a tropical paradise, but the fact is all this has to come in on the weekly barge. Nothing much worth eating grows here, except the odd coconut that might belt you on the noggin and a few scrawny papayas." He scowled. "We're not even allowed to catch a fish, these days."

"Really?" Jack frowned.

"The reef is a national park," Laura said. "We require a permit for everything—animal, vegetable or mineral—that we take out of it for our research, and there are strict limits and regulations on those. For example, we can only have a shark for three days. They get stressed and won't eat so they have to go back into the ocean quickly."

"Sharks?" Callie lowered her fork and stared out at the lagoon.

"Ah, don't worry." Kevin winked. "They're only little fellas with very small mouths."

Laura said, "Actually, some of them are quite large, but they're not interested in eating people." She paused and pursed her mouth slightly. "Usually."

Kevin added, "There's been some trouble the last few years, but not here. Not yet. Someone got a chunk taken out of 'em… oh, fifteen years back, maybe? But then, he was swimming in the middle of a baitball at the time." He quirked his mouth. "Probably just 'natural selection', really."

Laura shot him a sharp look.

Callie said, "Um, what's a baitball? So I know not to swim in one, like."

Laura answered. "Small fish swim close together when they're trying to avoid a predator."

Kevin grinned. "Such as a small-mouthed shark."

Jack and Callie laughed, but Laura didn't.

As they finished eating, Callie excused herself and stood. Jack watched her get into animated conversation with several guests, but her focus seemed to be a black-haired woman sitting with Baz, the guy who'd helped with the resuscitation.

Laura said to Jack, "That's Baz and Nina. You should talk to them, too, while they're on Stanford. They're doing turtle research over on Apostle Island."

Kevin said, "They usually eat with the staff when they're here, but I figured Baz deserved a treat after slaving over the patient with us this morning."

Callie's discussion involved hand waving, eyebrow raising and sympathetic looks. Several people were showing her their mobile phones and Callie nodded with interest. Next moment, Jack saw the familiar motions as she paired Nina's phone with her own. Transferring footage. That woman could charm a wildebeest off a lion.

<hr>

Jack was surprised to find the kitchen had been designed to hold a table just as long as the one used by the guests. Kevin and Laura had led them through for introductions.

Large glass-fronted fridges revealed a variety of meats and fish, fruits and vegetables, and cartons of long-life milk. The chef looked up from chopping a head of lettuce, nodded a welcome at Jack and Callie, and said, "Welcome aboard."

It was a busy scene as workers mingled and sat, while wait staff from the dining room carried in leftovers from the guest buffet to set on the stainless steel serving bench among the sandwich ingredients.

"Is it a 1:1 ratio—staff to guests?" Jack asked Kevin.

"No, one staff member for every two guests. That's a good ratio on a luxury resort. The rest are marine researchers. Still, we're a small crew here. A maximum of fifty humans on the island at full capacity."

Callie said, "And about fifty thousand birds."

Kevin grinned. "Actually, nearer two hundred thousand over summer, when all the seasonal breeders are with us. That's about twenty birds per square metre, for those playing along at home." He angled his head towards the table. "Come and I'll introduce you."

He tapped on a glass with a spoon, and the room fell quiet. "Team, this is Jack Metcalf and Callie Brown. They're journalists—working on a documentary. Please give them any help they need, but just tell them if they need to get lost for a bit. They got lucky on a cancellation so we've put them in Cottage 8." Good-humoured complaints erupted round the table.

When the noise settled, Callie spoke. "Thanks for having us here. We know you've had the Attenborough crew before, but we're a much smaller outfit. Just us, in fact. Simple equipment." There was nothing self-deprecating about the way she said it, and Jack thought how far she'd come since the argument they'd had on a New Zealand mountainside about that very equipment.

He added, "Reality television, but better. We'll just hang around, watch what you do, and sometimes ask you for an interview. We know you're not on holidays, so we'll try not to get in your way too much."

Baz with the blond dreadlocks had come in from the dining room behind them, and said, "Hey, you're not the ones that made that New Zealand flick that went viral—what was it called? *Poison Lake?*"

Jack nodded. "*Poison Bay*. That was us."

"Respect, man. That was awesome."

Another man nodded vigorously. "Yeah, it was amazing." He raised his glass of water in salute and looked around at his colleagues. En masse, the group reached for water glasses, raised them towards Jack and Callie and said: "Respect!" then tapped on their glasses with cutlery—a few seconds of loud clinking.

"Thank you." Jack found it hard to think of anything else to say. He glanced at Callie and noticed her eyes seemed extra-bright.

One of the women spoke. "Maybe you need to do an investigative report on this jellyfish invasion."

Jack said, "Invasion?"

Kevin twisted his mouth. "Yeah. We found three more."

"How could that happen?" said Callie.

Kevin shook his head. "We don't know. A big rain event might just conceivably wash one out this far, even though it's never happened before. But there's been none of the right weather so far this summer."

One of the staff said, "And four just about counts as a bloom."

Laura spoke in a firm tone to the whole group. "No one goes in the water without a full stinger suit, until we resolve the issue. In fact, if you can avoid the water by doing other tasks in the next couple of days, do so. I'll be going round now to speak personally to each guest to ensure they understand what's required and help them process what they saw this morning."

Kevin added, "If any guests talk to you about it, keep the conversation calm and avoid the sort of exaggerated stories you're always telling each other." A murmur of laughter went round the table. "But don't downplay it so much that guests ignore the risk." He looked stern. "I'm serious. If you joke around and someone gets stung, you create an insurance nightmare that could wreck everything for all of us, okay? So be smart, people. Be calm and be smart."

A small pause followed.

"On the plus side," said one of the men, "we've got four new specimens."

Another murmur of laughter. Laura cut across it. "The woman who was stung is in a stable condition at present. We're waiting for updates. If guests ask, she is recovering in hospital."

Kevin added, "We've put the word out. If there's some new natural phenomenon taking place, we'll know soon enough."

One of the men said, "They'll want us to solve it."

Others muttered agreement and a woman mimed answering a phone: "Venom Central, how may I direct your call?"

<hr>

Jack and Callie wandered toward the jetty past the gorgeous saltwater pool—an infinity design where the water seemed to go right to the horizon. It was full of guests who might otherwise have been out snorkelling. Callie stared out to sea, her demeanour intense.

Jack said, "We don't need to go in the water."

"Unless we have to wade out to a floatplane, of course. But Jack, I can't get the idea out of my head—what if someone put those jelly-fish in the water on purpose?"

"Why would anyone do that?"

"A researcher gone mad? Someone trying to put Stanford Island out of business? The whole thing is making me itch."

"How about we let the scientists figure it out instead of dreaming up conspiracy theories."

6

*C*allie wrapped her fingers around the strap on her safety harness as the helicopter blades began to turn. Even with headphones on, the noise was intense, and her ligaments vibrated like the strings on a cello. The other hand gripped her camera on her lap. Its thin neck-strap didn't really seem adequate. She'd been in plenty of helicopters for work, but that was just to get from A to B. This was her first doors-off experience.

She glanced at Jack in the seat beside her. His face seemed calm enough, but she detected tension in the arm that gripped his SLR camera with the long lens.

Up, like an elevator, and Callie grinned as the length of Stanford Island and its fringing reef unrolled beneath them. She wanted to say, "Wow," but couldn't—the wind from the spinning rotor had dried her mouth and throat.

The helicopter tilted its front dome towards the ocean to move forward, and she wedged her foot more firmly against the bag under her seat which held her hat, towel, and snorkelling gear. The lip on the door was substantial but it was hard to override that instinct.

Silas sat in the front passenger seat as though he was at home on his sofa, alongside Dean the pilot, a tall beefy guy with arms and legs like tree trunks.

Silas turned and spoke to them, his voice tinny through the headsets they each wore. "You have seen the Great Barrier Reef from the air before?"

"Only this morning," Callie said.

"I have," Jack said, "when I was a kid. One of those old amphibious planes. Landed on its belly in the middle of nowhere and water sprayed up all over the windows. And then there we were —right *in* the reef." He looked like a child remembering Christmas morning.

"Ah, yes." Silas nodded. "The flying boat. Our helicopter is more spry; we can access smaller reefs."

They buzzed over reef after reef, the pilot taking them low enough to glimpse larger creatures such as sharks and stingrays. Callie began to relax and lean into the experience, trusting her safety harness.

She felt a thrill of joy each time they encountered another crystal-clear aqua splotch erupting from deep, dark ocean. Some reefs were enormous—maybe two or three kilometres wide and five or ten in length. Others were much smaller, with a ring of shallow mottled aqua-brown coral encircling a turquoise lagoon no bigger than a family swimming pool.

Twenty minutes later, Dean set them down gently on a floating platform anchored to a tiny reef.

As the rotor blades slowed and then stopped, silence rose up to fill the cabin. Silas swung round to look at them, smiled, and tapped his ear with one finger.

Callie and Jack both nodded and smiled in return, but no one spoke. They sat for a full minute, then two, then three, as a warm, gentle breeze tickled exposed skin and the sea shooshed languidly along the rim of the reef, effervescing as it met the coral. It felt almost like a religious experience.

They could have been dozens or hundreds or thousands of kilometres from any form of land. In every direction, the horizon was empty and vaguely curved.

Coral encircled the egg-shaped lagoon, rising jagged above the waterline. The sandy centre of the egg held water in various shades of turquoise, clear as glass.

Everywhere, life pulsed. Five mottled fish, each perhaps as long as Callie's forearm, disappeared under the floating platform. Beyond, two stingrays converged without colliding, their underwater flight paths apparently at different altitudes. Above, dozens of birds, their wings forming two muscular vees, wheeled lazily. Callie zoomed-in on one, and was startled to discover that its expression was intense and it was looking straight at her.

Silas swung around again. "And now, we explore. We will walk first."

"Walk? Where?" Callie said.

"Among the tips of coral, we find trails of sand. You have brought the reef shoes?" They nodded. "Do not cut yourself on coral, my young friends. The tiny animals, they live in the cut. This I did, many years ago." Silas shook his head. "How long it took to heal!"

Dean pulled out a pack of cigarettes, apparently settling in to wait in the chopper.

"Don't throw it in the water," Silas snarled at him.

The three of them waded awkwardly through the sandy channels, high-stepping over and around obstacles, searching for a flat space large enough for a foot. A clam protruded from the wavy edges of its shell like five side-by-side sets of brown lips puckering for a kiss. Silas waved his hand near it and the animal retracted, then bulged back out again after they moved past.

A bright blue starfish ignored an orange crab that scrambled right over it. A drab sea cucumber nestled in a shallow, sandy pool. Silas poked it, hard, so that it turned inside out, disgorging its innards in a defence mechanism.

Jack wrestled with his drone—a recent purchase. Callie watched the tiny screen as he did a sweep of the reef, then circled back to fly straight at them before swooping up and over the chopper.

Silas said to Callie, "What do you think of our little reef?"

"It's incredible."

"Thousands of reefs like this stretch across more than two thousand kilometres of oceans." He gestured around him. "In one more hour, the helicopter platform only will be above water. That is why we must come at the lowest tide. If we left you behind and the anchor chain broke, you would be riding a slippery platform in the ocean waves." He seemed to enjoy this mental picture rather more than Callie did. She jolted as he clapped his hands smartly, twice. "Come! Let us snorkel."

Back at the helicopter, Callie and Jack reached for rashies—long-sleeved lycra shirts that blocked the sun. Callie wore one whenever she swam in the heat of the day, because her pale skin fried like bacon and because her best friend's father died of melanoma at fifty-three. Jack wore one over his olive skin, too, because he was Jack. Even at school when their friends had worn them only for protection from surfboard rash, tanning themselves bronze the rest of the time, Jack had persisted—and shrugged when anyone teased him about it.

Silas stared at them both. "There are no stingers here."

"They're not stinger suits," Jack replied. Stinger suits were made of similar fabric but covered the legs as well. "They protect us from the sun."

"The sun is nature's best gift."

"Statistically, it's the most dangerous thing out here."

Silas, obviously deeply convinced by Jack's reasoning, stripped to swimming trunks, revealing a torso the colour of mahogany, and led the way into the lagoon.

Callie slipped into the silken water with a sigh of pleasure. It was ages since she'd been snorkelling and, all over again, she had to overcome the body's natural panic response to opening the lungs when the face is submerged. Her first breaths were too fast and she surfaced, gasping, to tread water a while, her fins cycling languidly beneath her. She tried again and in a minute or two she'd found her rhythm, soothed by the gentle roar of her own breath through the snorkel and the gurgle of bubbles around her.

Visibility was extraordinary. She could see all the way to the end of the lagoon. The sections she'd thought might be shallow enough for wading would in fact be well over her head.

Jack swam up beside her wielding the tough camera and they posed for an underwater selfie, Callie's long hair spreading around them both like an orange Medusa.

She dived deep to swim among a school of tiny blue fish with yellow tails which fluttered around her, bumping the glass of her goggles. She surfaced and blew her snorkel clear, then swam on the surface a while. Around her darted more fish of all colours: electric blue, silver, black, zebra-striped, red with blue spots. Some wore kissy lips or supercilious expressions.

Silas called to them: "Come and see."

They swam to meet an enormous fish, a dull grey-green in colour, well over a metre in length with a thick, ponderous body and a hump on its forehead.

"This is Napoleon," Silas said. "I look for him every year, for thirty years."

"You've been coming here that long?" Jack said.

"Since I was a young man, with my father."

Callie said, "Who owns this pontoon, Silas?"

"I do, of course."

Of course.

They clambered carefully over the coral to snorkel along the outside of the reef. "The colours, when you dive deeper!" Silas's eyes were bright. "But take care. The current is stronger than you think."

Callie dived again and again, fascinated by the wall of coral that descended vertically into the darkened deep, filled with a cacophony of life and movement. Soft corals undulated. Anemones pulsed. Fish darted.

As she dived again, something smooth brushed along her legs and then bumped her shoulder. She glanced aside into the beady eye of a shark longer than herself. She surfaced too fast. Forgot to blow her snorkel clear. Inhaled water. Spluttering, she trod water gently, trying not to splash, trying not to look like prey. She looked for the others and electricity shot through her torso: she had been carried out into deep, deep, deep, dark-blue water.

She whipped around, her eyes reaching for a sight of the helicopter. The coral they'd walked over only thirty minutes before now sat much lower in the ocean, some of it already submerged as the tide rushed back in.

She finally glimpsed the dark slash of a helicopter blade against the blue sky, far to the right of where she'd expected it.

And then she saw Jack surface from a dive along the reef edge.

They hadn't left without her.

She peered below, till she spotted the shark gliding through the shadowy depths. Keeping it in sight, she swam slowly and quietly back to safety. She'd had enough snorkelling for one day.

7

This time when the helicopter rose, Callie shivered as the blustery wind through the open cabin chilled her damp swimwear. The sun had shifted toward the west, and its glare bounced from the ocean into her eyes. She had scraped her wet hair back into a ponytail but one strand worked free to whip her face and shoulders mercilessly, raising a memory of stinging tea-towel fights with her brothers in their childhood kitchen.

Yet more dollops of reef sprawled endlessly ahead. After twenty minutes, an island appeared.

Silas swung around and his voice crackled through the headset. "Eden Island."

Eden was many times the size of Stanford, shaped like a wobbly green croissant with forested hills and expanses of bright green grass. As they drew nearer, a sprawling resort became visible sprouting from the end of a long jetty, sending tendrils into the tree cover and unfurling along the sandy shoreline.

A group of people on the sand turned out to be a beach volley-ball game in progress. A large high-speed catamaran reversed away from the jetty and began a sweeping u-turn, water churning aqua and white.

"Inter-island ferry," said Silas. "Two hundred passengers."

Their pilot took them on a circuit as Silas pointed out winding walking trails. In the hazy distance toward the north, more large, hilly islands shimmered in the heat. To the west, mountainous mainland cloaked in eucalypt forest hummed in shades of blue. They overflew a golf course where three people in colourful baggy shorts were about to tee off.

On the highest hill, a couple stood cuddling at a lookout. They waved furiously as the helicopter swept past and Callie grinned and waved back, snapping their photograph as they struck a pose.

A grassy airstrip lay draped like a bacon rasher across the top, with a helipad marked alongside a simple white shed.

As they disembarked the helicopter, Callie struggled to grab all her gear while getting her wind-frazzled hair back under control, then rummaged for her hat.

A sign across the shed read in large hot-pink letters, "Welcome to Eden." Cartoonish palm trees had been painted either side.

A golf cart pulled up. "Welcome, Mr Delport," said the driver, a young man in crisp white shorts and a hot-pink polo shirt bearing the palm tree logo and a name tag that declared him to be Heath.

Callie hoped there might be some food in their future. It might only be a couple of hours since the luscious lunch on Stanford, but snorkelling had made her ravenous.

"Would you like to explore the hiking paths," Silas said, "or head into the resort for a cool drink first?"

Not wanting to appear lazy, Callie held her tongue—and her breath—waiting philosophically for Jack to choose the harder option.

But he said, "Actually, I'd love to get some footage of that volleyball game before it finishes if it's okay with you?"

Excellent. Volleyball had to be near the food.

They climbed aboard the golf cart, Silas beside the driver, Callie and Jack behind them facing backwards, and rattled off down the bumpy roadway. Poor old Dean got to stay with his helicopter again. The cooling shade of the trees closed in around them and golden sunshine cast a strobe-light effect through the branches.

A few minutes later, they drew up before a large-scale resort complex where loud pop music played and children laughed and screamed in a pool surrounded by elaborately-fake landscaping and mini water slides in bright colours. Callie puzzled over another sound in the mix until she noticed a line dancing class in full boot-scoot up the other end of the dining room. Perhaps they'd be doing the *Nutbush* soon.

The three new arrivals walked onto a broad wooden deck and a waitress in a hot-pink sarong said brightly, "Good afternoon, Mr Delport."

"Do you come here often, Silas?" Callie said. "Everyone seems to know you."

"I own the resort, of course."

Of course.

The waitress led them to the best table—just conveniently cleared—on a deck that extended out over the beginnings of the beach. They sat under a thatched umbrella reminiscent of an Elvis Presley movie—and possibly that old, judging by the musty smell.

Callie worried they might only be offered drinks but thankfully the waitress distributed full menus. Callie ordered a latte and a banana split ice cream sundae, smiling blandly at Silas when he looked at her oddly.

Silas ordered sparkling mineral water.

Jack ordered fruit juice and a side of sweet potato wedges—clearly, snorkelling had made him hungry, too—then disappeared to get some action shots of the beach volleyball game before their orders arrived. Callie anticipated how well the sounds and images would contrast in the final documentary with the quiet, understated luxury of Stanford.

When he returned, Jack said to Silas, "Do you mind if I use the drone here?"

"If you wish." Silas's lips curved slightly into an urbane smile. "But please do not crash it into my guests."

Moments later, the waitress placed a dairy catastrophe in front of Callie—an oval melamine plate piled with several flavours of unnaturally bright ice cream and splodges of whipped cream from a can, drizzled with chocolate topping, and another topping that glowed fluorescent yellow even though from her memory of the menu it was meant to be caramel. Beneath it all, she could definitely detect slices of fresh banana.

Jack grinned at her.

"It's a fruit portion," she said.

He snacked on his wedges of deep-fried sweet potato while setting up the drone.

She ate ice cream and watched his phone screen. "It's just like the movies." She swiped one of his potato wedges to dip it in the fluffy cream and batted her lashes when he protested.

The drone observed, from above, the sweaty volleyball players, swooped out along the planks of the jetty, and then curved back toward the shore as a snorkelling family passed underneath. Jack zoomed a little but the vision was jumpy.

"I haven't had much practice," he said with an apologetic smile.

She glanced over her shoulder. Silas was watching too, apparently fascinated.

Callie said, "Maybe change height instead of using the zoom."

He brought the drone sweeping along just above the surface of the water, rising smoothly to a safe altitude as it approached the families playing close to the shore. It flew over a father who stood hip-deep in the water throwing his child in the air, their mouths open in laughter; a moment of innocence.

At first, Callie thought the screaming she could hear was just part of the endless excitement that was Eden Island.

But then she saw a change in the way people moved between her and the waterline, an edginess, a turning, a domino effect of realisation that surged across the crowd.

Jack frowned and sent the drone back up, searching the shore.

There it was.

A mother and child staggering to the beach. The child was emitting a piercing sound that mingled with the pop princess chirping out another hit through the speaker above them.

A small child, screaming in terror and pulling at his legs.

The afternoon sun blasted through the open sides of the chopper as they headed back to Stanford Island, and there was no shady place where Callie could hide.

Beside her, Jack held his camera in his lap, silent. He roused himself as they approached Stanford Island and the camera came up again—it would look different from this angle and in this light.

Callie snapped a few half-hearted shots herself, while questions swirled in her head.

A freakish invasion of box jellyfish to one offshore island might have a scientific explanation. But two islands, so far apart, on the same day?

And if there was any worse person to see in agony than a new bride, it was a child.

Eden Island was closer to the mainland than Stanford was. The rescue helicopter had arrived fast. The island used vinegar, had anti-venom on hand and applied it quickly. Surely, the little boy would be okay?

8

It was a relief to focus on work right now. Jack immersed himself in the interview with Aaron the researcher, and temporarily closed his mind to box jellyfish and the suffering they caused.

Callie was a great interviewer. Somehow, people told her things that turned information into something richer and deeper. Jack's more direct technique was better for confronting politicians and con artists.

Two cameras on lightweight tripods were recording different angles as they stood beside a fibreglass aquarium that held a variety of small fish, and several beautiful cone-shaped shells about the length of a finger, coloured a soft pink with a warm-brown diamond pattern. The resident snail was visible in two of them, spreading out under the shell like a skirt. Its ruffle was patterned white and light-brown and almost-black.

Aaron explained the proboscis the snail used as a fishing lure, the hollow tooth on the end that injected the venom, and the unique and fast-acting form of insulin in the venom that might help scientists develop better treatments for diabetes. "Have you got a waterproof camera? If you lower it into the tank and move it like a fish, we might be able to get one to fire at you."

Jack fetched his tough little camera and adjusted a sling. They experimented but without success. Unthinking, he reached to retrieve it. Aaron locked his fingers around Jack's wrist, hard, and pulled him back.

Adrenalin flooded Jack's body. "Sorry. Forgetting myself."

"Easily done."

Callie said, "How dangerous are they?"

"The venom causes muscle paralysis. Shuts down the respiratory system. They've caused forty deaths in the past century—that we know of."

Callie leaned back a little, away from the tank. "Are you scared of working with them? Or do you get blasé after a while?"

"Neither." Aaron crossed his arms. "I respect them and try not to act like a fish in front of them. People either want a pretty shell to put in a bowl on their coffee table or they think these snails should be wiped off the face of the earth for human safety. They're just animals trying to live their lives in the ocean—a place that is not a human habitat. The harpoon is for catching fish so they can eat. They're not out to kill people."

Callie tilted her head enquiringly. "What brought you to Stanford Island?"

"I heard about this project just when I was finishing my masters degree, back in November. It's part of my doctoral research."

Callie said, "And why this research, over all the other projects you could have worked on?"

He rested the heels of his hands on the side of the tank and gazed into the clear water for a long moment. "I grew up in the Pilbara, in remote Western Australia—my father was in mining. My best friend's father was diabetic and he died at forty-seven from the kind of heart disease white men get in their seventies. A good man." Anger flashed into his eyes. "Did you know First Nations people are four times as likely to get Type 2 diabetes? Four times!"

"Really! That's huge," Callie said.

"Really." A small, sharp pause. "Anyway, he's why I chose medical research."

Jack tilted his head. "How is the research funded?"

"We grovel to people who look down their noses at us and see if they might spare a few cents after they've fuelled their private jets."

Jack said, "What about the mining companies? Surely they could help?"

Aaron's head jerked back and his nostrils flared. "Make a deal with the devil? They're too busy destroying the land."

Jack was thinking about where to take that next when Callie stepped in. "Do you think your research will make a difference?"

A little bit of puff went out of Aaron. "I… don't know. I hope so. I'm still working that out."

THE SUN HAD SLIPPED INTO THE TREES AND LATE-AFTERNOON bird noises were escalating by the time they emerged from the lab. Jack shot Callie a side-eye and she raised an eyebrow.

"That was interesting," she said.

"Yeah. A lot of layers."

She narrowed her eyes. "There's obviously a really sore spot in there somewhere. Or several sore spots."

Pause.

Callie broke the silence. "Aaron must have a good relationship with his father the miner."

Jack frowned, pondering. "Very."

They drew level with the island office, and through the windows Jack saw Kevin at his desk talking to Silas Delport. Both men looked sombre.

"Perhaps we shouldn't interrupt them just now," Callie murmured.

But Jack walked straight to the open door and knocked as he walked in. "How's it going?"

Both turned and Kevin spoke. "Oh, hi, Jack, Callie. How'd it go with Aaron?"

Jack said, "Brilliant." Pause. "And we got a lesson in social economics."

Kevin smiled though his eyes looked tired. "Yeah, Aaron'll keep you on your toes. Mostly by ramming you up against a wall with his hands round your throat."

Callie said, "Everything okay here?"

"Not really. We've heard from two other resorts. Multiple stingers, and there's a young bloke in intensive care who might not make it."

Silas shook his head. "An astonishing infestation covering three hundred kilometres, all in the one day."

"How awful." Callie leant on the back of an empty chair. "The other islands—do they usually get stingers?"

Kevin said, "They're not quite as far out as us, but they're outside the normal range."

"Global warming?" Jack said.

Kevin frowned. "They move further south each year. But further out? I'm not convinced. And this is so sudden." He rubbed the back of his neck. "I've had both the tourism and health ministers on the blower in the past hour, looking for magic answers I haven't got." He sighed and quirked his mouth. "We're Venom Central. They always turn to us for things like this." As if on cue, the phone on his desk shrilled and he picked it up. "Kevin Harris… yeah… uh-huh." His face relaxed. "Oh, that's amazing. Thanks, mate."

As he put the phone down they all looked at him, waiting.

"Our young bride is sitting up in bed, eating a cheese sandwich."

***

JACK JOGGED DOWN THE BEACH, HEADING EAST, AWAY FROM the resort and the late colours unfolding in the sky behind him. He'd been deeply exhausted by the day, but running refreshed him. The tough cam was strapped to his forehead. Without a gimbal the vision would probably be too staccato to use, but he had plenty of memory cards and he liked experimenting. He focused on smoothing his gait. Tonight's "reverse sunset" was just as beautiful as the western sky. Fluffy cumulus clouds tinged with pale gold sailed like a fleet of fat ships across a backdrop that changed colour by the moment, soft blue and pink to purple.

He was the only man in the universe, revelling in the coarse coral sand abrading his bare feet, free from any concerns about used hypodermics. These were not beaches that needed to be sifted by tractor-drawn contraptions every morning.

He didn't notice the black shape in the water till he was almost upon it. A seal? Not this far north, surely.

And then the seal stood up and walked out of the water, becoming Baz the researcher in a black wetsuit.

"Dude!" the seal-man said. "Good day for a run, hey?"

"Yeah. Not game to risk the water, though."

The wetsuit was the short type, leaving Baz's lower arms and lower legs exposed to possible jellyfish.

"Yeah, that was intense this morning, hey? But I can't stay out of it. I seen no one was down here, so I figured I'd do a few laps, while the tide was high enough to swim down this end." He grinned. "Might have been too obvious outside the main house, hey? Don't tell Laura—she'd go mental."

"No stinger suit?"

"Nah, never needed one. Coulda borrowed one, but then they'd wanna know why, and what was I gonna say? Didn't need to, for my work. But you've gotta be one with the ocean, man. It's out there like this great big wild animal"—he looked out at it and extended his arms wide and high like a bear, fingers splayed, then dropped them to his sides—"and you gotta respect it. Sometimes it hugs you, sometimes it bites you, and that's just the chance you gotta take."

"Has it bitten you before?"

"Oh yeah. Broke my back surfing in a massive storm couple of years ago. In Victoria. Wasn't even allowed to walk for a few weeks. The swells that day! Just howling! Seven metres. You a surfer?"

"Tried it, but it didn't take." Now might not be the time to mention that his fear of heights was strangely activated when he tried to stand up on tilting water. "You must miss it." There was no surf inside the shelter of the Great Barrier Reef.

Baz stared out to sea and nodded slowly. "Every single day."

"So, what makes you stay in a place with lots of sea and no surf?"

"I love the reef, man. And I can make a difference."

9

$\mathcal{I}$nterwoven clouds glowed purple, pink, orange and red, like someone had gone berserk with an 80s makeup kit, as Callie wandered along the jetty with Nina. "Which one's yours?" she asked.

"Down here." Nina led her down a flight of steps to a runabout moored alongside the water-level pontoon. She grabbed the mooring rope and pulled the vessel towards them, then stepped over the gunwale. "What type of videos would you like?"

"Can I see what you've got?"

"Sure." Nina rummaged in a locker under the instrument panel, powered up a tablet and navigated through the contents. "I think these are the best ones."

"Aha—in the folder named 'best'."

Nina looked at her sideways with a coy smile. "It's my own unique code."

"Some of these are fantastic." Callie nodded as she scrolled and tapped, thoughtful. "Not just the content, but the angles. The framing. You've got a really good eye. These underwater sequences with the turtles are extraordinary." She looked Nina in the eye. "I really mean that. Have you ever thought about a job somewhere in media, or do you prefer to keep it as a companion to the research?"

Nina seemed to flush slightly—or was it just the sunset? "I wanted to try for one of the big documentary teams, but… Baz…" —she raised one elegant shoulder—"wasn't in favour."

"Oh… that's"—at least a dozen responses were on the tip of Callie's tongue, none of them overly complimentary about Baz— "really unfortunate." She took a deep breath. "Well, if you agree, I'd like to take a copy of these three pieces. If we use any of them in the final film we'll give you a credit, of course."

Nina did agree, and there was an extra sparkle in her eyes as they paired the tablet with Callie's phone for the transfer.

"Ahoy there!"

Callie shielded her eyes against the setting sun that angled under the jetty and peered into the cockpit of a lean white sailing yacht moored on the other side. She discovered Mary the solo sailor, her collision partner from this morning, lounging feet-up along a bench seat, a white enamel coffee mug in her hand. "Oh! Hello, Mary." She grinned. "Looks like you're living your best life."

"Every single day. Care to join me for tonight's sky-show? You're both welcome."

"Thanks so much, but I need to get back," Nina said with an overly sincere smile.

Callie said, "I've got a few minutes, and I'd love to." She stood to attention. "Permission to come aboard, Captain?"

"Permission granted."

Callie looked up at the underside of the jetty and down at the several metres of water that lay between the two vessels. "Instructions for *how* to come aboard, Captain?"

Mary laughed. "Back up the top and down this ladder over here."

Callie clambered down the pitiful excuse for a ladder, made her ungainly way around various winches, cleats and wires, and finally stood safely in the cockpit. "Well, thank you for the adventure."

"The best adventures happen at sea."

"One day, I might even leave port."

"Baby steps, matey. Would you like a cuppa tea? I hope so, because I'm all out of coffee and I don't carry alcohol."

"Of all the options on your drinks menu, tea is my favourite."

Callie followed the Englishwoman into the cabin and gazed curiously around the cramped but highly functional interior. A blue-padded bench either side of a laminated table. A tiny metal sink. A gas stove with a railing high enough to give sliding pots a fighting chance if the ocean heaved. Recessed shelves with high sides and various elasticated nets holding a riot of useful and interesting items, from foodstuffs to equipment to maps. A radio set and other technical-looking things. Towards the bow, a door standing ajar revealed a double bed, neatly made.

"How long have you been sailing?"

"All my life, really, but only in smaller racing dinghies till last year. My job evaporated and I decided to use the severance package to buy the *Celestial.*" She smirked. "After I'd signed all the paperwork, my brother pointed out the unfortunate combination."

"Sorry?"

"Mary and *Celestial.*"

Callie frowned.

"The *Mary Celeste.*"

"Oh! It's been a *very* long day."

"My brother thinks it's effing hilarious." Mary rolled her eyes.

The kettle shrilled and they headed back out to the cockpit, each holding a fresh mug of tea. Fortunately, the sky-show was still playing as they got comfortable, one bench each. Callie snapped some photos on her phone.

"So," said Callie, "your job evaporated?"

"Downsized, I think the current euphemism is. So I upsized my life."

"What was the job?"

"Stockbroker. Blow drying my hair and putting on a suit every day to run round and round on the spinning wheel of rats."

"Bit of a change, then?"

"Yes, and not just the hair." Mary ran her fingers through her scruffy, spiky, distinctly non-corporate hairdo. They chatted about daily life on board a yacht. The beautiful places she'd seen. A wild three-day storm she'd weathered in the Indian Ocean with swells like mountains.

"And then there's all the other yachties who want to come aboard for a few sundowners." She grimaced. "I'm an alcoholic, so I don't particularly want to watch them get wasted. And every time a stranger approaches my boat, I get edgy—ever since the pirates."

"Pirates!"

"Middle of the night near the Cape of Good Hope, a bump on the hull. I went out, and there they were."

"How terrifying." Callie leant forward a little, eyes bright. "What did you do?"

"My… friend… had a gun. And he wasn't afraid to use it."

Of the seventeen questions that immediately popped into Callie's mind, she settled for, "So you weren't always solo?"

Mary shrugged. "We parted ways when we reached Australia. What work are you doing on the island?"

"I'm a television journalist. I'm here with a colleague, making a documentary about the medical research."

"Oh."

No follow-up questions. Was Mary judging her? "It's a freelance gig. I'm on leave from my job this week. Jack—my partner-in-crime —arranged it all. We made a documentary together after we got lost with a bunch of friends down the bottom of New Zealand a couple of months ago. That one sold pretty well, so we're hopeful this one will, too."

"Not planning to get lost again?"

"Hard to imagine how we could, on an island this size."

"How do you decide what goes in the film? Do you plan it all beforehand or just see what happens?"

"We prepare a list of interviews we'd like to get and the types of shots we'll need as overlay—we shoot quite a few hours of video to create just one hour of finished documentary. But we also respond in the moment to opportunities or things happening around us. Like these dramas with the jellyfish."

"Dramas, plural? I heard about the poor lass this morning."

"There's been others—further up the reef."

Mary's eyes opened wide. "I've been warned about the box jelly-fish—I even bought a stinger suit in Cairns, which makes me look like a collapsing zeppelin—but I was told they don't really get out to the islands. Sounds like I'd better be more careful."

"Definitely. At the moment, anyway." Callie glanced at her phone. "Yikes. It's dinner time. Are you dining ashore tonight?"

"I am. I decided I could do without dried veg and macaroni for one night." She added, airily, "Though I'll miss it, of course."

"Would you like to walk together? I'd better get moving or I'll be in trouble, yet again."

Mary closed and locked the cabin, and guided Callie as she climbed around and over all the obstacles and back up to the certainty of the jetty's floorboards.

As Callie stood upright she sighed her relief.

Mary said, "Look at that. Two sea adventures in one evening."

"And I've survived both of them."

———

SURVIVING JACK'S DISPLEASURE MIGHT BE HARDER. AS CALLIE arrived in the candlelit dining room—where a nearly-full table of guests sat before doors open to a lagoon that glowed from some hidden light source in the tropical dusk—she saw that he had showered, his damp hair was neatly combed, and he had donned long khaki pants and a white button-up shirt with the sleeves rolled up to a muscular mid-forearm. He'd never be a movie star but he scrubbed up pretty good.

Callie had bumped into Nina right after they left Kevin's office and had been nowhere near their cottage since. Therefore, she was still in the day's clothes, smelling of stale sunscreen and shedding random grains of sand.

"Late *and* unkempt," Jack said.

"I ran out of time because I was finding you an interesting story," she said brightly. She introduced Mary, and said, "Tell him about the pirates."

"Pirates! Where?" His eyes locked onto the Englishwoman's face.

Diversion complete. Callie perused the evening menu and considered the herb-crusted coral trout.

Mary gave a surprisingly short and hesitant account of her drama. Did Jack make her uncomfortable? Or was it the restaurant with its soft music and wealthy diners? *Or is the story a lie?*

"Sounds dangerous," Jack said, and looked like he was about to ask more.

Mary said, "I hear you two had an even more dangerous time in New Zealand."

So, Mary can do a diversion too. Callie let Jack give the background to their reunion gone wrong in the remote mountains of Fiordland National Park. The decade of bitterness and grief that had ripened into malice in the heart of an old schoolfriend. The friends who didn't come home.

"So, I'd been planning to make some kind of documentary," he concluded, "but it turned out to be a very different story to the one I'd planned. And Callie ended up working on it with me. My background is newspapers, not television, so it was great to team up with her."

"How could you carry all that equipment, though, on a trek?"

"We just used consumer-level equipment. Much the same as we're using here—minus the drone." He smiled and shrugged. "That one's new."

Callie added, "Small equipment produces big results these days, but we mostly focused on the storytelling. And we told the truth, instead of trying to make ourselves look good." She raised one eyebrow. "Which was extremely awkward at times."

Jack rubbed his face. "Yeah, that was a bit uncomfortable. But it's probably what made it fly. In these days where everyone is showing off on social media, people are hungry for something real."

"Maybe that's why they like reality television so much?" said Mary.

Callie laughed. "Yeah, except this story actually *was* reality."

"And you've done well with it?"

"Yes—it went viral online, thanks to Callie's crazy marketing ploy. We posted the low-resolution version, for free, and then television networks from around the world came knocking. They wanted to buy the high-res version, figuring that people would want to watch it all over again. Which they did."

"So, you made money out of your friends' tragedy?"

Pause.

Jack said, "We did our job. And the message was important."

Jack was hanging out of a helicopter over a cold, dark New Zealand lake and his harness was coming loose. He had no free hands to save himself—in one he held his SLR camera while with the other he tried to contain a wriggling, bawling baby. The man seated in the front of the helicopter turned to look back and Jack saw he held not a camera but a high-powered rifle and was raising its barrel to point at Jack's face.

He woke with a gasp; it was a dream, of course. But there was definitely a crying baby somewhere. A streetlight usually created a grid pattern on his wall but the bedroom was pitch dark. Weird. A blackout?

He fumbled for his bedside lamp and then winced as the brightness hurt his eyes. Oh. He was on Stanford Island.

He crept out to the verandah and saw a ghostly figure in a pale nightgown down the other end. It was Callie, peering into the bushes.

In the moonlight he didn't see the smile on her face so much as hear it in her voice. "Well, I guess this is the mutton birds. Kevin said to listen for a strangled sheep. To me it sounds more like a wolf playing the kazoo."

"Well, that's a relief. I thought it was a baby."

She laughed, but there was an edge to it. "We'd need a miracle for a baby, Jack."

"Were you asleep?"

"I'd just dozed off when the serenade started. Trouble sleeping. This whole jellyfish thing is messing with my head. It's like living through *The Day of the Triffids*, underwater."

"Yeah, it's giving me the creeps too."

"Keeping you wide awake, obviously?"

He shrugged. "My mother always says I could sleep on a clothesline in a cyclone."

"Speaking of cyclones, what about the one that's forming up north?"

"That's way up past Cairns, Cal. It's over a thousand kilometres away."

She was silent a moment. "Jack, you know how you told me to bring waterproofs?"

"Yeah."

"I brought the ones I took to New Zealand."

"Not that awful orange jacket?"

She snorted. "The one that matches my hair. Did you bring yours?"

"Um… no. It's missing an arm. I brought my old one."

"Oh. Of course." Pause. Maybe she was remembering the moment he had to cut the sleeve off the new one. "It's just that… when I was packing my orange jacket… well… the last time you and I went into the great outdoors together, bad things happened."

Callie never admitted weakness. He felt a surge of something vaguely caveman-ish and stood straighter. "We can postpone the documentary. Book a floatplane out of here tomorrow."

Silence, then: "And miss what might be the biggest story of the year?"

He laughed softly. "You and I are a special kind of crazy, Cal."

She gave him one of her Botticelli angel smiles and reached for his hand. He wove his fingers through hers, soft and smooth and warm, and they leaned on the railing and gazed at the ocean in the dark.

10

———

*T*he rising sun was just beginning to caress the infinity pool as Callie dropped her towel on a poolside lounge and slipped out of her sarong. It had been a restless and confusing night, from so many angles. Early morning was not her natural habitat, but a solo dip seemed infinitely better than continuing to toss in bed.

As a lumpy teenager, she'd always found swimming pools humiliating. That frizzy-haired tomboy still lived inside the television journalist, albeit forcefully cloaked in plastic glamour and stilettos. As if it should matter what she looked like! But when the camera rolled and the red tally light came on it did matter, even to her.

A salary that was decent, albeit not as high as most people imagined, had procured the sleek black one-piece she wore, artfully designed to emphasise or camouflage where needed. But oh, the joy of just being herself with the water and no one to impress.

She stood at the edge and gazed at the pool's glassy surface as it reflected the pearly sky of dawn, enjoying its stillness. She dived in, cutting the water smoothly, and came up for air with a minimum of splash. She swam breaststroke to the end of the pool, turned and swam freestyle back to the beginning.

As she turned to begin another lap, something on the bottom of the pool caught her eye. She hovered over it then launched into a duck-dive, trying to see what it was. A pretty shell—a cone with a criss-cross pattern in gentle hues, like the ones Aaron was researching. It must be a decoration that someone had accidentally dropped. She reached to pick it up and at the last moment noticed what looked like a frill moving around it. It was still alive! She snatched her hand away as fast as the water resistance would let her and scrabbled at the side of the pool, trying not to let her feet touch the bottom near that tiny assassin. She surfaced, gasping for air, and heaved herself out of the pool on wobbly arms.

She sat down hard on the stonework and tucked her legs close so they didn't dangle into that perilous water. She trembled as her mind filled with visions of what could have happened. Muscle paralysis. Respiratory shutdown.

What the hell was it doing in the pool?

Nearby, a large wicker box held a set of viewing tubes resort guests used when walking on the reef at low tide—a metal cylinder with glass at one end and handles at the sides, designed to eliminate surface reflections and give a clear view of coral and fish. She wrapped herself in her towel and retrieved one of the cylinders so she could confirm what she'd seen before raising the alarm.

Yes, it was definitely a cone snail. She tilted the viewing tube and began to check other areas of the pool. She gasped as she found another snail little more than a metre from the first.

Callie worked her way methodically around the pool and counted a total of five deadly cone snails on the pool floor. She stood, hands on hips. "*This* isn't global warming. A human did this."

She walked with swift purpose to the main house where a big red emergency buzzer would help her reach the staff member on duty.

<hr>

Jack's footfalls were muffled by sand as he jogged along the access track that meandered down the centre of the island.

Nothing beat the shock absorption or the pleasing crunch of running in sand. His was far from the only noise though. The twenty-four hour birds called and shrieked and flapped around him.

He'd seen a couple of buggies on the island but, as far as he could tell, this track served only one road-vehicle—a trayback utility he'd noticed on yesterday's island tour. He wondered how it got to the island in the first place, and how they protected it from rust. He wondered what they transported to the other end of the island in it. He'd ask Laura. It must be research-related.

It was going to be hot later and, even now, sweat stuck his shirt to his back like glue. If he was at home in Brisbane, he'd be running through suburban streets with Rufus trotting along at his side, tail up, ears forward. They would evade the first reluctant cars nosing out of driveways—tradesmen and shift workers and city commuters determined to beat the rush. And then he'd head back to his cramped childhood bedroom in his parents' simple house for prayer and meditation before breakfast. Its peace and clarity fortified him against the ninety-minute traffic jam that stood between him and his college lecture room.

Today, he'd pray on the run; it wasn't an activity his current roommate understood. His right hand rested on the camera slung around his neck to stop it bashing against his body with each step. For fun, the tough camera was on his forehead again, recording his jolting passage through the island. He focused on the rhythm of footsteps and breathing and didn't think about Callie Brown.

He veered off the road onto a narrow pedestrian path through the trees and slowed to avoid startling any wildlife that might be entering or exiting the ocean. He was through onto the beach, and the cool wind was glorious on his heated skin. He paused a moment to snap some shots of fluffy clouds, their edges backlit by the rising orange sun. He should have brought the tripod. A time-lapse of the sunrise might have made a nice establishing shot in their documentary. He'd do that tomorrow.

He set off again, keen not to let his heart rate drop too much. As he rounded a wind-blown shrub, he had to swerve to miss a photographer crouched in the sand. "Ugh… sorry!"

The man stood; Jack expected a tourist but it was Silas. "Don't worry. One thing is true about Stanford Island—always there will be another bird." He smiled and cradled his long lens in one hand. "I see you are here for the same purpose."

He mustn't have noticed the abundant signs of recent running but Jack decided to let it pass. "Are you getting some good shots?"

"Yes, in that tree a pair of egrets nesting. The colour of the light this morning—they look gold instead of white."

"May I see?"

The man manipulated the controls on his camera and scrolled through a series of shots that displayed on its rear screen. "Here. This one I like. And this one."

"Wow. I love the angle of its head. And the light in the eye. Amazing clarity for such a big zoom."

"Yes, the lens is very pleasing. Do you have any good pictures today?"

"Only the sunrise. But there's one on the camera you might like —a brolga. Dancing."

"Oh! I wish so much to see that." He was like an excited kid.

Jack pressed buttons and navigated to the shot. He smiled as he remembered how the lanky silver crane's awkwardness had disappeared as it lifted its wide-spread wings to dance for a potential mate. The fanned feathers were outlined in gold, backlit by the sun, making the bird pop from the dark background of distant rainforest.

Silas said, "Exquisite. This bird—where is the best place?"

"Um…" Jack rubbed his face. "This was up in the Daintree. Far North Queensland. But it's the state bird so we must have them in more places than that. I can check, if you like. Are you planning to do some touring, once you leave the island?"

"I am not sure, but I hope."

"Have you got many photos of Australian birds?"

"Oh yes, for many years. Indeed, my love for birds is from this island."

"You've been here before?"

"With my father. Perhaps I was your age, or a little younger. Before you were born, I think. Back then, we could not see the photograph till later. No instant picture, then! And these were not even in the imagination." He indicated the tough cam on Jack's forehead.

Jack had forgotten it was still rolling. He used it so much lately it seemed like part of his head. "I've done some film photography. At school. Our teacher thought we should learn the skills. We even had a darkroom—but only black and white."

"Ah, the darkroom." Silas nodded and smiled. "A playground. In the darkroom, we bend reality to our wishes."

Callie was standing with Kevin and Laura, staring into the water, when Jack walked onto the pool deck with a towel slung over one shoulder, camera in hand.

"What's going on?" he said.

Before anyone could answer, the crunch of gravel on the path announced the arrival of Aaron looking like fury on legs.

"Kevin! Laura! Someone has taken my animals. All of them. They're missing from their tanks."

Laura pointed mutely at the pool while Kevin sighed and rubbed the back of his neck.

"What! What are they doing in there?" He grabbed the viewing tube discarded by Callie and crouched at the poolside. "Are they still alive?"

Callie said, "They looked alive to me. I nearly picked one up."

"We'll have to get them out of there, fast. This pool is saltwater, not seawater."

Laura spoke sharply. "Aaron, settle down. I can understand you're upset about your animals, but that's hardly the only problem here."

"It's a pretty stupid prank. It could derail my whole project!"

Kevin's tone was steely. "A prank is gluing someone's ruler to their desk. Putting deadly snails in a swimming pool used by tourists is attempted murder."

That finally seemed to slow Aaron down. He sat back on his haunches and stared at his boss. "Who would do that?"

"And why?" said Laura. "Why would anyone do such an *awful*

thing?" Her face twitched as though a bunch of emotions were wrestling just under her skin. Callie felt a few emotions of her own when Jack walked over and put his arm around Laura. Laura turned into Jack's embrace and it became a brief, fierce hug.

The snail retrieval operation commenced and Jack hovered with his camera. Once two snails were out of the pool, Callie excused herself to go shower.

Jack said, "I'll come with you." A little way down the path he said quietly, "Want to do a piece to camera?"

Callie stopped and stared at him, then turned to see the backdrop he had in mind—up the tree-lined path, early sunlight slanting through the leaves, and beyond, the ongoing hubbub around the pool. She nodded, scraped her hair back into a band as neatly as she could and adjusted her sarong. "You've got some overlay of the actual snails in the pool?"

"Yes."

"Okay then. Ready?"

"Rolling."

She drew herself up tall and confident and looked straight into the lens. "3—2—1… I was taking a swim at dawn this morning when I noticed something strange on the bottom of the pool. It turned out to be the very same deadly cone snails we'd seen in the research centre yesterday." She held her serious expression for a few seconds, then flicked him a glance. "Got it?"

"Perfect. You're a one-take wonder." He smiled.

They walked back to their cottage in a silence crowded with potential topics. Finally, Callie chose one. "I'll tell you who would do such a thing. Someone who knew the combination to the research centre lock and could handle those snails without getting stung."

Jack nodded. "But who had a reason?"

11

The chef was deftly slicing the bright orange flesh of a pawpaw when Jack wandered into the kitchen, his hair wet from the shower. "Okay to grab some brekky?"

"Yes. Seven till nine for guests at the buffet, six till eight for the staff in here—though they all seem to be having a lie-in today. No one's feeling the lure of the reef." Jack detected the lilt of an accent. Irish or Scottish? Callie would know, but they sounded similar to him. "Help yourself to anything on that bench. And if you get the munchies you can help yourself any time of day from there, or that fridge." He pointed his knife at a tall, glass-fronted chiller at the end of the room. "The kitchen's never locked."

Jack peeled a banana and ate it while investigating the contents of the big fridge: loaves of sliced bread; huge catering tubs of Vegemite, peanut butter and margarine; bowls of fruit; dishes of what might be leftovers from last night's guest dinner.

He fetched a bowl of Weet-Bix and milk and slouched against the bench. "Mind if I talk while you work? I'm Jack, by the way."

"Sure. I can chop and talk all at the same time. It's just like magic." He spun the knife round his finger, grabbed it, and smiled with a hint of mischief. "Romeo."

Jack frowned at the last statement, puzzled. Was the chef having a go at him?

The chef smirked. "It's my name: Romeo."

"Oh. Sorry."

"Me too. It's one of those classic Irish boys' names."

"Is it?"

"Not even a little bit. My parents were in the theatre, thought it was poetic. You can imagine the poetry that welled up from the hearts of all the other dear little children at school."

"I can. But a bit of persecution is so character-building for a child."

"And would that be the voice of experience?"

"It would. I was the religious kid. And categorically uncool."

"Did you get over it?"

"Which? The persecution, the religion, or the uncoolness?"

"Any and all."

He considered. "Still uncool, but I don't care anymore. I guess I probably got over the persecution." He paused and wrinkled his nose. "Mostly. As for the religion… I'm about to start the second year of a Bible college degree. Wouldn't really call myself 'religious' though."

Romeo selected three oranges and started cutting thin slices for his fruit platter. "What would you call it then?"

"Being a believer. Having faith." He shrugged. "Religion is about rituals. To me it's about… relationship? Connection to something meaningful?" He nodded. "Life purpose." He put two slices of wholemeal bread in the six-slot toaster and peered at the switches. "Did you know about this cone-snails-in-the-pool business this morning?"

"Sure I did. Callie found me first. The only one up and breathing at that ungodly hour. Apart from her, of course."

"Any idea who did it?"

The chef shook his head. "It's a weird thing, right enough. Aaron's just about the angriest person on the island, but I doubt he'd risk the health of his own sweet snails in a swimming pool. More likely to stab a lad through the heart just for touching them."

"Who'd know the combination for the research centre lock?"

Romeo paused from slicing spiky skin off a golden pineapple, stared at Jack and shook his head slowly. "Only absolutely everyone on staff. We get the new passcode in a staff email once a week." He resumed cutting. "The lock is just to keep eejit guests from poking their hand into something that might kill them. The staff have to sign a thousand indemnity forms. Even I had to take the time to do it, though people were starvin'."

"How long have you been here?"

"Just before Christmas. They lost their chef right in the lead-up to the summer rush."

"A baptism of fire?"

Romeo raised his eyebrows but kept his eyes on the pineapple. "You could say that."

"Do you like it here, though?"

He shrugged. "The setting is grand."

"Yeah. Pretty nice office," Jack said, looking out the kitchen window at the lagoon. "How many would know how to handle the snails without getting stung?"

Romeo paused again and considered. "T'wouldn't be that hard, if you didn't care about hurting the creepy-crawlies. Meself, I'd use those long-handled tongs over there, put them all in a bucket."

"Oh. Did you see anyone else moving around this morning?"

Romeo shook his head. "No, just a mutton bird that nearly flew right into the side of my head. Eejit birds. I start at five, and the housekeepers don't do the restaurant till half-five. I've been hearing the sweet sound of vacuum cleaners, so they must be doing their job. You going to be a priest, then?"

"No, probably a missionary."

"And the journalism?"

"I'm on leave without pay from my newspaper while I study. But I'm not sure if I'll go back to that job."

"Don't you have to be a doctor or a monk to be a missionary?"

"Plenty of mission projects want communication officers."

"Is that the truth? And what does Miss Callie think of it all? She's your girlfriend, isn't she?"

Jack wondered how to answer. "Not exactly."

"Hello again, Romeo." Jack flinched. It was Callie's voice, and for a confusing moment he thought she was addressing him, with sarcasm, before he realised she was greeting the chef. He wondered if she'd heard his last comment and what she thought about it.

———

As they approached the office together after breakfast, Jack saw Kevin inside in serious conference with Laura. At the door, he discovered Silas Delport was in the room too.

"Any news?" Jack said.

Kevin answered. "We've notified the police, but they're not exactly rushing out here. Sunrise Island woke up with two stonefish in the pool and Eden had a box jelly in theirs. Two people have been badly stung and it might turn into a murder investigation before the day is out."

Callie said, "What about the little boy stung when we were there yesterday?"

"He's doing well. He was lucky—wasn't a big sting, and he got help fast."

Jack exhaled at that part of the news. "That's good, at least. What will you do if guests want to leave? What if one of them is involved?"

Kevin rubbed the back of his neck. "We asked the cops, but they said to just keep a copy of everyone's photo ID, and they'll get to it when they can."

Laura's face looked tight. "Our situation is less urgent, apparently, because no one was hurt. And they know where our creatures came from even if they don't know who or why." She sighed and sagged in her chair. "But we have to decide what to tell the guests."

Callie gave her a slight smile. "Crisis management. But it's not like you can do much to limit the damage now."

Jack added, "Not when whatever this is has become so widespread."

Laura sat up straighter. "Oh, so are we 'news' to you now?" There was hostility in her tone.

Jack frowned. "We're in the middle of a developing situation, and Callie and I will obviously need to do our jobs. I would hope that friends could respect each other's professionalism in a crisis."

Kevin sighed. "I s'pose we'd rather have you two doing it than some joker just walked in off the helipad."

"My television network will want a report later today when they realise we're in the middle of it," Callie said. "I'd like to interview you, Kevin, if I may, when we know a little more."

He shrugged. "Sure."

Laura stared at the floor.

Silas Delport had remained subdued during the discussion, and Jack wondered how worried he might be about the future of his resort at Eden Island. Was it just a coincidence that Silas was connected to two of the locations? Or was he the target?

12

Eight guests decided to leave during the course of the morning—two by helicopter, the others on a motor launch. Callie did mini-interviews with several guests who agreed to appear on camera; Jack operated the equipment.

The guests spoke with accents from around the world. Some were devastated by the abrupt end to the holiday of a lifetime. Others clearly vacationed at similar expense frequently—their reaction was nearer irritation, but with an edge of unease.

The luxury cottages had no phones and the office phone was running hot with Kevin's calls, so Callie and Jack used the wi-fi connection to make internet calls. Callie talked to her news director in Sydney. Jack did the rounds of several regional police stations and then spoke to state command in Brisbane. He called the hospital for an official update on the stinger victims. They both monitored the internet sites of other news services and poked around on social media, trawling for any new information that someone might have uncovered.

They arranged an interview with Kevin, with the main house and turquoise lagoon as a backdrop. "We'll keep this short," Callie muttered to Jack. "No time to sift through a long interview."

Kevin's Hawaiian shirt of the previous day had made way for a plain dark blue. His demeanour was statesmanlike, concerned, capable. Though rough around the edges, he was a much better player than Callie had anticipated. *You could be a very convincing liar, Kevin. I'm going to have to watch you.*

Callie recognised the sound bite she needed about fifty seconds into the interview and wound it up without ceremony. Back at their cottage, she wrote her script while Jack, tense and focused, transferred the vision she specified from their various cameras and phones. She even wove in a credit for Nina Tanaka, the researcher who'd supplied footage of yesterday's beach drama.

Callie commandeered Jack's laptop to edit a short piece for the late morning news. Jack was more skilled than she at the finer details of the professional video editing software but he wasn't fast enough for the deadline pressure of television news, and he yielded with good grace.

She said, "They can tidy it up down there if they really want to —and if they have time. They'll probably need to slot in some vision of the rescue helicopter arriving at the hospital anyway."

Finally it was done, and they began the upload to the television station. It seemed like a lot of staff might be using the wi-fi at the moment. The progress bar moved oh-so-slowly as news time inexorably approached. Callie said, "There's someone waiting in a news editing suite in Sydney who probably needs supplementary oxygen right now."

When the "upload complete" message appeared with only fifteen minutes till news time, Jack released a gusty sigh. "It's intense, isn't it?"

She smiled and raised an eyebrow. "Welcome to my world."

He grinned. "I think I'll stick to newspapers and doccos."

"Not just yet, you can't. We'll have to do it all again with an update for the evening news."

He groaned.

She did another scan of the news headlines. "Well, would you look at that."

"What?"

"You know Cyclone Sasha, the one that was wa-a-ay up the

pointy end of Queensland? It's changed direction. Heading south. Fast. And it's just been upgraded to Category 3."

He put his head in his hands and she heard a muffled, "That'd be right."

She flicked him on the arm. "Just wondering, Jack, how many other things will you be wrong about before this adventure is over?"

He sighed. "I'm not making any more predictions."

She laughed.

They arrived at lunch to find several staff members eating in the guest dining room.

Callie murmured to Jack, "Kevin's boosting the numbers."

"Smart."

She scanned the room. "I notice he's found somewhere else for Laura to be."

Jack frowned. "She's probably attending to something important."

Callie decided not to press the issue, but the Laura she'd seen a few hours ago would not be an asset to the resort right now. And she still didn't know what Laura really was to Jack.

<hr>

As Callie pushed her plate away, replete, she heard Silas say to Jack, "Would you like to see my flamingos?"

Her eyebrows flew up, but Jack said, "Yes, I would."

The older man tapped on a tablet that rested on the table amid the glassware. Even from her position on the other side of Jack, Callie could see that the shots were exceptional—not just the classic compressed pictures of groups of them dancing, but close-ups of their faces that hinted at the personality of individual birds. Silas was clearly a master photographer.

Jack said, "Amazing. Especially this one. And the angle here. South America?"

"No, Namibia. Although I also have seen them in South America. I have some vultures here, from Kenya." He swiped, scrolled and tapped, and another set of expert photographs appeared on the screen. The birds were haggling over the carcass of something once-beautiful, and while Callie could appreciate the excellence of the shot she didn't love the voracious look in their zombie-bird eyes.

She leaned forward to speak to Silas around Jack. "Do you travel a lot specifically for photography, or just when it fits in with your business interests?" Jack leaned back a little, out of her way.

Silas tilted his chin back and forth: one, two. "A little of both. I love to record the natural world." He gave a bleak little smile. "How long will we have it, if humankind keeps destroying it? And birds particularly are my great passion. Did you know they once were dinosaurs?"

Callie said, "*Jurassic Park* revisited. At least they won't eat us."

Silas gave a short, gusty laugh, and tapped the beak of the vulture enlarged on his screen. "This one will. But only after you are dead."

13

The normal business of the island seemed to have ground to a halt. "I doubt we'll get much sense out of anyone for the docco till they know what's happening," Jack said to Callie. "What do you say to exploring the island, getting some overlay?"

Callie nodded. "Jetty first? Some nice colours and shapes there."

He experimented with angles and close-ups as he moved along the boards of the jetty, using a type of selfie stick with a gimbal that smoothed the movement of his steps. The gaps between the boards let through flashes of the turquoise water beneath. "Check this out."

She watched it on the screen. "That is seriously cool. So smooth. It's like you've got a studio dolly but it's just that little thing."

A few minutes later she said, "Hey, Jack!"

He stood beside her at the railing and videoed a reef shark cutting through a cloud of tiny silver fish that were swimming so close they touched each other, moving as one, surging through the water as they fled the predator.

She made jazz hands. "Bait ball!"

"Don't swim in it."

The fish were somehow keeping a shark-shaped buffer between themselves and the shark. "It's like the sharks have a forcefield around them," she said.

"Reminds me of when you drag the reverse pole of a magnet through iron filings."

"Mary's gone."

"Huh?"

"She was moored right here. She must have left this morning."

"That's a shame. I'd have liked to see her yacht."

"I'd have liked to interview her. I guess it doesn't matter." As they left the jetty and continued along the shoreline, Callie made him laugh with her tale about the sleek white yacht, its coincidental name, its intriguing contents, and how elegantly she herself had boarded and disembarked.

Near the staff quarters they came upon Aaron at a shady wooden picnic table overlooking the water. He stared morosely out to sea, an empty coffee mug on the table beside him. Jack glanced at Callie, and she nodded. They slid into the benches.

"Are you okay?" Jack said. "Did your snails survive?"

Aaron glanced at them, unsmiling, then looked back out to sea and sighed. "They're okay."

Callie said, "Was it really that bad for them to be in the pool?"

"Well, it wasn't good for them."

"Does it make a big difference to your results?"

"Probably not." He rubbed his forehead. "It's just that… I don't know… I can't really afford to lose them."

Jack said, "What happens if you do?"

"It's so hard to get new animals." He looked from one to the other, his eyes fierce. "They make it so hard for us. Do you know that I have to fill in dozens of forms just to be allowed a handful of animals for research that might cure diseases, but someone selling the shells or taking live animals for people to put in their aquariums can take hundreds at a time?"

Callie inhaled sharply. "You're not serious!"

"Do I look like I'm joking? I might come up with a product that makes money. And if I do, the government wants their cut. Vultures!" He spat the word. "I could go out there"—he nodded towards the ocean—"and have a good selection in an hour. But I'd be better off just buying the animals out of my own money."

Jack said, "Could you do that? Just replace these ones and resume the experiments?"

"How will I organise that, with all this rubbish going on? And we're so remote; everything has to be planned in advance. It's not like someone comes sailing around the outer islands with a box of cone snails on the off-chance someone wants to buy them."

Callie said, "In the circumstances, could you just, you know, pop out there," she pointed at the water, "and switch them?"

Aaron stared at her, his mouth a flat line. "You mean, break the law."

She flushed. "Well, these are exceptional circumstances."

He gave no answer and returned his gaze to the horizon.

Jack said, "I think there's a lot about your work we don't understand. It's more pressure than I thought it would be."

"Who knows how long this delay will last? My funding is running out and there's no guarantee I'll get any more. I was making such good progress…"

Jack led the way down various paths until they reached the sandy road that ran through the centre of the island.

"How do you know where you're going?" Callie said.

He shrugged. "Just keep going east."

She laughed, and he looked at her for explanation but she shook her head.

The sand to the side of the vehicle tracks was softer and kicked up in pleasing heavy clouds ahead of his shoes. It had probably been ground into fine particles by the constant abrasion of wheels running over it. He was tempted to kick harder to see how far it would fly; he resisted the temptation.

They passed the staff quarters, then the lab. He glimpsed another building through the trees. "Where's that map of the island?"

Callie rummaged in her bag and opened out the colourful sheet —somewhat crumpled—that was handed to guests as part of their welcome pack to help them find the pool or lunch or their next massage. "This building isn't on the map."

It was a cabin, not unlike the guest cottages in size but with simpler external finishes. Through the windows he could see a small kitchen, with a dining table and lounge room beyond. Furnishings that were pleasant but inexpensive. Jack knocked on the door but no one answered. He turned to say, "I guess we'll have to come back later," but Callie was already walking around the side, towards the ocean.

On a picnic table on a deck at the back, with a view through leafy trees to the sea, sat Laura, head in hands, a pile of paperwork on the table in front of her.

"Are you okay?" Callie said.

Laura's head whipped around and she stared at them, unsmiling.

"Sorry to interrupt," Jack said, and shifted weight to the other foot.

Laura sighed. "It's alright. Want a cuppa?"

They followed her inside and, as the kettle boiled, Laura unpacked the dishwasher, putting plates and mugs away, sorting cutlery, rearranging the teaspoons in the drawer one by one so that they lay on their sides in a neat row, each tucked into the curve of the next.

Callie said, "Is this where you live?"

"Yes—me and Kevin. We're the only ones who don't live in the staff quarters. Although there's a third bedroom here if we needed to accommodate another senior staff member. Or we can use it when family and friends come to visit." She pulled out three coffee mugs she'd just put away in a cupboard, opened the fridge, and stared into it for at least twenty seconds, before picking up a carton of long-life milk that stood at the front in plain sight. "It's nice to have somewhere to get away from everybody, now and then."

"Is this your parents?" Callie pointed at a framed photo on a higher shelf.

"Um, yeah." She opened the drawer again and took out one of the nested teaspoons. "My mum and stepdad."

"Do they come to stay sometimes?"

"No. No they don't."

"Oh. Do you get to go and see them sometimes?"

Laura didn't answer, but turned and led the way back to the deck with a large cafetiere of fragrant coffee and a plate of simple biscuits. "Sorry about the packet biscuits. Sometimes I get tired of the rich food in the dining room."

Callie smiled. "We all grew up on milk arrowroots. The best comfort food."

Laura was silent a long moment, then said in a tone that was slightly singsong with a harsh, sour edge: "Today's the day for comfort food."

"You must be exhausted," Jack said.

"Yeah." Pause. "What's coming next though?" Pause. "And then what will come after that?" She shrugged. "If the situation gets any worse it could kill the tourism side of things for ages. Without tourism, we can't fund the research."

Callie said, "Don't supporters like Silas fund the research?"

"Partially. But it costs an absolute fortune to keep a remote island running. A lot of our biggest current projects could probably be done on the mainland, to be honest. And that might be where we end up if the resort falls apart." She sighed. "And that would break Kevin's heart."

"And you?" said Callie.

"I guess I can always find another job. But I'd hate to leave here."

Jack felt a stab of impatience. "You're letting your imagination rule your head. It's not the end of the world just yet."

Callie shot him a glare.

Laura stared at the table. "Perhaps you're right. We'll wait and see what happens." She gave him a tight little smile and sipped her coffee.

Jack headed back to the roadway and led the way towards the reef flats that he knew must have been exposed by the ebbing tide by now. He had an idea for some overlay looking back over the coral to the outline of the island.

"Very sensitive, Dr Phil," Callie said.

"What do you mean?"

"Laura was upset. Couldn't you see that?"

"She was overreacting. It's not like her. She's usually quite logical."

Callie made a noise that could best be described as a snort, but there was no humour in it as far as he could tell. "How many times have you seen her when her home and livelihood are under threat from random murderers?"

"They're not murderers. Nobody died. You found the snails in time."

"Whoever put them there—and the critters on the other islands—clearly doesn't care if anyone dies, and that's much the same thing."

"Maybe."

"And she must be asking herself why they've been targeted."

"Probably."

"I suppose we'll find out. Whoever did it is probably proud of it."

"You think so?"

"It doesn't strike me as the type of thing you do and then keep secret."

"What are you thinking? A ransom?"

Callie shrugged. "I hadn't really thought of it in those terms. But it's attention-seeking behaviour, you have to agree with me on that— even if it's your day to disagree with me about everything else."

"What are you talking about?"

She continued on her own theme. "It was meant to create a splash." Pause. Side-eye. "So to speak." He gave a half-smile, which was more than the pun deserved.

They walked in silence for a while, and then she said, "Did I say the wrong thing about the photo? Are her parents dead? Or, I don't know, divorced? Alienated from her?"

"What? No, I don't think so. Last I knew, everything was okay." Jack had a sudden thought. "Did you bring your reef shoes?"

She rummaged in her bag. "Um, no. Should I have?"

He sighed. "I'll wait here." He looked around. "I'll get some shots of the birds in the trees."

He knew it would take her a while to a. Find their cottage, b. Find the shoes, and c. Find her way back to him.

By the time she returned with the shoes, flushed and puffing slightly, he had set up the drone and become engrossed in the up-elevator style shots he could get with it as the drone ascended past flapping birds, nesting birds, screaming birds, and out the top of the tree canopy.

"Look," he said.

She peered at the vision on his screen and grinned. "Cool! Especially this one." She seemed to enjoy the new toy as much as he did. "Shame you can't hear them properly."

"I recorded sound with my phone. Hopefully it'll be clear enough, but we can do voiceover on those pieces of footage." He shrugged.

"Will you use the drone down the end of the island, too?"

"Yeah, I'd like to. Better save some battery."

"Have you got a spare?"

"Yeah, but only one. And they don't have very much juice in them."

They began walking again and she said, "Do you think we'll still be able to make the original documentary? Or are we just here to cover news, now that all this has happened?"

"I don't know. But I think we should go ahead as if we'll make the docco—get the overlay and the interviews we need. Whatever this turns out to be, there's a good chance we'll make a docco about that if we don't make the original one, don't you think?"

"Another viral docco?" She raised one eyebrow.

He gave a half-smile. "We seem to keep finding ourselves in the middle of viral documentaries."

She sighed. "We're supposed to *report* the news, not *be* the news."

14

They could have played with the drone all afternoon if they'd had more batteries. Callie was bewitched by the vision on Jack's tiny screen as the drone swooped over the fringing reef and then down the centre of the island, revealing glimpses of the roadway they'd just walked up, the lab, the utility and resort buildings, the communication tower, the glowing pool, the jetty with its motor launches and glass-bottomed boat but no longer hosting visiting yachts. How different it all looked from above. Serene. Perfect.

As the vision travelled back down the island towards them, Callie said, "Who's that going into the lab. Is it Kevin?"

"Might be. I don't think I'll take the drone down to check." He shot her a wry look. "Might make him jumpy to have it hovering next to his head, with all that's going on."

When they called into the lab on their way back, Kevin was engrossed in something on a computer screen.

"Are you happy to see us at the moment, or would you rather not?" Callie raised one eyebrow.

He gave a sardonic half-grin. "I'm working on some research. It's nice to lose myself in some of the good stuff for half an hour."

Jack said, "It would be great to get an interview on camera. What do you think?"

"For the news?"

"No, for the documentary. We'd still like to make some progress. We've only got a week and this… whatever this is—might hold things up."

He agreed. They managed to get him out to the wet lab—the outdoor deck with the sea tables and the big tank full of jellyfish. The sun was lower in the sky, the light gentler.

"Could you do the thing where you pick one up, like you did yesterday?" Jack said.

"Only if you don't tell Laura on me." He grinned.

"Hang on. I'll get set up."

"Ready? There's one coming to the surface now."

The camera rolled as Kevin's hand darted into the tank and seized the jellyfish. He held it high and looked up at its transparent bell in his hand as its long, lethal tentacles trailed down to water level where they then flared in the gentle current.

He explained for the camera why he could hold it this way without getting stung, and then gave Callie a cheeky grin. "Would you like one to take home as a pet? Perfect for the home aquarium."

Callie laughed. "The home aquarium of a serial killer, maybe."

Back inside, they set up the cameras again in the lab, with Kevin sitting at a computer screen covered in a colourful graph, a lab full of scientific clutter spread out behind him.

"Tell us about the heart research and what jellyfish have to do with it," Callie said. A blunt and open-ended question was often the best beginning, especially when she hadn't done quite enough pre-reading.

"The simplest way to describe it is probably that the toxin causes an incredible surge of electricity in the heart, and there are heart conditions where we need better control of electricity. So we isolate the compounds in the venom and figure out which combinations are responsible for what. Can we manipulate their combinations and quantities to steady the heart instead of stopping it?"

"How do you figure out which things to investigate," Jack said.

"We guess." He gave a cheeky grin. "We follow hunches. We see something that's happening and it brings to mind something that happens in a medical condition, a disease pathway."

Jack nodded. "Not a quick process."

"No way, mate. Takes forever. It can take months or even years to follow a hunch long enough to find out that it's not the right hunch. But we have to keep searching." He wiggled his fingers and said in a spooky voice, "The truth is out there."

"Laura said you could probably do a lot of this research on the mainland," Jack said.

He gave a half-shrug. "Yeah, maybe. Particularly since we've switched to the box jellies, because they don't even inhabit these waters." He snorted sarcastically. "Not till this week, anyway."

"So…" she said.

"It's a constant juggling act, to make sure the resort generates enough profit to cover the other stuff. It's expensive and inconvenient to live and work out here but it has a bit of glamour, which the investors like—looks good in their annual reports." He spread his hands. "So, you weigh it up. The lab was already here, so why not use it. And most people that go home from here, whether they came for a holiday or to work, care more about the reef when they leave. And that's gotta be a good thing."

"Makes sense," Callie said. "So, it was a heart condition that your mother had?"

"Ah, no." He scratched the back of his neck. "She had early-onset Alzheimer's. There's an enzyme the venom inhibits, and it's an enzyme we want to inhibit with Alzheimer's. So we're looking into that."

Callie said, "Two research projects?"

"Oh, we're running multiple projects here at any one time, but the heart one is the main one for the jellyfish. It's shown the most promise so far, which means it's more likely to make money sooner so it's easier to get funding. I do the Alzheimer's one on the side, basically."

"A passion project." Callie tilted her head.

"Yeah, you could call it that."

"It must have been a hard time for your family," she said.

He was silent a moment and stared at the bench. "I was away at uni. When I came home for the winter holidays she made a chocolate cake and it was horrible. Sounds stupid—but my mum made the best chocolate cake in the world, bar none." He rubbed his thumbnail along a crease where there was a join in the bench. "Then I saw other things. Losing stuff. Wearing clothes that didn't match." He looked up. "I think Dad had been making excuses for a while."

"How did you cope with it, out here in the middle of the ocean?" Callie kept her voice gentle.

"Not easy. But easier than when they had to leave here and move to the mainland, to a tiny apartment that was stinking hot, no ocean, no breeze. She'd lived here since they were first married—most of her adult life. At least here she had half a chance of knowing where the hell she was."

"Not possible to stay here?" Jack said.

"Ah… no. There were"—he paused, and his eyelids flickered—"things that happened around that time."

"Is your dad still alive?" Callie asked.

"Nope. The strain of it was all a bit much. Wrecked his health. He only lasted about five years after her." He scratched his neck again. "Got a bit tired of living without her, I reckon."

"And this research?" she nudged.

He raised his hands as though about to deliver a speech, let them fall, and sighed. "Ah, you know…" He looked her straight in the eye and then shook his head slowly. "If we could save some other family from going through all that, how good would that be?"

15

In the end, the biggest story didn't come in time for the six o'clock news but the late news.

The guest dinner was served buffet style instead of the usual evening a la carte, and five or six staff members were boosting the depleted number of guests at that long and sociable table. Callie was surprised to see Romeo among them.

Jack murmured, "Who's looking after the kitchen?"

"I guess with a buffet most of his work is already done. He's a good choice, though. No better anti-depressant than an Irish accent."

Jack said, deadpan, "And if things get messy, he's good with knives. But what about Aaron? He's a revelation."

"Yes, he's really settled down. He'll never be as chatty as Romeo, but when he's not obsessing over his snails he's got a calm strength about him that's reassuring."

"Kevin seems to know the mettle of his team."

"That man is proving exceptionally good at crisis management." Callie refrained from mentioning the continued absence of Laura. "Speaking of our great leader, I wonder where he is? Should we be checking we're not missing something important, instead of feeding our faces?" She tilted her head and considered the slice of lush chocolate gateau on a plate before her. "Nah." She spooned a sizeable piece into her mouth.

Jack said, "We need to keep our strength up," and had a spoonful of cake himself.

She was enjoying a reviving coffee when Kevin entered the room looking especially serious. Still no sign of Laura. Callie watched Jack discreetly set his phone camera going, propped against his coffee cup and pointing towards the end of the table where Kevin stood. *Good man.* They wouldn't broadcast a stealthily-obtained video without discussing it with Kevin—apart from being unethical, when he found out about it he'd probably stop cooperating with them. But the energy in the room would change if the recording process was drawn to everyone's attention.

Kevin said, "Excuse me, ladies and gentlemen. Friends." He gave a reassuring smile. "I hope I can call you friends."

Not sure about the "friends" thing, Kevin—might be too much. Too oily.

"We've just this minute had a call from the police and I'm afraid it's not especially good news, but we have a plan to deal with it." Guests glanced at one another. "A group of eco-terrorists has claimed responsibility for what has taken place here on Stanford Island"—Kevin had to increase volume to be heard over the exclamations that met this statement—"and there have been incidents at several other resorts along the Great Barrier Reef. In the circumstances… please, friends, let me speak… in the circumstances, we believe the best course of action is to evacuate the resort. We want to ensure the safety of all our guests."

A woman stood to leave and spoke sharply to her partner. "I told you we should have left this morning!" Others began to push back from the table, a cacophony of chair legs groaning on the timber floorboards.

Kevin fought to regain control of the room. "A moment more of your time, please. Friends. Please, just a moment."

The sharp-voiced woman muttered, "We're not your friends."

Her husband grasped her hand and said gently, "Come on, love, sit down for a minute."

Kevin said, "We're sorry that your visit to our island home has ended so unpleasantly. You will of course receive full refunds, and an invitation to return for a complimentary week in the future when our peaceful way of life returns. I will arrange a launch to carry all of you to the mainland, departing at nine in the morning. Please have your bags outside your cottage at 8.00 am."

One man said with a frown, "Why can't we leave tonight?"

"Night travel through the reef is not ideal, and the police don't feel there is any imminent threat tonight."

Callie noticed all the things he didn't mention in that statement but, at a glance, the guests seemed reassured enough.

Kevin continued. "Two members of staff will be available here in the main house at all times tonight, and we will keep the lights on. You are welcome to come here at any time through the night if you wish, or to stay in your cottages. Other members of staff will patrol the resort in pairs. For now, I suggest you go to your cottages and pack while I brief my staff. I came to you first because you deserved to know." The words sounded a little contrived, but they seemed to come from the heart.

A melee of confusion followed. The short tropical twilight had long-since ended, and some guests were clearly nervous about walking to their cottages in the dark. The splendid isolation that had brought them here no longer seemed so attractive. Others were anxious to be active, and packing gave them an outlet. One guest—owner of a family business whom Callie had chatted to at lunch—walked up to Kevin and said, "I realise this would be awful for you. Thanks for everything."

"Thanks, mate." The two men shook hands.

Jack stopped his phone and began a new video recording. Kevin seemed to be edging his way towards the door into the staff area, one guest at a time. Callie moved that way too, behind Jack, and Silas Delport appeared beside her. She said to him, "A nightmare, isn't it?"

He shook his head briefly. "It is very bad."

"Will you go to the mainland tomorrow with the other guests? Or head to Eden Island to look after your own resort?"

He pursed his lips. "Today I engaged a crisis manager to handle the media reports about Eden. And I have been speaking to my resort manager. I chose her very carefully. She has the evacuation under control, I am thinking. A much larger crowd, but also much closer to the mainland." He shrugged slightly. "A manager often does a better job when allowed to do the task they were hired for, and not be watched by the big boss, do not you think?" He looked at her with a questioning smile.

"I've never done that particular job but I guess it might be true. When I'm in the middle of reporting a big story, I certainly don't want my boss sticking his nose in. I'm the one on the ground who knows what's going on and what's possible."

He nodded. "I can be on Eden very quickly with my helicopter." He shrugged. "The mainland seems too far from either of my interests, so I think I will stay here on Stanford at present." He paused. "And do not say so, but the food is better here on Stanford, no?" He smiled like a naughty child, eyes bright.

It was the first evidence of a sense of humour that Callie had seen from him and it startled her into a grin. A guest frowned at her, and she carefully formed her lips back into a more serious arrangement.

"What about you?" he said.

Callie raised one eyebrow. "I'm a journalist. It's a massive news story. What do you think?"

He nodded, and even seemed pleased.

She asked, "Will you be pulling out of your investment here?"

"Perhaps. And yet, this may not interrupt the research if they are dedicated to continue."

"I imagine it will take a long time for tourism to recover—both here and on Eden—even if it ends with no damage to infrastructure."

"My resort is well insured. And here, they may see it as an opportunity for greater focus on research for a time."

Kevin had finally made it to the staff door and they followed him through it.

At the tables to the side of the kitchen the entire team was assembled though it was way past the staff dinner hour, and she realised suddenly that gathering the team was what Laura had been doing.

Kevin didn't need to call for attention. Everyone fell silent and stared.

"The police tell us eco-terrorists have claimed responsibility for what's going on. I'm shutting down the resort and all guests will depart on a launch at nine in the morning. We'll keep the research centre open for any who feel a need to stay. If you want to go, there will be a seat on the launch for you. Go and pack what you need, now. If you want to stay and help keep things operating, you'll be welcome to do so. Laura and I are staying at present, and we'll continue to monitor the situation in case a full evacuation becomes necessary."

Laura said, "Don't go anywhere on your own, especially in the dark; find someone else and travel in pairs. We have ten walkie-talkies—ensure you have one with you, wherever you go."

One of the women said, "What if they blow the place up in the night?"

Kevin said, "The police seem to think if they were going to do that, they'd have done it first. But there are no guarantees. Be watchful. Report *immediately* anything suspicious that you find—*anything*."

Laura added, "Not just a ticking package, but a door open that shouldn't be. A utility item out of place."

Kevin continued, "We're going to keep the main house open with the lights on all night, in case any guests want to be around other people. You can join them or stay in your rooms. We need a roster of staff willing to patrol the resort tonight and to take turns staying awake in the main house."

Laura said, "I have two printed lists here. On this one, mark beside your name whether you are staying or leaving in the morning. On this one, write your name in a timeslot if you're willing to be on the security roster tonight."

Kevin turned to Callie and Jack. "You also have a choice. You can leave at nine in the morning, or you can stay."

They glanced at each other. "We'll stay," said Jack.

Callie added, "And we'll take our turn on the roster."

ONCE THEY WERE OUTSIDE AND ALONE, JACK SAID TO CALLIE, "I want to get back to the cottage. Those terrorists might have released a video."

"Better make the most of the internet connection while we have it."

"You think we'll lose it?"

She shrugged. "If I was going to attack an island like this in an ongoing way, I'd take it down."

He nodded. "Okay. Although they may have finished what they came to do and be a hundred miles away by now. If they're against tourism on the reef, they've certainly done plenty of damage to that today."

"Zealots don't usually stop at the bare minimum though, do they?"

At their cottage, Jack did a quick check of the rooms for anything out of place, then fetched a small case from the backpack he'd used as a cabin bag.

"What's that?"

"Satellite phone. After New Zealand, I decided never to be without communication again. Thought I'd better make sure it's charged."

"Before we lose electricity."

"Exactly."

She raised one eyebrow. "How about you charge it somewhere out of sight?"

He followed her gaze to the extensive windows surrounding them, now blank against the darkness outside. After a moment's consideration, he went through the motions of getting some clothes out of a drawer and bundled the case among them, then walked into the bathroom and shut the door.

When he returned from the bathroom, Callie was at her laptop.

Jack said, "Anything?"

"You were right." She indicated the news website open on her browser.

He leaned over her shoulder and read aloud:

"'Terrorists have claimed responsibility for a series of attacks on the Great Barrier Reef since yesterday that have left one person dead and three more fighting for life.' That's a shame, one of the box jelly victims from the Eden Island pool must have died. But who are the three fighting for life? I thought our bride from yesterday was sitting up and eating."

"Yes, but 'one dead, two fighting for life, and one sitting up and eating' doesn't have the same ring to it."

He rolled his eyes and deadpanned: "Journalists."

"Anyway, there's a video. It's downloading."

Once the video was saved to her desktop, she pressed play. A man in a mask and black t-shirt appeared. The background was nondescript—could have been anywhere.

A distorted voice said: "You have plundered the Great Barrier Reef for far too long. It is a living creature, a complex and beautiful ecosystem, not a circus act. Your waste and brutality have gone on long enough. The continuation of life on this planet—all life, not just depraved humans—depends on the survival of this natural wonder. You have seen what we can do. All tourist resorts on the reef must close immediately, or we will do more of it. More islands will be targeted if all resorts are not vacated within twenty-four hours. We have shown you a small sample; we have a vast army ready to do our bidding. The tourist next to you might be working for us. Researchers may continue their work, because they seek to save the reef, and they understand the need to tread lightly on this planet. But tourism must stop. Stop killing the reef or the reef will kill you."

The video stopped and they stared at the final freezeframe.

Jack said, "Why is research allowed?"

"And 'a vast army'. Why say that?"

"Maybe because it's not true? Maybe it's just two people and a jetski."

She snickered. "A pretty good jetski, if it can cover three hundred kilometres of ocean in one night."

They continued to stare at the screen, each lost in their own thoughts.

Callie turned to look at him, her brow furrowed. "Surely the tourism industry does far less damage to the reef than a lot of other things—it's so highly regulated. What about shipping, for instance? And the big industries—coal and gas, always dredging to extend the harbours. Farmers with their pesticides running off the land when it rains. Why pick on tourists?"

Jack pondered. "I suppose they're an easier target."

She nodded slowly. "A newsworthy target. International media attention. Every country will have citizens caught up in it. But how can it do anything to save the reef?"

He rubbed his face vigorously and then plunged his hands into his pockets. "Maybe it's just the first stage."

16

When they arrived at the main house at midnight for their turn at the roster, Callie saw the plush rattan armchairs with their bright birds and flowers had been moved aside to make room for a row of mattresses on the floor. The concertina glass doors were folded back to maximise airflow and lights glowed at the bottom of the steps into the lagoon. Last night, those lights had looked enticing, like the underwater lights of a swimming pool on a hot night. Tonight they seemed eerie—and yet they would clearly silhouette anyone trying to approach the building from that angle. Last night, they'd been turned off at eleven, but she guessed that tonight they would glow till dawn.

Inside, the lights were dimmed and guests had taken up residence, in some cases two to a mattress—space limitations or emotional comfort? Suitcases stood near their feet. She glimpsed the turquoise of staff polo shirts on several of the recumbent forms. Dressed for tonight's duties or dressed for the morning? They had baggage alongside, too.

Half a dozen people sat at one end of the long dining table in brighter light, talking quietly. The kitchen door swung outwards and Romeo elbowed through with a tray of mugs and a pot of fragrant coffee. Callie's nose twitched.

Jack murmured, "Get yourself caffeinated, girl."

She needed no invitation.

As Romeo handed her a steaming mug he tilted his head and smiled. "Need a heart-starter, Miss Callie?"

"I prefer to think of it as rocket fuel for the brain. What have we missed?"

"Oh, well, there was some hand waving, and then a little useless discussion. That dear lady over there"—he tilted his head towards one of the mattresses—"had a fit of the hysterics, but I was able to calm her down eventually with a glass of hot milk and a bit of blarney." He leant in close. "Don't you be making any racket, now. I think she might even have gone to sleep at last."

She raised a finger to her lips. "Quiet as a mouse."

Beyond him, she saw Laura walk in from the pathway. Jack went to meet her and they had a quiet conversation. Callie suspected a lot of commotion behind the "calm" face Laura was now projecting. Jack reached out to touch Laura's arm. He held the contact for a few seconds. She put her hand over his and nodded.

Romeo turned to follow Callie's line of sight. "Ah, the deputy returns." He poured another mug of coffee and held it out as Laura approached and Jack disappeared outside.

"Thank you."

Callie said to Laura, "How's it going out there?"

"A bit crazy down at the staff accommodation. Most people are packing to leave. They don't know how much to take. A few of the researchers are trying to finalise their records. It's hard to know what to do with their animals. We showed them a video from the terrorists… researchers are not being threatened, apparently."

"Yes, Jack and I saw it online."

"Oh, did you? Well, they're not convinced. They want to be away from here if anything else is going to happen."

"What about you? Would you rather be away from here?"

She shook her head with energy. "Oh no, I couldn't leave the island when all this is going on. Or Kevin."

"I noticed you and Jack chatting."

"Yes, he's very good company in a crisis."

"It sounds like you've known each other a long time."

"We grew up in the same church."

"So you're pretty good friends, then."

"I should think so. We discussed marriage a few years ago."

"Oh. He never told me."

"He hasn't said anything about you, either." Her face was very still.

Callie recalibrated. "Where did he go just now?"

"I think he wants to get some video of the packing up."

So much for teamwork and always travelling in pairs. Callie gave Laura a bland smile and sipped her coffee.

<hr>

CALLIE WANDERED THROUGH TO THE STAFF DINING ROOM with her mug. She found the remote-island researchers Baz and Nina grazing through the fridges. Nina looked sheepish. "Caught in the act," she said.

"Surely you're allowed to eat here anytime, like everyone else?" Eating after midnight didn't seem odd to Callie. She perched on a seat at the staff table, close to a couple of half-empty coffee mugs.

Nina came to sit near her, and for the first time Callie noticed the bulges in the cloth bag the other woman slung onto the floor under her seat. "Oh, I see. A few extras." Callie grinned.

Nina gave her a coy smile. "The diet on Apostle can get a bit… samey." She gathered her curtain of long, straight black hair at the nape of her neck, and with a few expert flips and twists had tied it into a hair knot. The gleaming, elegant do wouldn't have looked out of place at a cocktail party.

"How did you do that?"

"Oh, it's easy." She undid the knot and showed Callie the step by step process.

"Gorgeous. Mine's too frizzy. It'd probably stay that way till I cut it off."

Baz put a bulging fabric shopping bag on the floor beside Nina. "I'll go talk to Aaron."

"Sure," Nina replied, and when he'd left the room she said to Callie, "Hair discussions aren't that interesting to Baz." She looked sideways at her. "As you can probably tell by looking at him. But one of the beautiful things about coming to Stanford is the chance to wash my hair properly. We're on rainwater over at Apostle so two-minute showers are the rule. No desalination plant like they've got here. And our electricity is much more limited—so a hair dryer is pretty much impossible, too."

"I guess you'd get sick of that, but it sounds strangely nice to me. I resent the amount of time I have to spend on mine."

"One of the hazards of your job."

"Oh yes, I live in Plastic World. Who cares about the truth, so long as the hair and makeup are okay."

"The one you did in New Zealand was fantastic, though. No hair and makeup in that one."

"Oh, thanks." She grinned in recollection. "I wore a baseball cap as much as possible when I had to go on camera, to hide the grease."

Nina laughed. "It sounds like you're more attached to your appearance than you think."

"Stockholm Syndrome. Hey, do you mind if I do a little interview with you about life on Apostle Island, while we're here?"

"Right now?"

"Yes."

"Oh… okay. But I have to get my university's permission before you use any of it."

"No problem." Callie fished in her bag and set up her phone on the other side of the table, attached to a tiny bendy tripod not much bigger than her hand. "Nina, what was it like when you first went to live on Apostle Island?"

"Oh, that first week was quite overwhelming. But you do get used to it over time, and even get to enjoy it."

"How does it work? How long have you been there?"

"We do a six month tour as island managers, and they like to have married couples for the job—it just makes it easier."

"I guess you get to work on your marriage, too."

"Yes indeed."

"How remote is it?"

"Coming over here to Stanford Island is a trip to the Big Smoke for us, even though it's so small. It can take us hours to get here sometimes, depending on the waves and the wind."

"Why do you come here?"

"The barge can't get to us at Apostle, so we collect our supplies from here. No one has blasted a channel through the reef like they did here back in the Dark Ages. Except for an evacuation by air we can only get out when the tide is high enough, so we can be stuck there for a week or two at a time."

"That would be tricky if you were sick, or in a cyclone, wouldn't it?"

"It can be. We have access to the Flying Doctor, and a long list of procedures for every type of risk situation. We're monitoring Cyclone Sasha at the moment, just in case."

"Has anyone ever been stuck there in a cyclone?"

"Not yet. One of our newer buildings is cyclone rated." She shrugged—a slight movement of one elegant shoulder. "Only to Category 3, though. I wouldn't like to be there in a Category 4 or 5. I lived through Cyclone Yasi back in 2011, when I was in north Queensland."

"That was a big mother of a cyclone, wasn't it?"

"It was Category 5 and utterly massive—nearly as big as the United States." She gave her sideways look again. "I remember the media graphics. Journalists love that kind of thing."

Callie flashed her an unrepentant grin. "You bet we do! What was it like?"

"Very, very loud. And very, very scary. I was in a shelter—at the local sports hall. And it was just as well we evacuated because the storm surge went right through our house. My kitchen was full of sand when I went home. There was no beach left."

"Or there was, but differently arranged."

"Precisely. But Sasha is smaller, and so far it doesn't look like it will track this way. We have four researchers due to join us, so we have to consult with our director back at the university and decide whether to put them off."

"I imagine that has a lot of repercussions."

"Yes. They plan for a long time before they come to us. You can't come to Apostle on a whim. We're about to enter a week where the tides will keep us island-bound, so that adds a little more pressure to the decision."

"Why don't they dig out a channel, to make it easier?"

Nina became still. "Because it's a revolting thing to do to living creatures."

"How did you end up on Apostle Island?"

"I met Baz at university. We got married. And then he wanted to come here. So I came."

"What are you researching?"

"Climate change."

"Is it promising?"

"I wouldn't call it that."

"What would you call it?"

"Depressing. The reef is dying. Ours will be the generation that presides over its demise."

"What can we do to stop it?"

"I'm not sure. It might already be too late."

"Are you shocked by these terrorist attacks?"

"Yes and no. It's unfortunate that people are being hurt. It's also unfortunate that the reef is being hurt."

"Do you think killing tourists is a reasonable way to fight for its future?"

Nina's mouth thinned to a straight line. "That's not what I said. If you'll excuse me, I need to finish packing."

17

Jack keyed in the entry code and pushed open the lab door to a scene of tense activity. Four researchers were busy in the space but there was little conversation. When they did speak to one another it was in lowered voices, as though afraid of being overheard.

He'd briefly called at the staff quarters on the way through, where the opposite seemed to be true. There, people were yelling down corridors to each other and a man and woman were comforting a teenage girl awash in noisy tears.

There, he'd done a walk-through with his tough-cam in the headstrap, and he did the same thing here at the lab. He captured vision of people moving to and fro and continued on out onto the aquaria deck. The tanks sparkled under bright lights and a woman was attending to some harmless sea cucumbers.

Jack said, "How will this affect your research?"

She sighed. "It will set me back for weeks, probably. But at least I've uploaded all my data to the cloud."

"You didn't trust the guarantee that researchers would be okay?"

"I was in Bali when it was bombed. I left the nightclub early, but my best friend was in the middle of it..." She trailed off and shook her head.

Jack had been a kid at the time and only saw the aftermath on television from the safety of his family home, but he remembered the horror and creeping fear of that endless Sunday and the days that followed. So many young Australians among the hundreds dead. Others struggling to find friends, to get home. He couldn't blame her for avoiding anything similar.

"What will you do with the critters?"

"I'll release them out the front here. The tide is high—I won't have to go far."

"You're not concerned about box jellies floating around?"

"I'll wear pantyhose."

"That's enough protection, is it?"

"Yes. I always have a pair in my kit. They're thick. I wear them when I need to wade around inshore waters over the summer months." She placed the last creature in a bucket.

Jack looked over his shoulder at the scene of busy distraction in the lab behind them. "Would you like me to keep you company as you take them out?"

She made direct eye contact for the first time. "Oh, would you?"

She quickly pulled on pantyhose over her shorts and shoved her feet into a pair of reef shoes. He held his torch out to the side so it lit her next footsteps as she led the way down a narrow path through the forest and onto the beach.

They nearly collided with a large sea turtle heaving its way up the sand. "Quick! Turn the light off!" she whispered. "And don't make loud noises. We mustn't disturb her while she's deciding where to lay her eggs. Just give your eyes a chance to adjust to the moonlight."

They stood and waited. Jack's camera was still running but he knew it would record no vision now the torch was switched off. His night-vision version lay uselessly in his camera bag back in their cottage. A salty breeze wafted off the ocean, carrying to his ears the gentle shushing of the waves and the labouring huffs of the turtle. Behind him, mutton-bird calls rang out in the forest. Jack began to make out the line of the horizon and then the white foam edging the small waves. He looked behind, but the forest still appeared impenetrably black.

The researcher whispered, "Can you see now?"

"Sure."

They walked carefully and quietly along the soft sand in the dark, giving a wide berth to the turtle—just a large, dark, oval blob on the pale beach. The researcher waded into calf-deep water, gently lowered her bucket and released the sea cucumbers. Jack was struck by how tender she could be towards them when she must have been so afraid.

As they turned to head back, something caught his eye. Red? He stared towards the uninhabited end of the island and waited. There it was again. A tiny red dot appeared and disappeared. At first his heart clenched as he thought it might be a rifle scope. Were they in someone's night-vision sights? But no, it came and went.

Someone down there was smoking a cigarette. Someone who probably couldn't see them at all in the darkness.

Someone where no one should be tonight.

Jack murmured near Callie's ear, "Come with me a second."

"We're supposed to be on duty here in the main house."

Jack raised his eyebrows and angled his head towards the long dining table, and the crowd of staff and guests still chatting quietly round it even though it was nearly one o'clock in the morning.

Callie snorted. "Well. Yes. Okay."

Gravel crunched under their feet as they walked outside. Jack kept his voice low. "I've just seen someone smoking a cigarette. Up the other end of the island. We need to check it out."

In the dim glow of the resort-path lighting, he saw her lip curl. "Are we the Tobacco Police now? Who cares, with everything that's going on tonight?"

"Concentrate, Callie. This was right up the end of the island. On the edge of the forest. A long way from any of the buildings."

Pause. "Oh."

"I saw it when I was helping one of the researchers release some animals into the ocean."

"Can we be sure it wasn't one of the staff?"

"Why would they be so far up there? At this hour? Kevin ordered everyone to stay close to home tonight."

"Do you think they know they've been seen?"

"Not sure. They might not have seen us at all. We were walking without lights. Because of a turtle."

"Because of a turtle?"

"Light confuses them. Can mess up their whole egg-laying thing."

She shook her head. "The world is ending and you're worrying about turtle eggs."

"No reason the world has to end for that turtle. Or its young."

He saw the flash of her teeth as she smiled. "You're a softie, Jackson, and that's the truth." He didn't know how to respond to that.

"So, are you coming with me?"

"Of course. Do we tell anyone where we're going?"

"What do you think?"

After a short pause she shook her head again. "No. Got the night-vision camera?"

He held up the head strap in his hand.

She said, "Let's just call past the cottage and get my cap. It'll hide my hair."

"Good idea."

"I draw the line at putting dark smudges on my face, however."

When she was ready, he led the way to the lab and then the twisting, uneven goat track beside it that took them to the beach. When she stumbled on a tree root he grabbed her hand to steady her. He murmured, "We'll have to turn the lights out when we get to the beach, so they can't see us. Just let your eyes adjust."

"They've probably finished their ciggie break by now. But we could have found them if you hadn't gone off on your own."

"Huh?"

"We were supposed to be travelling in pairs tonight." There was an edge to her voice.

"Are we really going to talk about this now?"

They emerged onto the beach in the dark and stood in silence. Jack reach up and switched on his night-vision camera. The turtle was higher up the beach, and stationary now. Among the other night noises he heard the swish and scrape of its rear flippers as it laboriously dug a hole for its precious cargo.

He whispered, "Can you see now?"

"Yes, enough."

"If we can find my tracks towards the waterline we might be able to figure out where I was when I saw it."

"But won't we be easier to see against the sand?"

"Got a better idea?"

"We could creep along the edge of the treeline and stop every now and then to watch. If it's someone keeping a lookout, we can hope they're a chain smoker."

"Okay." Jack led the way again, but progress was much more difficult than it had been earlier on the beach. His foot slid on a patch of grass, connected with a rock, and he grunted softly as pain shot up the side of his ankle. As they approached a curve of the bay, he stopped, and reached back for Callie's hand. She took it and seemed to understand him. She stood close behind him. He could feel her breath on the side of his neck and her warmth just near his left shoulder though their bodies didn't touch. He stared into the darkness, trying to judge the location. Just to the right of where he was looking, a red dot glowed and disappeared. He gave her hand a brief squeeze and got an answering squeeze. She'd seen it.

They stood another few minutes and saw the red glow come and go several times. *What do we do now, Columbo?* If the cigarette belonged to a terrorist, he or she could be armed with any number of weapons. And they had nothing but a couple of tiny hiking torches and a camera. He cursed himself silently. They hadn't even brought one of the walkie-talkies.

A faint noise. Was that a splash? Callie squeezed his hand sharply, then laid her other arm across his shoulder from behind so he could follow the line of her pointing finger. Towards the ocean. He stared and saw the glint of moonlight off a long curved shape. A boat! He squeezed Callie's hand again and she took the pointing hand away. As he watched intently, he saw the faint glow of a small white patch beside the boat. It came again. And again. His puzzlement cleared. They were rowing. Another glint of moonlight glanced off an outboard motor raised at the back—to give them enough clearance to get over the island's fringing reef? The tide was still high. It was just a dinghy. Probably aluminium.

Jack stared out to sea, wondering if there was a larger vessel out there. No one travelled ninety kilometres offshore in a dinghy. Nothing visible, but he did a slow scan of the horizon anyway, hoping the night vision camera on his forehead might pick up something the human eye could not.

A soft, grinding crunch brought his gaze and his camera back to the shoreline as the rower grounded the boat. There seemed to be just one person in the dinghy. A dark figure made its quiet way down from the trees where he'd seen the cigarette. Impossible to be sure of gender.

The person on the beach leant forward and seemed to give something to the rower. Or take something from them? Again, Jack hoped the camera might see what he couldn't, although they were too far away to hope for much detail.

The figure on the beach shoved the boat off the sand, then moved swiftly back up the beach and blended into the trees as the rower headed out.

How long should they wait? Jack felt a firm nudge to his shoulder. They released hands and recommenced the laborious obstacle course along the forest edge.

Jack had fixed his eyes on a dark rock at the waterline just this side of where the boat grounded, hoping to use it as a marker. As they drew closer, he realised the dark blob was higher than before. Another sea turtle. Bless the animal, it would be moving more or less parallel to the path the person had taken. A couple of metres beyond its trajectory should take them straight to the smoking spot.

18

Callie collided so solidly with Jack's back that a gentle, "Oof!" escaped her lips. *I hope no one heard that!* She'd only looked away a moment to check out the turtle below them, and that's when he'd come to a sudden stop. They must be near the smoker's position now. Could they risk turning on a torch? What if the occupants of the boat were watching the shore? And even worse, what if the smoker still lurked?

She felt Jack's hand reach for hers again. She peered into the forest but it was dark and formless. She gazed out to sea, and at that moment over the night-bird noise behind her she heard a gentle rumble followed by a sound like a throaty mosquito. They squeezed hands simultaneously. *The outboard motor.* She scanned, and detected the dinghy's frothy trail glowing white on the surface of the ocean. It curved away into the distance and the sound gradually grew fainter. Even once they couldn't hear it anymore they stood silent in the night breeze, holding hands, breathing gently, as the minutes passed.

Jack turned his head towards her. She nudged his shoulder: *Let's go.* A hesitant metre or two forward, Jack stopped and crouched low with his back to the beach, flicking on his torch but shielding its beam with his hand. He edged along while Callie kept watch, following the faint glow the light cast into the trees, searching for any human-shaped objects on the move.

Jack reached forward and picked up something from the sand. Then another, and another. Just as he put them in his pocket, Callie glanced up and saw one of the trees move. She inhaled sharply and the torchlight flicked up towards the movement; Jack had seen or heard it too.

The person ran and Jack ran too. She wanted to cry out, to tell him to stop, but the words stuck in her throat as she realised she must be silent. She followed him into the forest, seeking the direction of the darting torch and the pounding footsteps, trying to move fast as branches hit her face and roots grabbed for her feet.

"Agh!"

She heard the cry but didn't know who it was. She couldn't see the bobbing light anymore.

She stopped and tried to listen but the blood pounded in her ears, her own breath rasped in her throat, and the confounded birds were making such a racket. Should she turn on her torch? *Jack. Where are you, Jack?*

A bird flew up, squawking. Its wings hit her face, soft yet raspy on her skin, and she reeled back. *Jack! Where ARE you?*

She stumbled forward, lurched into the sticky leaves of a tree. Her foot caught in a hole in the ground and she half-tripped but kept moving. The ground seemed smoother. A path! But which way was Jack?

She saw a faint glow at ground level and moved towards it. Was it Jack? Or a trap? She edged closer and closer. Her foot connected with something solid. Something soft and warm.

Jack.

She crouched and felt along his body. Could she call his name, see if she could get a response? Or was someone still listening, maybe even someone who didn't know who it was that had chased them in the dark?

She found his shoulder and shook it firmly. She heard a moan. He was alive!

She felt for his ear and leant down close to murmur, "Can you hear me? Are you okay?" She put her mouth right at the opening to his ear and hissed, "Jack! Are you okay?"

He sighed and started to move.

She murmured again, "Stay there and recover."

She fumbled for his torch. She could see now that it had slipped, still lit, into a bird burrow. She flicked it off.

They stayed there as seconds and minutes ticked by, Jack lying prone, Callie crouched beside him. She scanned the forest in all directions but saw nothing larger than birds moving. What if they were still being watched? If she went for help would the assailant get her, too?

Her mind roamed the possibilities of everyone she'd met on this island. She had no way of knowing who might be in league with the enemy.

<hr>

"HOLD STILL!"

"But it hurts."

Callie flicked him a glance in the mirror. "Well you should have thought of that before you went running off. Do it again and I'll kill you myself." She picked up her hiking torch to study the wound on the back of his head again. Why was the light in posh hotel bathrooms always so dim?

"But we needed to know who it was."

"And do you know who it was?"

"Well… no."

"Well then." She poured a generous amount of antiseptic lotion on another cotton ball and pushed it through his blood-matted hair with perhaps a little more firmness than was strictly necessary. He winced and sucked in his breath. "You might have concussion. How are we going to get through this thing if you've got concussion?"

"Why would I have concussion, Doctor?"

"You lost consciousness, idiot. I grew up with two brothers who played football. I know about concussion." She could hardly breathe in the close tropical air, fogged now with the sharp sweetness of anti-septic. It didn't help that the bathroom door was shut against the acres of glass that allowed the night to look in at their cottage from all directions. It had been a stumbling, fearful, endless journey through the dark forest back to this doubtful refuge. She sighed. "I think maybe we should wash it with some water. We need to get the blood out of your hair or everyone will see it."

As he bent over the bath, hands propped on the edge, she used the shower hose attachment to sluice the evidence from Jack's head. "This was a good idea. I can see it better now." A superficial wound. They always bled like crazy—she remembered *that* from her brothers' footy days, too.

"Good thing you brought that first aid kit."

"Yeah, I guess." Her eyes pricked. She might not have learned CPR, but at least she'd beefed up her travel medicine kit, inspired by the one Erica the nurse had taken with them into the New Zealand wilderness.

With Jack seated again on his chair in front of the mirror, she pressed another wad of lotion-soaked cotton on the wound and held it there, hoping the bleeding would stop.

Jack went strangely still and she looked up at him in the mirror. He was staring at her.

"It was one of the staff."

"How could you tell?"

"I heard the walkie-talkie, just as he hit me."

19

Callie sipped hastily made instant coffee from the minibar and stared unblinking at Jack's laptop screen while the night-vision recording played: black and white with a tinge of green. She smiled as the shot lingered a little longer than necessary on the first turtle laying her eggs.

Then the sweep of the beach. The edge of the forest. A bird flapping up in front of them. The thin, frothy line of the ocean hitting the perimeter of the reef in the middle distance.

Callie said, "Pause it! There's the dinghy approaching, but we hadn't seen it yet." It was too far away to make out the person aboard. "Okay, keep going."

"There's the smoker." The glow of the cigarette was bright. It was impossible to gauge even the person's gender, and no comparison to give height.

The handover took place at the water's edge. Jack said, "Is it a box or a bag?"

"I think it's got a handle, by the way they're carrying it. A small case of some kind. A piece of equipment?"

"And it's on the island now, whatever it is." He deadpanned, "Too small to be an assault rifle, at least."

Callie said, "No guarantee there's none already aboard the good ship Stanford, though."

Jack sighed and rubbed his face. "How do we get ourselves into these situations?"

They watched the dinghy head back out past the fringing reef, and the brightness of its wake when the motor was eventually started. It grew smaller and smaller. And then it stopped.

"There must be another vessel out there," Callie said.

"Is that… I think that's a mast."

She peered. "Can you zoom in?"

He fiddled with the laptop keys but the zoomed image was too blurry—less clear than the wider shot.

"Can't you press a couple of keys and instantly have an image so clear we can read the boat's registration number?" She fluttered her eyelashes at him, and continued breathlessly, "Like they do in the movies?"

"And the brand on their cornflakes packet. But no, this is the real world, sorry."

"Keep playing it and maybe we'll get lucky." The person on board must have been hitching the dinghy to the other boat. The distant vessel turned.

Jack hit pause and pointed at the screen. "That's definitely a mast."

"So we know it's a sailing yacht, not a hot-water boat. That's something, at least."

The vision bleached white while Jack collected cigarette butts in the sand by torchlight, and then there was the sudden jerk as he looked up at the watcher in the trees. The chaotic run through the forest that followed made her seasick. A collision with something—a tree branch?—jarred the camera and tilted it up and away from Jack's field of view.

He huffed. "What a pain!"

Callie felt that stronger language might have been justified in this specific case. Now all they could see were branches and flapping birds lurching by above Jack's head, to the soundtrack of his heavy breathing and pounding footsteps.

A resounding thud, rather like the sound a brick might make if it hit a piece of concrete, preceded Jack's fall to the ground, and then they got a glimpse of feet running away followed by a long static shot of rainforest debris.

"They hit you with the case."

But in the blur of the fall something else was visible for a moment. Jack rewound and stepped slowly through it, frame by frame. "Is that…?"

"That has to be the island logo. It's a staff shirt."

"So were they carrying that walkie-talkie I heard because other staff are involved? Or just because it happened to be on their hip at the time?"

Callie extracted a notebook from the muddle on her desk. "Let's make a list of what we know. The terrorists have a sailing yacht with an aluminium tender. A lot of them prefer inflatables, so maybe that's distinctive? We don't know how many are aboard the yacht."

"There's at least one of them on the island, working on staff, and they now have something in a metal case. A handgun? A radio? A satellite phone?"

Callie tapped her pen on her lips. "They must already have a communication device. Otherwise how did they talk to the yacht?"

"Could they have used the island radio when no one was looking?"

"Maybe. We need to check how it works."

"And why not have a gun with them already? There's no security check here."

A pause. Callie said, "You know, that antivenom Kevin brought out for the bride was in a black case with a handle."

Jack raised his eyebrows and nodded.

They both stared at nothing for a while.

Jack shook his head. "Let's keep moving. The person on the island smokes French cigarettes." He nudged the three butts that now resided in a snaplock plastic bag.

"Yes… is the person European? Romeo, maybe? Or Silas? He was pretty vague about where he comes from." She shook her head. "What am I thinking? Silas wouldn't be wearing a staff shirt."

Jack said, "Could just be a pretentious Australian."

"Or someone who travels. They don't look like something you could pick up at any old smoke shop in regional Queensland. I'll go online and do a search for the brand." She opened her own laptop. "And I'll check the news while I'm at it."

"I'll upload this vision to the cloud. We don't want to lose it."

They worked quietly a while, and then Jack spoke again. "You know, if they're killers I'm wondering why they didn't kill me."

Callie stared at him. "Maybe they tried and failed."

<hr>

JACK RUBBED HIS FOREHEAD JUST ABOVE HIS EYEBROWS AS THEY drew near the main house. His head ached and his vision was slightly blurry, but this didn't seem the time to tell Callie about it. "A lot of these people are health nuts as well as greenies," he said softly. "Surely there wouldn't be that many smokers? And they wouldn't leave the butts lying around for animals to eat, either."

She said, "I guess it narrows the field."

Callie had already established that the smoker most likely brought the French cigarettes in from overseas or ordered them online. And she'd found pictures, so they knew to look for cigarettes that were yellow all the way along the stick, not just at the filter tip.

As they passed the pool a sudden gust of laughter made Jack jump.

Callie veered off and he followed her.

"Oh, hi guys," she said. "Getting into the cancer sticks, are we?"

Romeo, Aaron and Laura turned to watch them approach. Even in the gentle glow of the pool lights, he could see that every single one of them had a cigarette in hand.

Romeo said, "Medicinal purposes."

"It's been a strange day," Laura said. She wouldn't make eye contact with Jack. "Where have you guys been?"

Callie said, "Sorting some stuff in our cottage. We were rostered on duty in the main house but there seemed to be quite a crowd. Anything new to report?"

Romeo shrugged. "The natives are still restless in there. But on the plus side, morning is only about three hours away now."

Laura sighed. "This night seems to be everlasting."

Aaron said to Jack, "So, are you going off-island in the morning after all?"

"No, why?"

"Didn't you just say you were packing?"

Callie answered. "No, checking our videos and planning. What have you guys been up to?"

"Feeding the troops to keep their spirits up," Romeo said. "Hand-holding the distressed. Partaking of caffeine and nicotine."

Callie said, "We'll leave the nicotine to you guys. But we might head in and look for some better coffee." She yawned.

Once they were out of earshot of the smokers, Jack said, "All smoking yellow cigarettes."

"And it was such a good clue."

"The attacker probably shared them on purpose."

"Could it have been a woman that hit you?"

Jack pondered. "Too tall to be Laura." He paused beside a clump of palms that hid them from the view of those by the pool. "At least, I think so. But I doubt she'd get involved in anything like this. Can you remember who left the main house when I first went up the beach?"

She frowned. "Romeo was taking coffee around. And I spoke to Laura. I don't remember seeing Aaron."

"I saw Romeo with the coffee, so he could have left after that."

"So could Laura. I went to the kitchen and did an interview with Nina, so the staff could have been anywhere. Baz went off. Said he was looking for Aaron, but who knows? We need to keep an eye on Baz and Nina, by the way. Something about them raises my hackles. Why are they here at exactly the time of the terrorist attacks? I got Nina nicely riled in my interview and she didn't have a lot of sympathy for the victims."

"You got her off-balance?"

"Yeah. We were bonding over hair products and then, whammo!" Her eyes sparkled.

"Why?"

"Just following a hunch. She was a bit too helpful with that video of the jellyfish incident." She wriggled her shoulders. "I mean, she really does want to be a photographer, I suspect. But there was something about it."

"I've barely spoken to her. I'll look forward to seeing the interview. You know, to anyone else it might look convenient that *we're* here just when this is happening." He shook his head. "It's impossible to know who to trust."

Callie made a beeline for Kevin. "Could we get a quick interview with you for the early morning news?"

"Sure."

Callie looked at Jack. "Perhaps down the end of the dining room, with the sleeping guests in the background?" He nodded. She steered Kevin through a gap where they'd have to avoid a potted palm and took the chance to move close and quietly take a deep breath. No clinging scent of cigarette smoke that she could detect. "Tough night, huh?"

He nodded. He was still projecting a strong presence but he couldn't hide the fatigue in the corners of his eyes.

"Rolling," said Jack.

"Kevin, tell us how this night has been."

"It's been a long night, Callie, but our guests have taken it in their stride. Most have chosen to sleep in the main house, as you can see behind me. Staff have been making patrols around the resort through the night. We're all looking forward to morning."

"What's the evacuation plan?"

"All our guests and the majority of the staff will leave in the morning. A few staff will stay to keep the island running until this crisis is past. And a couple of the researchers will continue with their important work."

"Stanford Island has been special to your family for many years, hasn't it? How does this attack make you feel?"

She saw Kevin's eyelids flicker. He obviously hadn't expected something so personal and it wasn't particularly relevant to hard news—but there would be a documentary to come. "It's very painful. But the safety of my guests and staff must come before any feelings of my own tonight."

"If you could send one short message to the terrorists, what would it be?"

Kevin paused a fraction then turned to stare down the barrel of the camera lens. "Stop hurting innocent people."

20

The story for the early news was written, produced and sent, and it was a masterpiece of atmosphere and contrast. The noisy chaos of the staff quarters against the hushed, controlled panic in the research centre. The dim and restless slumbers of the figures on the main-house floor against the raw statesmanship of Kevin as he fought to save everything he'd worked for over so many years.

All the while they put it together, Callie's mind rattled with everything they *couldn't* tell the world—yet—about the events of this endless night. She watched Jack rub his forehead while they waited for the interminable upload to complete and thought of all the things they couldn't even say to each other.

"Have you got a headache?"

He glanced at her and then looked back at the progress bar on the screen. "Yeah, a bit."

"Well, why didn't you tell me? I've got paracetamol in my kit." She stared into her own hollow eyes in the bathroom mirror as she waited for the glass to fill. Was she his nurse or his mother as she pushed the tablets out of the blister pack into his waiting hand? She put a hand on the warmth of his shoulder as he swallowed them, to comfort herself as much as him.

"Thanks. I didn't know…"

"Have you been worried about it?"

"Well, you said I might have a concussion…"

"Maybe. I think you'd have been vomiting and stuff by now if it was really bad. Just don't hit it again, okay?"

Later, after a beautifully-prepared breakfast that few people ate, she followed cameraman-Jack down the long and sombre queue of travellers snaking down the jetty, waiting to board the launch that had arrived fifteen minutes late. Had Kevin kept them all in the main house till the last minute for their comfort or to minimise the amount of time they were open-air targets?

She touched Jack's shoulder and drew him to the other side of the jetty. "Quick reality check: are we doing the right thing by staying?"

He slouched against the railing but his eyes on hers were intense. "Almost no researchers left for us to keep working on the original concept. Is the group on the launch the bigger story? But there'll be other journos waiting for it to reach the mainland so we're not needed for that. My hunch is that we need to see it through on the island. What about you?"

"I have that feeling you get when you're running towards the sirens instead of away from them. And no idea how to do it any other way."

He grinned. "What's wrong with us, do you think?"

"Mental instability. Something amiss in our upbringing."

They returned to the long queue of leavers and paused several times to do a quick vox pop with a guest or staff member. Callie asked variations of the inane "how do you feel" question because inane got the best results with inexperienced interviewees when you only wanted a five-second soundbite.

In contrast to the brilliance of the day she and Jack arrived—was it only two days ago?—this time they worked underneath the kind of sulky summer skies that when she was growing up in Brisbane always made her mother stare out the window and say, "There must be a cyclone up north." Without the sunshine, the ocean lost its jewel-brightness and its clarity. A huge stingray slipped past under the jetty, and she could see it only dimly through the dull reflections from above.

At the edge of the island's encircling reef, the white line of the ocean meeting it was thicker, with visible splashes—testimony to the restless heaving that had delayed the launch's arrival. There would be some uncomfortable stomachs among this crowd in the next couple of hours before they hit the safety of the mainland.

The luggage was loaded, the vessel ready to receive. The queue started moving up and over the gangway, flowing into the rows of seats like blood through veins. Ten guests, sixteen staff and researchers, two crew—and two police in black armoured vests.

Jack, camera rolling, did a walk-through of the loaded launch behind Kevin and Laura, who farewelled each row of passengers with just the right mix of confidence, gentle urgency, and empathy.

Callie waited beside a chunky police officer with biceps like hams, but didn't look at him or the hardware he carried. "Good to see you guys here," she said. "I thought there weren't enough resources to send any police out to the island?"

He kept his eyes on the passengers. "We were sent up from Brisbane to assist the local force."

Back on the jetty, Callie felt as though fifteen spiders ran down her spine as the engine revved and the launch pulled away from the jetty. She waited in silence as Jack panned the camera down towards the water that swirled and roiled around the jetty pylons in its wake. *We can always leave tomorrow.*

After the launch left the reef channel and entered the gentle buffeting of the open ocean, Jack turned the camera towards Baz and Nina. They were moving about on their own small boat alongside the jetty, checking things, as it rocked on the wake from the larger vessel. They seemed irresolute. The cyclone had slowed and changed direction again and it looked as though both islands might be safe from Sasha.

Callie had heard second-hand over breakfast that a cancellation had come through this morning from Apostle Island's impending group of researchers. Apparently, those scientists—or their insurance company—didn't have much faith in terrorist promises.

When Jack pressed the off button Callie said, "Did you get some shots of the police officers?"

"I did indeed. How come they've suddenly got enough staff resources to cover an evacuation when they didn't have any to investigate an attempted murder yesterday?"

"They're up from Brisbane. I wonder how many they're bringing in from around the state? Or around the country. This is a big story, Jack."

"And it's not over yet."

"I wonder if your attacker just left on that boat."

"I know. We'll have to leave it up to the police to catch him now. But at least it might be safer here, if he's gone."

"So long as he hasn't left any ticking presents behind."

21

*K*evin summoned everyone to a meeting in the dining room. Romeo poured coffee with his usual blarney but Callie accepted the steaming mug with a frisson of impatience—she had another news deadline approaching.

A call on the walkie-talkie had been enough to bring Silas from who knows where but Kevin had been forced to send Laura to the research centre to fetch Aaron, who seemed oblivious to any risk other than that of losing momentum on his project.

Finally, they were all assembled. Only nine people sat around the long table now. The island was simultaneously empty and yet pressing in around Callie. They'd be 'seven stranded castaways' after Baz and Nina left, but Gilligan's Island it wasn't.

Walkie-talkies lay on the table in a neat row—enough for them to have one each. The beverages and pastries weren't fooling anyone. This was a council of war.

Kevin began, and Aaron was first in his sights. "Keep your walkie-talkie on you at all times and answer it immediately—I don't care what you're doing. If you have to drop a snail on the floor and stomp on it, pick up that walkie-talkie." He didn't use a single profanity, but you could feel them underlining every word. Apparently, calm-statesman-Kevin had left on the launch with the guests.

Aaron's broad shoulders swayed slightly in unease or possibly even belligerence, but all he said was, "Okay."

Kevin looked around the table. "We are here to maintain the island's systems until this crisis is past and we can bring more staff back to help prepare for normal operation. We don't know how long the situation will last. The media are in a frenzy about it, worldwide, and no doubt feeding the terrorists' agenda." He looked at Callie and Jack.

She ignored the implication and said, "Can we continue to work on the story we came here for?"

Jack said, "Yes, we had to do the news stories when the situation arose, but there's no reason not to keep working on the documentary."

Kevin stared at him. "Okay. But we need to keep in mind that we can't be sure the risk has ended with the departure of our guests."

Beside him, Silas said, "You will continue your research, yes?"

"Yes." Kevin's jaw was set.

On his other side, Laura nodded. "We're in the middle of several crucial experiments. Hopefully, we can maintain the flow of those."

Kevin said, "But wherever we are, we all check in via walkie-talkie every hour on the hour. Baz and Nina, what's your decision?"

Baz answered. "Our director has told us to stay here for now. If the cyclone changes course again it will be easier for the authorities to evacuate us all from one place." As he spoke, Nina stared at the table, but when she glanced up her eyes flickered round the group.

"Okay. Romeo, I'm assuming we're all right to continue mealtimes?"

"Of course. I've no wait staff, so it would help if everyone could pitch in."

"Okay. And let's be precise about times today, people. Synchronise watches. I'll see you all back here on the dot of twelve noon for lunch, but first walkie-talkie check is 10.00 am. Do not miss it."

<hr>

Jack scrolled back and forth through the vision they'd recorded, making swift selections of sound bites and overlay as he conferred with Callie. On the laptop beside him, her script seemed to be almost writing itself. After years working for a regional newspaper with weekly deadlines, the deranged intensity of television timeframes had almost given Jack a heart attack at first. But now they'd found their flow. The connection was more intimate than if he'd kissed her.

The piece was done and the grinding upload to the television network's servers began.

Callie said, "Much faster than last time."

"A lot less people using the microwave link."

"I meant the editing. But yes. If we've got some bandwidth to play with, how about a background check on our playmates? See if they've got reasons to stay that they're not telling us about."

"Good idea."

Callie drew up a list in her notebook and, one by one, they input the names of the seven other people still on the island. The researchers appeared on scientific websites and social profiles. Baz and Nina seemed to be connected to some of the more vocal environmental protection groups. "That may or may not be significant," said Callie. She listed the name of each group on her pad.

Aaron had only fourteen "friends". Callie said, "Why am I not surprised?"

"He'll need to become a better diplomat if he wants more funding."

Kevin popped up in local news reports about the island stretching back several years—various research projects, new developments at the resort, comment on global warming and the future of the reef. If he wasn't who he said he was, he'd been pretending for years.

Callie said, "What about Laura?"

"I've known Laura forever." He received a pointed stare from Callie. "Oh, all right." But there was nothing that seemed unusual about her and he recognised quite a few of the faces she was connected to.

For "Silas Delport", they found a swimmer and a Presbyterian minister, but no one that looked like their Silas Delport. It was frustrating rather than odd to find that such a man wasn't a fan of social media. Jack said, "Even a business profile would have been handy. I wish we knew what country he was from."

"Yeah, he was evasive about that." She wriggled her shoulders. "It bothers me."

"Me too." He clicked through fifteen browser pages, but they found nothing more satisfying.

Romeo O'Farrell was a revelation. Callie said, "Explain to me how *that* man has only forty-two friends."

Jack scrolled. "Am I reading this right? He didn't even create a profile till a few months ago."

"Print it to a PDF. So we can check some of the details later if we lose the wi-fi."

"How will we check the details if we lose the wi-fi?"

"Good question. What did people do in the olden days? Maybe we could, like, make a phone call?" She angled her head and fluttered her eyelashes at him, twice.

"It might have to be the batphone if the microwave link goes down." His eyes slid to the hiding place they'd settled on for the satellite phone case—under the mattress in his bedroom. So few hiding places in a hotel room.

"Is the case waterproof?" she said. "I wonder if we should bury it in the sand or something."

The "upload complete" message popped up on their screen just as the walkie-talkie burbled. Jack's eyes flicked to the time stamp on his laptop. It wasn't the regular hourly call.

Kevin barked, "Can you all come to the office immediately, please? Everyone to the office, now."

———

The first thing that struck Callie as she entered the office doorway behind Jack was not the naked distress on Laura's face but the incandescent fury on Kevin's. Was he looking at her? What had she done? Was it one of their news stories?

She fumbled for a chair as Jack put his hand on Laura's arm and squeezed it gently, all concern. Baz and Nina were leaning against a bank of filing cabinets. She turned to see that Silas, Romeo and Aaron had come in right behind her.

"The vessel with all my staff and guests on it just sank."

Kevin's arms were crossed and he was now staring at a section of his desk. He seemed to be waiting for a reaction.

Baz said, "Oh man! No. That's just wrong."

Nina's mouth was open, eyes wide. Stunned mullet. Callie struggled to classify the response of the others.

Jack said, "How?"

"A fire. Someone's luggage exploded."

Callie said, "How do you know so soon?"

"I heard the mayday call." He hooked a thumb towards the marine radio behind him.

She said, "Are they okay?"

"No idea. The captain was deploying the life rafts and calling for all shipping in the area to divert." His eyes slid from her to the floor beside her. "A captain I've known twenty years. A mate I've drunk beer with. A father and grandfather." *He's accusing someone in this room. Who does he suspect?*

Baz shook his head. "There's nothing more scary at sea than fire."

Nina said, "We could have been on that boat!"

Kevin swung in his seat to glare at her. "Friends were on that boat. Innocent people. Not to mention my island and my future."

Laura moved to his side. "Kevin, don't." Her voice was thick. He batted her comforting hands away.

Aaron said, "Why do this now? It doesn't make sense. We were complying with the terrorists' demands." He didn't look anxious but frustrated.

"Good question." Kevin was looking at his desk again.

Jack sighed. "Publicity. This story was already huge. It will be stratospheric now."

Callie nodded. "There were citizens of a dozen nations on that boat. That's a dozen nations reporting it as their own story."

"Surely they already had enough publicity." Nina seemed to be studying the floor near Callie's feet. "They didn't need to do such an evil thing." There was a tremor in her voice.

Jack said, "Yeah, I know. But media coverage is oxygen to terrorism. It amplifies panic. Especially now that everyone with a phone and a hashtag is a reporter."

Callie added, "It's round the world in seconds. Before anyone even has a clue what's really happening."

Jack rubbed his forehead. "I wish it wasn't so. And I don't know how to fix it."

Silence cloaked the room.

Romeo said, "What do we do now?"

Kevin said, "I don't know. Do whatever you like." He planted his hands on his desk, shoved back and up, and stalked out of the room.

"Kevin!" Laura started after him but Jack put out a hand to stop her.

"He needs to cool down on his own for a bit. Let him get over it."

She looked at him with huge eyes and Callie saw her throat wobble as she swallowed. "How can he ever get over this?"

"Are Laura and Kevin a couple?" Callie asked Jack as they approached their own cottage once more. Even with her long legs she almost had to run to match his pace.

"What? Don't be stupid. He's old enough to be her father."

"Have you even *seen* them together? Or are you just too busy waltzing down memory lane with her?"

Jack ignored her and strode to his laptop, flicking the lid up to bring it to life while he was still in the act of sitting.

"What are you doing?"

"I want to know who Silas is. His island's been targeted. His research has been targeted. What if someone expected him to be on that boat today?"

"We tried to find Silas before. He's a ghost."

"He said he was on the island back in the eighties with his family. I'm looking for something that happened to the island back then." He typed into his browser window.

Callie leant over his shoulder and read *delport stanford island 1980s* in the search bar. She pulled her chair over and waited while Jack scrolled through the results. He shook his head, tweaked his search terms, and searched again. Then again.

He clicked.

She leant in close and read silently as he scrolled. "So a Simon Davenport bought the island. A hostile takeover."

"Very hostile, by the look of it. Must have been hard for Kevin's parents. They didn't just lose their home and their business. The island was more to them than that."

"I wonder if the stress caused his mother's illness. Could Simon Davenport be Silas Delport? An alias?"

"He'd only have been in his twenties. Probably too young."

"Although it was the decade of the young tycoon."

"Hmmm. Maybe. Or his father? Silas told me he came here with his father. Learned to love bird photography here, he said."

"Why change his name?"

Jack rested his chin in his hand and stared at the screen. "Trying to get away from what his father did?" When he turned to her, they were so close she could see the lighter colour on the tips of his eyelashes and feel his breath on her face. "Why would Kevin seek out Silas? Why ask for investment from the family that destroyed your own?"

She pursed her lips. "An olive branch? Emotional blackmail?" Her laptop burbled and she turned to it. A video call from William Green in the newsroom in Sydney. Only a few months ago she'd thought he was the love of her life and had laughed at the prospect of becoming Callie Brown-Green. She clicked to accept the call.

And there he was with his perfect hair and chiselled chin, inescapable. "Callie. The scanners are picking up something about a boat sinking. What do you know?"

"It's the ferry that was evacuating Stanford Island. A fire on board."

"I'm on air in a minute and we'll cross live to you. Fix your hair. There's no time for makeup."

"I don't have many details."

He smirked. "Since when has that ever stopped us? You're the best we've got. But they'll probably all survive, anyway."

"How disappointing for you."

"Don't be stupid. You know the rule. 'If it bleeds, it leads.'"

She stood in one fluid movement and stalked out onto the verandah.

The computer screen shouted after her. "Callie! Where are you? Quick, we're on in forty-five seconds. Huh? Who are you?" She swivelled to see Jack seating himself in front of her laptop.

"Jack Metcalf. No 'e' on the end of Metcalf. Callie's had to step out. I'll do it."

"Oh. Whatever. Cyrus, get Callie's name off the super." A pause. He'd be listening to a request in his earpiece. "Who cares? Just 'live from Stanford Island' will do." Then a faint, distant voice through the laptop speakers—"Twenty seconds" from the floor manager.

Callie stayed on the verandah though the freshening wind was whipping her hair painfully against her skin, but her eyes were glued to what promised to be a train wreck. What did Jack know about live television? The small-time newspaper guy she was trying not to love and the national celebrity she used to love, face to face seventeen hundred kilometres apart, live across Australia and likely to be syndicated worldwide by the end of the day. What a treat.

She heard the floor manager's distant voice again, counting down from five. He wouldn't say the "one", he'd just point. She couldn't see William clearly from this angle, but she knew his face would be morphing so that compassion glowed from his eyes. Changing colour like a lizard.

"Welcome back. Tragic news just in from the Great Barrier Reef in the midst of this terrorism crisis—we're getting reports that a large vessel, possibly a ferry, is sinking. Let's go live to Stanford Island, where Jack Metcalf is at the epicentre of this unfolding crisis." Oops, he said crisis twice. "Jack, what can you tell us?"

"Thanks William. The details aren't clear at the moment, but we've just come from a meeting with island manager Kevin Harris, where he's told us that the launch that left the island this morning is on fire and sinking."

"A further act of terrorism?"

"Again, we can't confirm that as yet, but Mr Harris seemed to regard it as the most likely cause. Apparently, the fire started with some form of explosion in the luggage compartment."

"Any news on survivors?"

"According to Mr Harris, the captain is deploying the lifeboats and has put out a call to all nearby shipping to assist. There were thirty people aboard when it left Stanford Island at nine this morning, including guests, staff, crew and two specialised police officers. Until we hear any different, I'd suggest we hope for the best. They're in good hands and the vessel is well-equipped."

"What's the mood like on Stanford Island at the moment?"

"The handful of staff who've remained here to keep the island going are obviously devastated. These people were their guests and friends. The terrorists had given an undertaking to leave people alone if they evacuated immediately, and it seems they may have broken that promise. We're all wondering who or what might be next."

"Thank you, Jack. We'll talk more as the situation unfolds. That was Jack Metway, live from Stanford Island."

Jack shut the lid of Callie's laptop and stood abruptly. He switched on the stainless steel electric kettle that stood in their minibar. He didn't look at her.

She walked in off the verandah. "I usually wait till they've given me the all-clear before I disconnect the call."

He shrugged. "Good for you." He put a tea bag into a mug and ferreted for a sugar sachet.

They stood there, two metres apart, staring at the kettle while it hissed and rumbled. It took thirteen millennia to boil and still they stared at it.

The kettle clicked off and Jack flicked her a glance. "Want one?"

She exhaled. "Yes, please. Better make it tea. My blood is forty per cent java after last night."

He made one for her, just the way she liked it, and handed it to her on his way out onto the verandah. She followed him and they stood at the railing watching the ocean thrash at the edges of the reef.

He said, "Did I embarrass you?"

"You were surprisingly brilliant. I didn't know you had it in you."

He flicked her a glance. "I can't work around you all this time and not learn *some*thing."

The corners of her mouth turned up in a tiny smile. "They won't like the fact that you made it sound less deadly, though. That's not the sort of thing that glues people to their televisions."

"I was thinking of the relatives who might be watching it. They deserve the truth, not the beat-up."

"I know. One of the things I like about you, Jack Metway."

He huffed a laugh. "That's only my stage name."

She quirked her mouth. "It probably doesn't matter, since the world didn't see your name onscreen anyway, Mr 'Live From Stanford Island'." He laughed again.

Silence lengthened and stretched thin. "What's wrong with us, Jack? Why can't we make it work? I thought we were good together."

He propped his elbows on the railing and stared into his tea. "I thought so too. But our lives are heading in different directions."

"What do you mean? We're here, working together. Couldn't we do more of that?"

He sighed. "Bigger things than that. Callie, you're an atheist. I'm a religious nut. We want different things."

Some of her tea slopped over the edge of the mug. "Hang on, are you telling me you're rejecting me on the basis of *religion*?"

"I wouldn't put it like that."

"How would you put it? One minute you're such a nice guy, and the next you're a total bigot!" She flung the contents of her mug across the sand in a dark swathe and stalked back inside to plant it on the table with a crash.

He followed her. "So I'm a bigot for having different beliefs to you?"

"News flash, Jack. People of different beliefs have been getting on well for ages now. Is this why we never went to the next level?"

"By 'the next level', I assume you mean sex. You don't even understand that, to me, sex is for marriage."

"What are you? The world's oldest virgin?"

"So, you think it's cool to make fun of stuff that matters to me. How do we make that work, oh Queen of Tolerance?"

She wanted to storm out of the room, slamming something in her wake, but this confounded cottage was full of sliding doors. "I wish you'd told me this is what you thought when we were in New Zealand. William wanted me back, you know. I could have done much better than *you*."

He stared at her. "You were news for a while, and William wanted to use you again like he'd used you before."

That's when the noise started somewhere beyond the trees, drowning out the pounding of her angry heart, the wind-flapping leaves, the clamour of the birds. Loud and roaring, then grating and shrill, going on and on, metal on metal. "What the hell is that?" she said.

Jack's laptop pinged and she glanced across at its screen.

The message said: "Internet connection lost."

23

Callie stood on the path outside their cottage, irresolute. The noise had died away—she didn't know which direction it had come from. And for the first time in her adult life she felt a reluctance to run towards danger. Anyone who could sink a boatload of tourists was a loose cannon on a scale she'd never yet encountered in the flesh. She didn't want to be a journalist anymore. She just wanted to be at home on her sofa.

Laura appeared round a bend in the path. "Did you hear it?"

From behind Callie, Jack said, "Yes. Which way?"

Callie roamed towards a small gap in the trees and scanned the sky. "Where's the tower? Yesterday, I could see the tip of the microwave tower from here."

Laura followed Callie and stared. "Oh no!" She ran.

Callie shouted, "Isn't the tower this way?"

"We need to stay on the paths."

"You must be kidding. Do you think this terrorist is sticking to the paths?" But there was no one left to hear her because Jack had followed Laura at a flat run. She ploughed into the forest, pushing aside curtains of the huge, bird-dropping-encrusted leaves.

Fifteen seconds later, the ground disappeared underneath her and she fell heavily. She lay on her back, winded. Overhead, dozens of birds wheeled across glimpses of grey sky from one branch to another and another and back again, yelling and screaming without pausing for breath. She was panting, mouth open to the branches— and the birds. *Better close it.*

She sat up and looked about. Which way was the path? Dense foliage surrounded her in all directions, and more and more birds.

She was breathing much too fast. *Calm down, Callie. Think.* There, that was definitely the bird burrow she'd tripped into. And there beyond it was an indentation that was probably one of her footprints. And another. The opposite trajectory would be the tower, more or less.

She stood carefully and tested her right ankle. Sore, but not excruciating.

She walked on, careful now, limping a little as the ankle grabbed, looking at the ground as often as she looked ahead. A glimpse of something brown and then she was up against the back of one of the utility sheds. A rumbling noise, like an engine. Was it a generator?

Left or right? She chose a direction and moved. A flash of turquoise. She looked up and made momentary eye contact with another human through the forest. Romeo, maybe? Whoever it was had melted away into the trees.

She rounded the corner of the shed and emerged into a clearing. Laura and Jack, still as statues, stared at the source of the noise. The island's utility vehicle at a crazy angle, engine running, driver's door open. Its front end was so crumpled she was amazed the engine still functioned.

Under its chassis and sprawled across the clearing and beyond that into a swathe of broken, freshly-felled trees lay the mangled communication tower. The top was tilted back, its dish snapped in two so that it resembled a huge and useless fortune cookie.

Callie followed Jack, using the path this time. "Wait up. Where are you going?"

He glanced back at her and then beyond her, but didn't answer. Close to his side he held a small shovel from the utility shed.

Back at their cottage he went straight to his bedroom, pulled out the satellite phone case and opened it. "It's still here."

"What are you going to do?"

He looked at her properly at last, his mouth a grim line, and spoke softly. "We can't lose this, too."

She nodded. "I've got just the spot. But we need camouflage clothing."

He pulled off his white t-shirt and opened a drawer. Callie went to her room and rummaged. The best she could do was a grey top and khaki cargo pants. She wound her orange hair into a snake on the crown of her head and carefully covered it with the black base-ball cap.

"Have you hurt your foot?" He stood in the doorway.

"Yes. Come and I'll show you why."

The bird's burrow made a perfect hiding place. They smoothed sand over the disturbance and marked three surrounding trees with the shovel so they could find it again themselves.

It felt like they'd buried their relationship along with the phone.

24

Jack flicked the camera on his forehead into record as they walked into the staff quarters. Right now, it was good to have a specific task. He murmured to Callie, "Do you know which one is his?"

She pointed at a noticeboard. A floor plan, with names on it.

"Excellent. Didn't see that before." Then he bellowed down the corridor, "Hello! Anybody here?" Callie turned to him slowly with one eyebrow raised. He shrugged. "Easiest way to find out."

He counted seven doorways and turned left into Romeo's room. It was a single. Romeo must be considered a senior staff member if he didn't have to share a room. Callie began quietly opening drawers but Jack went straight for the end of the bed where a jacket lay casually draped. It was much easier to lift than the luxury mattress in his room at the guest cottage—a light foam-rubber number, not an innerspring pillow-top.

And there it was. He clicked his fingers to get Callie's attention before he pulled out the hard-shell black plastic case and laid it on the bed. It was about the size of a small laptop case, but thicker. She pointed to the corner. He wouldn't have seen it himself. Three strands of hair stuck in a join in the plastic, and a smear of something shiny. Probably blood. He moved closer so his camera could get a close-up of the evidence. He didn't need a DNA test to determine that he was looking at a little piece of himself.

There was some kind of dial in the centre under the handle. Like a combination lock but with no numbers. He frowned at it and tried to figure out the mechanism, then looked about for anything that might help him prise the case open.

She opened her eyes wide in sarcasm and mouthed, "Open. It." She walked to the door to look up and down the corridor.

He pulled up the sturdy clips on each side and, behold, the case opened. He lifted the lid tentatively, stared a moment, then lifted it to show Callie as she glanced back from the doorway. She became still and her face settled into resignation.

They didn't know brands or details but they didn't have to. There was no mistaking the outline of a pistol in the dense foam. An outline that was empty.

———

As they emerged onto the path Jack said, "Now what?"

"Research centre. I want to know what's in that 'nothing much' room."

"What's that got to do with Romeo having a gun?"

"I have no idea. But they didn't want us to see it. So I want to see it."

As they checked the various zones of the research building that were easily accessible, she said, "It feels like the laboratory of the zombie apocalypse."

"What do you mean?"

"All the people are gone. All the animals are gone, except for these hideous jellyfish and cone snails. And the fridges and filters just keep humming."

Jack looked around. "Looks like a partially empty lab to me."

"The people who ran it are probably on the bottom of the ocean."

"No, they're probably in well-equipped lifeboats or already on board rescue vessels."

"I should have gone with them, then. Instead of being stuck on an island with a guy with a gun and who knows what else."

She didn't say "and stuck here with *you*", but even Jack could read *that* sub-text.

He came to the door beside the photo of Kevin's parents and stared at the combination lock. He looked about for a utility cupboard.

"What are you looking for?"

"A crowbar or something. Maybe we can jemmy it open."

"We don't want to broadcast our suspicions. Why don't we try the combination instead? It's probably not much different to the other one."

"You think?"

She shrugged. "People are people, even on an island doing 'important research'. They're lazy about passwords."

She pressed a sequence into the keypad. Nothing. She tried again. And again. To his surprise, the lock clicked. She didn't open it immediately but looked at him and whispered, "What if someone is in there?"

He felt stupid for not thinking of that. He lifted his hands in a half shrug.

She pulled the door wide and descended confidently into a room that had a subterranean feel to it even though it was only down four steps. There was no one there and Jack pulled the door closed behind them.

He asked her, "What would you have done?"

She shrugged. "Bluffed."

They stood in a room of glimmering tanks that all seemed to contain box jellyfish. They were lit by a network of bright lights. He said, "These must simulate daylight. They're probably on a timer." There was almost no natural light. A wall full of fixed steel louvres on the ocean side of the building allowed dim bars of illumination to enter but were probably mostly for ventilation. The gap between louvres was too narrow to see out, but Jack felt the movement of air coming in off the blustery ocean.

The benches contained similar scientific paraphernalia to the dry lab upstairs—test tubes, cabinets, warning messages. He lifted the lid on a humming freezer and peered at meaningless groups of test tubes. Cold air rose in white tendrils into the humid atmosphere.

He pressed the spacebar on a computer but it brought up a password window. He tried the door code but it declared: "Password incorrect". Callie nudged him aside and keyed in a few combinations. Nothing worked.

"No filing cabinets," she said.

"It must all be on the computer."

On one bench, several cages of mice emitted a rank, yeasty odour.

Beside them on the bench, a glass-walled cabinet measured about a metre tall and half that in width, but was completely empty. Spray nozzles hung from the ceiling of the box. The locking mechanism appeared simple so he pulled it open, but he had to apply pressure. Was it airtight? An acrid smell wafted out and he shut the door quickly. He felt a pricking sensation in his nostrils and his eyes watered. He followed tubing that led from the nozzles to a pressurised tank standing alongside. It announced in large letters: Danger.

"What have I just inhaled!"

"I don't know, but it looks like these guys have been on the laughing gas too."

Several mice in one cage sported red-rimmed eyes. In another, two mice scratched at angry welts on their skin.

He shook his head. "What has this got to do with heart research?"

"No idea, Dr Jekyll." She paused and stared into one of the swirling tanks, arms wrapped around herself. She took a couple more steps and stopped dead in front of another door that opened at the same level as this lower lab. She looked back and forth around the room. "It's gotta be Aaron's snail lab on the other side of this door. The other day, Laura told me this was storage. Why did she lie?"

"Probably just avoiding the curiosity of journalists."

She turned on him, her expression fierce, and hissed, "Whatever is going on in this room, Laura knows about it."

"What's your problem?"

"Why are you so blind to her faults? If this is something dodgy she's in it up to her armpits."

She reached for the door, turned the lock, flung it open, and collided with Aaron.

———

Jack's mind was completely empty of words but Callie said, "Oh. Hello Aaron. What are you doing here?"

"I work here. What are *you* doing here? Where's Kevin?"

She said, "I don't know, I haven't seen him for ages."

On cue, the walkie-talkies on each of their hips burbled for the hourly check-in. By the time they'd all answered, Jack had recalled the English language and he tried for a straightforward tone. "Aaron, do you know what the mice are for? And this glass cabinet?"

Aaron walked in and stared at the mouse cages in silence. The three of them stood in a tableau while the pause lengthened, and finally he said, "Why do you ask?"

"I couldn't understand why it would be necessary to spray mice with something if they're doing heart research. I got some of it up my nose when I opened the glass cabinet and it hurt. Is it dangerous?"

Aaron flicked him a glance. "I wouldn't worry too much. I think it might just be capsicum spray." He turned and walked back into his own lab, picked up a clipboard and began attending to something in one of the tanks.

Callie looked at Jack with one eyebrow raised. He lifted his shoulders in a slight shrug. She turned and followed Aaron, and Jack followed her, closing the door behind him.

She said, "How is your research going? It must be hard to concentrate with everything that's been going on."

"Not really. It gives me something else to focus on." He kept his eyes on his clipboard. "But I was only halfway through uploading my latest results when the microwave link went down."

Jack said, "Would it help to back it up to one of our laptops?"

He sighed. "It probably doesn't matter."

Callie said, "Are you coming to lunch?"

"Not right now. You guys go on ahead and I'll finish up here."

<hr>

As they walked down the path, Jack muttered, "Capsicum spray? Why would they be using capsicum spray?"

Callie said, "I don't know. But does Aaron really know or is he just guessing? And why did he stop challenging us?"

"Probably because you acted like we were meant to be there. Well played, by the way."

She pursed her lips. "I don't think he was convinced by that. But for some reason he stopped worrying about us. I can't figure it out."

As they neared the staff quarters, the outer door burst open and Baz erupted from the building followed by Nina's voice: "Don't you dare walk away from me!"

He stopped dead and stared at Jack and Callie, his mouth a thin line, and then staggered as a clunky sandal hit him squarely on the side of the head. He clutched his ear and turned back to face the open door. "You bitch!"

"This is not what I signed up for! I want out of this, Baz. Get me out of it *now*!" She stood before him, majestic, hands on hips, chin at an imperious angle—and then did a nearly-comical doubletake as she noticed Jack and Callie.

Callie said, "Hi." She had her lips pressed together and seemed to be only millimetres away from a smirk.

Jack said, "We'll see you at lunch." He grabbed Callie's elbow and steered them both past the warring couple.

Callie said, *sotto voce*, "She's got a good arm, that Nina."

He ignored her, saying nothing till he knew they were out of earshot again. "Have you got any theories about the spray?"

"Well, the only other things in that room are jellyfish. Could it be jellyfish toxin?"

"They've got plenty of tentacles nearby if they were using the mice to develop the antidote. Why would they need to spray it?"

"No idea. But it'll be interesting to see if Aaron reports us to Kevin and Laura."

As they neared the office, Kevin walked out and stared at them.

Had Aaron been on the walkie-talkie already? No, of course he hadn't or they'd have heard it on their own handsets. Could he have used another channel?

But Kevin pointed back inside his office. "Look." He seemed to be breathing harder than usual.

They stood in the doorway and stared. Pieces of what used to be the marine radio lay smashed and scattered across the gouged and chipped credenza and the floor. In front of it, in the centre of Kevin's desk, its blade deeply embedded in the gleaming timber surface, was a fire axe.

25

*L*unch was the weirdest meal Callie had ever eaten—and she'd eaten ferns in the wilderness with a bunch of starving killers, so that was saying something.

The faces around the table at the Restaurant of the Apocalypse varied from morose to angry to blank. She had a hunch that at least some of them knew or thought they knew who'd planted a bomb on the launch and destroyed their communication with the outside world. Heck, maybe all of them knew. But the elephant in the room would have to take a seat and wait till after lunch.

The chicken, veggie patties and salad were perfectly prepared and beautifully presented. Romeo had even somehow found time to knock up a batch of warm crusty bread rolls, presumably all while juggling his concealed firearm. The axe in the antique desk was vivid in her mind's eye. That was pure malice. It occurred to her that Romeo might even poison them all—who knows why?—but he was eating it himself…

Laura put a small portion on her plate and then picked at it. Callie on the other hand knew she needed fuel for whatever lay ahead, so she ate heartily. And it was delicious. Across from her, Jack was taking the same approach.

Baz, whose left ear was purple and swollen, cleared his throat. "We think we might leave after all." Beside him, Nina kept her head down but her eyes—half concealed by her dark fringe—flitted uneasily.

Laura said, "Are you mad? That sea is heaving."

Kevin shook his head. "You'd better wait till the weather settles. You could have done it this morning, but I wouldn't advise it now. If you can't make headway you don't want to end up stuck out there after dark."

"Let them go, if that is their wish." All heads turned towards Silas. Who made him boss? Callie tried not to stare as he loaded a bread roll with butter several millimetres thick.

Then she saw that Aaron hadn't looked up. He only had eyes for his chicken. Did that mean anything? Possibly not. It was good chicken.

Silence lengthened. Callie's mind roamed around possible conversation topics and flicked them aside one by one. She couldn't ask any of her real questions, and to pretend an interest in the heart research right now would be ludicrous. She finally found something. "Kevin, how will we manage if the cyclone changes direction and comes this way? Have you been through a cyclone here before?"

He looked her full in the face. She could have sworn he was almost as relieved as her that she'd found a topic. "There was one when I was a kid. The wind was unbelievable. We wore wetsuits when we went outside, because of the sand. My dad was out for a while securing the boats and when he came back his ankles between the wetsuit and his shoes were all swollen and red. They'd been sand-blasted."

Jack said, "Did you know it was coming?"

"Weather forecasting wasn't as accurate back then—they were harder to track. We knew the barometer was dropping, but the weirdest thing was when we got up in the morning and there was no low tide. Mum got pretty noisy when she saw that, I can tell you. Everyone else had already gone so it was just us three." He put on a girlish voice. " 'I told you we should have left yesterday.' " Kevin at this moment was the most relaxed Callie had seen him for days.

She said, "No low tide?"

"Yeah. Storm surge. That's when we knew it was coming for us. And it was too late to leave by then."

Romeo said, "What did you do?"

"Dad's big old desk—the one in my office …" He paused a moment, then regrouped. "It was the most solid piece of furniture we had, so the three of us dragged it to our cabin and hunkered down under it with mattresses piled all around." He shook his head slowly. "That noise. Insane! Like being trapped inside the engine of a 747. And it was dark—why do they always seem to hit at night?— and then water started pouring in under the mattresses. At first we thought it was the rain because the roof had gone, but it was the sea. Waves were breaking at the front door of our cabin, right over here." He pointed with his fork. "Then it went really quiet. That was the eye of the cyclone passing over. Dad went out to have a look and when he came back he said the kitchen shed was gone." His face saddened. "Mum cried then. My mother never cried. It was quiet for maybe twenty minutes, no wind, no birds… and I remember the sound of her sobbing. Knowing the cyclone was coming back soon and we had to go through just as much again before it would be over."

No one ate for at least a minute. Then Jack said, "But you obviously made it through okay?"

"Yeah. But everything was destroyed. Our boat was gone, even though Dad had pulled it up as high as he could and tied it down. Sheets of corrugated iron embedded in the pylons of the jetty, like knives in butter." Or axes in desks. "Dead birds everywhere. Every tree shredded—my dad was pretty much the tallest thing on the island. He walked right to the other end to check things and from the highest point up here you could see him all the way, even over the piles of dead trees."

Jack said, "How did you leave?"

"They sent a boat for us two days later. The sea had settled a bit, but it was still a rough ride. We were pretty glad they came, I can tell ya. Our rainwater tanks had been blown to bits, and we'd used up the water containers we took in under the mattresses with us, even though we'd been rationing it. We'd set up a contraption to distill some sea water, but that's a slow process. And it was so hot. No shade anywhere. And the dead birds were stinking." He shook his head.

Callie said, "But you rebuilt."

"We did." Kevin looked her full in the face again, the light of battle in his eyes. "The Harrises will always fight for Stanford Island."

———

When Kevin rose to leave at the end of lunch, Callie stood and followed, keeping her manner casual. Baz and Nina had headed to the staff quarters to pack their gear. Others were still talking as they helped Romeo clear the tables.

She shot a glance over her shoulder at Jack. He caught both the glance and the hint.

Outside on the path, they had to put on a burst of speed to catch Kevin, who had just passed his vandalised office and was still walking with a purpose.

Jack's headcam was in place and rolling, and he said to Kevin, "What happens now?"

Kevin gave them the barest glance. "I'm heading for the island launch. I'll use its radio to let the mainland know what's going on here."

Callie said, "Do we need to evacuate after all?"

"I hope not. That sea's getting bumpy and it's a long way to safety. I'll see what they say."

After a few more paces, Jack said, "Kevin, what are the mice for?"

Callie held her breath.

Kevin stopped dead and stared at him. He began walking again and muttered, "Testing the anti-venom."

Jack said, "Anti-venom, or antidote? I think I heard you call it an antidote."

Kevin threw out his hands in a dismissive movement. "Same thing."

Callie said, "Wasn't the anti-venom an accidental discovery?"

"Yeah. What of it?"

"So, why did you have mice here?"

"We're a research station. Sometimes we need lab mice."

Jack said, "But the spray cabinet… that doesn't seem like something you'd have for heart research."

"We needed it. We built it." He strode out ahead of them onto the jetty and down the ramp to the pontoon—the floating platform where two small launches were moored. They followed, and though Callie stayed on the pontoon, Jack clambered aboard behind Kevin, no doubt to record the important radio call on his camera.

He was about to enter the cabin when Kevin burst out of it with a face like thunder, his tongue dripping with curses. "They've taken it, the mongrels!" He shouldered Jack aside, leapt out of the boat with more nimbleness than Callie would have suspected was in him, and crossed the pontoon to the smaller craft, the one that belonged to Baz and Nina.

Jack followed Kevin, but Callie clambered aboard the first craft to peer into the cabin they'd just left. Her eyes took a moment to adjust to the dimmer light within as she scanned a driver's seat, a wheel, and a panel of equipment, like a cross between the dashboard of a car and the instrument panel on a light plane. There were gouges in the panel and in the middle was an ugly hole from which wires protruded helplessly.

She heard more swearing outside, and emerged to see Kevin kneel on the pontoon's edge and peer into the water. He held something long in his hands; another of the viewing tubes the tourists used. She wanted to see Jack's reaction but he didn't look at her, and she realised he'd have to keep the headcam trained on Kevin's movements.

Kevin swore again, stood and pulled off his shirt and shoes. Despite his bulk, his body cut the water cleanly as he dived. She wondered if any box jellyfish still lurked and hovered anxiously, watching his movements wobble as they were refracted by the water's movement. Moments later, his head broke the surface, water streamed from his hair, and he gripped the pontoon with one hand, bringing the other up to dump two black boxes on its deck. Trailing from each was the unmistakeable cord and handpiece of a radio. Both the boxes and the handpieces were smashed, the gleam of electronics visible through their shattered shells. Kevin clung to the pontoon with whitened knuckles and stared at the destroyed radios right at his eye level, breathing hard.

"We can't go yet. I can't find my phone." The voice was Nina's and she sounded just a little shrill. As the path ahead of Callie began to curve around within throwing distance of the lab, she prepared herself to duck in case the woman's aim was about to be tested again.

Callie and Jack were silently trailing Kevin, like bridesmaids behind a man carrying the strangest bouquet: a radio in each hand, cords trailing, water dripping from his clothes and his burden. For some reason, it evoked a dystopian steampunk version of the bridal scene in *Great Expectations*.

"Well, hurry up and find it. We don't want to be stuck out there in the dark."

They rounded the corner a few steps behind Kevin, and Callie watched another tableau unfold. Baz and Nina, standing either side of a large trolley piled with gear, swung around at the sound of their approach and stared. Kevin stomped up to Baz, said, "Here, have your radio," thrust a mangled electronic mess at him, and continued on down the path.

Throughout, Callie watched Baz's face cycle from anger—towards Nina?—to confusion as he beheld the metallic tangle in his hands, and then something that looked a lot like fear.

Nina's face paled. "What is it? What's happening?" She looked to Callie and then Jack, seeking… information? Reassurance?

Jack said, "They've been hacked out of both of the boats."

"Who by?"

"How would we know?"

"And that's our radio?" She indicated the mass. "The radio from our boat?"

All four of them stared at it in silence.

Nina pressed her fingertips to her chin, hands together in the prayer position, pushed them away from her and shook her arms, shifted her weight from one foot to the other and back, and again. "We can't go, Baz. We can't go out there into that"—she indicated through the trees at the wild ocean—"with no radio."

"We can't stay here." Baz's voice was deeper, rougher than usual. "We have to get to the radio and the wi-fi on Apostle."

"What if they've already been there, too?"

He looked up from the remains of the radio in his hands and pinned her with a glare as he ground out the words. "Find. Your. Phone."

"Can we help?" Callie said. "Do you know when you last had it?"

Nina looked at her with desperate eyes and pressed both hands to her chin again.

Jack said to Baz, "Can I help you with anything else while they look for it?"

"Um, yeah, maybe. We should probably carry some extra water, in case we get stuck for a while. Could you help me get it?"

The two men walked off and Callie moved alongside Nina. "Just take a deep breath and think. There'll be a memory in there some-where. Where is it normally?"

"Well, it's always in this bag." Nina picked up a large, tie-dyed, pink and orange cloth bag with a long strap in the same fabric—the one she'd had in the staff dining room last night—and held it towards Callie. Her movements were slow and deliberate, but her fingers trembled as she pointed inside. "It goes in this pocket, right here."

"Maybe it's fallen out into the main part of the bag." They care-fully turned out the contents onto the top of the pile of gear and sorted through notebook, pen, comb, tissues, purse—but the phone wasn't there. Callie was close enough to hear Nina's ragged breathing hissing in and out.

They searched the lab and then Baz and Nina's room in the staff accommodation. On the way past the pool to check the dining room, Nina stopped dead and pointed. "Look." She started to shake and weep in soft, gasping whimpers.

Callie turned towards what Nina had seen and tried to understand what she was looking at. From the wooden countertop of the outdoor bar, a long piece of metal protruded. Walking closer, she realised it was a crowbar. Impaled by it against the timber in a bright orange case studded with diamantes was a mobile phone.

"Oi! What are you doing?" Jack turned at the abrasiveness in Romeo's voice, and hesitated.

Baz continued hefting a plastic vat of water from the bottom shelf at the back of the storeroom.

"Did you hear me? I'll be having that back on the shelf where you found it, thanks all the same."

Baz dumped the water container on a small trolley and stopped to stare at the chef, his mouth a grim line. "What's your problem? We need some extra water for this trip."

"Then you'll be getting it yourself from the tanks and putting it in your own containers."

"We don't have any more containers."

"Not my problem." Romeo shifted his weight, and at his sides his hands fisted slightly, then stretched.

Jack said, "Are there any spare containers they could use?"

Romeo thrust his chin forward and glared at Jack. "Does this *look* like a department store?"

Baz ground out, "Stop me!" and yanked the handle of the trolley, heading for the door.

Romeo slammed the whole side of his body into Baz, who cannoned into the shelving and lost his grip on the trolley handle so that it overbalanced and rolled back towards Jack, who leapt out of its path in the nick of time. Bottles and jars tumbled over. A huge jar of olives rolled off the shelf, bounced on the lino floor without breaking, and continued rolling as Baz turned to grab Romeo by the shoulders, forcing him back against the opposite shelves, where catering-sized boxes of cereal teetered and fell.

"What the hell is going on in here!" The roar came from Kevin, standing red-faced and fiery-eyed in the doorway, and the two combatants staggered apart like naughty schoolboys. Kevin swore viciously, in imaginative ways that questioned their intelligence and their parentage, and finally ran out of steam. He muttered, "As if we haven't got enough problems." He stabbed a finger at Jack. "You. What's it all about?"

Jack rubbed his face, then plunged his hands into his pockets. "Um, Baz wanted to take some water. Romeo didn't think it was a good idea."

Kevin sighed, and his posture deflated as though the anger was draining out his feet. He looked around at the mess.

Romeo took a step forward, his chest thrust out. "We've got a lot more people to keep watered than *he* has"—flinging a hand in Baz's direction—"and I'll not be letting our emergency supplies go running off. Who knows what else might happen before this circus is over?"

Kevin scratched his neck and gazed at the floor. Silence lengthened. "Let him have it." He turned and walked out.

<hr>

As they wheeled the trolley towards the infinity pool on their way back towards the lab and the jetty, Jack spotted Callie and Nina side by side on a sun lounger. Nina seemed to be crying. Callie had an arm round her shoulder.

Jack wouldn't have thought Nina was the crying kind. Or that Callie would be her chosen comforter.

Baz stayed on the path, making a show of holding the water trolley upright, which was probably unnecessary. He could have wheeled it over near his wife, anyway; the pool surrounds were paved.

Jack walked towards the women and threw Callie a questioning look.

Callie said, "Good news." Her face was expressionless. "We've found Nina's phone." She angled her head towards the bar.

Jack squinted at it then walked over and stared.

Baz materialised beside him. "Oh, man." He studied the impaled phone for several long moments, then turned to Nina, who gazed up at him, her eyes awash. "We gotta get out of here, babe."

She nodded mutely.

"I don't blame you for wanting to get out of here," Jack said. "In fact, I wouldn't mind joining you. But are you sure it's safe?"

The sweep of the ocean was on full display. As recently as yesterday, there'd been only gentle swaying in the waters around Stanford. Between here and the edge of Australia's continental shelf many kilometres to the east, reef after reef ran interference on the Pacific Ocean, taming it, turning down the volume on its power. Today, waves whipped up by the distant cyclone were beginning to be too much even for the Great Barrier. Long swells topped by whitecaps were heaving past Stanford, roiling and leaping as they connected with the island's own coral perimeter.

Baz didn't look at the sea or Jack. He just stared at the phone. "Can't be any worse than staying here."

"Even with no radio on your boat?"

Baz scratched his chin stubble. "No radio on this island either, mate. No phone. At least we've got those back on Apostle." He looked up and out at the sea, then, and considered, and nodded. "Gettin' a bit gnarly out there but I reckon we can do it. We probably should've went yesterday. Come on, babe." He held a hand toward Nina; she took it and their eyes locked as she stood. "We'll be home by dark, easy."

Jack and Callie went with them to the jetty and helped transfer their gear down onto the pontoon, and then into the small half-cabin cruiser that would be Baz and Nina's escape pod.

Baz brought out two life jackets and laid them on the bench.

"What about the EPIRB?" Nina's voice was husky, but she seemed to be trying to look positive.

Baz unlatched a compartment and showed her a bright orange device.

Boom! Jack's mind flooded with memories of a similar locator beacon, of pulling so hard at it trying to get it to work that he tore the skin along his thumbnail and it hurt for days; of a perilous New Zealand mountain ledge with a seven hundred metre drop; of a murderous wind that screamed and slapped. Wind buffeted his arms, but it was warm, not cold, and he returned to the now and the here. He took a deep, steadying breath, and found Callie looking at him, her eyes gentle.

"Well, I think we're ready." The active certainty that had emanated from Baz while they packed the boat seemed to dissipate. He propped against a corner of the gunwale and shifted his long legs uneasily.

"Might just go for a pee before we leave." Nina smiled uncertainly.

"And maybe a cuppa and something to eat," Callie said. "Energy for the voyage."

To Jack, Callie's smile seemed a little too cheerful for the occasion, but the two researchers turned to her like she'd just announced their winning lottery numbers.

"Oh, yes."

"Great idea."

The four of them clambered off a boat that was all shipshape and ready to sail—apart from the gaping wound in the control panel—and headed back to the main house.

There was coffee and tea and fruit juice full of ice among the small selection still kept on the dark teak dresser, and there was cake and fruit, and then there wasn't much else they could do but leave.

Laura strode briskly into the dining room just as all their chairs were scraping back from the table. "Oh. I thought you guys had gone."

"Just leaving now," Baz replied.

"Super!" She turned to Jack and Callie. "Could you help us? We're going to have a go at repairing the radio dish."

"Sure," Jack said, but he saw Callie's eyebrows fly up before she got them under control.

"Happy to try," she said.

"Just need some extra hands," Laura said.

They all walked out together and down the four stairs to the path. Laura moved quickly in the direction of the utility sheds and turned to check if her helpers were following.

Baz and Nina wandered towards the jetty path and seemed almost to be fighting a gravitational force that wanted to anchor them to the main house.

"Do you need any more help before you go?" Jack said.

"No. No, mate." Pause. "I think we're good to go." Baz smiled, but it was a low wattage affair. "Hope you guys will be all good here."

"Thanks. We hope so too. Safe journey." Jack held out a hand, and Baz shook it, then Nina.

Callie copied him, but her handshake to Nina turned into a hug. "When you get there, notify someone about what's going on here, will you?"

They both spoke at once. "Yeah, sure, mate." "Yes, we certainly will. So long as our communications are still working…"

With a brief, awkward wave the two researchers set off towards the jetty, Baz in a slow loping stride, Nina hugging her arms around her body. They put on a burst of speed and disappeared around a corner into the dense tree cover.

As Jack followed Callie who followed Laura down another densely forested path, Callie said to him, quietly, "I hope they've made the right decision."

Jack said, "Well, they know their boat, and this ocean. They've probably done difficult trips before."

"I almost wonder if we should have gone with them."

"I know what you mean. At least they'll be out of reach of this… this random maniac."

She muttered back over her shoulder, "Random? That thing with Nina's phone… that was personal."

He was still thinking about that when they emerged into the clearing that contained the group of utility sheds and the collapsed radio dish. The ute that had pushed it over stood off to one side, its bonnet staved in, one headlight broken.

"You managed to get that out of the way?" Jack said to Laura.

She smiled. "It still runs, would you believe?"

Kevin looked up from a toolbox and some building materials he'd been piling near the dish. "A lot of the wiring actually seems unbroken," he said to Jack and Callie. "I figured if we could try to mend it"—he shrugged—"maybe we could somehow hoist it above the trees and see if it picks up a signal." He gave them a long, sarcastic look. "Nothin' better to do with the afternoon, anyway." He turned to Laura. "No Romeo?"

"No. His walkie-talkie's charging in the kitchen. I can't search the whole island for him. I thought about asking Baz and Nina, but they need to get on the water more than they need to do"—she paused and indicated their task with fluttering hands—"this, or they'll miss the high tide at Apostle."

Kevin looked surprised. "They haven't left yet?" He angled a questioning glance towards Jack and Callie.

"They had some dramas getting away," Jack said. He didn't want to tell them about Nina's phone and he wasn't sure why. He didn't know who to tell about his satellite phone, now that it might be the only functioning communication device on the island.

Or maybe not the only one…

He turned his head towards Callie, wondering how to seek her opinion, and she caught his gaze and shook her head, slightly, just once. Was she psychic?

"That thing must weigh a tonne," Callie said. "How are we going to lift it?"

"Laura, where's that other power drill?" Kevin held one in his hand but continued to rummage through the assembled items. He looked back over his shoulder towards the open shed, then walked towards it and peered at the outline of various tools on a hanging frame. "We had another one that was better than this."

"How should I know?" She went to the shed and started opening drawers and shifting tools in a fairly useless manner.

"It does look extremely heavy," Jack said. "Should we get Silas to help?"

Kevin didn't even look at him. "He's probably in a hammock somewhere. Drinking cocktails."

There was something about the set of his jaw that surprised Jack. He turned casually towards Callie again and she caught his look and slowly raised one eyebrow two millimetres.

"What about Aaron?" she said to Kevin. "Surely we can get him to stomp on a snail or two and get over here pronto?"

Kevin looked fully at her and emitted a gust of laughter.

Laura said, "He refused to come. He says it's a stupid idea. He's probably right."

27

*a*aron *was* right. Jack had thought it probably wouldn't work, but there was comfort in the four of them being together and working on a shared task while the world collapsed quietly just beyond their embracing shield of bird-filled trees. And it would make an interesting piece of footage.

Getting the dish back together was a challenge beyond their skill. Had they succeeded, hoisting it high enough to clear the treeline would have been an altogether different challenge. It was massively heavy and had probably been put up there originally by some kind of crane. They maybe could have tried something with ropes and the ute.

About ninety minutes later, sweaty, bruised, tired and disgruntled, they all gave up on the microwave dish and returned to the dining room.

The huddle of food items displayed on the teak dresser seemed to have been refreshed since they'd been there last but Romeo was still out of sight.

The concertina doors stood open onto the deck. Gusty winds swirled through off the ocean.

Jack flopped into one of the embracing rattan armchairs with a long, cool glass of iced water. He started peeling an orange and thinking about the last time he'd sat in that particular armchair, after the box jellyfish incident—was it only a couple of days ago? Seemed more like a couple of weeks.

Callie took another chair, along with a glass of juice and a slice of orange-and-almond cake that she ate with a fork.

Kevin slumped into a third chair with a cup of coffee.

Laura walked straight past them all onto the deck, shaking her head. "It's getting rougher." She adjusted the concertina doors to lessen the wind's disruption inside.

Jack levered himself out of his chair and followed her out, popping an orange segment in his mouth. He continued past her down the steps that led into the lagoon and watched a large turtle glide past under the glinting surface.

In the late afternoon light he scanned the reef surrounding the island, and the way the water leapt as it collided with it. All but the very tip of the jetty was hidden from inside the main house by the curve of the island, but out here he could see almost all of it. Halfway along it, moored beside the jetty, the island's motor launch rode heavily in the swells rolling down the channel, and it was a good thing it had several padded fenders protecting it from the pontoon's movement. All the visiting yachts and pleasure craft were long gone, and even the small practical craft used by the staff in their work had been dragged ashore. The launch looked rather naked, sitting there on its own.

"Hey, there's at least one piece of good news." Jack returned to his armchair and his orange. "It looks like Baz and Nina finally got away."

"Are you sure?" Callie said. "I was almost expecting them to walk back in here for another cuppa."

"You might still get to see them for a late dinner," said Laura, "if they can't get over the reef at Apostle."

"Oh, that's right," Callie said. "She told me there's no channel. How does that work?"

"Imagine trying to get a boat in down the other end of this island," Laura answered. "You can do it—if the boat's small enough —but you have to wait for a tide high enough to get safely over the fringe reef. It's a king tide tonight, so that's in their favour. But the more bumpy the sea is, the less clearance you have between swells."

"Huh?"

Laura reached out her hand above the surface of the coffee table and mimicked the sea's movement. "The coffee table is the bottom." She moved her hand along in a kind of sine wave. "Like this if the seas are calm. Like this if the swells are big—higher peaks, lower troughs."

"Oh."

Kevin gazed into his coffee. "And they're carrying a load. And it'll be nearly dark at full high tide." He half-sighed then shook his head. "I couldn't force them to stay." This man seemed the sober twin of the wise-cracking Kevin they'd encountered previously.

"It's almost full moon, at least," Laura said. "And they do know that reef backwards."

He scratched the back of his neck. "Yeah, I s'pose. Sometimes you just have to time your run, cross your fingers, and hope for the best."

DINNER WAS SIMPLE AND HOT. SOME KIND OF BEEF STEW WITH a lot of vegetables and maybe red wine. Warm bread rolls and cold butter. No vegetarian or vegan options. Had Baz and Nina been the only non-meat eaters? And if so, how did Romeo know? It felt odd to think of him monitoring what they all ate, but Jack guessed it was probably his job to notice things like that.

Conversation was minimal. The usually loquacious Romeo stared at his food and ate steadily. Jack had detected coolness between him and Kevin. The issue with Baz and the water wasn't going to be forgiven anytime soon, by the look of it.

Cutlery scraped on plates. Wind buffeted the building and fluttered the leaves of a potted palm and whistled softly through the narrow gaps in the hinge-points of the concertina doors, now only partially open. Outside, the evening sky show was beginning: purple and pink.

Kevin cleared his throat. "I've made a decision to evacuate the island. We'll head for the mainland in the morning. Pack a smallish bag—remember we've all got to fit on the launch and the less extra weight the better—and be here for breakfast at 6.00 am. We'll finish up the island lock-down tasks as fast as we can and get away mid-morning, hopefully."

Judging by Laura's expression he hadn't discussed it with her, but she didn't speak. She looked resigned more than surprised.

Aaron pushed his empty plate away. "I wish you'd decided that at lunch time. We could have been on the mainland by now." No mention of his snails, for once.

Kevin didn't look at him. "At lunch time, we still had communications."

"What about the cyclone?" Romeo said. "We can't even check if it's coming this way. Maybe we should leave tonight."

Kevin scowled. "Navigate the reef on a rough night with no radio? What a genius plan."

Before Romeo could respond, Laura cut in. "The last track map we saw this morning had us getting some bad weather here, but not in the direct path. We're in the Watch area. I agree with Kevin that leaving tonight wouldn't be wise. Let's do as much as we can tonight to get ready."

Jack wondered again about declaring the satellite phone buried in the trees, but just as he started to angle his gaze toward Callie beside him he felt the pressure of her foot against his own. Very firm pressure. She raised an eyebrow just slightly, shook her head slightly, just once, and looked away. She definitely must be psychic.

<hr>

"What are you going to do?" Jack said to Aaron as they stepped down onto the path. The researcher seemed hesitant and unfocused—quite different to every other time Jack had seen him.

Aaron sighed. "Release my snails and pack up my project."

"Need some help?"

Aaron gave him a long, considering look. "Sure." He was less welcoming once they reached the lab and Jack's camera went into position on his head. "Do you have to film *every*thing? Surely the documentary is cancelled by now."

Jack shrugged. "Maybe. Maybe not. But if I don't film it, I've got no options later." He didn't ask permission to continue and Aaron didn't challenge him again. It seemed more like apathy than acceptance.

A few minutes later, the snails were in a bucket getting ready to make their second journey in as many days—or was it three journeys? One out to the pool, one back to the lab, and one back to the reef where they belonged. Yes, three.

Down on the beach, they worked together to carry an aluminium dinghy to the waterline. The tide was nearly at the high water mark where various pieces of marine debris formed a wavy line. The sky above was now a sullen purple with an alien-planet glow as the last of the light faded.

Aaron glanced upwards and shook his head. "Don't like the look of that sky. That's a cyclone sky, I reckon."

"Coming our way?"

"Not sure. I'm no expert on Coral Sea cyclones. I'm from the west, remember."

Jack sat towards the front and took the oars and rowed while Aaron guarded the bucket of snails between them. He had to pull hard against the currents and the dinghy jolted frequently on the rough surface. The difference between now and a couple of days ago when their floatplane had landed on a mirror surface was exceptional.

Jack said, "Your dad works in mining?"

Aaron shot him a look, his eyes narrowed.

"You told us about him, in your interview."

"Did I?" The researcher's shoulders relaxed a little. "Yeah. Iron ore."

"What does he think of your research?"

Aaron glared at his hands on the bucket handle. "Thinks I'm witless. 'A waste of a good education' I think he said. He's more worried about the money he spent on my good education, if you ask me."

"He doesn't think medical research is valuable?"

"He thought it might be till I told him how it worked. Saw him at Christmas. Explained how long it takes and how many false trails you might have to follow before you find the right one. How hard it is to get funding. Now he thinks I'm wasting my life and his money. 'How are you ever going to raise a family on what you earn?' What if I don't want to raise a family?"

They drew over a coral bommie just visible under the glinting water and Aaron said, "This'll do."

Jack used the oars to try to hold the boat steady—with limited success—and looked over the gunwale with interest. "This is the kind of place they like to live?"

"Who gives a stuff?" Aaron emptied his bucket over the side much more carefully than his words might have implied, then sluiced it out in the water.

"What happens to your project now?"

Aaron placed the empty bucket precisely in the centre of the dinghy's floor and rested the tips of his fingers along its rim. "Probably lose my funding." He paused, staring into the bucket. "Probably have to go work in the mines and drive a really big truck."

On the way back to his cottage, Jack saw an opportunity to get some night vision of the endlessly flapping and jostling and screaming birds. He'd been ruminating about extending the camera overhead on a selfie stick, right alongside the nesting avians. He'd wanted to try it since they first arrived, but it kept getting put off during the rolling series of dramas.

Now that the fundamental nature of their film seemed likely to shift towards the sinister, the creepy Hitchcock vibe of the night birds might be just exactly right.

He left the path and stepped carefully, using his torch to check for tunnels and bird nests in the sand. Once in the thick of the trees, long drooping leaves brushing his arms and clinging to his neck, he extinguished the light, extended the selfie stick upwards, and began filming. He experimented with different movements: side to side, rotating on an axis, or smoothly up and down. The red light of the

Bluetooth switch on the handle seemed too bright so he covered it with his fingers. Above, the faintest purple glow remained in what sky he could glimpse through the vegetation.

Above the screeching and crying he heard footsteps on the path. Brisk, determined footsteps. He peered through the leaves and in the last gloomy light saw a man walking this way, just passing the lab. He would soon walk past, only a couple of metres away from Jack's location, but would probably be unaware of his presence. Kevin, maybe, heading for his house? The only building out this way. He prepared to call out a greeting but something made him stop.

It wasn't Kevin. Wrong build. Not tall enough for Aaron. Wrong hair for Romeo.

The hair on the back of Jack's neck stood to attention. Was it a stranger, a terrorist?

No. As the man passed, the close-cropped hair and firm bearing were unmistakeable. It was Silas. Carrying something—a duffle bag, maybe, or a small backpack?—and heading swiftly away from the resort in the gathering dark.

<h1 style="text-align:center">28</h1>

<hr>

Callie emerged from the steamy bathroom to collide heavily with Jack as he closed the front door of their cottage. The contact was not unpleasant.

"Sorry," he said.

"What are you looking for?"

"A little broom or something. There's sand all over this thing." He held the phone case in his hand.

"Does it matter? Can you get the phone out safely?"

"Probably. But I hate dropping sand on the floor." He shrugged.

She grinned. "Even I agree with you on that." She fetched the box of tissues from the bathroom and helped him dust it down as they stood in the entryway. "You're not going to tell anyone you've got it, are you?"

He paused in the cleaning process and looked at her. "I've been wondering about that but we never seem to get a chance to discuss it. What do you think?"

"I keep thinking: which one would we tell? I don't trust any of them."

"Kevin and Laura?"

She shook her head. "They're the best of the bunch but there's something creepy going on in that lower lab. I can't quite put my finger on what's wrong with it. And even if they're okay, once they know about it, how long till the phone ends up with an axe through it?"

"You don't think it's someone else doing it?"

"What do you mean? A stranger hiding on the island?"

"Yeah. It's not a big island, but it's crowded with trees. Lots of sheds and different buildings. Plenty of places to hide. And we've already seen a small boat access the far end at night."

"True. But even if there's someone else here with us, I just get the feeling that"—she lifted her shoulders high and shook her head, floundering for the right way to explain it—"well, that even though they always seem surprised by each individual bad thing that happens… they don't somehow seem surprised that, generally, bad things are happening. Do you know what I mean?"

He gazed at the case in his hand and nodded slowly. "Yeah." He sighed. "And we have to protect the phone if we possibly can."

Silence stretched, thin and fragile. "Who are you going to call?"

"Well, I thought about making a report to the police, but if they didn't do anything about cone snails in the pool will they care about people destroying radios? With all that's going on around the islands just now. We already know they're strapped for resources."

"I suppose it's just property damage until we can prove anything else. Could just be someone with a personal grudge. Nothing to do with the terrorists." She paused and raised an eyebrow. "Or someone using the terrorists as cover for something else…"

He looked at her and narrowed his eyes. "Yeah." Pause. "I thought I'd send an email to a mate, so at least someone knows what's going on here. And I want to check on the cyclone—and try another search for Silas. I saw him just now, where he shouldn't really have been, and I don't know what it means." He told her where he'd seen Silas.

"That *is* odd." It had to be really odd if even No Conspiracies Jack had been alarmed by it. "Does that thing connect to the internet?"

"Yep. Just tether it to my laptop like a normal phone." He crouched down to mop up some sand that had scattered onto the floor.

As he stood, she held out her hands to take the crushed tissues from him. "I'll get rid of those for you."

"Oh. Thank you."

"You're welcome." She rolled her eyes at herself as he walked away. They could start a charm school for marooned journalists who used to be in love.

<hr>

THE THOUGHT OF SLEEP WAS SO VERY ALLURING, EVEN WITH the world falling down around their ears. It was a while since she'd pulled an all-nighter, and it was telling on her. Used to do it all the time in her teens and early twenties. When had it started to get hard? Now she thought about it, the night before the all-nighter had been pretty short, too. And the one before. She prepared for bed to the soundtrack of the shower running, followed by muffled thumps as Jack sorted himself out in his room. He must have taken the laptop in there.

As she threw back her sheets to get into bed, she startled at the sight of a man in her doorway. "Hello," she said.

Jack said, "Hello."

"Find anything?"

"They've put out a new track map for Cyclone Sasha. Category 4 now, heading south, fast." He rubbed his face. "We're not exactly on the current track, but we are now in the warning area, not just the watch area." He looked at her sideways.

"Oh. Great." She took a deep breath. "And Silas?"

"Nothing yet. The connection's slower than I hoped. I'm doing a reverse image search."

"Do those things actually work?"

"With the right software, they do."

"How did you get the right software?"

"I have my ways."

"When did you get a clear photo of him?"

"A still from the beach yesterday. He was talking about birds." He pointed at his now-bare forehead. "Tough cam was rolling."

"You and Silas seem to be bonding nicely."

He shrugged.

She said, "So…"

"I'm going to let it keep searching while we sleep."

"Good idea."

"I wondered… do you think maybe we should sleep in the same room, with all that's going on?" He angled his head. "My room, since the laptop is in there."

She stared at him. "Me, in your room? Are you sure you'll be safe?"

He sighed loudly and walked away.

She gathered up a pile of pillows and followed him. He was hunched over the computer screen but glanced up as she made a careful wall with them down the centre of the king-sized bed. "Just to protect you from my insatiable desire to take things to the next level." She got into the bed and pulled the sheet up carefully, lying to face away from him.

"It's not funny, Cal."

"You're right. It's not funny at all."

She heard him slide the bedroom door shut and lock its flimsy catch, then he climbed in on the other side of the pillow wall and flicked off the light with what sounded like a vicious snap. "Why do you have to make fun of things that are important to me? I'm not the only person in the world who thinks this way, you know. I get that everyone else thinks I'm a freak, but why do *you* have to treat me like one?"

"Maybe I don't enjoy rejection all that much."

The light snapped on again but she wasn't going to look at him.

"Rejection? What's it got to do with rejection? When have I ever rejected *you*?" The final word had a strangled sound and she considered looking at him, but she considered too long and the light snapped off again.

Silence stretched in the dark. She found a small voice to say it with. "You think I'm cheap."

He huffed. "When have I ever said anything like that?" Another pause and then his voice was softer. "When would I ever think such a thing of you?"

"Well, you think I'm unsuitable, at least."

"No, Callie, I think we're unsuited. That's a completely different thing."

Silence welled up again but she had to ask. "How do you do it? How do you not think about it?"

"About what? Sex?" He was waiting but she couldn't reply. "Oh, Callie. If you only knew how often I think about it." His voice became so quiet that she struggled to hear it past all the pillows. "And how it's always you that I think about."

Outside the window, a mutton bird started wailing.

29

*W*hen Callie woke, Jack was hunched over the laptop. Early light seeped through the wind-whipped trees outside the window.

She rubbed her eyes and yawned. "What did you find?" He didn't answer; just glanced at her and left the room. She stumbled round to the computer and peered at the screen. No wonder Jack had nothing to say. It was unmistakably the same man, though a little younger. Jack's new friend, Silas, smiling proudly, rifle in hand, beside the carcass of an elephant.

As they walked to breakfast, she said, "He was younger in that photo. Maybe he doesn't do that anymore."

Jack shrugged.

"Did you find anything else?"

"No, it's still searching. Still grinding away. Maybe the cloud cover slows it down. Or maybe the software needs more bandwidth."

Kevin had ordered breakfast at six: be there or miss out. Callie didn't think her stomach could possibly accept food at this hour, but then the aroma of frying bacon assaulted her nostrils and she reconsidered. It was a mystery how Romeo could keep cooking up a miracle each mealtime with everything else going on.

She and Jack were last to arrive. They received a muted "Good morning" from several people—manners had not yet deserted them all. Jack filled a bowl with a sensible serving of Weet-Bix and fruit but Callie went straight for the bacon and eggs, adding a fried tomato for colour and movement, and a couple of pieces of crusty white toast. The yolks were a little more runny than she preferred, but they spilled onto the toast in a pleasing golden surge, and the bacon was crisp and delicious. The combination crunched in her mouth and echoed in her head and must be audible to everyone inhabiting the sombre silence of the room.

The glass doors onto the verandah—usually folded back to allow the full cooling benefit of any available breeze—were closed. They rattled and creaked in their tracks with each new gust. In the distance, beyond the lagoon, she could see the ocean leaping high and white as it collided with the fringe reef. The clouded sky above it glowered with a weird pale-bronze light.

When Laura opened the door to walk out onto the verandah a blast of air entered, and she struggled to shut the door behind her. In a moment she was back, and this time she didn't shut the door. "Kevin! Come and look. Right now." The tone of her voice arrested all the eaters, who streamed out onto the verandah behind Kevin, into the wind, as floral arrangements on the dining table flapped and shifted.

Laura pointed at the lagoon. Callie peered down to see that it lapped at one of the teak steps. It was hard to see through the water today because of the surface gleam reflecting the cloudy sky—a pewter overlay—but she could make out a few more steps beneath.

Callie glanced at Kevin. He walked all the way down till he stood on the bottom step and stared at the water lapping against his thighs. Were his shoes waterproof?

Callie said, "What's wrong?" She had to speak up, over the gusting wind.

Laura looked at her with a furrow between her eyebrows. "It's high tide, and Kevin is now standing on the high tide mark. It's a storm surge. The cyclone must have changed direction. The air pressure difference forces the water up"—she curved her hand—"like the edges of a bowl." To Kevin she said, "What should we do?"

He rubbed the back of his neck. "We could shelter in the upper lab. But we still might be better to head for the mainland. Complete our lock-down really fast." Callie stared at the leaping ocean in the distance and her inner eggs and bacon performed a selection of tai chi. "It'd be a rough ride, but we could probably do it in five or six hours. What do you think?"

Laura said, "What if we can't outrun it? Would we be better to head for Apostle and use their radio to call for a helicopter evacuation?"

"We'd be a couple of hours further into the weather by the time we got there. I doubt they'd be eager to put a chopper in the air. And the helipad is so restricted on Apostle." He turned to wade back up the steps. "I'd rather be stuck here than there."

Callie leant on the timber railing and looked east towards the jetty, visible from here where the verandah jutted out over the lagoon. She could see swells rising and splashing as they hit the pylons. She remembered how flat and smooth it had been when they arrived. Was that only four days ago? She wondered about Baz and Nina alone on Apostle Island—if they had even made it safely—and whether they might already have called for an evacuation and be secure on the mainland.

Jack had his camera in the headstrap, though Callie knew the audio would be hopeless with this wind in its microphone. He said, "Won't they come for us when they realise the cyclone has changed course?"

Kevin stood on the verandah, water dripping from the hem of his Bermuda shorts and streaming from his shoes. "No, the protocol is to wait for us to make a decision and notify them. They don't know we can't do that. If a cyclone moves in too fast to evacuate, we have a lock-down procedure."

"Surely Baz and Nina will have told them we've lost the radio and microwave link," Jack said.

Kevin's face relaxed slightly. "Yeah. Yeah. They might have done."

Callie asked, "If we can't leave, then what?"

Kevin said, "The lab is cyclone rated to Category 4."

Jack crossed his arms. "What sort of damage might we experience if Sasha is Category 5?"

Kevin half-shrugged, a movement that seemed foreign to the set of his shoulders.

Callie said, "Can you tell how far away it is?"

Aaron's voice broke in, harsh and sharp. "Kevin, where's the launch?"

Kevin's head whipped around toward the jetty. He swore. "It must have slipped its moorings!"

Kevin could move, even in soaking-wet shoes. He left glistening footsteps behind him through the dining room, skidded on the polished timber as he took the corner, and slammed open the front door to head out to the path. He pulled a stampede in his wake, as though they were all connected by ropes. Jack and Aaron collided in the doorway. Callie might not be very athletic, but she had longer legs than Laura and trailed her reasonably closely as they pounded the paths, her breakfast jolting with each pump of her legs.

The jetty vibrated and thundered as they ran onto it and she stopped, panting, her ankle burning fiercely from yesterday's fall. She looked right and left, but could see no vessel adrift or grounded on coral. Near the lab, she could see an aluminium dinghy pulled up on the sand, just above the waterline—but they could hardly all make it to safety in that. Laura ran all the way to the end of the jetty and looked back, tension evident in the lines of her body as she scanned the shoreline.

Kevin paced up and down, his face almost purple, using what oxygen he had left to swear again and again and again.

Laura jogged back, breathless. "It must have washed away in the night. I can't believe it!"

Jack leant on the railing and peered downwards. "Kevin!" His voice was deep and harsh. "What's this?"

Callie ran to him and saw a large dark shape looming underneath the pontoon beside the jetty. He started down the ramp to the water-level platform, and she followed. There was no doubting that shape. In all their panic, no one had thought to look underwater for the boat—and why would they?

She looked behind her for Laura and Kevin but they hadn't

followed. They were still up on the jetty, Aaron beside them, mute. Laura gripped the railing with clawed hands and her tan seemed almost greenish, or was that just the weird light today? Kevin stood beside her like a statue, staring, his arms hanging limply by his sides.

The surface reflections were a menace. Callie grabbed a viewing tube from a utility box and pressed the glass end to the water so she could see the submerged boat more clearly. As she did she noticed something weird on the other side of the pontoon in the shadow of the jetty.

"Jack!"

Another boat. She crossed the pontoon, pressed the tube to the water and looked, in fascinated dread. Two large creatures lurked in the cockpit—sharks? But then one of them rolled in the current and she realised she was looking into the open, staring eyes of Nina as her long black hair writhed.

30

$\mathcal{U}$sing snorkels and clad in full stinger suits against the possibility of loitering box jellyfish, Laura and Aaron entered the water to retrieve the bodies of Baz and Nina.

Laura had lost it for a bit—and lost her breakfast over the railing —when Callie first announced her grim discovery, but she seemed to have pulled herself together.

Callie and Jack monitored progress through more viewing tubes, ready to help haul the flaccid forms out of the ocean's embrace.

The snorkellers had to dive again and again. Baz and Nina seemed to be entangled in ropes, and it dawned on Callie that they'd been tethered to the wreck of their craft.

Was this a "kindness", allowing their bodies to be recovered for the sake of the families instead of drifting away to be eaten by reef creatures? It felt more like a warning. Or an omen.

Romeo had melted away at Callie's first shout about the deaths, she wasn't sure whether Silas had even followed them to the jetty, and Kevin seemed to have abdicated. When his staff had first rushed off to prepare for the retrieval, he had plonked down on a bench at the head of the jetty and stared at nothing. He was still in that position half an hour later when the four pallbearers came back down the jetty trundling two baggage carts.

They paused in front of him. Aaron said, "It looks like they were shot. In the back."

Laura said, "There are multiple holes in the hulls of both the boats. This was on the sand." She indicated a power drill with an auger attachment. "I think it's the one from the utility shed. They won't be easy to patch. Do we try to float one of them?"

Kevin still said nothing. He seemed to be in some kind of fugue state.

Laura said, "We're going to put the bodies in the coolroom."

The grim procession continued down the path toward the main house and when Callie glanced back over her shoulder, Kevin was still staring at nothing.

Jack said, "I think we should lay them out straight."

Laura caught her breath on what might have been a sob. "We can get the carts in here if we move some of this stuff. Why not just wheel them in and be done with it?"

"It'll make it harder on the families to have to identify them in this position. They might… set. We should arrange them as nicely as we can."

Callie said, "Why don't you go and grab a couple of sheets, Laura, to cover them with. We'll sort them out."

After she'd gone, Jack said, "That was a good idea. Thanks."

Callie waggled her head. "She's not coping very well. Better to get her out of here. Were they close friends, Aaron?"

He was moving a box of pineapples and melons aside and didn't even pause in the task. "Doubt it. I don't think she even liked them much. Especially not Nina."

Jack said, "Let's get the fruit out of here. It'll give us more room. The fruit will keep for a few days, which is hopefully as long as we'll need it."

Aaron's head snapped up at that and he let the box fall awkwardly. A ripe rockmelon rolled across the cold concrete floor, hit the sharp edge of a shelving bracket, and split open. The sweet caramel-like smell filled the air. "Do you think we're going to be stuck?"

"Don't you?"

"Someone has to start wondering why they haven't heard from us. When they can't get through on the phone or the marine radio, they'll come and check."

"Will they?"

Aaron studied his foot as he kicked gently at the steel upright of the nearest shelf. "I don't know. I've only lived on a remote island for a few months. I've never been through anything like this."

"What if they don't come? What if they can't? Won't they assume we'll use our own boat to evacuate?"

Aaron looked up again and stared at him for five beats. "I've always thought if I was stuck here in a Category 5, this coolroom would be the best place to wait it out. Or the walk-in freezer, but it's too cold. Even if you turned the power off, it would hold the cold for too long."

Jack said, "You've given it some thought, then?"

"I've been through cyclones in the Pilbara, so yes, you think about it. Shipping containers usually survive. The weight and the shape—the wind goes around them. These big fridges and freezers look a bit like shipping containers."

Callie said, "But Kevin said the lab is the cyclone-rated building."

"Not Category 5. And it's not the highest place. This is."

Jack shoved his hands in his pockets. "So what are you saying?"

"Maybe we shouldn't put the bodies in here. I don't want to weather a cyclone in a morgue."

As he stared at the floor and Jack stared at him, the compressor clicked off and the lights went out.

31

Two long rows of solar panels. An axe hole through each and every one. Callie knew they were axe holes because the fire axe was still embedded in the last one on the right.

Two more holes through the main workings of the generator. Round holes, those. Bullet holes, maybe. The generator emitted steam and dripped oil in a widening puddle on its concrete base, and it wouldn't start.

"It's a lot of work," Jack said.

Callie frowned at him. "What is?"

"All that business with the axe. If you've got a gun, why not smash the solar panels with that?"

Aaron fingered one of the gouged panels. "Limited bullets?"

Callie stared at the array. Then the axe. "Or maybe just unlimited anger."

Laura stood to one side, a chaotic tangle of bedsheets clutched to her chest with both arms. She had converged on the island's power factory at the same time the other three arrived, but it didn't prove she hadn't been wielding an axe there a few minutes earlier. Aaron was the only one they could be sure hadn't done it. Kevin, Romeo and Silas were absent, still.

The four stared at each other.

Laura said, "That means the desalinator is no longer working. It runs on solar power." Her voice was a curious blend of matter-of-fact tension.

"How much other water have we got?" Jack said.

"There's the rainwater tanks on the main house but they're not especially drinkable." Her knuckles were pale, so tight was her grip on the bedsheets.

"Why not?" Callie said.

"Bird poo." She moistened her lips. "We could boil and filter it. The pump system is electric, so there'll be no water to the taps. There's a few big flagons of drinking water in the storeroom. We'd better conserve."

Aaron said, "We always conserve."

Laura said, "We need to conserve more."

Callie looked at Jack and was pretty sure he was also thinking about the vat of water now probably resting uselessly in the submerged hull of Baz and Nina's vessel. Could they retrieve it, if things got desperate?

Laura was still reviewing the practicalities. "Our only functioning bathrooms will be the communal ones in the main house—they run straight from the big tank. They were deliberately designed to keep working even if all the power sources fail."

She turned on her heel and walked jerkily away, towards the main house.

Two long shelves in the walk-in freezer emptied, their contents shifted unceremoniously out to the passageway.

Two long bodies—one a little shorter—carefully wrapped in bedsheets, and respectfully laid on the emptied shelves, like it was some sort of cold, hard double bunk.

Their flurry of activity completed, the four living people sweating in that cold, cold room stood irresolute, shifting their weight and fiddling with their hands.

"Do you want to say a few words, Reverend?" Callie meant the nickname gently, not maliciously, but nevertheless she saw Jack's face go tight. *Kain used to call him that.* She remembered that other time, not so long ago, when he'd been asked to do much the same thing on the spur of the moment. That time it had been an old friend, on a mountainside, in a sleeping bag.

Jack turned to the two researchers.

Laura said, "That would be nice," and half-smiled.

Aaron said nothing, just gave Jack a long, considering look.

"Okay," said Jack. He cleared his throat awkwardly, and Laura bowed her head and clasped her hands in front of her while Aaron still stared at Jack. Callie decided to follow Laura's lead.

Jack's voice was a little rough. "Lord, we don't know what's going on here, but you do. These two have died too young. We entrust them to you now. Have mercy on their families. Have mercy on us. And please don't let the murderer win any more rounds." He said no more.

"Amen," Laura murmured after an awkward silence.

"Amen," Callie said vigorously, feeling more sincerely religious than she had in a very long time.

Jack pushed past her to exit the freezer and headed swiftly in the direction of the path to their cottage. Callie ran after him.

"Hang on!" she called. "Lady with a twisted ankle!"

He paused a moment, turned to look back at her with an expression that said *hurry up* more clearly than any words could have done, no doubt embellished with more swear words than Jack generally used, then resumed walking.

"What are you going to do?" she said, walking just behind his left shoulder and puffing.

He glanced back past her to see if anyone was near, then muttered, "I'm going to make that phone call. They *have to* come now. And we need to get them out here fast, before the cyclone closes down their options. Our options. I hope it doesn't take too long to get a clear connection with this cloud cover."

"How long does the phone battery last? Now that we've lost power."

"It's been on the charger all night while it was searching, so it should be okay for a while." He shook his head. "I hope it didn't get fried by a power spike when the generator went off." He shoved open the door of their cottage and strode into the bedroom.

She walked right in behind him, fast, but he had stopped dead and she cannoned into his back. "Oof. Sorry."

He lurched but regained his balance, and turned to her with hollow eyes.

She looked past him to the laptop on the dresser. There seemed to be more space around it than there'd been earlier.

When he spoke, his voice was as hollow as his eyes. "It's gone. The phone… it's gone."

"Who do you think took it?" Callie said, once again addressing the back of Jack's left shoulder as he strode back towards the main house. She winced as her ankle tilted. She was getting mighty tired of this path.

"How should I know?" Then he paused a moment and seemed to repent of his abruptness. "You got any ideas?"

"Not sure. A bad guy who wanted to stop us having access to it? Or a good guy thinking we might be bad guys because we had it and didn't tell anyone."

He started walking again and kept his voice low. "Just exactly who are the bad guys and good guys anyway? Do you think Romeo shot Baz and Nina?"

"I don't know. What if his gun isn't the only one on the island? But I do know that the only person who couldn't have wrecked the generator was Aaron."

He stopped again and looked puzzled. "Laura as well. She was with us."

"No, she was getting sheets."

"Oh." He paused, but didn't dispute her Laura-suspicion for once. "Would she have the strength for the axe? Those panels are pretty hard."

"She's pretty tough."

He started walking again.

"Where are you heading?"

"Water. Pool or lagoon. It's always close to water that we find the messages."

"Messages?"

He didn't answer her. They rounded a corner near the pool deck and she saw Romeo standing on the stonework, staring into the water, a viewing tube held loosely in one hand, dripping water onto his left shoe.

Jack walked straight up to him, grabbed the viewing tube, crouched and peered into the pool. Callie bent and looked over his shoulder. It was unmistakably Jack's satellite phone she was looking at on the bottom of the pool. Jack muttered to her, "One of the bad guys, then."

"That your satellite phone?" Romeo's voice had a hard edge.

"Yes." Jack turned to look up at him from his crouched position. "Did you put it there?"

Romeo shifted weight and his expression was unpleasant. "Now, why would I be doing that?"

Jack said, "So we couldn't use it to call the cops."

"Who are you and why are you so conveniently here just at this time? Why are you always after snooping around? And why did you have a satellite phone and keep it all to yourselves?"

"We're journalists. We snoop for a living. It's easily verified." Callie's tone was frosty.

Jack stood up and planted his feet squarely. "Who are you, with your brand-new social profiles and only forty-two friends, and why are you here so conveniently just at this time? And why do you have a gun?"

Romeo's eyelashes flickered infinitesimally but he said nothing.

Callie moved to stand firmly beside Jack, shoulder to shoulder. "Did you kill Baz and Nina?"

Romeo seemed almost insulted. "Hell no. Why would I be doing a thing like that?"

Jack said, "You tell *us*."

Callie added, "Someone did."

Jack said, "Why do you have a gun?"

Romeo sighed. "I didn't kill the hairy vegetarians. And I have a gun because I *am* a cop. I'm with Interpol. I'm here… on an investigation."

Callie was madly rearranging her mental furniture as all the questions fought for the chance to be first out of her mouth.

Jack beat her to it. "Show us some ID. Did you know the terrorist attacks were coming? Why didn't you stop them? Why didn't you protect Baz and Nina?"

"Plucky, aren't you, little man? I didn't know. Not really. I was expecting something… different."

"Like what?"

Romeo didn't answer.

Callie said, "You can't seriously hold out on us now. Not when all our lives could depend on it."

"And I want to see your ID," Jack added.

He sneered, "I don't carry ID when I'm undercover."

"I don't believe you. It's a posh resort, not a gang of Mexican drug dealers." Jack's jaw was set hard.

Callie took a chance. "Are you investigating Silas Delport?" Well, it had to be one of them, and Silas was an elephant-killer.

Romeo's eyelashes flickered again. Bingo.

Jack must have seen it too. "What has he done?"

"I don't rightly know just yet. But when an international arms dealer starts taking an unhealthy interest in a tiny tropical island off the coast of Australia, I pay attention."

Callie and Jack looked each other in the eye for one-and-a-half beats but neither of them said it out loud: international arms dealer.

Jack said, "Who's helping him?"

Good recovery!

"Thought it might have been you two, actually."

"Us? We only met him three days ago."

"Four days ago," Callie said, brightly. "It's Thursday."

"Is it really?" Jack raised his eyebrows in an interested way.

"Time flies when you're having fun." She turned back to Romeo. "Is Silas the target of the terrorist attacks or the instigator?"

Romeo narrowed his eyes, and stared at her, hard. "Instigator. I think."

"Why attack his own island?" Jack said.

"You mean Eden Island?"

"Yes. And his own pet research project here on Stanford?" Callie added.

Romeo shifted his weight. He crossed his arms in front of his chest and rocked slightly onto the balls of his feet, then back again. "What do you say to weapons testing?"

Callie and Jack stared at each other for nearly three beats this time, then turned in unison to stare at Romeo. Silence lengthened.

"They're not exactly weapons," Jack said. "They're animals."

"Well then, testing compounds that could be weaponised, if you want to be precise."

Callie thought about the global media coverage and the mice with the red eyes. "Maybe. He'd need help. Up and down the reef, of course, but even just here on Stanford. Jellyfish. Snails. He doesn't strike me as a do-it-yourselfer. Who helped him here? Kevin? Laura?"

Romeo waggled his shoulders slightly. "Not sure. They'd be the obvious answer. But something's off. They can't be the whole answer."

"They can't have killed Baz and Nina," said Callie, "because they were with us at the time. Trying to rebuild a satellite dish."

"Can we be sure exactly when they were killed?" Jack said to her.

"Pretty sure. Remember that their boat was already missing when we all came in for a cuppa after working on the dish. It must have been underwater, even then."

Jack raised his eyebrows and nodded. "And the drill with the auger bit was already missing when we started."

"Is that so?" Romeo pursed his lips. "Useful to know."

"Who else do you suspect, then?" Jack said.

Romeo said, "Well, you two arrived about five minutes before the jellyfish, which seemed a little too convenient to me." He glared at them.

Jack shrugged, but Callie said, "It *is* odd timing when you think about it, isn't it?" Nascent thoughts began to germinate in the back corners of her head.

"I wondered a while if it might be Baz and Nina. I saw them talking to him t'other night in the dark, and I can't think why they'd have anything to chat about otherwise. Could also explain why they're dead now. A falling out."

"Why would they get involved with someone so dodgy, though?" Callie frowned.

"They were tied up in some pretty extreme environmental groups. It's not a terribly long leap from there."

Callie thought about Nina's anger in the staff dining room the other night, and about her saying, "Get me out of this, Baz," and about the fear in her eyes when she saw her impaled phone. Could it be true?

Jack was on a different tack. "Who's helping you? Who delivered the gun to you? And why did you belt me over the head with the case?"

"Ah. Yes. Sorry about that." He gave a little smile that didn't look particularly sorry.

"Who delivered it to you? Who's got a yacht?"

Memory rushed in on Callie and she took another chance. "It was Mary, wasn't it? Where is she?"

Romeo's eyelashes flickered again. This dude should seriously not play poker.

Jack looked at her and she elaborated.

"Mary. From England. On the *Celestial*." She turned back to Romeo. "Romeo dealt with some pirates that attacked her yacht somewhere down the bottom of Africa. I'm guessing he shot them and threw their bodies overboard."

Romeo said nothing.

Jack said to Romeo, "That yacht could probably carry all of us, couldn't it?" He indicated the leaping ocean beyond the edge of the wind-ruffled infinity pool. "And handle these seas better than any motor launch. Why don't you get her here and let's evacuate before this cyclone hits."

Romeo crooked his finger in a theatrical "come hither" manner and led them to the other end of the pool. He spread his hands in an expansive flourish that concluded with his right foot extended forward and his right hand pointing down towards the pool, where Callie could just make out through the reflections a dark blob resting on the bottom.

Romeo said, "Because that, my darling ones, is my radio."

"Aren't the portable ones waterproof?" Jack said.

"Correct. They float, too. But not after someone's smashed 'em to bits with a hammer." He crossed his arms and grimaced. "Totally banjaxed."

Jack and Callie stared into the pool for at least six beats this time, and then at each other.

Callie turned back to Romeo and said, "Still got your gun?"

Romeo was sporting a loose Hawaiian shirt today instead of the turquoise staff polo shirt, and his right hand twitched toward his waist.

32

*D*uring a cobbled-together lunch of sandwiches and leftovers, Romeo for some reason told no one else about the communication devices still resting on the bottom of the pool. For some reason, Callie and Jack didn't mention them either.

Callie tried very hard not to stare at Silas, who chewed a ham sandwich with both literal and figurative relish as though he was at home at his own dining table and they didn't have gusty winds pummelling the glass doors and a double-bunk worth of bodies in the freezer.

To help her not to stare at him, she distracted herself by occasionally making eye contact with Romeo, who gave her a series of innocuous smiles. She also watched Laura, who had finally recovered her appetite enough to make it through two full chicken-salad sandwiches, and a mango which she ate rather curiously with a knife and fork, including peeling it. Now, that was something Callie would give worlds to get on video.

She must have watched a little too hard. Laura said with a tight shrug, "The juice irritates my fingers."

Kevin had regained his voice, and concluded the awkward meal by recommending sleep for all this afternoon in preparation for whatever the night might bring in the way of weather. Well, he almost ordered it, really. And he refrained from mentioning any of the non-weather troubles the night might bring. There was a lot of not-mentioning going on around that table.

Back in their cottage, Callie said to Jack, "Feeling sleepy?"

"Not even a little bit."

"Is Silas here to create weapons out of box jellyfish toxin and test them on mice—and people?"

"It's a good question to ask. Should we go ask him?"

Callie recoiled. "If he's just put a bullet in two 'hairy vegetarians', as Romeo so charmingly calls them, why not us, too?"

"Another good question to ask. Should we go and look for whatever he buried down the eastern end of the island, while he has his nap?"

"I doubt he needs a nap. Probably sleeps like a baby all night. He might be having a reunion with his buried treasure right now. And how would we find it?"

Jack sighed. "Yeah, it's not as though we could track his footprints or anything." He rubbed his face.

"What do you think it is?"

"Most likely thing would be a firearm or a radio or other communication device, wouldn't it?"

"Why not keep them in his cottage? No one's going in his cottage."

"We would."

"We might."

"He could have watched us searching Romeo's room. Or any of the other nosing around we've been doing. And figured it was too much of a risk."

Callie's arms prickled with goosebumps, and she rubbed them with her hands while casting her gaze around the endless windows that allowed the leaping sea and the writhing forest to look in on them. "How about we go into the bedroom and talk."

"Good idea."

They ended up settling on the floor in a spot where they were not visible from outside the cottage, side-by-side but not touching, leaning back against the bed.

Callie said, "Is Silas behind the whole terrorism thing? Why do that? If he shoots elephants he can't care *that* much about the environment. And, apart from anything else, it's a lot of work."

"I've been thinking about that. It's incredibly effective, cheap, global advertising if you're trying to draw attention to a weapon you want to sell."

Callie pondered that a while. She didn't quite know how to introduce the next topic. "If Silas is making weapons from venom, he's not doing it without researchers."

"That had occurred to me." His face was set.

Silence stretched taut. Callie *really* didn't want to be the one to say that the woman Jack had once nearly married was probably implicated.

Jack said it for her—almost. "It would help account for the nature of Kevin and Laura's shock when things started going south." He sighed. "As you said, they were shocked not that things were happening but by the types of things that were happening."

Callie offered, "Maybe they didn't expect anyone to die."

"Let's hope that's the case."

She stared at the floor and picked at the threads of the grass matting. "Do you think we'll die?"

She sensed his movement as he rubbed his face. "Oh, Callie. I hope not."

Silence stretched again.

He rubbed the back of his fingers gently, briefly against her wrist. "I'm sorry I hurt you by not continuing the relationship. I didn't know how to tell you, once I'd figured out it wouldn't work." Pause. "And I didn't know for sure if it mattered that much to you."

She met his eyes. "It mattered." They held the eye contact for several heartbeats. He looked away first.

His voice was deeper than usual when he continued. "I know the way I see things doesn't make much sense to you… but I want a life partner, not a fling. And if I end up going to"—he shrugged—"India, say, to do mission work, would you want to come with me? Work alongside me? Cheer for me?"

She frowned slightly and then gave him a sideways look. "Could you maybe pick a cooler climate?"

He huffed half a laugh, then became serious again. "My faith is not just an 'interest', where we could each have our own separate interests, as well as interests we shared. It's the guiding principle of all my decisions. All my life goals. I want to share that fundamental drive with my partner. The conflict in our life-direction would be just too destructive. Eventually, we'd tear ourselves apart."

She swallowed hard but kept her voice light. "So, no long-distance relationships between Delhi and Sydney, then?"

"I…" He shrugged, but there was resolve on his face. "I want more than that."

Silence. "I'm sorry I hurt you by saying you're weird. With the sex stuff. I mean, you are weird. But I like weird. Whatever happens with us, I actually admire you for sticking to what you believe." She snorted in self-deprecation. "As for me, I seem to think the same as whoever I'm with at the time."

He shot her a wry, lopsided smile. "Unless it's me."

A moment of genuine laughter connected them, and then dispersed, gently.

She fiddled with her phone, woke it, hunched over it and started flicking through various images she'd taken over the past few days. The glorious helicopter trip. Eden Island. The lab—

She jolted upright and stared at Jack.

He shook his head. "What?"

"The lab. My voice recorder was running."

He looked puzzled. "When?"

"When you were waiting for me to arrive for lunch, on the first day." She flicked the photo app out of the way and dived into the voice recorder with several quick, stabbing taps. "Remember? I left my phone on the bench and then went back to get it. It was recording, the whole time. Kevin and Laura had a conversation, right near it, about the Day of the Jellyfish."

CALLIE TURNED THE SOUND RIGHT UP TO HELP THEM HEAR IT over the wind buffeting the walls of their refuge. She moved through a seemingly endless silence on the recording till they finally located the sound of the outer door opening, followed by the clomping footsteps of Laura and Kevin walking across the lab.

The whole thing makes me so uneasy.

That was Laura's voice, followed by tapping sounds and a beep-clunk. Callie said to Jack, "That's probably the keypad for the lower lab." He nodded. Though Laura seemed to be muttering, it had come through loud and clear on the recording, probably because she was so close to the phone by then.

You worry too much. That was Kevin.

A sound like a gasp. *And you don't think I'm right to worry? Are you serious!* She almost hissed that one.

More clomping as they descended the steps into the lower lab. A crunch as the door swung to, but it hadn't shut properly. Their voices were softer now that they were further away.

Look, if everything works out, it'll be well worth any of these risks.

And just how much are you prepared to risk? How many lives *are you prepared to risk? If I'd known it would come to this, I'd never have helped you.* She swore, and there was a thump. Did she trip, or did she punch something? Or someone?

Of course I don't want to risk any lives. This whole thing is about saving lives. You know that. Why would you say that to me?

He's a loose cannon. What were you thinking?! You seriously cannot trust that man. Especially once he knows what you've done.

Callie looked at Jack and opened her eyes wide. What had Kevin done?

Stop being such a drama queen.

Drama queen? He must have made this whole circus happen this morning, Lord only knows how. He must have. There's no other explanation for it. What if that poor woman dies? Is that enough drama for you? And then what else will he do?

More muffled sounds of a door opening, a voice saying *Hello?* and softer footsteps this time. "That would be me, arriving," Callie said.

And it's so dangerous to use the antidote when we haven't finished testing it!

It was a golden opportunity right there in front of our faces and I wasn't going to let it go past. And besides, it worked, so what are you whinging about?

Don't you dare patronise me. You can talk it up as a big success in front of Silas Delport if you want, but don't imagine you can deceive me. She's not out of the woods yet and as for potential side effects—

He interrupted her. *Did you really think we wouldn't need to test it on humans one day? How naïve are you?*

Silence, then something that might have been a muffled sob or just a foot scraping the floor.

Yes... I know... but it's just that... it was horrible. You weren't the one doing CPR. I thought she'd die and it would be all my fault. And they were so happy, hanging all over each other at the beach this morning...

We always knew it would be hard. Kevin's voice was much gentler now, and his volume had dropped. Callie and Jack both leaned closer to the phone's speaker. *We can't give up now. Think how many lives could be changed by this.*

Can I help you?

Jack jolted at the loudness of Aaron's interrupting voice, and so did Callie, as though he was catching her out all over again. She fumbled to stop the player and tried to control a fit of the giggles.

"Nothing else worth listening to?" Jack said.

"I don't think so. Just Kevin introducing me to Aaron, and me covered in awkwardness at being caught eavesdropping." She shook her head. "Aaron must be a ghost. Did you even hear his footsteps?"

"No, I didn't." Jack scratched his face. "You know, he might walk very quietly, but I didn't hear the outer door open, either. It would be harder to do that without any sound."

They took the recording back to the moment Callie entered and listened very carefully from there.

Callie stared at Jack. "Do you think Aaron might have been in the lab all along?"

"What do you think?"

She thought about it. "If he was, he must have been hiding. I didn't just say hello, I looked around that room to see if anyone was there before I walked into it. He's six foot two and he was wearing a bright turquoise staff shirt when I met him—I distinctly remember it. Something like that's not easy to miss, even with all the shelves and clutter."

Jack stared at the phone. "What does it mean?"

"I don't know." She shook her head in puzzlement. "Could he be… somehow tied up in it with them?"

Jack shifted his shoulders. "Maybe. But then again, what if he was spying on them?"

33

They found Aaron in the staff quarters, lying on his bunk, hands folded on his chest, eyes staring upwards. Was he dead?

The researcher cut his eyes to where they stood in the doorway and Jack huffed in relief. "You're not dead." Had he actually said that out loud?

Judging by the sarcastic look he was getting from Callie, yes, he'd said it out loud.

"No." Aaron had gone back to staring upwards. "Not yet. But there's a murderer on this island and a cyclone about to pound us. And we can't get away from either one."

Jack pulled out a plastic chair and plonked into it. "How's your nap going?"

"'Bout as well as yours, by the look of it." Aaron sighed, and levered himself upright as though he was a hundred years old. He swung his legs around and sat hunched on the edge of the bed, legs akimbo, arms bent, hands resting on the edge of the mattress.

Jack said, "Who do you think the murderer is?"

He replied, "Why? Do you think it's one of us?"

Callie pulled over the other chair and said, "Do you think there's a stranger somewhere on the island?"

"Could be. How would we tell?" He sighed again. "But I was right down the far end at about the time Baz and Nina must have been shot, and I didn't see any boats."

"Boats?" Jack said. "Where?"

Aaron grabbed a notebook and pen and turned to a fresh page, where he drew a surprisingly detailed outline of the island. "I was at the eastern tip, here, where it narrows. From there, I have a view of the beach nearly as far as the cottages on the southern side, here, and to the lab on the northern side, here. I can't see the whole jetty, just the tip. If someone wanted to kill Baz and Nina at this hidden part of the jetty, and they weren't on the island already, and they didn't want to be seen, they'd have to come ashore over the reef somewhere. You'd be foolish to do that near the cottages or the main house, so we can rule out the whole western end. You can't get over the reef safely at low tide, especially when the sea's running like this, so they'd have to stay here quite a few hours. And I wouldn't be out in that"—he indicated toward his window which had a view only of the draping leaves of trees, but it was more or less the direction of the ocean—"in a dinghy, would you? But even if their boat was small enough to pull it up high, it would be hard to get it into the tree cover. If I'd seen a strange boat on the sand anywhere up either side of the island, with everything that's going on I'd have paid attention. Plus the tide was too low for a quick getaway. Baz and Nina's boat was at the jetty when I walked to the eastern end, and missing when I came back. I noticed; I thought they'd left. So it must have been sunk in that timeframe, and it seems to have been sunk with them on it, so that must be when they were killed."

A thorough analysis. Jack appreciated Aaron more with every day that passed.

After a pause, Callie said, "There were delays, too. Baz and Nina didn't leave right after lunch, like they'd planned. A visiting murderer would have had to keep hanging around and watching for an opportunity when no one else was looking. Impossible if you were relying on the tides."

Aaron nodded. "So it must have been done by someone already on the island. Maybe someone hiding. But most likely one of us."

"Which one?" Callie said.

He stared at Callie then Jack, and folded his arms across his chest, sitting up a little straighter. "All this started happening after you two arrived. Could be you."

Jack said, dismissively, "Yeah, nah."

Aaron actually smiled a little at that. "Yeah, nah. You're a moron, but you're an honest moron." Jack felt oddly flattered.

"Kevin and Laura were with us," Callie said, "trying to fix that stupid dish, for an hour or more from the time Baz and Nina headed off to the jetty."

"And they were still with us," added Jack, "when I saw their boat had left." He grimaced. "Or I thought it had left."

Callie turned to Aaron. "Could be you, though. You've just admitted you were by yourself when they were killed." She raised an eyebrow.

He gave her a blank look. "Why would I do that?"

She shrugged. "I don't know. Some conflict we know nothing about."

"And then sink both the boats so we're stuck here in a cyclone?"

"Well yes, there's all of that." Her heart didn't really seem to be in it.

Jack said to Aaron, "So if it wasn't you, that leaves Romeo or Silas."

"Or both of them working together. Or one or both of them working with Kevin or Laura, or Kevin *and* Laura." Aaron sighed again.

Callie said, "You think Kevin and Laura conspired with one or both of the others to murder Baz and Nina? Why? For what purpose?"

Aaron put his notebook back on the desk beside his bunk, lining its edges up square with the edges of the table, placing the pen parallel. "I don't think it, really. Kevin ran to look for the island launch this morning. Kevin doesn't run." He'd stated it baldly, not as a joke, but Callie snickered very quietly. "And he and Laura seemed gutted when they saw the bodies." He shrugged one shoulder. "But I'm not that good with people, so how can I tell?"

Callie said, "I thought they were gutted, too." Pause. "But I still think they're up to something."

"They're definitely up to something."

Jack and Callie glanced at each other and then looked at him. Jack said, "Like what?"

Aaron narrowed his eyes. "Not sure, exactly, but that business in the lower lab. That's not necessary."

"That's what I thought," said Callie. "What's with all the Secret Squirrel stuff?"

Aaron nodded at her. "We all sign confidentiality agreements anyway. No one would dare share anyone else's research without permission. You'd never work in the industry again if you did. And why keep box jellyfish under artificial light when we've got a perfectly good aquaria deck in the sun? And why have so many of them?" He shook his head again. "That's just showboating for Silas. Nobody needs that many animals once you've figured out the compounds."

Callie flicked Jack another glance, and he said, "You think it's all just to impress Silas?"

"Yes."

Callie said, "But why would they do that? Would it get them more money?"

Aaron tilted his head. "I guess if it looks more impressive, it might help." He gave them a flat look. "Scientific research rarely looks impressive. But do you get to his level in business by being a moron? Wouldn't he see through it?"

"Why do you think the stuff in the spray cabinet is pepper spray? When did you see the cabinet?" Jack saw Callie shoot him a quelling glance, but he wanted to know now. "Have you got access to that lab?"

Aaron snorted. "No, but their security codes are so easy to guess." He looked at Callie. "Even you figured it out." From anyone else the remark would have been teasing, but from Aaron it seemed a bland statement of fact.

She shot Jack a grin. "So easy, a journalist could guess it." Then back to Aaron. "So why did you want to know what was down there?"

"Because they didn't want me to see it and I couldn't see a good reason for that." His expression became intense. "Did you know that there's not a single researcher working on this island who was here at the time they set up the new project downstairs?"

"Really?" Jack shifted in his chair.

"So …" Callie stared at the floor. "Whatever they're up to, they've been planning it a long time."

"Seems like it."

Jack still needed his answer. "What do you think the spray cabinet is about?"

"If it didn't sound so idiotic, I'd say it looks like they wanted to give the impression it's box jellyfish venom."

"What possible use could there be for that?" Callie said.

Aaron shrugged. "Some weirdo treatment no one's ever thought of? I can't think of one. For the research they're supposedly doing… it's the type of thing you'd need to have internally. Systemically. I thought about heart meds they spray under the tongue… but on the skin? As it stands, I doubt it would act on the skin, anyway. It has to be injected. That's how the jellyfish operate. Thousands of tiny hypodermics on each tentacle." He furrowed his forehead and stared into space. "Although I s'pose if you added something to it, to help it cross the skin barrier…"

Jack said, "But… you don't think that's what they've done?"

"No."

"So why use pepper spray?" Callie said.

"Make him think it was doing what they promised, maybe?" Aaron spread his hands and then let them fall back in his lap. "But how does that help? In the long run, Silas isn't going to pay for a drug that doesn't actually work."

Jack and Callie looked at each other. How did all this fit with Romeo's allegations? He wondered if they should tell Aaron. What they should tell Aaron.

"Maybe they were stalling for time," she said.

Aaron wrinkled his nose. "Possible. Stupid, though."

"What made you think it was pepper spray?" Jack said.

"I opened the door and sniffed. I know what it smells like." His eyes went hard. "I know what it smells like because my mate and I got sprayed with it during a protest outside a mining conference a few years ago. My father hired a fancy lawyer to get me off, but my friend ended up with a conviction." His whole face turned into granite. "A conviction on his record. For taking part in a protest. And none for me. Because I'm white and he's black."

Jack said, "What will that do to his career?"

"He got invited to address a conference in Stockholm last year, but he couldn't get a visa."

Jack felt like he'd been punched. "That's awful."

Aaron pressed his lips together and stared at the floor, and Jack figured he'd probably said the wrong thing, but as the silence lengthened it wasn't a particularly unfriendly silence.

Callie was the one to break it. "Aaron, does Silas know about the pepper spray?"

"Yes. He asked me about it."

"How did he come to ask you about it?"

"He walked in on me in the lower lab, yesterday. I figured I'd be in trouble because I don't have clearance for that lab, but he just seemed to want to ask questions." He frowned. "Maybe he assumed I was working on it too. Hadn't thought of that."

"And he directly asked you what was in the tank that feeds the spray cabinet? Or did he already seem to know?"

"No. He said, 'Is this cabinet safe enough to contain it?' I think those were his words. Seemed to think I knew what we were containing. I said yes, it should be safe enough, since it was just pepper spray."

Jack looked at Callie and she tilted her head and opened her eyes wide.

He said, "Can you remember exactly when this was?"

"Just after Kevin called us all together about the fire on the launch. I went in there to see what else I could find."

Jack said, "You thought there might be a link between the firebombing and that project?"

Aaron shrugged. "Lots of weird things happening. What if the weird things are connected?"

"Did you find a connection?"

"No, but I still think it's weird. They've got gas masks and hazmat suits that look like they've been worn. You don't wear them till there's an incident and there haven't been any incidents. Not on the log, anyway."

Callie said to Jack, "That conversation would have been just before the axes started flying."

Aaron looked puzzled. "Do you think Silas has something to do with the axes?"

Callie said, "Don't know for sure. But if he found out they were cheating him he'd probably be pretty angry…"

"Angry people yell, or sue, or remove their funding. They don't go round bashing things with axes." Aaron frowned. "Unless they're psychopaths. But it still doesn't explain the murders. Baz and Nina had nothing to do with the jellyfish project."

Pause.

Jack said, "What do you think of Silas?"

"He's a narcissistic creep."

Jack sat back in his chair. Even by Aaron's standards it was a blunt statement.

"Reminds me of my father. All smiles and compliments, but it's just to get you to do what he wants. And then when you let your guard down, he sticks the knife in."

34

When Aaron popped the lock on the lower lab and swung the door wide, Jack watched Kevin and Laura turn in alarm. They stood over the far side of the lab, next to an aquarium. In the gloom resulting from the power outage, both wore headlamps, and the glare of the LED lights blinded Jack for a moment. The room was filled with a weird, pulsing half-light and felt more like a cavern than ever.

Callie muttered, "Bluebeard's den."

"What are you doing here?" Kevin challenged as Aaron led the way down the stairs.

"What are *you* doing here?" Jack challenged in response. Strapped to his chest, the small camera was rolling. "You told us to have a nap to prepare for the cyclone."

"Yes," said Aaron, walking steadily towards them around the end of the row of fibreglass tanks. "Why aren't you napping?"

Jack felt movement at his feet and glanced down in astonishment to see water swirl around his shoes.

Callie's feet, beside his, were shod in sandals. "Where's the water coming from?" Her voice was strong but he glanced up to see a shadow of alarm in her eyes.

Laura pointed at the end wall. "The Coral Sea." Fixed steel

louvres let in another howling wind gust, along with a swirl of frothy water. "It's the storm tide." Her voice was flat, her face hard to read.

Callie said, "Has it ever come into this room before?"

"No. But we've never had a direct hit from a cyclone. Not since this lab was built."

Aaron paused and rested his fingers on the edge of the nearest aquarium. "What are you going to do?" His tone wasn't challenging but questioning.

Jack added, "And do you need any help?"

Kevin shook his head. "We're not sure what to do with them." His voice sounded thinner than usual; strained. "They're getting no daylight equivalent in here since the electricity went off. If we shift them to the tank on the outdoor deck, they'll get shredded by the cyclone. If we release them, how will we ensure none of us get stung, if the water rises or when we finally evacuate?"

The answer was obvious to Jack. "How about we prioritise human life right now and leave them exactly where they are." He cast a glance to the cages just visible over Callie's shoulder. "And the mice, too."

Laura narrowed her eyes. "You've been down here before."

"Of course we have. Wouldn't you, in our situation?"

She looked at Kevin but he ignored her and said, "If the water rises high enough, they'll be swept out of these tanks."

Jack considered. "If we put them in the other tank, upstairs, will that be safer?"

Aaron answered that one. "The rainfall from a cyclone would probably be enough to overflow that, whether or not the storm tide reaches it."

Callie swayed slightly beside Jack. "What do you suggest?"

Aaron said, "How about we lower the water levels in the outer tank, put them all in there, and cover it with a tarp?"

Laura bristled. "They'll be injured if you put that many in one tank!"

Jack just stared at her and he had a sense that the others were doing the same.

Callie spoke sternly. "So how about you tell us what's going on. All three of us would like to know."

"All four of us would like to know."

Jack whipped around and inhaled sharply at the sight of Silas standing in the doorway, a pistol in his hand. He walked calmly down the steps into the lab and stood between but slightly behind Jack and Callie, an unpleasant smile on his face. Callie gave Jack an intense look and edged away. Jack angled his body so the camera could capture Silas. As best he could tell, the gun was aimed straight at Kevin.

"What are you doing?" Silas spoke conversationally with a charming smile. "And why did you think you could do it to me?"

Kevin raised his hands to shoulder level, palms forward, in a gesture of semi-surrender or appeasement. "Now, wait a minute. Our research didn't get the results we wanted but we still have something of value to offer you."

Silas's top lip curled momentarily. "I am not the fool you think." The smile continued but his voice took on an edge of a hiss. "You have set out to deceive me from the Day 1." He indicated around him with his free hand. "All of this. A charade. You betrayed me. And now you will have your reward." His eyes swept around each person present. "I am sorry, my friends, but you will all now have to receive the reward for the sins of Kevin Harris."

Callie interrupted. "Did you organise all this, Silas? The so-called terrorist attacks? The bombing?" She had moved back from him a little further.

Silas gave her a formal half-bow, but the gun stayed pointed at Kevin's heart, his grip firm.

She continued, "And did you take us to Eden Island on purpose? Did you organise it so we'd be there when that child got stung? So we could film it and get it on the television news?"

He smiled charmingly. "Of course."

"Well that was pretty clever," she said. "Must have taken some planning."

He tilted his head and his eyes crinkled in a deeper smile. "I strive for excellence. I am glad you enjoyed it."

"You must have quite a team." She was obviously engaging him to buy time, and Jack only wished he knew what to do with the opportunity.

"Yes, indeed. But it becomes smaller day by day." He shot an icy glance in Kevin's direction.

"Including Baz and Nina?"

"Of course."

"What did they do to get themselves shot?"

"They betrayed me. I do not like that."

"How will you get off the island before the cyclone, once you've dealt with all of us?" Her voice was calm, interested.

"I will summon my team. I will not be here for the cyclone. I do not like cyclones."

"Are you sure you can trust the other members of your team? Where are they?"

Another warm smile. "They are near enough to be here as soon as I need them. And they are much too intelligent to cross me." His voice turned harsh. "Now it's time to reduce my team to only those I can trust."

Jack's eyes fixed on Silas's hand, only perhaps thirty centimetres from Jack's own elbow. Just beyond it and below it, in his peripheral vision in the half light he saw a shadow rise in the dully-gleaming tank before him. As Silas's fingers began to tighten on the trigger, Jack's hand shot into the tank, grabbed, lifted and flung.

Jellyfish tentacles flipped across Silas's hand and the noise of the gun exploded, drowning out a guttural roar from Silas.

Callie screamed and kept on screaming, and the sea rushed past and over Jack's shoes.

35

Callie's foot was on fire, the fire of a thousand suns and the burning wouldn't stop and she couldn't stop, couldn't stop screaming and how would she breathe and why hadn't she worn closed shoes. She drew breath and screamed again, her voice hoarse and thin.

Beside her, Silas was falling falling falling to the floor, and Jack had the pistol in his hand now and was staring at her, reaching for her, his eyes wide. He threw the gun from him and it arced through the air into the tank and sank from sight.

Across the room Laura was screaming, "Kevin! Kevin!" and there was something dark on his shirt and it was so gloomy in here.

The water swirled over her foot and carried the jellyfish away from her and back towards Silas where he lay writhing on the floor and pulled it along his bare arm. The noise he made was like a wild animal enraged, maybe like that elephant, and he clutched his chest and she screamed and whimpered. Jack grabbed her arm and grabbed her other arm, no that was someone else, and she turned and it was Aaron.

"On the bench!" That was Jack's voice maybe, but it sounded hoarse and strange. And together they lifted her as something tumbled to the floor—the mouse cages—and Aaron had shoved them aside and the mice screamed too in tiny tiny voices and she said, "The mice! The mice!"

Aaron muttered something about the mice that wasn't very nice and grabbed a big plastic bottle and then he was up on the bench too and started pouring it over her foot and it still burned and she waited and hoped and it still burned.

She began to get her breath and Jack was gripping her hands so hard it hurt. "Callie!" he said. "Oh Callie, I'm so sorry!"

Her eyes were blurry with tears and she sobbed, "The mice." She had a mousetrap in the cupboard under the sink at home but they were creatures too and why should they die and why should they burn? He looked down at the floor and let her hands go and grabbed their cages, one in each hand, and looked around wildly and lurched to another bench and dumped them on a pile of papers.

Jack roared, "Laura! The anti-venom! Where is it?"

Laura wasn't listening. He could only just see her head over the tanks. She was hunched on the floor beside Kevin who had slumped down against the bench that ran along the back wall. She was pressing her hand against his shoulder, and Jack could see blood trickling down between her fingers. Kevin's face looked two-dimensional and his eyes were half-closed.

She shot Jack a look over her shoulder with desperate eyes. "Help me!" She turned back to her patient. "Kevin! Don't die on me. Don't you dare die!"

Aaron yelled, "Look out! The jellyfish."

Jack spun and saw it in the sloshing water, being carried oh-so-surely towards Laura and Kevin's bare legs.

"Catch!"

He whipped back at the sound of Aaron's voice and grabbed the broomstick the other man had thrown, just as it was about to sail past him. He swirled it like a bullfighter's cape and stopped the jellyfish, sweeping it firmly but carefully, pulling it back towards him, trying not to let any tentacles detach. "Light!" he shouted at Laura, and after a half-second of confusion she realised what he wanted and angled her head so the torch beaming from her forehead shone on the animal.

He slowed himself, stood perfectly still, breathed, waited his timing, and plunged, plucked the bell and lifted, gently but surely. *Don't rush this part, Jack. Slow. Slow.* He raised his hand high and those endless tentacles draped down nearly to the floor, but he kept them away from his body, even with the wind blustering through those louvres. He moved steadily towards the nearest tank.

"Jack!" Aaron was offering him a plastic bucket now. Was the man a walking cleaning cupboard?

Jack grabbed the wire handle and dropped the bucket carefully to the floor, bracing it with his feet to hold it still against the moving water, then let the jellyfish concertina into it, slowly, inexorably, down all the length of its tentacles. No further risks: he lifted the bucket and tipped it carefully into the nearest tank.

He turned again to Laura. "Anti-venom?"

Behind him, Aaron said, "I wouldn't give her anti-venom."

Laura was gulping air but she managed to say, "Are you sure?"

Aaron said, "Chuck me Kevin's torch so I can check. He's not using it."

Jack strode the few steps towards the huddle of Kevin and Laura, swiftly pulled his t-shirt off over his head, folded and wadded it into a makeshift wound pad and thrust it at Laura as he reached for Kevin's headlamp and pulled it off. She seemed to have trouble unclenching her fingers from the wound, as though they'd gone into spasm, so he bit the headlamp strap in his teeth to free his other hand, gripped her wrist, pulled her hand away, shoved the wadded t-shirt under it, and pressed her hand back into Kevin's wound again. "You're doing well." While he was there, he felt under Kevin's chin for a pulse. It was steady enough, if a bit faint. Maybe he was in shock. He was sitting in seawater and he needed a blanket.

Jack spun around again and delivered the torch to Aaron, then joined him in inspecting Callie's sting. She was on the high bench, pressed back against the wall, knees bent, feet pulled towards herself, as far from the watery floor as she could get. Two raised red-purple trails passed across the instep of her right foot.

Jack looked up into her red eyes and said gently, "Does it hurt anywhere else?"

She shook her head but couldn't seem to get any words out.

"Your other foot's alright?"

She nodded.

He reached up and cupped her face with one hand, then turned his fingers and ran the back of them along her jawline. She grabbed the hand as it reached her chin and squeezed and held it. Squeezed it so tight it hurt, actually.

He said to Aaron, "You sure she doesn't need anti-venom?"

"I wouldn't use it on myself for a sting that size. Her pulse is less erratic now. She'll be pretty sick for a while but I don't think she'll die. Anti-venom can be dangerous if you have a bad reaction to it, so you don't use it unless you're going to die without it."

"But we still need it for Silas. He's got a bigger sting." Jack turned to where the man was lying then realised he wasn't groaning anymore. "Oh no!"

"Let him die!" Laura's voice was shrill.

Jack whirled on her. "That might be who you are, Laura Jensen, but it's not who I am." His voice was cold and hard and she flinched.

"Help *me*," she bleated, and her eyes filled with tears.

Aaron said, "We all need to get upstairs out of this lab." He leaped down from the bench, pulled Callie roughly towards him, bundled her into his arms and carried her upstairs to dump her unceremoniously on the nearest chair. Jack felt cheated; he should have been the one to carry Callie.

Aaron was back in moments and he gripped Silas under his armpits while Jack grabbed his legs. In thirty seconds, Silas was lying pale and still on the vinyl flooring up in the dry-lab while water pooled around him from his wet clothes, and the pair headed back for Laura and Kevin.

Jack said, "Kevin, can you walk?" He was a very big man, and the more he could help them, the better. "Come on, mate."

With help, Kevin levered himself up from the floor, then leaned heavily on Jack as Laura continued to press his shoulder wound. His colour was slightly better, or was it just the light?

Aaron said, "You got it from here, Jack?"

"Yes."

"I'll get the defibrillator for Silas." He pounded back up the stairs and disappeared.

"And some blankets!" Jack shouted after him.

As they made stumbling progress across the lower lab to the stairs, Laura said in a thin voice, "We've got some standard anti-venom in the fridge upstairs. You could use that."

It seemed to be a peace offering, and then Jack realised something. "You had standard anti-venom all along and you trialled the new one on that woman the other day?" And then he thought some more. "And you had a defibrillator all along?"

He stared at her, and her face crumpled.

36

*C*allie clutched a shiny silver space blanket around her trembling shoulders while she held an ice pack on her foot and watched the resuscitation crew work on Silas. She had no power in her arms or legs. Her heart felt jumpy in her chest. And the pain, the pain. She felt like very stale leftovers, wrapped in foil.

Across the room a couple of metres or a couple of miles, the leftovers of Kevin was wrapped in foil too. A Kevin kebab.

The movements and quiet shouting made a confusing swirl all around her, a swirl that she was in the middle of and yet far away from. The injection of anti-venom into Silas, the urgent voices, the pumping of the CPR, the standing clear while they applied the defibrillator.

At least there was more light up here, thanks to the wide, wide glowing glass windows at the end of the room. The light coming in was gloomy because of the clouds, but it was brighter, so much brighter than the cave downstairs.

Bright enough to see every single one of Silas's neat, close-cropped, pepper-and-salt hairs on the back of his head as they bent and twisted where they pressed against the vinyl of the floor as the CPR crew pushed and pumped.

Her seat was high, a seat for a bench not a normal chair, and she felt like she might topple all the way off it and fall right into the white vinyl floor. Her foot was still on fire but under the ice pack it was a less ferocious burning. Aaron said she wouldn't die, so she wouldn't die. Aaron seemed to be a bloke who told the truth whether you liked it or not.

And he spoke again now and it wasn't a truth Jack liked, she could see that: "It's not working. He's dead."

"I thought the protocol was to keep doing CPR. Doesn't the venom wear off?"

"It wasn't a huge sting. I'm surprised."

"Heart condition." A rough, gravelly voice she didn't recognise. Who? Kevin. Kevin was speaking. Was Kevin better, in his foil? "He's got a heart condition. That's why he supported the heart research…"

"Well, doesn't that mean the venom's stopped his heart and we need to start it again?"

"We've tried the defibrillator five times."

"One more time?" Jack looked sad. So sad.

Aaron the truth-teller retracted his earlier truth and gave it one more go. But Silas kept on lying perfectly still as the room around Callie swayed and heaved.

Jack stood and rubbed his face. From her high, toppling seat, she reached out her hand and batted his elbow with her rubbery fingers and he turned. She reached for him, pulled him to her and reeled him in and enfolded him in her arms, all safe and warm.

She said into his beautiful, kind ear, "I should have… worn my… closed… shoes."

37

Silas was irretrievably dead and it was Jack's fault and his stupid heroics hadn't even saved Kevin from being shot and he'd injured Callie as well.

But he had to think about all of that later. Much later.

For now, Kevin needed dry clothes and proper first aid, and Callie certainly couldn't be left alone, so the five of them made the world's weirdest space-blanket parade along the path through the flapping, writhing, maniacal trees, and into the house where they'd drunk coffee and eaten milk arrowroot biscuits on the deck a couple of days ago.

Aaron carried the first aid kit from the lab in one hand—because it was more comprehensive than the one Kevin and Laura had in their house—and with his other arm he supported Kevin.

Whether Laura was propping up Kevin on his other side or being propped up herself was debatable. She had full first-aid training, Jack was sure of that, but she seemed to have become a bit useless.

Jack shuffled behind them, his arms tenderly around Callie in her weirdly crackling coating. He held her ice pack crumpled in one hand and his hand started to ache with the cold. She was walking okay now, just seemed a bit off the planet. Whether that was the effect of the venom or the pain or the shock, he couldn't tell. Maybe all three.

Inside, he bundled Callie onto a corner of the cushy sofa, repositioned her ice pack, unfolded a wrap that lay on an ottoman, and tucked it gently around her.

"The bleeding's mostly stopped." Aaron had unwrapped Kevin's shoulder, keeping the rest of him inside the space blanket. "Find him some dry clothes while I bandage it."

"The stove is gas," Laura said to Jack in a fractured voice. "There's a stove-top kettle in one of the cupboards. And a tank of water in another one. We all need something hot and sweet." She disappeared down the corridor.

Aaron threw over his shoulder, "I'll have some of that hot water in a bowl first. And some clean tea towels or something."

Jack initially plugged in the electric kettle from sheer force of habit, and came to his senses only when it didn't light up. He found the other kettle in the cupboard under the sink. It took him a while to get things started because he wasn't used to a gas stove, but he finally got it happening without blowing them all to bits. He brought the hot water while the kettle boiled again, and handed Aaron implements as he needed them, darting back to stop the kettle when it whistled, then back to assist Aaron.

"Should we try to get the bullet out?" Jack said.

"This isn't the Wild West." Aaron didn't even look at him.

They worked quietly together till Kevin's wound was bathed, disinfected and securely bandaged, and the man looked just slightly better. They helped him into the dry clothes Laura had brought, the women, even off-planet Callie, looking discreetly elsewhere even though the patient didn't much seem to care about his privacy just now, and, eventually, everyone sat down with a hot drink.

The packet of milk arrowroots was back from the dead, sitting on a plate in the centre of the coffee table. The last few days' humidity had not been kind to them, but hey, they were food and would help with the shock.

Laura retrieved a bag of glucose jellybeans from a drawer in the kitchen and held them out to Callie, whose face brightened. She took three and stared at their vivid colours in her hand. "Eat them,"

Laura said, force fed a couple more to Kevin, and then tossed the packet on the table.

Jack said, "Has anyone wondered where Romeo is?"

"I have," Aaron said.

"Did you know he's with Interpol?"

Laura gasped. "What?"

Aaron looked interested; Kevin just stared, his face hollow.

Laura said, "How do you know?"

"He told us this morning. Said he was tracking Silas."

Aaron said, "Why did he tell you?"

"We asked him what he was up to when he found his radio handset in the pool."

"Beside our satellite phone," Callie mumbled, her mouth full of jellybeans.

"Satellite phone?" Laura glared at Callie and then at Jack. "Have you got a satellite phone—all this time—and you're keeping it to yourselves?"

Jack sighed. "It's a long story."

"Oh, well, please do tell. We've got so much time to listen to your stories of virtue and superiority."

Jack said, mildly, gazing into his coffee mug, "It's no use now, anyway. It's on the bottom of the pool." And then he raised his gaze and looked her dead in the eye. "And you can hardly blame us for not knowing who to trust."

Silence stretched and a flurry of sand hit the windows, making a metallic tinking noise on the glass. Jack looked out to the line of shrubs edging the top of the beach—shrubs that were far above the normal high tide mark. He saw a splash of water leap among their stems, and then a wave surged right through towards him. He went to the window and watched it run across the pillowed sand towards the house, soaking in and leaving a dark undulating stain on the soft sand.

"We can't stay here," he said. "The storm tide's coming in."

Aaron joined him at the window and stared at the same thing. "The walk-in fridge next to the main-house kitchen. It's on the highest point—it's our best chance."

Kevin groaned and put his head in his hand. "Oh dear God.

We're all going to die. How did I think I could do that to a gun-runner and get away with it?"

Jack said, "How about we don't die? And what exactly did you do?"

"I… I told him we could weaponise it." He shook his head. "It's not true of course. It doesn't penetrate the skin without the barbs in the tentacles."

"What if you added something to it to cross the skin barrier?" Aaron said.

"I'm not sure. We told him about that issue and that we were looking for a solution, but we didn't look very hard because we didn't want him or anyone else to have access to such a terrible thing." He shifted uncomfortably in his chair. "I'm sure there'd be better and cheaper chemical weapons anyway. It's ridiculously hard to harvest box-jelly venom. The whole thing was only ever just for show."

Jack said, "You've been playing this game a while."

"A long while. It's been exhausting, keeping up the act. I don't know why he had to move here and watch us the whole time. We could have just sent him reports."

"Silas is a bit more hands-on about his investments than that." It was Callie, and though her voice sounded tired it was good to hear her making a bit more sense.

"Why Silas?" Jack said.

"We needed funds, and he has funds, and… I… I wanted revenge. He ruined my family." Kevin's jaw set hard.

"That worked out well," Jack said.

"Yeah."

"But how did he know?" Laura stabbed another glare at Jack. "Did you tell him?"

"No, I did." Aaron was still standing and he stood very upright indeed. "He asked me about it and I told him I thought you had pepper spray in the cabinet."

"When?" Kevin's voice was hoarse.

"Yesterday, after you told us about the ferry blowing up."

Silence lengthened, and sand flicked the glass again. Kevin said, very, very quietly, "Baz and Nina. He must have thought they were in on it."

Jack said, "They weren't?"

"Well, they knew nothing about our research, or the deception. But I'm pretty sure they were helping him somehow. I have a hunch they supplied the box jellyfish we found in the lagoon."

"Maybe they thought they were helping an eco-warrior." Jack rubbed his face with both hands. "And regretted it when they realised how far he was willing to go."

Water leapt through the shrubs again.

Callie said, "Are there any buildings further that way?" She pointed vaguely towards the east.

So, maybe not making so much sense after all.

Laura shook her head. "No, this is the last one."

Callie persisted. "Not even a little tiny structure?"

"Well, there's the shelter for the seawater pump, but it's only waist-high, and full of pipes, so I don't see how that can be of any use."

Aaron said to Jack, "Let's move those jellyfish and then get Silas into the freezer."

"Good idea, while we've still got some daylight. Then we can get the fridge set up for the night before the rain starts." Jack drained his cup, stood and grabbed another stale biscuit from the plate and a couple of jellybeans, too—the energy burst from the glucose would come in handy. He looked towards Laura, who was curled up on the other sofa beside Kevin, leaning her head against his uninjured shoulder. "Can you look after these two while we do that?"

She seemed distant, but she nodded. Not much of a supervisor but she was the best they had.

"Is he your boyfriend?" Callie said.

"What? No!" Laura glared at her and then sighed. "He's not my boyfriend. He's my father."

38

*J*ack and Aaron worked together quickly, deliberately and almost silently to siphon off about a metre of water from the top of the huge outdoor jellyfish tank. Then back into the downstairs lab where the jellyfish one by one were carefully netted, carefully transferred to a plastic bucket, then carefully tipped into the big tank.

During the whole process, Jack's mind kept circling back: Kevin was Laura's biological father. There was even a resemblance. Once you saw it, you couldn't unsee it. He would talk briefly to Aaron about something essential to their task and then, there it was again. Why had she never told him? Why had he never thought about her biological father at all? He'd known that the man he'd known as her father was her stepfather, the man married to her mother, a man who could not have been the source of any of her genes. But he'd never thought about where the other half of those genes had come from.

And why did he get caught out every single time he didn't listen to Callie about one of her hunches?

"Don't lose any tentacles," Aaron said, but nothing he said could have made Jack more cautious.

Each time they made another transfer they had to skirt around

Silas's body lying cold and grey on the floor, his face covered neatly with a lab coat Aaron had produced after their resuscitation attempts failed.

"Have we missed any?" The transparent jellyfish were so hard to see in the clear water. Both men did another careful circuit of the tanks, shining torches into them at various angles, trying so very hard to be sure. In the tank nearest the door, Jack stared at the refracted outline of the handgun on the bottom and wondered if it would still work.

"A tarp," Jack said.

"Should be one in the utility shed."

"You want to get it and I'll go check the patients?"

"Okay." Aaron didn't stop to chat.

Jack used the net one more time after he'd left.

<hr>

AT THE HOUSE, THE TWO INJURED PEOPLE—WHO WAS HE kidding, it was Callie he needed to check—were looking much the same. But Callie's mind seemed sharper.

"Did it work out okay?" she said.

"Yeah, we've nearly finished over there. How's the pain?" She'd discarded the ice pack.

"Still burning, but it's not as bad as before. And I don't feel quite so deranged."

He wandered to the window. Even in the half hour they'd been busy in the lab, the water had reached nearly as far as the edge of the timber deck. Less than a metre below the height of the floor on which he stood. The shrubs and trees were no longer just flapping but bowing and writhing.

"Wanna play some fifties music?" Callie said. "The whole island is doing the Twist."

The comment was more like vintage Callie, and he felt encouraged enough to give her a bigger smile than the joke deserved.

Kevin's colour seemed better. Jack looked at Laura. "How is he?"

"Much the same."

"I'll be back as soon as I can."

Back at the lab, he and Aaron wrestled with the tarp, which kept getting away from them, dancing in the wind, whipping their exposed skin, even within the high, sheltering walls of the outdoor deck. Eventually, they had it subdued, anchored firmly with a rope rather skilfully knotted by Aaron.

"You a sailor?" said Jack.

Aaron actually smiled, with teeth. "Boy Scout."

As respectfully as they could, they shifted Silas to a large baggage trolley and trundled up the path towards the main house. The long, usually-droopy leaves of the trees were flying horizontal like flags.

Something felt off-balance. What was it? Amid all the rushing, whooshing and rustling noises of the wind, the birds were silent.

"Why are the birds quiet?" Jack said. "Have they left or are they just getting ready for the storm?"

Aaron looked around at the trees. "Kevin might know. But where would they go? It's a long way to the mainland, and they've got young."

Earlier, they'd left the freezer door open to avoid freezing the bodies solid in the retained cold—but now it was shut. Had the wind blown it?

In the punk symphony of noises—howling wind, snapping leaves, thundering ocean, rumbling trolley wheels—it took Jack a moment to figure out what he was hearing. A banging noise? Metallic. Something blowing in the wind? He looked around. No, it seemed to be coming from somewhere beyond the freezer.

Aaron, ahead of him, stopped dead. Jack collided with the back of the trolley, banging his shins.

Aaron backed around the side of the trolley until he was level with Jack and then shot him a glance filled with what Jack would have thought was superstitious dread if it had been anyone other than Aaron. "Did we make a mistake? Were they not… dead?"

There was the sound again. A steady metallic banging. And it was coming from the freezer.

Jack strode forward. There was a broomstick jamming the door handle. He pulled at it, tried another angle and wrenched hard. It came free, he slid the door open, and Romeo fell heavily against him, swathed in plastic and cardboard.

"Wh-where were you? I thought you'd n-never come." Romeo's jaw was trembling so hard that Jack could actually hear the man's teeth clattering against each other.

"What is all this crap you're caught up in?"

"In-insulation. Packaging. Best I c-could do."

"Let's get you warmed up." Jack started to lead Romeo into the main house past the Silas-laden trolley, but Romeo reeled backwards.

"What's h-he doing here?"

Jack found it hard to answer and Aaron stepped in. "He's not doing anything. He's dead. Jellyfish sting." He shrugged slightly. "Or heart attack."

"C-couldn't happen to a nicer b-bloke." Jack shot him a reproving look. "H-he p-put me in there." He sounded more like a petulant five-year-old than an international crime fighter, but it might have been the hypothermia talking.

A few minutes later, a pot of water was boiling on the gas stove in the main-house kitchen and Aaron had returned with blankets.

"You must have been in there at least two hours," Jack said.

"I don't know, but it was a long time. I thought I was g-gone." He was speaking more clearly but another shudder rippled along his entire frame.

"Just as well the power was off. I guess it holds the cold for a long time, though."

"And I had such fabulous c-company in there."

Jack made hot, sugary tea without asking for preferences and passed it to Romeo without comment.

Romeo curled his lip in distaste at the first mouthful but Jack just said, "Drink it. You've got hypothermia." He frowned. "I wish we could get you into a hot shower." The hot water systems were gas, but the water pumps feeding the showers were electric.

As the ice man sipped, Aaron said, "A hot bath. We could boil the water here and take it to the tub in the closest cottage."

"Don't waste d-drinking water."

"Seawater. Or pool water."

Jack pondered. "It would take too long. I guess there's no hot water bottles on this island?"

Aaron frowned. "There might be some of those instant-heat packs in the first aid kit." He returned a minute later with a couple, but it wasn't enough.

Jack emerged from the cupboard under the kitchen bench. "What if we fill some of these big jars with hot water and pack them around him?"

They relocated Romeo to one of the big rattan armchairs, arranged him with blankets, and carefully tucked two heat packs and half a dozen sealed glass jars full of hot-but-not-boiling water around him.

"How are your fingers?"

"I think they're okay." He extended them and bent and wiggled his fingers. He grinned. "Kept them in me armpits. Not sure about me toes, though."

"Hopefully your shoes helped with that." Jack turned to Aaron. "We'll have to get the others up here. Night is coming." He looked out at the ocean. "Night, and Cyclone Sasha."

"Can't they get themselves up here?" Romeo muttered.

"Um, no." Jack rubbed his face with both hands. "Long story."

"Not that long," Aaron said. "Kevin's been shot, Callie's been stung, and Laura is off her brain. Oh, and Laura is Kevin's daughter."

Romeo stared at him blankly.

Jack gave him a wry smile. "You're not the only one who's had an interesting afternoon. How did he get you in there, by the way?"

Romeo sighed. "I had my gun on him and was going to put him in the freezer myself. But, sweet Lord above, that man can move. Took my pistol, gave me a shove, locked the door, and disappeared."

"Why didn't he shoot you?" Jack said.

"Oh, right, thanks then."

"No, I mean it. He enjoys shooting people, so why not you?"

"Probably saving bullets." Romeo rolled his eyes. "He's apparently keen on preserving the earth's resources."

Aaron said, "He knew he'd need at least five bullets for the rest of us."

Jack frowned. "Surely he had his own gun if he shot Baz and Nina."

"Obviously not handy if he took Romeo's."

Jack sighed. "Whatever. We'll need to get everyone up here and prepare some hot food."

He turned to go but Romeo said, "Hang on. Where's my pistol?"

"On the bottom of a jellyfish tank."

39

allie surfaced from a tortuous dream, where flocks of jellyfish flew through Norwegian paintings, to a noise. A different noise. Not birds or wind or projectile-sand or waves. She looked at Laura, who seemed to be asleep on Kevin's shoulder. Both of them were asleep. But it was definitely a mechanical noise.

Could Silas's crew have come looking for him by sea or air? Had he sent a signal before he went to the lab? Or did they have an agreement to come if they didn't hear from him by a certain time?

She stood, rubbed her eyes, and peered out the window to the water that was now surging across the deck. How long had she been asleep? Each time the sea receded as a wave ebbed, it seemed to recede less.

She struggled against the gusting wind to open the door onto the deck, looked out, looked up, and listened as the wind butted past her into the house. No, it was coming from somewhere else.

A loud bang and the shattering of glass. She leapt out of her skin and back into it again, but in a slightly different order.

"What are you doing? Shut the door!" Laura struggled up out of the lounge and ran to the kitchen. "You broke it! You broke it."

Callie followed her and stopped in the doorway at the sight of a picture frame, face down, and shards of glass across the floor. Laura picked up the photo of her parents, shook it free of glass fragments and clutched it to her chest.

"I'm so sorry. Here, let me help you."

"Leave me alone!"

Callie was just grabbing a broom that stood in a gap beside the fridge when she was distracted by a flash of unnatural colour through the trees outside. Red. Her blood ran cold, then hot, then away from her brain into her extremities, leaving only dizziness.

A car was pulling up out front with a grinding, shattering noise.

It was the island ute with its crumpled bonnet and one headlight hanging loose.

Jack and Aaron stepped out of it and strode towards the house, and Callie dropped the broom to clatter onto the floor and stumbled out of the kitchen to sink into the lounge and put her head in her hands. She drew a deep, shuddering breath, and then another one.

"Cal! Are you okay?" Jack was standing beside her, touching her shoulder, but she couldn't look up at him.

"I heard… I heard an engine. And I didn't know…"

He was sitting beside her now and she looked into melting brown eyes that were all concern. "I'm so sorry. We would have tried the walkie-talkies, but we thought you might all be asleep. Hoped you'd be asleep, actually."

She leaned back against the lounge and closed her eyes. "You were gone so long."

"Yeah. Sorry about that. We found Romeo. Locked in the freezer."

That wormed its way into the central processor of her brain and her eyes popped open. She stared at him. "Is he…?"

"He's okay. But it took us a while to warm him up. And now we need to get everyone up to the walk-in fridge for the night. We can't stay here. We brought the ute so we can carry blankets, mattresses, pillows. For protection, and to try to make us as comfortable as possible…"

"Time to get moving." Aaron's voice was even brisker than usual. "We have to organise food, and it won't be straightforward." He walked to the windows, examined the ocean, then spun around. "Laura. Blankets and mattresses. Should we take them from here?"

She took a couple of steps towards him from the kitchen, looking like a ghost in an old black and white movie, the photo frame still pressed to her chest. "I…" She looked towards Kevin but he still seemed to be asleep.

"No," Jack said. "Their mattresses are probably inner spring, like the ones in the guest cottages. Let's get some foam rubber ones from the staff quarters. They're lighter."

Aaron frowned. "Have you been doing a mattress survey?"

"We were looking under some of them earlier." Jack made it sound as though that was something anyone might do, and Callie stifled a giggle.

It took some time to rouse Kevin enough to walk. Callie wondered at first if he might have died but it seemed he was just in shock, or pain, or maybe feverish.

Aaron got behind the steering wheel. Kevin was carefully arranged in the passenger seat. Jack helped Callie clamber on rubbery legs into the tray of the ute beside Laura, among blankets and pillows and various food items, including the packet of stale biscuits that seemed destined to haunt them forever.

<hr />

Callie curled into a rattan armchair in the main house and watched the sea through the concertina-glass doors.

Jack and Aaron had deposited her there while they went off to collect a ute full of mattresses so they could set up a bunker for the night. Laura had been left nominally in charge of the three "invalids". Callie was pretty sure she was in better mental shape than Laura in spite of the jellyfish venom. But in the end she didn't have the energy to resent it.

The doors were closed tight against the approaching storm and rattled in their tracks. If she slumped down low she couldn't see just how high the water had risen. She could pretend the horizon was always that high. She could pretend that the water always shot long white tendrils up against the railings, and that the waves always pulled in long and rough above the reef.

It was better, anyway, than watching her neighbours in the other armchairs.

Romeo had left the room and she wasn't sure why, but then the door from the kitchen swung open and he limped through, bearing a tray of cheese, breads, and crackers, and even a few pieces of fruit. She appraised it out of the corner of her eye as he held it in front of Laura with a small stack of plates. Very good quality cheese.

He said, "Might as well eat it. Won't keep much longer."

Laura, unsmiling, put a selection on a plate and shoved it towards Kevin. He seemed to consider it as through a fog, but eventually took it from her with his good hand, balanced it on the arm of his chair, and went back to gazing blankly at the sea.

Laura stood, held the back of her hand against his forehead, sighed, and disappeared into the kitchen.

Callie was regarding a good spread of snacks on her plate by the time Laura returned, bearing a first aid kit. "Is he okay?"

Laura didn't answer, just rummaged in the kit and extracted what turned out to be a thermometer. She inserted it in Kevin's ear, and when it beeped she looked at it and sighed again.

"What's wrong?" Callie said.

"I don't know. Could it be infection, this soon?"

"How high is it?"

"Only a few points up, but still."

"Stress, maybe?"

Romeo had crunched and chewed throughout this little presentation, and now he stood and dumped his empty plate onto the big teak coffee table. "I'll go and help the lads."

"Are you sure that's wise?" Laura looked disapproving more than concerned. "Shouldn't you rest?"

"Do you want to take my temperature, too, nurse?"

Callie couldn't work out whether he was being insulting or joking or if he really wanted to know. Either way, Laura clicked a new hygiene cover onto the thermometer, took his temperature, looked at the screen and said, "Oh. Alright. It's nearly normal."

"Nearly Normal"—Romeo took an elaborate bow—"at your service." He turned and scuffed his way to the end of the dining room and out the front door, closing it firmly behind him.

Callie pulled herself up out of her armchair and stood beside Laura, swaying ever-so-slightly. "What will you do about Kevin?"

Laura flicked her a nervous look. "Um, we've got a Flying Doctor kit in the office. There are antibiotics in it. I could give him some, just in case. Watch him, while I go get it?"

"Will you be okay out there?"

"I'll be fine. He can't be left alone." She gave Callie a stricken look and followed the direction Romeo had taken.

Callie eased her phone out of her pocket and switched on the video recorder. She pushed the tray of food out of the way and sat heavily on the big coffee table, right in Kevin's eye-line. She drew a deep breath and looked directly into his eyes, but they didn't seem to be focused on her.

"So, are you going to just fade away and die or are you going to fight for your life?"

Now they were focused on her. "What do you mean?" His voice was hoarse.

"You're not trying. Just sitting around like a big pile of rancid butter, no use to anyone." She indicated with her chin the direction Laura had just gone. "She'll be devastated if you die—you know that, don't you?"

Now they weren't focused on her. "She'll be better off without me. Look what I've got her involved in. What sort of a father does that?"

"Bit of a moron, probably." And there his eyes were, focused on her again. "Maybe all this is just 'natural selection' in operation." Her eyes were hard and he flinched. "Although I'm trying to believe you meant well."

"It was a way to fund the research."

"Which project?"

"The Alzheimer's research. I'd tried so many other angles and the resort was going down the gurgler. Running costs, insurance costs have gone through the roof."

"Well, you seem to have come up with a great solution."

"Yeah." His gaze shifted to his hands. "After tonight, there probably won't be any resort left, anyway." He flapped his injured arm and winced. "And I can't even do anything to secure it. Those young blokes aren't even thinking of protecting the buildings. They're just worried about finding us somewhere to shelter."

"Silly boys."

"If I was in better shape I could do a lot in an hour. Tape the windows. Pack stuff up high for when the water rises. Lock down the lab and all that expensive equipment."

"I'm finding it hard to care much about the resort or the lab when there are two young humans on ice in the freezer."

He flinched again but didn't say anything.

"This little game of yours has cost people their lives. And a lot more."

"I know."

"So, how about you do something to save the lives that are left."

"Like what?"

"Like: pull yourself together, eat that food your daughter gave you, and start being a leader."

40

A pile of foam rubber mattresses from the staff quarters towered above the back of the ute, anchored with ropes intricately knotted by Aaron. This time, Jack drove. He turned left instead of right and pulled up beside the lab.

Aaron said, "What?"

"Just checking."

He entered the code and eased the outer door open. He almost put a finger to his lips to silence Aaron, then realised Aaron wasn't a person who needed to be shushed. The door on the other side of the room into the lower lab was slightly ajar.

He walked as silently as he could but couldn't match the silence of Aaron behind him. The man really was a ghost. He could feel his presence rather than hear him.

Jack checked through the sliver of an opening then pulled the door wide and said, "Looking for something?"

Romeo swore explosively and bolted upright from where he'd been bending over one of the far tanks. He considered them in the doorway for a long moment. "Where is it?"

"Not in there anymore. Surely it won't work after it's been in the water anyway?"

Silence. "It might." He tilted his head. "I think we oughta find out, don't you? What if Silas's goons come ashore? Do you want to be without any protection?" He narrowed his eyes. "Who's gonna protect your girlfriend?"

Jack grinned. "She's pretty scary all on her own. Are you coming? We need to hurry." As he turned his head to go, he saw the photo of Kevin's parents on the wall and grabbed it.

Romeo thumped something and swore viciously. "Where is it, you little toad?"

"Yell all you like. I'm not giving it to you. So you can stay here and drown or you can come with us and get some food and shelter and maybe survive the night." Jack didn't wait to see his response, and Aaron strolled out beside him as though they were going to a cafe for a macchiato.

As Jack turned the key in the ignition, Romeo stalked out of the lab, his face like thunder. He pulled up short when he saw the mountain of mattresses. "Where am I supposed to sit?"

Jack exchanged a quick glance with Aaron, who stepped out of the passenger seat. Apparently, he shared Jack's feelings about letting Romeo find his own way back.

Romeo climbed into the seat and looked straight ahead, jaw clenched. Just behind him, Aaron swung one long leg up, wedged his foot into a small gap beside the mattresses and balanced the other foot on the edge of the tray. He gave a quick knock-knock on the roof.

Jack put the car into gear and tried not to smile while Romeo fumed.

<hr>

WHEN THE THREE OF THEM WALKED FROM THE BREEZEWAY into the kitchen, Romeo hanging behind, Kevin was up and about and seemed to be giving orders.

"We'll need enough food for three days, not just overnight."

"Why three days?" Laura looked flustered.

"First rule of disaster prep. If we can make it last longer than that, so much the better."

"Oh. Oh yes, of course."

Callie walked out of the storeroom and dumped a box of long-life milk cartons on the bench. She smiled. "How did you go with the mattresses?"

"Good," Jack said. "How about we get the coolroom ready while you sort out supplies?"

"We might need to get more water from the rainwater tanks," Kevin said. He glanced out the window. "And the sooner the better. I'm not sure how many of those big flagons of drinking water we've got left."

"We can always hop out and get the one that's under the jetty," Romeo said, his face like concrete.

Kevin stopped dead, glowered at him, his eyebrows a straight line, and then turned back to the task.

"Romeo," Jack said pleasantly, "shut up, and come and help."

He was surprised when the chef actually did follow him. Together with Aaron, they worked at clearing space in the walk-in fridge. It was a carbon copy of the walk-in freezer alongside—like a small shipping container, about the size of a very small single garage, with a sliding door on the short end nearest the kitchen door, steel shelving down both sides, and a walkway down the middle. It was still cool, but not unpleasantly so—for Jack, at least. He couldn't speak for Romeo.

They discovered that the right-hand row of shelving was free-standing. Removing it would make more room for six humans to spend a cramped night together. And maybe more nights after that.

The three men worked swiftly to sort the contents of the shelves, silent apart from Romeo's decisions about what to keep, what to discard. Some was dumped unceremoniously outside, too perishable to be worth keeping. Whatever was deemed potentially useful for the days ahead was relocated to the left-hand row of shelves.

Fifteen minutes later, the space was cleared.

"Looking good." Kevin stood in the doorway, a woman either side. "But we shouldn't leave this lot out here to become projectiles." Behind them was a trolley loaded with cartons of long-life milk, large plastic flagons of drinking water, long-life cartons of juice, and various canned goods.

Aaron fiddled with the sliding door and examined its latch. "We'll have to figure out how to hold the door partially open."

"Open!" Romeo said. "Are you deranged, man?"

Aaron gave him a blank look. "This structure measures twelve cubic metres, which means with six people inside we'll suffocate in approximately one hour."

Callie grinned at Romeo. "If you ever need to weather a cyclone in a fridge, take a scientist."

He gave her a sheepish smile. "I didn't think of oxygen."

She laughed. "Me neither."

"Carbon dioxide." Aaron said it as though it was self-evident.

Judging by the expressions of the others, it was not self-evident.

Aaron frowned and persevered. "Carbon dioxide poisoning will kill us long before the oxygen runs out. We exhale it. We need to vent it."

Kevin cut into the science lesson. "We can't leave this shelving out here, either. It'll become a projectile, too."

Jack said, "Where do you want it?"

"Dining room, maybe? There's space there."

Aaron said, "If those glass doors blow out, the wind could push these round in circles, make a complete mess of the place."

Kevin looked like he'd been punched, but all he said was, "Yes, they might."

Laura said, "What about the office? Could you carry them that far?"

They weren't that heavy and the office was only just the other side of the pool, but the biggest issue was the time it would take. The sky was already glowing with the first tinges of sunset colour.

Aaron walked to one end of the shelf, and Jack promptly joined him at the other.

When Romeo went to assist in the middle, Kevin said, "Before you go…" They stopped and turned. "While you're down that way, get what you need from your rooms." He turned to include the women. "Everyone needs to pack a small bag each—basic toiletries, essential medication, a change of clothes. And anything you can't bear to lose. We don't know what will still be standing in the morning." He said to Laura, "Can you grab some stuff for me?"

"Yes, of course." She seemed more focused now.

"Romeo, what do you suggest for dinner? It's probably the last decent meal we'll have for a couple of days. Can I start getting some of it ready while you lot are busy?"

"Oh, well, okay then. I thought maybe a good old-fashioned spaghetti bol?" His eyes slid to the walk-in freezer. "Erm, maybe you could grab some beef mince from in there. Put a big pot of water on to boil. I'll see to the rest when I get back."

Kevin nodded. "I'll see everyone back here at… six-thirty?" He raised his eyebrows.

An uneasy series of looks passed among the group.

"Yes."

"Okay."

"Six-thirty."

Jack looked at Callie. "Think you can walk as far as our cottage?" She nodded. "See you in our room in ten." Then to the rest. "Come on, you lot. Let's get this thing done."

―――――

Callie had both their laptops and several other items in a waterproof Otterbox by the time Jack arrived. "He said a small bag. How much do you think?"

He grinned. "Well, I'd rather do without undies or toothpaste than leave any of our memory cards or camera gear behind."

She snickered. "Suit yourself, you lout, but I'm definitely taking my orange rain jacket." She turned abruptly away as tears gathered under her eyelids and behind the bridge of her nose. Was it just reaction to the jellyfish sting?

"Cal."

She looked back and he pulled her into his arms for a long, fierce hug.

Ten minutes later, they each had a small duffle bag loaded with cameras, computer gear and a few clothes.

Callie gasped softly as she pulled a sock over the burning sting on her foot, then again as she pushed the foot into a sneaker.

"You okay?"

"I'll be fine. But we need to find Silas's gun."

"What? How on earth are we going to do that?" He frowned. "Or do you think it's in his cottage?"

"No, I think it's in the shelter for the water pump."

He stared at her a long moment then nodded slowly. "What if we pass the others on the way?"

"We go up the other side of the island. With any luck, we won't run into anyone." She grimaced. "Island staff or otherwise."

He sighed and rubbed his face. "How fast can you walk with that foot?"

The western sky glowed lurid purple and red behind them as they strode past the remaining guest cottages and onto the sandy path that curved along the southern shoreline towards the eastern tip of Stanford Island. The long leaves of the trees reached out sideways in the wind, grabbing like sticky fingers, slapping Callie's bare arms.

In one place, the path dipped a few metres to run close to beach level. The ocean was surging and hissing over this section, at least knee-deep.

Callie stopped dead and stared at it. Her shoes weren't waterproof. Jack led the way, clambering carefully through the undergrowth on the high side, clearly trying to miss any bird nests, and reaching back to offer a steadying hand as she followed.

She said, "How high do you think the storm surge will rise?"

"I don't know."

"Remember when Laura said if there was a tsunami, we'd drown?"

"A storm surge isn't a tsunami."

"No. But it's not even raining yet and look how high the water is already."

"Kevin's family got through a cyclone back in the day by sheltering up on the highest point. We probably will, too."

"What if this cyclone is worse?"

"What if it isn't?"

They walked on in silence. They passed a segment where the tree cover opened to a small group of low sandhills, and sand whipped Callie's bare legs like a million hot needles, taking her mind off the pain inside her shoe for a moment.

Jack stopped suddenly. "Here's the road. Is that Kevin's house over there?"

She peered through the trees. "Yes, I think so. Where do we think the pump shelter is?"

"It needs to be accessible."

"So we follow the road."

It was accessible—just a couple of metres from the roadway—a waist-high wooden structure. Jack knelt and pulled open the door.

Inside was a small black backpack.

He looked at her, then pulled it out. He seemed reluctant to try the zip so she did it herself.

There were several things inside. Something that looked like an 80s cordless phone with a thick stubby antenna. She said, "What's that?"

He pulled it out and examined it. There was a charging cradle, too. "A radio I think. I wonder if it works?"

"Well, maybe don't try it just yet, till we know we're not summoning a horde of demons."

There was also something wrapped in a chamois. She unfolded it to reveal a silver pistol. And a metal tube about the same length— probably a silencer, she suddenly realised. And two cartridges of bullets.

Jack didn't say anything, and she looked at him but his gaze was fixed on the gun. He seemed incredibly tense. She touched his arm but he pulled it back.

"I killed a man, Callie. I killed him as surely as if I'd used this gun."

"No you didn't. You acted to save Kevin and the rest of us and, in the process, Silas died. It's unfortunate, but it's not the same thing as setting out to kill him. You couldn't know he'd have such a bad reaction."

He looked away. "I just wanted to distract him. I figured… if I could get even a tiny part of a tentacle on his hand, it would be enough to startle him so one of us could get the gun off him." He shook his head. "But then he fell… and got another sting…"

"You heard what the others said—it still wasn't a big enough sting to kill him."

"But it did kill him. And Kevin got shot anyway."

"Kevin got shot in the shoulder. Where do you think that bullet would have ended up if you hadn't jolted Silas's hand? You reckon Silas is the kinda guy who misses?"

He looked up at her for a moment and then looked down at the gun again, silent for several beats. "You were stung…"

That one was easy to deal with. "Think of the story I'll be able to tell at parties. Maybe even a fancy scar to go with it." She touched his arm again and this time he didn't pull away but looked her in the eye. "Thank you for saving my life, Jack. Thank you for saving us from that man."

41

They ate around the staff table as rain lashed the windows right along the ocean side of the kitchen and pounded the steel roof, a steady, thrumming resonance that seemed to make the bones in Callie's skull vibrate. During short periods of respite when the rain eased—comparatively—it just sounded like someone was outside flinging bucketfuls of gravel at the glass.

The rain had arrived just as Romeo was dishing up an extra-tasty bolognaise. Was it extra-tasty because of his special recipe or just because she'd almost died today? She sprinkled grated cheese on her second helping as she considered the question, and smiled at Jack when he offered her the big bowl of tossed salad. His plate was of course a well-balanced blend of food groups in a range of colours, and he probably assumed she actually wanted salad.

If Callie had been in charge of the kitchen, her pre-cyclone Stormageddon meal would probably have amounted to opening a couple of cans and telling everyone to eat them cold and eat them fast. Whatever else Romeo was, he had to be a real chef. He had even bothered to make garlic bread: crisp-edged and dripping with real butter. She tore off another piece. She'd need strength for whatever lay ahead.

The rain had also brought with it the night, at least half an hour early. A battery-powered lantern spilled a circle of light around the other end of the table. At Callie's end, someone had stood a torch on its base, shining up to the ceiling in a way that gave everyone weird upward nose shadows and big eyebrows. It felt like camping, and she almost expected someone to tell a ghost story.

Conversation, however, was awkward, firstly because they almost needed to shout above the noise of the battering-ram rain, and secondly because no one seemed inclined to make the effort. Some gusts sounded like they were about to lift the sheets of corrugated steel overhead. It was raining not cats and dogs but panthers and wolves, and they were wrestling to the death on the roof.

Callie sat opposite Laura. Occasionally their eyes collided, and every time this happened they exchanged strange little Nancy Reagan smiles. Callie started doing it on purpose and was delighted to observe the slightest glint of laughter in Laura's response.

Callie pondered why Kevin hadn't chosen to eat at his beautiful polished dining table one last time, since there was a reasonable chance no one would eat at that particular table again. But perhaps the deck chairs and timber sun loungers, brought in off the verandah and stacked along the edges of the big room where they lurked in deep shadow, were too depressing. They gave it the feel of an old-time holiday camp, closed for the winter… or forever.

It was most definitely not winter. She'd adapted in recent years to Sydney weather, where rain often meant a drop in temperature. In the tropics, rain just meant even more humidity.

"That was delicious," Jack said, as he placed his knife and fork side by side on his empty plate and pushed it away. "What can we wash these dishes in?"

"Don't waste water." Romeo's face was flat.

"Could we get some seawater in a tub, maybe? It might not be that hard to get some from the verandah right now."

"Seawater won't lather. Just stack them in the sink, and if we get through this thing we'll wash them tomorrow." He paused. "If we still care about dishes."

Callie shot a glance towards Kevin, who said, "You'll get drenched getting a tub full. Don't get wet unnecessarily."

Laura added, "And you could fall in. Which would be a nightmare for all of us."

Silence followed—or at least, absence of conversation. The panthers and wolves were still busy upstairs.

Jack picked up the small black backpack at his feet. He looked at Callie and she nodded. He eased it open, drew out the radio, and put it on the table.

Laura said, "Is that…?"

Kevin said, his voice sharp, "Where did you get that?"

"It was in the water-pump housing," Jack said.

Callie added, "We think it belonged to Silas."

"When did you get it?" Kevin looked furious.

"Just a few minutes ago. We took the long way back from our cottage."

"And you didn't bother telling us you were going up there." He thumped the table with his good hand. "We've told you the truth. Why don't you trust us?"

She saw the tendons roll across Jack's knuckles as he gripped the edge of the table with both hands. "We're telling you now. And excuse me if a few forced admissions don't exactly give me one hundred per cent confidence in your honesty and integrity."

Pause.

Callie said, "The important question is: should we try it? Could Silas have rigged it to connect automatically with his team? Could it be dangerous to use it to call for help?"

Laura reached for it and picked it up like it was ticking, turning it over in her hands. "It looks like a normal portable marine radio. I think he'd have been selecting the channels as he needed them. We should be able to put it on Channel 16." Her eyes flicked to Jack and Callie. "That's the emergency channel." She looked at Kevin. "What do you think?"

He held out his hand and she passed it across. Kevin examined it and his finger paused over the on button.

Romeo said, "What if they're monitoring Channel 16?"

Aaron said, "Anyone idiotic enough to be out there tonight would be monitoring Channel 16."

No one spoke for maybe twenty seconds. Tick tick tick.

Kevin huffed. "I've made so many mistakes. What's another one?" He flicked the radio on and selected Channel 16.

A rattle of static and then: "—estial Celestial, *mayday mayday mayday.*"

"That's Mary!" Romeo wrenched the radio from Kevin and pressed transmit: "Mary, it's Romeo, where are you? Over."

More static. "*… wave and it … the mast. Over.*"

"Can you get to Stanford? Over."

Nothing.

"*Celestial,* this is Romeo, can you get to Stanford? Over."

"*… can't do … am really …*"

Another voice. "Celestial Celestial Celestial *this is Marine Rescue, Marine Rescue, Marine Rescue. Report your position. Over.*"

They didn't hear Mary's reply, but it seemed Marine Rescue did. "Celestial, *activate your EPIRB. Do you have a life raft? We cannot launch till the weather system passes. Over.*"

Marine Rescue made a few more attempts to contact Mary, but judging by the side of the conversation audible in the resort kitchen they weren't getting a response.

Romeo looked like someone had let all the air out of him.

Kevin took the radio. "Marine Rescue, Marine Rescue, Marine Rescue, this is Stanford Island, Stanford Island, Stanford Island. Request assistance. Over."

"*Stanford Island, this is Marine Rescue. Where have you been? Over.*"

"Marine Rescue, we are under attack. No radio, phone or internet since yesterday. No electricity. No boats. We have six people trapped on Stanford. Three dead. Some injured. Cannot evacuate. Repeat, cannot evacuate. Can you help? Over."

There was a protracted silence during which Callie guessed someone at Marine Rescue was grabbing a pen or information, or maybe just swearing inventively.

"*Stanford Island, did you say you are under attack? And—no— boats? Over.*"

"Marine Rescue, our boats were sunk by terrorists. Three people dead. We have had no weather report since yesterday morning. Please advise. Over."

Another silence. Maybe they were consulting a map. *"Stanford Island, you are in the direct path. Repeat, you are in the direct path. Cyclone Sasha is now a Severe Tropical Cyclone—Category 5. Repeat, Category 5. It has enlarged and intensified. Expect wind gusts above 280 kilometres per hour. Storm surge to five metres or more. Expect the eye to pass within three to four hours. Shelter securely on high ground. Repeat, shelter securely on—high—ground. We cannot put a chopper in the air till the cyclone passes. Over."*

Kevin's face looked dead. It took him a moment to press the transmit button again. "Marine Rescue, we are preparing to shelter in the walk-in fridge beside the main house. Winds already gusting to ninety-six kilometres per hour. Tide currently two metres above normal. Please retrieve us urgently when possible. Medivac or Flying Doctor. Gunshot victim. Over."

"Stanford Island, did you say—gunshot—victim? Over."

"Marine Rescue, yes. Me. I've been shot in the shoulder. Wound is dressed, taking antibiotics. Please come and collect whatever is left of us as soon as the storm has passed. Over."

"Stanford Island, we will be with you as soon as possible tomorrow. Good luck from the team here. Over."

"Marine Rescue, thank you. We cannot recharge this radio and will preserve battery. Over and out."

He thumbed off the power and stared at the radio in his hand for a long, long moment.

42

The new-look coolroom made Callie think of a padded cell, Hawaiian style. Foam mattresses clad in hibiscus-patterned fabric of red, pink and gold covered the floor and stood upright against the walls and shelves.

At Kevin's insistence, the mattresses had been stacked two deep on the floor, so that if their storm bunker began to disintegrate they could raise one layer and hide under it for some meagre measure of protection from above. This made for an especially unstable floor when they tried to walk on it.

There'd been more mattresses than they'd needed and Kevin had also insisted the rest of them be stored carefully on a bench at the back of the kitchen. If the group survived the night, they might come in handy tomorrow.

Horizontal rain now filled the breezeway, so they had all been drenched making the dash across.

The fridge was so well-insulated that it still held the cold, even half a day after the power went off. The blankets and pillows would be welcome, if Callie could ever settle down enough to sleep.

Kevin was resting up the back, possibly asleep, despite his initial determination to take a position nearer the door. Jack had said, "The best way you can lead us right now is from the rear. Rest and heal, because we're definitely going to need your expertise in the morning."

Laura lay beside him, reading a book by the light of her head-lamp. The other three men were playing cards, the battery-operated lantern between them.

Thanks to the present wind direction, the fridge's sliding door was tied fully open and Callie stood just inside it, trying to catch a glimpse of the ocean in the gloom. If she leaned out too far, she risked being hit in the eye by fat raindrops travelling fast as bullets, or maybe shredded vegetation or even clumps of sand and rocks that went skittering past. Through the thinning shrubs at the end of the walkway, she could see breakers where no breakers should be, the water level perilously close to their current altitude.

She became aware of Jack at her shoulder. "Maybe don't poke your head out," he said. "If that rope lets go, the door could shut in a hurry."

She pulled her head back in fast, eyes wide.

"Want to join us for cards?"

"I don't know how to play poker."

"How about 500?"

"Well, yeah, but I haven't played it for ages… you'll probably have to remind me of the rules."

"Doesn't matter."

They made room for her in the circle and she sat cross-legged opposite Jack, the only one willing to be her partner. Their friend-ship was about to be sorely tested.

With the distraction of the shrieking, howling, wailing winds, and the thundering of the rain, she kept forgetting what she'd played and what was trumps. Once, she saw Jack's face flush when she played the wrong card, but he didn't say anything. Aaron was counting cards, she was sure of it. Maybe they all were, except her.

Laura produced a large block of chocolate, broke it into pieces, and passed it around. Callie felt her respect for the woman increase by seventy-two per cent—thirty-five per cent for thinking to pack chocolate, and thirty-seven per cent for having the decency to share it. See? She *could* count.

The rain began to change angle, and they adjusted the door so it was only slightly-open.

Aaron kept bidding *misere*, where the bidder's partner doesn't participate and the goal is to lose the maximum number of tricks. She had always found this an unsettling way to play a game because she had to try to remember to lose. She wasn't particularly competitive about cards but she didn't want to lose, either. A situation where everyone could win, that would be her favourite card game.

Jack shuffled and dealt, and as they picked up their cards, Romeo said to Aaron in a conversational tone, "If you bid *misere* again, I'll pick you up by the legs and hurl you out into the ocean."

"Why?" Aaron looked blank rather than offended.

"Because when you bid *misere*, I don't get to play at all, you eejit."

"But we get a higher score if I win a *misere* bid. We're more likely to win the game."

"True. But I don't enjoy sitting here watching the three of you play."

Callie said, helpfully, to Aaron, "It's just a game." And then all three of them stared at her. She rearranged her cards and moved her jaw from side to side as her ears popped.

Jack pinched his nostrils closed and his Adam's apple went up and down as he swallowed. "The air pressure's dropping."

"Is that supposed to happen?" Romeo said.

"Yeah." Jack wobbled his jaw and yawned. And then they all yawned.

On the wall of the fridge, above the "mattress line" where Callie could see the metal lining gleaming dully in the gloom, humidity was beading, sliding, making tracks. It definitely wasn't cold in here any more. Warm and damp and… suffocating. Even the surface of the fabric beneath her felt… moist.

Three more hands of 500—none of them *misere*—and her eyelids were growing heavy. Lack of oxygen or just plain tiredness?

Jack rubbed his face. "I think I'm going to try to sleep for a while."

"Should we let some more air in first?" Callie glanced at Laura but she was already asleep, her headlamp extinguished. Kevin was probably asleep too, though he didn't look comfortable.

They manoeuvred the door wide open and due to the wind direction it didn't really put fresh air in so much as suck stale air out, but that was good enough for Callie. It would remove the deadly carbon dioxide.

Within minutes, the door was secured part-open again. Four humans arranged themselves in a row beside the sleeping two, legs cluttered because the space wasn't long enough for their height, rummaging for pillows, some bothering with blankets. The light went out.

The noise. So intense and so terrifying, now that there was nothing more interesting to distract her from it and no one to make eye contact with. No one to make her feel like they were all in this together, that it was an adventure, not a catastrophe.

The rattles and shrieks and occasional shudders in especially strong gusts, when she wondered if a structure like this could just peel apart at the seams. The insulated walls and roof were thick, but what was joining them together?

As she lay there in the dark it was impossible to relax. How could anyone sleep? And yet they seemed to be sleeping—everyone but her. The dull-sharp burning pain in her foot from the jellyfish sting, successfully forgotten while everything else was happening, amplified one decibel for every minute she lay there, awake and alone in a row of bodies. She still had her shoes on, not wanting to be caught barefoot in whatever crises lay ahead. If they had to make a run for it from here, there would be debris. So much debris. So sharp and so brutal.

And where could they run to, anyway?

She edged across the hibiscus print towards Jack beside her, and rested her head on his chest, listening in vain for the sound of his heartbeat above the cacophony. She covered her other ear and pressed against his muscles more deeply. There it was, just. Dub-dub, dub-dub. She felt the vibration more than heard the sound.

There was something comforting and true and mundane about the rise and fall of his deep, even breaths.

She rearranged her shoulder and snuggled against him—ridiculous in this clammy heat. Gradually, her breathing slowed and synchronised with his.

———

A GUNSHOT! SO PAINFULLY LOUD IN HER EARS. AND SIRENS! OR screaming?

Callie struggled to her feet, desperate to locate the threat in the darkness, but the ground was soft and clinging, like marshmallow beneath her feet, sucking her downwards. She couldn't balance.

There were people around her, and movement, and Jack was beside her—she could sense him. She grabbed and got his arm.

"It's okay," he said. "The door slammed."

Finally, Romeo flicked on the little lamp, and she scanned the frightened faces as they grasped, one by one, what had happened. Laura looked shattered and Kevin was breathing heavily—she could see his chest moving—as he clutched his wounded shoulder, his face contorted. Maybe he'd jolted and hurt it. Or was it a heart attack?

Aaron stepped over Romeo to help Jack find a solution for the door. They couldn't leave it closed or they would suffocate.

Outside, the wind shrieked and howled, and the rain still flew horizontal like a billion vengeful sea sprites determined to strip the flesh from their bones. The men would be drenched before they'd been out there even three seconds.

Would this night never end?

43

Jack stirred and wondered what had woken him. Silence. Silence had woken him. Silence that rang in his ears and crammed the corners of his skull.

His clothes still clung to him, damp from the earlier wrestling match with the door in that wilful rain. How much earlier? What time was it?

Sleeping with shoes on for a ready escape was never going to be comfortable, let alone wet shoes. His legs were bent to fit into the too-short space. How much more uncomfortable it must be for Aaron and Kevin, so much taller than he was.

Someone was moving and he propped on an elbow. Who? Laura.

She clambered over the tangle of legs and finally made it to the door, where she peered out the narrow ventilation gap. He grabbed his headlamp, put it in place and switched it on.

She startled at the light and looked at him. "We're in the eye. I want to see out. We might not have long."

He clambered upright and helped her with the ropes. As he slid the door wide, letting bright moonlight flood the bunker, he was aware of more sounds of movement behind.

"Is it over, then? Have we made it through the thing?"

He glanced back at Romeo and quickly tilted his headlamp up as the man squinted from a direct hit. "No. It's the eye of the cyclone. It'll be still and quiet for a few minutes, and then it all starts again."

Callie, unfolding her legs to stretch them up the wall opposite, sighed deeply and muttered, "We're only halfway through."

Romeo swore lavishly. "You've got to be kidding me." He fell back against his pillows, arms folded across his forehead. "Who wouldn't want a tropical holiday?"

Laura said, "If anyone needs the loo, now is the time to make a dash for it. But don't dilly dally."

That seemed to cause more action. Jack rummaged for his tough cam and the night-vision camera and headed out the door.

"Where are you going? It's not safe to wander about!"

He ignored Laura and strode past the freezer towards a tumultuous ocean he could now see clearly, where a few hours ago a row of tall shrubs would have blocked his view. They'd been reduced to a few desperate looking stems, standing limp.

He might have twenty minutes before it started again, or only five. He began filming upwards with both cameras, unsure which would get the better view. He slowly turned to capture the majesty of the eye-wall which reached up into the heavens on every side, framing a perfect circle of deep-blue, star-studded sky. The moon was full and bright and shining straight into his camera lenses. It lit the banks of encircling cloud so the edges looked soft and white and fluffy and harmless.

He did a very quick check of the footage—it was perfect in the wide angle on the tough cam—then repeated the experiment with slight adjustments.

"The jetty." He started at Callie's soft voice. She must've snuck out behind him, defying Miss Laura's instructions. "We can see the jetty."

He turned east and looked, training both cameras again. Would the moonlight be enough to light his video? He'd been too engrossed in the spectacle above to notice the devastation below. The jetty, reaching out into the roiling water like a supplicating hand, shouldn't be visible from here. But it was. Its deck, usually far above the surface, was barely visible above the waterline, and then a wave broke along its length. Some of the trees that had blocked it from sight were now trunks bearing a few shredded leaves; others were gone altogether. He had a clear line of sight to the pool, too, and it wasn't just trees that were missing. He pondered a moment before realising the changing shed that usually stood between it and the main house had gone. The bar was still there, but its roof had blown away.

Beyond, the far end of the island was not in the calm eye with them, but trapped in the fury of the eye wall. From here, its wind sounded like moaning—a lower register. What was left of the trees down that end writhed in the force of the wind and flailed whatever leaves remained. He tried not to think about the birds. And the turtles. And the turtle eggs, so tenderly laid just a few nights ago.

"Piece to camera?" he said.

She didn't waste time discussing options but stood where he indicated and pulled herself up tall.

"Rolling."

"We're in the eye of the cyclone now, and all is calm. We know this deceptive peace will end all too soon, and we wonder what is still to come in this endless, terrifying night."

He panned the camera round to the left and ended on a shot of the banking clouds that were approaching, wild water leaping beneath them. When he clicked the off button she said, "Okay?"

"Yep, good."

"I thought the sea would be calm in the eye, somehow."

"Me too." Together, they stared at the waves crashing into each other out in the deep water. It was hard to judge without anything for comparison, but they were flying maybe five storeys or more into the air as they collided, twisting and turning in all directions.

Unauthorised breakers thundered towards the shore. He thought of how Baz could have been hanging ten out there tonight… and then stopped thinking about that. It was now several hours after high tide, and the fringing reef should have been beginning to emerge—but the storm surge had swallowed it whole.

"Is this the highest the surge gets?"

"I don't know. I hope so." He turned to film a wave that broke across the edge of the pool.

Callie said, "It really is an infinity pool now."

He gave her the side-eye and walked carefully to the end of the concrete path, filming through the remnants of the shrubs just as a larger wave pushed through them and ran down the breezeway.

"Jack! Callie! Get back inside." Laura's voice seemed an octave higher than usual.

"Look at that!"

He followed Callie's line of sight and zoomed in with the night vision camera on the cloud wall that was approaching fast, about to reach the fringing reef—and the saltwater fury that travelled directly underneath it.

He slipped the tough cam into his chest strap, already recording. The water level, already so high, was mounting, and upon it came a curling wave, its hollow centre black under the dying moonlight.

They glanced at each other, turned, and ran. "Everybody inside!"

He shoved Callie ahead of him through the door, and said, "Is everyone back in?"

"Aaron! Where's Aaron?"

Jack leant out and bellowed, "Aaron, hurry!"

Aaron appeared out the main-house mens' room door a few metres down the walkway, glanced toward the ocean, and lunged toward their bunker just as a low wall of frothy water caught him mid-shin. He staggered, took two more high, leaping steps, and grabbed for the edge of the fridge as the force of water pushed his feet from under him. Jack reached for Aaron's other hand as arms circled his own waist from behind, and somehow they hauled Aaron in and fell into the bunker in a painful tangle of arms and legs and swearwords as the sliding door rammed shut in their wake.

"What's happening?"

"Get off me!"

"Light!" Laura yelled, and then there was light.

The battery-operated lantern was growing dim but it was enough to see Callie inside the door, panting, leaning hard on the handle, trying to hold it closed as water forced its way through in a spurt.

Jack disentangled himself from Aaron and… Romeo, it was Romeo who'd hauled him in… and staggered across the mattresses to Callie's side to help.

He lost his balance and lurched into the wall, shoulder first. A huge shuddering thud, like they'd been hit by a wrecking ball.

"It's the freezer! It's loose!"

"Open the door!"

"What?"

"What!"

It was Kevin's voice, stern and commanding. "Open the door. We do *not* want to float. We could end up anywhere if we float. We could roll. Open the door!"

"Hang on everyone!"

"The shelves! The shelves are bolted in. Grab one."

"Grab the shelf. Can you reach it?"

"Kevin, stand up! Can you stand up? You have to stand up."

Jack wrapped his arms around Callie from behind and they pulled the door open together, as gradually as they could. Foaming seawater surged inside, across the ludicrous hibiscus mattresses, chewing their legs and battering everything in its wake. It swirled under the pack of playing cards and tried to lift them back out as it ebbed, but Romeo lunged and caught them. Jack looked at him and Romeo grinned as he shoved them into his pocket and held tight to the shelving he could just reach above the mattresses.

Another huge shudder and the ground beneath them shifted. How far? Were they reaching the edge of the concrete base? Were they going to roll?

Another shudder, another grating slide. Their angle toward the building had changed, no longer perpendicular—but they were still upright.

Another low wall of water entered the bunker on top of the first and slapped them, reaching their lower thighs this time. Over his shoulder, Jack saw Laura trying to hold Kevin upright. Aaron followed his gaze, changed his hand-hold, and helped her.

The rain began again, even fiercer than before, a different direction, driving straight in the open door, biting Jack's face. The wind shrieked and moaned and howled, and then another noise. A tearing, grating, explosive noise, both deep and high at the same time, incredibly loud, even above the maelstrom.

"What is it?" Callie said over her shoulder at him, squinting against the biting rain.

Jack held her even tighter as the steel roof of the walkway right along this side of the main house lifted and curled, pulling out of its fasteners, bang, bang, bang-bang, right along its full length, folding past them with a demonic swipe that made them throw themselves sideways into the boiling water to avoid it, lodging itself viciously into the steel framework of the opening where their heads had been a moment ago, before the wind pulled it out again like a rotten tooth. It made wobble-board noises as it sailed off, the strangest Aladdin's carpet, into the fury of the Coral Sea.

The wave ebbed with relentless suction, pulling him and Callie with it as they lay sprawled and vulnerable across the padded floor. He locked his hands around her waist and rammed his feet against the inside wall to hold them, and then there was another wave, washing right over their faces. And then another.

Jack struggled for enough leverage to push them both high enough to get their heads clear of the water and he could see Callie was working her legs to gain purchase against whatever part of the structure she could access. He wanted to get them standing upright but there was nothing to hang on to, nothing to pull with—only more wet mattresses sagging away from the sheer wall beside them.

Another wave ebbed, and this time the water level was lower. And again, and lower still. Another, and they were down to about ankle deep, although the power of it at that depth was still extraordinary. And then it was gone.

Rain still pelted them like a thousand pebbles through the wide-open doorway. He staggered to his feet, he and Callie helping each other, breathing hard, coughing. The saturated mattresses underfoot were like quicksand.

The ocean outside was now only a few centimetres deep across the concrete walkway. Was the surge finished? Please God, let it be finished.

Jack grasped the door and forced it closed to give them some brief respite from the driving rain, and even a break from the noise, while the team worked out what to do next.

In the comparative quiet, he could hear sobbing. He figured someone else could check who that was.

He lurched to the other side, the side near the freezer, reached up for a shelf in case of any more jolting, and with the other arm pulled Callie to him. She wrapped her arms around his waist and leaned into him, her face buried in his shoulder, breathing hard.

Their bunker shuddered again, but this seemed to be the wind, not water. Was it… pushing them back the other way? A ringing sound, steel on steel, like a sword fight in a tumble drier, and a… a triangle… appeared in the white wall opposite. A triangle? Hammering, on the roof, wild and furious. He squinted at the triangle in the dim light of the failing lantern. A trickle of water appeared below it. Was it… roofing steel? A sheet of roofing steel had pierced the thick wall opposite, embedded, anchored, and protruding as far as a loaf of bread inside. How big was the part they couldn't see, the part whipping around outside? It would act like a sail! *Please God, help us.*

More hammering and the triangle changed shape, became smaller. Another shudder, and it pulled back out and disappeared, leaving a dark, diagonal gash in the wall, maybe the length of his forearm.

Water spurted through the gap, forced by the furious rain, and wind shrieked through it playing Stravinsky for beginners.

On the other side of Romeo, Aaron caught his eye. "We'll need to seal that. Water will get into the foam insulation. Could weaken the structure."

The sobbing became louder.

44

Too much. Too much. Callie clung to Jack, slumped into the lines of his body, afraid her legs would fold. She'd felt his body tense when that weird slicing, banging, tearing noise began, and a bit later she'd heard Aaron's voice, raised above the racket, and someone was crying, but she could do nothing about any of it. She didn't want to look and she didn't want to know.

She felt trembly and cold. But it wasn't cold in here. It was the opposite of cold. Why would she feel cold?

No more cyclone. It could end now. She just wanted to get into her bed in the cottage, if she still had a bed, or a cottage, and go to sleep. If she was still alive in the morning, good. And if not then so be it.

Jack eased Callie away from him and looked at her face. She was trembling and couldn't seem to raise her eyes to his.

He looked towards Laura, wanting to ask if she still had any dry blankets anywhere, but she was preoccupied with Kevin.

It was Kevin who was sobbing.

Aaron said to Jack, "How's her pulse?"

Jack fumbled with her wrist and finally found the right spot. He shook his head. "Erratic."

"She's in shock. She's still got jellyfish venom in her system, remember. It can make her sick for a couple of days."

Laura spun towards them. "We've got to get them both dry, somehow. They can't sleep on these mattresses."

She was right. These mattresses, bulging with seawater, were like the swamp of an alien planet. In the low light of the fading lantern, the lurid hibiscus patterns looked like a disease.

Jack wondered where they would get dry bedding in the above-ground whirlpool they currently called home. And what to fix first—the sick people, or the hole in the wall? "Laura, have you still got those glucose jellybeans."

"Yes! I have!" She felt around on a high shelf and, miraculously, the packet was still there, and there were at least fifteen left.

They force-fed several to Callie and Kevin. Jack said, "Hold it in your mouth for a while. The glucose gets to your brain faster." At least, that's what his running coach had said. Each of the able-bodied had one as well.

Jack said, "There's those extra mattresses we left in the kitchen. I wonder if they're still dry?"

Aaron said, "There's newspapers in the recycle bin in the kitchen. We could use those to stuff the hole in this wall, even if they're not dry."

"Wouldn't they just wick water into the insulation, though?"

"Wouldn't be as bad as what's happening now."

Jack considered the rain gushing through the gap and had to agree. If the wall of their bunker disintegrated they would be in so much trouble.

With difficulty, he persuaded Callie towards the end where Kevin had slumped down against the wall and Laura was tending him.

Callie clung to Jack and didn't seem to want to let him go, and he didn't want to leave her. He managed to get her huddled alongside Kevin.

"Blankets?" he asked Laura.

"We've used them all." Her face was a mask of distress. "They're all wet. Every single one of them."

Jack thought of the two foil emergency blankets so carelessly discarded in Kevin and Laura's house earlier and wanted to punch himself in the face. They'd brought the lab first aid kit with them but not retrieved those foil blankets.

He had a sudden thought and groped his way back along the shelves. Thankfully, he and Callie had put their duffle bags up on the highest shelf, and the mattresses had held them in place. He pulled out a dry t-shirt and her fluoro orange rain jacket, and managed to get her into both, though she baulked at the rain jacket for some reason. It was only a waterproof shell with no warm lining, but it would help.

Laura managed something similar from Kevin's bag.

The four healthier castaways then stood in a close circle for a conflab above the roaring of the storm. The slit in the wall was now playing like a carillon. At least it was an improvement on the shrieking.

Romeo said, "Is there more than one place we store blankets in this tropical paradise?"

"Well, they're in the cupboards in the accommodation buildings, or the linen closet next to the office." Laura shook her head. "It's too far. Too much risk."

Aaron said, "What about the ones we used for the guests who slept in the main house the other night? Where did they end up?"

Laura's face lit up. "Yes! I don't think they were put in the laundry yet. Were they? I don't know where they are, though…"

"Getting the mattresses back dry…" Jack tailed off.

Aaron said, "Those tarps. Did we have some left? Where are they?"

A quick rummage produced a stack of cheap blue tarps. They'd been on a lower shelf and thus were wet with seawater, but it would still be better than transporting unprotected mattresses across the horizontal waterfall currently roaring through the gap between the bunker and the kitchen door.

Now that her first aid training seemed to be coming back to the fore at last, Laura was assigned the care of Callie and Kevin.

Jack staggered across the squishy floor, steadied himself against the door, then carefully pulled it wide. More rain-bullets pummelled his face as he squinted towards the kitchen door, gauging the distance, the number of steps. The change of wind direction had been bad enough, but they were also now minus the shelter of the walkway roof.

He steadied himself, switched on his headlamp, leaned forward ready to dash, then crashed backwards into the bunker, hard and fast, slamming into someone who'd wrenched him right off his feet as a metallic bonging noise filled his ears. It took him a moment to register that a steel rubbish bin had bounced along the walkway—like a bowling ball ricocheting off the gutters of its lane. It would have cleaned him up like a skittle if not for Aaron, whose hands still gripped his upper arms from behind.

Romeo stood flattened against the mattress-wall opposite. "Interesting," he shouted, eyes wide.

Aaron released Jack, who threw back over his shoulder "Thanks, mate," and then—he'd think about it later—launched into the rain. With the wind pushing from behind him, every step threatened to send him flat on his face onto the concrete.

He was already dripping wet from the ocean dip he'd taken with Callie minutes before but, if possible, he seemed to be even wetter as he lunged through the kitchen door. His shoulder felt bruised by something that had crashed into him—he didn't know what—and something slimy clung to his arm. He pulled it off—a leaf. Underneath, he saw blood welling. Probably just a graze.

The vinyl floor was awash. From the storm surge? Maybe, but also from the rain thundering out of the sky directly into the line of steel sinks along the front under where the windows used to be. The windows were gone, shattered, and a swathe of roof was missing. His headlamp glinted off shards of glass across the floor.

Over the racket he didn't hear Romeo or Aaron enter, but there they were, panting and drenched like him. He shouted: "Glass on the floor," turned towards the back of the room, where they'd left the mattresses, and tripped over... a piece of coral. A jagged piece of fresh coral the size of a cauliflower heart lay on the kitchen floor. He regained his physical balance quickly, but when he saw a fish flopping under the bench and then another near it, it took a moment of pointless staring to regain his mental balance.

Aaron was at the recycle bin, hauling out a bundle of newspapers.

"Dry?" Jack called.

"Dry enough."

The mattresses had been stacked on their long edges on top of the bench at the back of the kitchen, and apart from the first one, which had borne the brunt of the rain sheeting in through the broken windows earlier, they proved to be relatively dry—certainly drier than the ones slurping in the bunker.

Jack approached the two-way swinging door through to the dining room. It was thumping wildly in the wind. He steadied it with some effort, and pushed it far enough to see what lay on the other side but hopefully not get his head taken off by anything shooting by.

The concertina doors hung every which way in the gloom, torn from their connections. The outdoor furniture that had been brought in from the verandah lay strewn across most of the floor, like a giant's game of pick-up sticks gone very badly wrong.

The gorgeous solid-timber dining table, so very long, and glossy with the rain that must have flown in from the lagoon when the concertina doors gave out, stood firm. The shift in wind direction meant the threat now lay in the opposite direction, from the front of the building, from the direction of the guest cottages, which could well be peeling apart and disintegrating into so many missiles. The windows on the front of the main house seemed to be holding—so far. The swinging kitchen door probably wasn't being blown so much as sucked—by the wind outside the now-open verandah and the roofless, windowless kitchen.

He poked his head around the door and did a quick sweep with his headlamp. He couldn't see the blankets anywhere… but what if they'd been stacked on the floor? The breakers that rode the top of the storm surge would have washed them away.

As he withdrew back into the kitchen, Romeo called, "Blankets?"

"Can't see any. You try? But watch out for missiles if those front windows go."

Romeo stilled the thrashing door, pushed, thrust his head and shoulders past it and scouted, but he wasn't gone for long. "Someone must have put them away."

Across the room, Aaron stood in the door to the storeroom. "Hey, look!"

Miraculously, the roof was still fully intact over this smaller room, and the upper shelves were dry. Up there, along the top shelf, was a row of neatly folded blankets. In an even greater modern-day miracle, they located a pack of large plastic garbage bags to put them in.

They gathered close to discuss.

"One thing at a time across and set it up, or shift everything first?" Romeo said.

Aaron said, "Could we carry it all in one trip?"

Jack said, "In the wind they'll act like sails, especially the mattresses. We'll probably need all three of us to get each thing across. And we'll have to crouch low."

The three men stared at each other a moment, and Jack for one was absorbing the potential implications and recalling how dangerous it had been just to get to the kitchen in the first place. He wished he'd realised how dangerous this short expedition was likely to be. But what difference would it have made? They needed the items; that was all there was to it.

"The ute?" Aaron said.

"What! How?"

"Use it to block part of the walkway. Block the wind."

"It might not be there anymore. It might not start. We'd have to cover open ground to get to it."

Romeo shook his head. "Blowing a hooley out there. Roofing iron everywhere."

Jack said, "How about we make them as aerodynamic as we can?"

As they worked together to wrestle each mattress into a roll, like enormous sushi wrapped in blue tarps instead of seaweed, Jack said, "I wonder if the manufacturers ever considered aerodynamics."

Romeo grinned. "Judging by the colour of these hibiscus, I'd say they were definitely flying high at the time."

45

Those jellybeans were a miracle. Callie, feeling thirty-two per cent better and tired of being a passenger in her own life, was up and active, pulling at the soggy mattresses on the floor, trying to make space before the men returned. They were hugely heavy with the weight of water.

"Help me," she said to Laura.

"Should we get rid of them? What if the other ones are no better?"

"If they're not, these two"—she indicated the ones standing up against the shelves—"will be drier than these. We've got to get Kevin onto something better, fast. In fact, if we can get these out of the way, we can get him resting on one of these before the men get back."

They wrestled the first one to the door. Laura stopped and pulled back. "If we put it outside it'll end up in the ocean."

"Maybe." Callie paused, puffing hard from exertion. "You got a better idea?"

Laura looked crestfallen. "No."

"Maybe they'll snag on what's left of the bushes down the end. Come on."

Even over all the noise, Callie still heard the thrashing raindrops as they landed with sharp cracks on her dreaded orange rain jacket. She pulled her hood up over her hair, looked left and right, checking both what was coming out of the wind in one direction and, in the other, whether the men might be about to emerge from the kitchen.

Impossible to tell, either way.

"Fore!" she yelled. And they shoved it outside. It must have weighed as much as two of her, but as soon as she wrested it high enough for the expanse of mattress to be flat on to the gale, the wind grabbed it and off it went, cartwheeling down the concrete walkway. "Whoa." She angled her head slightly to watch it, saw it snag a hopeful moment on the remains of the shrubbery, then pull up and flop wetly onwards, disappearing into the sea. She grimaced with regret, then turned back inside. "Next."

They sent a second mattress after it, then pulled the remaining mattresses from the back of the fridge toward the door, standing them up along one side to allow the water still lurking in the base to drain out. Then they wrangled one of the standing mattresses into position so that the driest portion was available for Kevin's upper body, and got him lying down and as comfortable as possible. He groaned, apparently involuntarily, as they laid him down, and his face was ashen.

Callie looked at Laura, ready to offer suggestions, or failing that, commiserations, but Laura was fixated on the upper shelf unveiled by moving the mattress.

"Look!" She reached up to pull down the top item from a stack of folded newspapers. "Where did these come from?"

"Oh, yes. I put them there. Thought they might come in handy for cleaning up or lighting a fire or whatever." She slapped her forehead. "I didn't think of it when Aaron was talking about newspaper."

"We could make a blanket for Kevin."

"Or should we pack the hole in the wall?"

"Why not do both?" Laura delivered the friendliest smile Callie had received from her all week.

As the tallest of the two, Callie took charge of the wall, grabbing large sheets of newsprint, crushing them, and packing them into the wide slit cut by the roofing steel. She pulled her hood up again to protect against the rainwater spurting through more and more forcefully as its passage became restricted by the growing plug. Piece by piece, she forced more and more into the gap. As the paper absorbed water and compacted, it felt as though it might turn into something like papier mâché… or concrete. Breathing hard with the effort of reaching up over her head, she forced the last piece in, taking care not to slice her fingers on the jagged steel.

She looked around for any praise that might be forthcoming, but Laura was too busy swaddling Kevin. She was layering flat paper, with crushed paper between the sheets to create more insulation. When she had finished, a story about the local football team graced his chest. He looked like a particularly newsworthy mummy and as Laura stood, Callie gave her the double thumbs-up. Laura grinned, inspected Callie's effort, and returned the gesture.

If they could cheat death with some simple newspaper, maybe they'd survive after all. They reached out and hugged each other, somehow friends now. Hope could do that to a person.

JACK SAID, "OKAY, SO WE RUN AS LOW TO THE GROUND AS WE can?" The three of them were gathered behind the kitchen door, the rolled, tarpaulin-swaddled mattress held like a torpedo, a man on each side and one behind.

"Sounds like a plan," Romeo said.

"Let's go."

Progress against the force of the wind was even harder than he'd anticipated. Jack staggered backwards, lost his grip and skidded towards the end of the path and the ocean, learning what it felt like to be literally blown off his feet.

"Lower!" said Aaron.

They crouched and laboriously crab-walked the first of the rolled mattresses to the bunker. Jack's mouth filled with rain and he could barely see. The door was wide open, and dark, and they lunged inside, toppling into a painful heap. The squishy mattresses he'd expected to land on were simply not there.

It was so dark inside, and Jack fumbled for his headlamp, but it was gone. It must have blown right off his head.

Suddenly, it was light. Laura shouted over the noise, "Sorry, just changing the batteries."

At the end of the bunker, Kevin lay still and covered in something… grey? Was he dead?

Callie wasn't with him.

He cast around. There she was. Standing upright, grinning at him. Over her shoulder, he could see the gash in the wall was now blocked.

"We found some newspaper," she shouted.

***

CALLIE WAS IN A NESTING MOOD, AND LAURA SEEMED MORE than willing to act as accessory.

The men obeyed their demands to rid the bunker of the remaining drenched mattresses. They returned item by item with several fresh and dry-ish mattresses—enough to create sleeping space for all—a big bag of blankets, and even more newspapers.

Eventually, everyone was inside. The door was secured just open enough to ventilate. The new injuries were assessed and found to be only a cut arm that might need stitches later (Jack), and badly grazed knees from a windblown fall (Aaron). They were cleaned and dressed with the contents of the first aid kit.

It had taken well over an hour to achieve all this since the storm surge receded, and the cyclone was quietening by subtle increments. It was still deadly out there, but not quite as deadly. Could something be degrees of deadly, or was it one of those words like pregnant, where you could only be pregnant or not-pregnant? Callie wasn't sure and decided not to pursue the thought.

The wind still screamed like the souls of the damned, but maybe one octave lower. The soprano souls had finished and the altos had taken over. She'd heard more missiles hit the bunker at erratic intervals, but so far none had pierced right through to the inside. And so long as Cyclone Sasha didn't turn in its tracks and head back for Stanford Island again—which cyclones had been known to do, but she was adopting Jack's "what if it doesn't?" approach—the storm should continue to moderate.

Laura administered another dose of antibiotics to Kevin, and accepted Jack's offer of a Vitamin C tablet as well. It might help, one never knew.

Laura produced more of her famous chocolate for the rest of the team. It was melted around the edges now and rather damp with seawater, having been on a lower shelf during the wash cycle but thankfully not washed away, and it tasted like ambrosia.

This time, Aaron took point position near the door, where rain continued to spurt in through the gap. Romeo was beside him, then Jack. Callie lay between him and Laura.

Within moments of lying down, Jack was snoring ever-so-softly. Callie snuggled into his chest and fell into a deep and dreamless sleep.

<h1 align="center">46</h1>

*C*allie woke with a mouth like the bottom of a bird cage, and a raging fever. Or was she just hot?

A thick synthetic blanket clung to her damp skin. She flung it off. Her left forearm hit something. Hit it with a fair amount of pressure. Something yielding. Something that said, "Ugh!"

She looked left into hazel eyes, a woman's eyes, Laura's eyes, just a few centimetres from her own. "Oh. Sorry."

"Um. That's okay." Laura rubbed her stomach and floundered around, trying to sit upright.

Callie followed her lead and surveyed a bunker full of arms and legs, all trying to stretch and disentangle. Aaron seemed to be lying on an angle across much of Romeo's space and even a bit of Jack's, possibly to stretch his long legs or maybe just to escape the rain that had been driving through the door's ventilation gap for the past few hours. The two displaced men seemed slightly startled to find their legs intertwined in strange configurations, and fairly eager to untwine.

Beyond Laura in the half-light, Kevin's eyes were open, staring at the ceiling. Callie watched him for endless seconds till he blinked—just to be sure.

The grey light of dawn was visible through the ventilation gap. It was still raining, but in gusting flurries now instead of a driving wall, and it wasn't spurting inside like it had earlier, just intermittent spray.

Jack staggered upright, rubbed his knee, stepped over the other two men, and wrestled the door open.

Early light reached in along with spattering rain. It took Callie a moment to process what she was seeing outside. A small aluminium dinghy. Right there on the breezeway, among shredded vegetation, broken branches, and a yellow plastic bucket. The dinghy's pointed prow was partially embedded in the main house's timber wall, its belly at least a hand's length deep in water. Had it washed ashore? No, it couldn't have. The water had receded before they'd gone to sleep. It must have blown there. But the wind was now blowing from the island, not the sea. Perhaps it came from a storage space on the island?

Romeo sat up straight and stared at it. He clambered out and approached it, hesitantly, touched the dented gunwale in a long, slow connection, then stepped right into it. He sat on its bench in the driving rain, his sneakered feet ankle deep in water, and hunched forward over his knees, gasping for breath, his hands on the back of his head.

That's when Callie saw the name on the stern. It wasn't one of the island dinghies. It was a tender, from a yacht.

The name on the stern was *T/T Celestial*.

"WHERE'S THE RADIO?" LAURA'S VOICE WAS HIGH AND SHARP.

Callie said, "Don't tell me it washed away!" She joined Laura near the shelving and started moving things around, peering into the gloom for anything yellow.

"No, I put it on the top shelf, right up here."

"Are you sure?"

"Yes, I'm sure."

"It couldn't have been knocked off?"

"No." She drew a shuddering breath. "Well, there were those jolts in the night…"

"Don't worry if you can't find it." The creaky voice came from Kevin, still on the floor. "They said they'd send a chopper this morning. It'll be daylight soon. The wind is weaker. They'll come." He reached awkwardly to pat Laura's ankle, near his shoulder. "Don't worry, girl. We'll be okay."

Laura rested her head against the pillar of the shelving.

Kevin cleared his throat and spoke again. "Why don't you see what's still usable in the main house. Everyone will feel better with some brekky."

Amid the chaos of the broken building, the long, long, solid dining table still stood. It was awash with rainwater and bore several gashes along its dark surface, and it had shifted a couple of metres across the room, but it had survived.

Part of the roof was missing in that section of the building, but with the wind currently blowing from behind, not from the ocean, there was enough to shelter a significant stretch of table—plenty of room for six people to sit undercover at one end while rain splattered onto the other end.

Callie and Jack mopped dry the sheltered half of the table with newspaper from the recycle bin, while the others poked around among the tangle of furniture and debris spread across the huge room, looking for usable chairs.

Romeo did his best to contribute but he seemed about two sizes smaller than yesterday.

"Callie, can you help me bring Kevin over?" Laura said.

"Sure."

As they crossed the remains of the kitchen together, Laura muttered, "I'm afraid someone might have taken that radio."

"I've been wondering about that. But who? And why?"

"What if they… called Silas's team? Could there still be someone here working for him?"

They paused inside the kitchen's outer door and stared at one another.

Callie said, "What would they call them about?"

"To let them know Silas is dead, maybe, and won't be giving any more orders? To get them to come here and... I don't know... collect them? Or... finish us off?" She gulped a little on the last words.

"Well, we're left with Romeo and Aaron, really. Which one do you think it is?"

Laura's hands twitched by her sides. "I don't know."

"I'd be surprised if Aaron turned out to be a good liar."

"Don't confuse frankness with honesty. They're two different traits."

Callie had a think about that. "What should we do about it?"

Laura sighed. "I don't know."

"Let's just keep our eyes open and not get complacent." She snapped the hood up on her orange jacket and stepped out the door into the wind and rain again, but she didn't head for the bunker.

"Where are you going?" Laura called over the noise of the weather.

"Just looking. You get Kevin ready. I'll be there in a minute." She stalked down the walkway past the door of the big walk-in freezer, now lying at an angle on its base, and continued close to its leeward side, picking her way carefully over piles of debris. The rain was no longer horizontal, but it was still at enough of an angle that the height of the freezer gave her protection.

She surveyed the ruined island in the grey pre-dawn light—a clear view all the way to the eastern tip. Piles of vegetation and the shattered remains of structures. Neither natural nor manufactured features seemed taller than a single storey this morning.

The lab building had survived, the upper parts of its steel panelling exposed to her view now that the trees that sheltered it had been stripped. The office had lost its roof. Towards the centre of the island, the utility shed seemed mostly intact among the remains of the forest.

The ocean end of the jetty was missing—just bare pylons sticking up out of the water. But there was probably enough jetty still remaining, reaching out into the channel that had been carved from the coral decades ago, to allow a small vessel to dock. With the destruction of the tree cover between here and there, it would be hard for anyone to sneak up on them by sea, at least. And the sheer quantity of garbage in the lagoon would make a seaplane landing extremely hazardous.

A helicopter would be the easiest way to access Stanford Island right now, and the weather had probably even moderated enough for an adventurous pilot to take the chance.

<hr>

KEVIN SAID, "WE HAVE TO CLEAR THE HELIPAD." HE COUGHED —a harsh, gargling sound—and pressed a hand to his injured shoulder. "Please."

He'd been leaning heavily on the women when they'd brought him in, one on each side, and was now sitting at a slight lean in a dining chair beside the big dining table.

Jack went to the front glass door to look towards the helipad he'd taken off from just a few days ago to go snorkelling in the sunshine. The trees that had then stood back from the big H in a respectful semi-circle were now lying flat and broken. The helipad itself seemed to be knee-deep in the rubble of island life. Jack blinked as another furious gust of wind splattered rain at eye-height onto the glass.

He blinked again when Aaron spoke unexpectedly close to his left shoulder. "They can't land on that. Let's get it done." He reached past Jack and turned the handle, pulled the door in and stepped briskly through, pulling the door smartly to, behind him, to keep the wind out.

Jack pulled his jacket hood up against the rain and followed him out, just in time to help him shift an enormous palm frond that obstructed their path across the deck. He paused a moment at the railing to view the remains of the guest cottages. The first three still stood but looked like a giant had kicked them in the night. Which is what had happened, in a way. The next four were entirely roofless— just the walls still standing. The three on the end, including the one he'd shared with Callie, had been reduced to mere structural timbers extending above the mangled trees.

Callie said from beside him, "Gardening gloves."

"What?"

"We need gardening gloves to shift that lot." She indicated the piles of corrugated iron, broken glass and vegetation littering the helipad. "I wonder if I could get to the shed?"

"No need," Laura said. "I collected some yesterday."

Jack nodded. "That was smart."

"It was Kevin's idea, actually. Even with everything, he was still thinking strategically." She drew a deep breath. "I'll go grab them."

The gloves were wet—they'd obviously been on a lower shelf in the bunker—but they were undeniably useful. This task was a tetanus infection waiting to happen. There were only four pair of gloves and Romeo seemed to be mostly standing around staring, so it was almost a relief when Laura sent him off to think about breakfast. He must have really loved Mary. Jack found himself wishing he'd drunk tea on that yacht before it sank, though he couldn't figure out why that should seem important right now.

All four of them were needed to shift a felled palm tree that lay diagonally across the helipad. It was so much heavier than he'd anticipated—waterlogged. Jack scanned the mutilated forest, wondering where it had blown from.

Aaron said, "I think it used to be near the main house. Over there." He indicated with his chin.

"But the wind has been blowing the other way for the last few hours."

"Yes. It would have blown across this way, and then blown back again."

The strength of the wind that could do such a thing…

A pile of rubbish grew at the base of the main house promontory. Strips of roofing steel curled like apple peel. Tree branches. Bedding from the cottages. Palm fronds. Pieces of splintered timber.

A huge stingray lay on its back and Jack bent over it sadly, about to pick it up, when the tail flicked towards him.

"Watch out!"

He stepped back and said, rather obviously, "It's still alive."

"Here. Let us do it." Laura stepped in and Aaron joined her. They lifted the creature carefully and gently, stilling its tail. Its mouth opened and closed. They carried it tenderly to the edge, where the water was above high tide, though high tide was still an hour away, and slipped it into the water. It flapped once and disappeared into the murk. The crystal water of yesterday was now full of sand and vegetation and all kinds of natural and artificial debris.

They worked fast and as a team. Eventually, a more-or-less-flat platform emerged. A wash of sand, nearly ankle deep in places, lay across much of it. This part must have been thoroughly underwater at the height of the storm surge.

"Do you think the sand matters?" Jack said, as the four of them stood in a circle, puffing, rain splashing off their jackets.

"It won't stop them landing."

"But it will stop them seeing it's the helipad. The H is obscured."

Jack and Aaron took hold of one of the palm fronds and dragged it through the sand to clear a fairly effective H. They dusted off their gloved hands and headed as one for the main house and a well-earned breakfast. All except Callie, who stood a moment longer, staring at the H.

"If we build it, they will come," Jack said to her with a smile.

She didn't smile back. "Yes, but *who* will come?"

47

Breakfast was a hotchpotch of things assembled from anything that had survived the night in the kitchen or storeroom. Romeo apparently hadn't made use of any of the supplies they'd so carefully carried over to the bunker yesterday.

Cereal and long-life milk were standard enough, but there were a range of spreads on the table and no bread to go under them. Baking was obviously out of the question, but Callie knew there were multiple loaves of commercial sliced bread in the walk-in freezer. She'd seen it in there yesterday. Was it safe to eat bread that had spent the night in a partially-defrosted freezer that was being used as a temporary morgue?

There was long-life fruit juice and moderately clean glasses to drink it in, but no water. She was fanging for a cup of coffee, even instant would do, but Romeo didn't seem to have boiled anything, even though he'd had at least twenty minutes while they were clearing the helipad.

She said quietly to Jack, "Should we get one of those water tanks from the bunker? Make some hot drinks?"

Kevin must have heard her. He looked at her, his face pale, and nodded. He cut his eyes sideways to Romeo. He seemed to be trying to send a message but she wasn't sure what it was.

Jack scooped up the last of his Weet-Bix in one big mouthful and stood to help her while he chewed. They collected a small trolley from the kitchen and wiped it dry-ish with newspaper.

Out on the walkway, the dry-ish trolley got immediately drenched in the rain and Callie suddenly realised what Romeo didn't want to walk past. That dinghy.

She and Jack stopped next to it as the rain beat on their faces, looked at it, looked at each other, then looked at it again. Together, they tried to pull its bow out of the wall but it was too heavy with the weight of water within it—and getting heavier all the time, even though the rain had slowed to a steady roar and was now falling on an angle rather than horizontal.

"Hang on," Jack said. He got down low, close to the bow, and pushed hard.

Callie joined him, and with a tearing groan it broke free of the wall. She tried to get her hands under it and lift from the bow to empty the water, but Jack said, "No, too heavy. From the gunwale. Then we don't have to lift as far."

Another pair of hands appeared and she discovered they were attached to Aaron. Had he heard them or was he just psychic? Between the three of them they were able to lift it enough on one side that the water started cascading out. It streamed across the walkway, more and more, until they were able to lift it fully perpendicular and empty the water in a huge sluice. Suddenly lighter, it was blown by the wind, hard, and cracked against Callie's knee. She swore under her breath and hopped.

"Sorry!" Jack said.

"Put it down!" Aaron said.

They put the dinghy back on its base and worked as a team to shove it to the end of the walkway, pushing it into the wind, scraping loudly against the concrete, and then around the corner onto the sodden, water-flattened grass at the front of the main house.

"Upside down," Aaron said. "More aerodynamic."

Callie decided to stand back and let the men wrangle it while she clasped her throbbing knee. And that's when she heard the engine.

Jack stood back smartly to avoid the dinghy as it crashed into its new position—and nearly collided with Callie who was limping towards the helipad. She sidestepped but otherwise ignored him, looking up and out, scanning the sky, every line of her body tense.

"What is it?"

"Can you hear that?"

Over the noise of the wind and the waves, he did hear something. Something… mechanical. Throbbing. Missing a beat sometimes. But it wasn't coming from the direction of the mainland…

She spun around and headed back towards the kitchen. She broke into a run as she hit the walkway along the side of the main house and he followed, with Aaron close behind.

She passed the bunker, skidded on the wet concrete in front of the walk-in freezer, grabbed the corner of it to save herself, then disappeared behind it.

Jack rounded the same corner and slowed. The ground was littered with debris, some of it potentially dangerous. He followed Callie to the vantage point and stared.

The outer third of the jetty was just pylons this morning, without boards or railings. A vessel was pulling in alongside what remained, nudging something in the water that might have been a mattress. The boat was partially concealed by the jetty. The hull seemed to be white and sleek, the shape of the upper structure hard to discern.

"I think it's a sailing yacht," breathed Callie. She shot Jack and Aaron a glance. "Can you see?"

She ran towards the kitchen, opened the door and yelled, "Romeo! Come quick!"

The chef came through the swing door from the dining room, hesitant, puzzled.

"There's a yacht," she said. "I'm not sure… I think it could be… it could be Mary?" She shrugged, suddenly afraid that she was raising his hopes and about to break his heart all over again. What if it was just some random sailor seeking any port in a storm?

Or Silas's crew.

He stood very still and spoke very quietly, as though the words were afraid to leave his mouth. "Where?"

"The jetty."

He walked towards her, stumbled over a large piece of coral on the floor, looked down at it, then up again at Callie. And then he shoved past her, out the door and down to the path that led toward the jetty.

Once again, Callie found herself running down that path as a member of a stampede. It had been hard enough yesterday with a sprained ankle. Today, she had a still-not-healed sprain, a burning jellyfish sting, a throbbing dinghy-battered knee, an Olympic-level sleep deficit, and a million and one obstacles to hurdle in pouring rain. Palm fronds and other trash littered the paths. One extended puddle was ankle deep. She had to keep slowing so as not to slip.

She was about to run onto the boards of the jetty in the wake of Romeo's thundering footfalls when Jack grabbed her arm from behind. "Wait. The jetty's damaged. Move carefully."

He turned out to be a prophet when Romeo tripped on a missing board and went sprawling, but then he was up again—moving a little more circumspectly but still hurrying.

It was indeed a sailing yacht. Its steel mast was brutally bent over sideways, embedded through the cabin and part of the gunwale, then touching the water on the port side. The vessel listed to that side. The mainsail seemed to be still attached to the remains of the mast, but torn and flapping in the wind. Other sail fabric stretched under the bow into the water.

A person stood at the helm.

Romeo stopped still and called, "Mary?"

The person threw their arms wide and called back, "Wherefore art thou, Romeo?"

"Mary!"

The chef clambered over the railing, dropped awkwardly to the deck of the yacht, scrambled to the back and pulled the woman into his arms.

Callie, Jack and Aaron stood on the jetty above them and grinned at one another.

JACK WENT WITH CALLIE TO THE WALK-IN FREEZER TO GET bread, smiling and mostly ignoring her prattle about health and safety and thawed bread in morgues. All smiles faded and prattle stilled, however, when they wrenched the door open to find a sheet-wrapped body sprawled on the floor. It must have been thrown there in one of the structure's jolting sideways shifts through the night. At least the seals had functioned, however, and the freezer was dry.

He looked at Callie and was startled to see her eyes full of tears, her lips pressed together in a wobbly line. She took a deep breath and said, "I guess there's only a certain number of miracles available today. Come on. Let's sort it out."

It turned out to be Nina, and they carefully lifted her back onto the bottom shelf, arranging her limbs with respect.

They dashed back through the rain to the kitchen with two loaves of bread. Jack stepped in after Callie, automatically removed his jacket and shook it out the door to avoid trekking rain inside, then put it back on again—a ludicrous procedure given the current state of that floor, and the roof.

His nostrils were assailed by an unmistakeable aroma, and he turned to a cosily surreal tableau of Romeo at the stove holding a rain-splattered umbrella over his head, or maybe holding it over the gas burners, while bacon and eggs sizzled in a large pan and water simmered in a pot. At a bench under the shelter of the remaining roof, Mary sat on a stool while Laura, first aid kit open before her and headlamp illuminating a nasty wound on the other woman's head, said, "Did you lose consciousness at all? You'll need to be checked for concussion."

"I'm not sure. I don't think so."

Jack started walking towards the toaster, remembered that it was electric, and stood mid-stride and undecided in the centre of the kitchen.

Romeo noticed him and gesticulated with the long-handled tongs. "You'll find a metal tray in that cupboard—we can cook toast in the oven. Dry the tray with newspaper. But first, you'll be washing your hands." He pointed at a metal bowl on another bench, a cake of soap and towel beside it, then continued flipping bacon.

As they sat down to the feast, with Kevin looking brighter and Mary's head bandaged, Jack thought about all the different meals he'd eaten at that long table and how this might be the best one yet.

Broken furniture and battered walls and windows surrounded them as they lived out Kevin's father's concept of house-party guests at one big table—multiplied to the power of ten by all they'd endured together and all they'd meant to each other in the life-and-death struggle of the night.

They had to speak up over the sound of rain thumping the other end of the table, the floors, and what was left of the roof. The weather had now moderated to the level of a heavy storm, but seemed like the merest sunshower in comparison to what had gone before.

Laughter surged around the table as Mary turned her night's terror into a series of funny anecdotes and the Stanford Island team reciprocated with their own now-hilarious recollections and observations. The meal ended so quickly.

The sun had risen at last—Jack could see it angling in under the heavy cloud as golden rays outlined the breakers leaping out in the ocean.

And that's when Romeo scraped back his chair, stood, and pulled out a gun.

"I'm really so terribly sorry to finish like this, it seems very bad-mannered and ungrateful, but I really do have to ask you for that toxin, Kevin. And the antidote as well."

He shrugged and he even did look sorry. Mary rose with an equally apologetic smile and a slight movement of her hands, and moved to stand slightly behind Romeo.

"Oh, and I do also have this." He pulled out the portable marine radio, then shoved it back in his pocket. "Sorry about that, too, y'know. We just, well, we need a little time to get away…"

Callie was extremely glad that Jack had set a camera rolling earlier without drawing attention to it.

There were only storm sounds for fully twenty seconds.

"What?" said Kevin, eloquently. He looked flabbergasted more than angry.

"I think you did hear me. Laura, could you get it for us, perhaps?"

Callie said, interested, "Why?"

Romeo shrugged again and quirked his mouth. "Not much money in police work, unfortunately."

Callie continued, "So you joined forces with Silas?"

"Hell no!"

Jack had leant forward and put his interested face on, too. "Who will you sell it to?"

"I have my contacts. Laura?"

Laura looked at Kevin, who gave her a thoughtful look in return and then nodded. She smiled slightly and stood to go with them.

"Erm, probably better if the rest of you stay in here, if you don't mind." He waved the gun, but in an explanatory rather than threatening way. "Sorry again. And, erm, thanks for all the help. You know." He hovered, uncertain.

Mary said, "Romeo," and stepped back. As they headed through the swinging door after Laura, Mary looked back, possibly to check they were all staying put, and gave an odd little wave of farewell.

They did stay put. And they all looked at each other. Aaron seemed particularly confused, which wasn't an expression Callie was used to seeing on his face.

When she was quite sure they'd left the building and were out of earshot, Callie said, "He wasn't there. He doesn't know." She sat back and grinned.

———

Maybe fifteen minutes had passed—fifteen minutes of coffee and speculation—when Jack heard what could have been an engine. It was hard to tell over the swirling roar of the storm, so he eased his arms back into the rain jacket hanging over the back of his chair and headed again for the sheltered nook down the side of the walk-in freezer.

The *Celestial*—or what was left of it—was nosing slowly down the channel through all kinds of floating debris, a considerable quantity of sail canvas still wrapped under its hull, and still listing to port.

Appearing beside him, Callie said, "Bon voyage."

"Yeah." Pause. "You know that was Silas's gun he had?"

"I wonder when he got hold of it."

"Who knows? Such a messy night."

"Where's Romeo's gun?"

Jack gave her a small smile. "Bottom of a *really* big tank of box jellyfish."

She shifted weight. "Should we retrieve it? Would it still work? Might come in handy if we have any… unwelcome visitors."

"If it did work, and if the bad guys did come, you'd have to be ready not only to use it accurately but to shoot first, and shoot to kill. Nothing less would stop Silas's buddies." He kept watching the departing yacht. "Think you could do that?"

After a long pause, she said, "Have you got an alternative?"

"I'm hoping the rescue chopper will arrive for Kevin soon. If anyone else shows up before they can collect the rest of us, I think we'd be better off to hide till they find what they want and go away." He indicated the scene spread out before them. "What's the chance they'll want to search all this?"

Callie surveyed the shattered island and blew out a long breath. "They won't find what they want, though. Because Romeo's just taken it."

"Good point." He frowned. "I wonder if they know what it looks like."

"Are you thinking of a decoy?"

"Maybe. Let's talk to Laura about it."

They returned to the walkway just in time to see her enter the kitchen ahead of them.

She spun as she heard the door open behind her but then gave them a smile and continued on into the dining room.

"Okay?" Kevin said.

"They're gone. I'm not sure what will happen when he offers pepper spray to international arms dealers, but I guess that's his problem."

Callie snorted as she sat down and reached for another piece of toast.

Jack said, "What about the loss of the anti-venom?"

"We've got the formula," Laura said. "We can always make more."

Kevin added, "It's not proprietary. Everyone shares anti-venom. So even if he did manage to find a buyer it wouldn't make any difference."

"Two useless things to sell." Laura smiled.

Jack grimaced. "I don't really want anything that bad to happen to him."

Laura stared at him. "He's just robbed us. At gunpoint."

"Yeah, I know. But he's part of the reason we're all alive this morning." He shrugged.

There was a small silence. Maybe Laura and Kevin had thought of some other people who had done bad things.

Callie said, "He might blame the people who gave it to him."

There was a slightly longer silence.

Jack said, "Will they even get that far in that yacht?"

Laura shook her head slowly as she answered. "I don't know. It looks dreadful. It might be seaworthy enough, if they stay inside the outer reef till they can repair it. And if they don't get any more big storms."

"How was the lab?" Kevin said, quietly.

Laura sighed. "It's still standing, but it's a mess."

"How high did the water go inside?"

"Pretty high."

Callie said, "Why was it the cyclone-rated building when this building is higher?"

"It was the last one built." Kevin shrugged. "The other buildings were older. Different building standards."

Laura nodded. "When we rebuild the other buildings, they'll be cyclone-rated, too."

Kevin muttered, "If we rebuild."

"Kevin," said Callie, "who did your dad win this island from in that card game? Was it Silas's dad?"

Kevin shot her a glance that might have had a question in it, then looked down at the table. "Yeah." He grimaced. "But he got it back."

"Was his name Simon Davenport?"

Another glance. "Yeah."

"How did he do it?" Jack said.

Kevin sighed. "He waited twenty years, till Dad borrowed big money to develop the island. Built this main house and the cottages. Then Davenport worked on all our suppliers so they put their prices up or just 'couldn't supply us anymore'. He put around rumours that deterred tourists. Persuaded universities to dismiss our research. And when Dad defaulted on the loan, he moved in and bought it from the bank at a knock-down price." He stared at the table, his lips pressed together. His nostrils flared. "My parents had to leave their home. Then Davenport let it sit empty for five years before he sold it again, and everything deteriorated. All that hard work…"

Callie nodded slowly. "This happened while you were away at uni? And your mum's dementia was developing."

"That's right." He ground out the words.

"I'm sorry," she said, and his eyes flicked up to meet hers, and held. "I'm so sorry about everything."

Jack said, "How did you end up back on the island?"

"About ten years ago, it sold again. The resort and research managers both left within the same week. I came to the new owners with my vision—Dad's vision, really. I could manage both the resort and the research station, so they didn't need two senior staff, and I could do a lot of the renovation work myself—one cottage at a time. They liked the plan. And it was working." He ran his fingers over the texture of the timber in the tabletop. "I heard last year that the owners were thinking about selling, and I was looking for a way to raise some capital to maybe buy it myself…" He slapped the tabletop and turned to stare out toward the choppy ocean.

Jack turned to Laura. "You found what you needed for Romeo and Mary, in spite of the damage?"

"Yes, the locked cabinets were still intact and they'd kept a lot of the water out. I managed to give them something that looked like a toxin and an antidote."

"Do you have a second set?" Jack said.

"Why?"

"I'm just thinking it might be handy. We don't know what Silas might have told his team. Do they know it's not genuine, or did he keep that to himself? We don't know who might turn up here."

Kevin turned back. "I wouldn't want you to gamble your lives on the chance of them accepting something like that. Now that I've seen what Silas was capable of, I think his crowd are just as likely to kill any witnesses"—his voice turned sour—"even if they believe you that it's a weaponised toxin."

"I agree," said Jack. "But if they search for themselves and find what they think is the toxin and the antidote, I doubt they'll keep looking for us. It's not a big island but it's not that easy to search it in a hurry, especially in its current state."

Callie added, "They might just assume we've been rescued already. Or that we drowned."

After a pause, Laura said, thoughtfully, "I've got extra vials of both things. But we only had one of those fancy plastic cases, and I—"

Aaron interjected. "There's a case in the storeroom."

It was on the top shelf, pushed to the back where only a very tall person could see it or someone with a step ladder, and it turned out to be the case from Romeo's gun—the one with a sample of Jack's scalp on one corner.

The foam outline of a pistol was not allowed to be a problem for long. "We can cut a new lining from one of the mattresses," Aaron said. He produced a pen knife and proceeded to do just that while Laura ran to the lab. He cut without measuring anything, and it fitted perfectly.

By the time Laura returned, their stage prop was ready to receive the four convincing-looking stoppered-glass vials she brought—two of each. Finally, the case stood sealed and ready on the long wooden table among the butter and spreads.

"Do we leave it in plain sight or hide it?" Jack said.

Callie tilted her head. "They'd expect it to be locked away, wouldn't they?"

"Back to the cabinet in the lab, then," Laura said.

Callie stood. "I'll come with you."

Jack and Aaron sat back down, to keep Kevin company and to listen for an engine.

"BE CAREFUL." LAURA LOOKED BACK OVER HER SHOULDER AS they entered. "There's a lot of broken glass. Chemicals amongst it, too."

Callie rejoiced in her closed shoes, even though they squelched wetly and rubbed mercilessly on her jellyfish sting. The roof seemed to have survived but some of the cupboard doors hung open, their contents strewn across the floor. Judging by the arrangement of mess in here, the water in the upper lab must have risen to about hip height. From the bench tops upwards, the lab was still relatively neat.

"Look out for box jellies." Laura began to descend the stairs to the lower lab. She paused on the third step, produced a torch, held it down low and shone it through water that swirled shin deep. "They seem to have been washed out of their tanks."

"Didn't the guys put them all in the big tank out on the deck?"

"Oh. Did they manage to do that? I didn't realise." She began to move into the water, then paused. "Are you absolutely sure?"

"Um. I think so." Callie wriggled her shoulders. Had she understood Jack correctly? She'd been off her brain with jellyfish venom last night. "Not sure I'd stake my life on it… or yours. How far have we got to go?"

"The locked cabinet over there." She pointed to the opposite side of the room. "You stay there. No point both of us taking the risk." She moved down one step.

"Wait!"

Laura spun around. "Why?"

"A stinger suit. Or pantyhose. Surely you've got something here?"

Laura's eyes opened wide. "Of course we have." As she climbed back up the stairs and Callie moved out of her way, she muttered, "That cyclone has obliterated my IQ."

From a dry shelf at the top of an otherwise waterlogged cupboard she produced a pair of thick support pantyhose and pulled them on right over her sneakers, up her legs, and then over her shorts.

As she moved carefully back across the upper lab, sliding her nylon-covered feet tentatively on the wet vinyl, Callie sang a few lines of *I'm Too Sexy*, and Laura laughed and struck a pose.

"Actually, I'd better make sure I don't slip." Laura kept up some chatter as she descended the steps and waded across the lower lab. "I shouldn't really wear them like this, but I'm afraid if I take my shoes off I'll never be able to put them back on again."

From the doorway, Callie said, "Wet shoes are the height of comfort. They were especially good to sleep in. I might keep it up when I get home."

"Must be so awful on that sting of yours." She had the cabinet open now.

"Yeah, not great. But, you know."

The decoy was in place, cabinet locked, and Laura on her way back. "Yeah, I know. Sort of."

Safely upstairs, Laura stripped off the pantyhose and looked towards the deck. She glanced at Callie. "Mind if I check on them?"

"Sure."

Island and ocean trash littered the deck but the blue tarp had held firm, its elaborate system of knots secure. "Shall we let them breathe?" said Laura.

"Sure." Callie helped her—very, very carefully. They couldn't tell whether the water level inside the big tank had risen, potentially bringing tentacles within reach of their probing fingers.

"There's no filtration without electricity, so I guess they'll die anyway."

The two women stood and stared silently into the tank as the shadows swirled. There was a dark blob on the bottom, but Laura didn't seem to notice it and Callie decided not to say anything.

Laura wrapped her arms around her own shoulders and sighed.

"Things to do," Callie said, brightly. "Come on."

She led the way back outside and pondered possible conversation topics. Scanning the battered landscape as they picked their way back up the littered path towards the main house didn't provide much inspiration for upbeat discussions.

Callie finally said, "You know you've had a good holiday when you can't even remember what day it is."

Laura snorted. "I think it's Friday."

"Is it really? Excellent. Any plans for the weekend?"

Laura said quietly, "Just surviving would be nice."

"We've made it this far." Was that too trite?

Maybe it was too trite, because Laura didn't say anything for a while. Then she said, "Even if I get off here safely, it's not over for me. It's just beginning."

Pause. "You mean the legal consequences."

"Yeah." Pause. "And facing the families."

Callie's mind roamed around the possibilities of that, looking in awkward corners, turning over rocks and logs, and not much liking what lurked. Not just the loss of Baz and Nina, but the many tourists and workers and businesses impacted in so many desperate ways. No matter who committed the actual crimes, it all traced back to a stupid idea Kevin and Laura once had, to deceive a very bad man.

"I wish Romeo hadn't taken the marine radio," Callie said. "Could we do anything with the walkie-talkies?"

Laura seemed to take a moment to latch onto the change of subject. "Um. They might reach as far as Apostle Island, if we were really lucky. But there's no one there."

"How far is Apostle? Could we get there in a dinghy?"

"I wouldn't care to try it in these seas."

"But technically possible?"

"Why would you want to try?"

"Wouldn't there be a radio at Apostle?"

"Oh. Yes. I guess so. Although Apostle would have copped the storm surge as well."

"Isn't the water level highest under the eye? At least, that's what happened here. It dropped as soon as the eye passed."

"I guess." Laura frowned. "Might have been lower there. It's a long way to go on the off-chance."

They drew level with the pool. On the far side, it was filled to the brim and above with sand, shaped into sculpted mounds where yesterday the infinity edge had dropped abruptly to the rocky section of beach a couple of metres below. The murky water that remained in the inland half of the pool reminded Callie of a giant soup tureen full of chopped vegetables. Something moved in it. Maybe it was *fish* soup.

And then she saw the fin. "Is that a shark?"

"Oh." Laura gazed at the pool. "The poor thing. It won't survive in there." Her eyes looked moist, but she didn't suggest any heroics for rescuing the creature.

"I used to think sharks were one of the scariest things in the world," Callie murmured.

Laura looked at her, and then dropped her eyes. "People are much scarier."

They started walking again.

"Are things okay with your parents?" Callie said.

Laura shot her a glance then returned to watching for hazards on the littered path. She sighed. "They weren't very happy about me wanting to come here to work with Kevin. He didn't treat my mother very well when she found out she was pregnant. Suggested I could be someone else's baby. Told her to get rid of me."

"Oh." Callie processed that. "Why were you so keen to be with him, then?"

"Mum never told me his name, but I found it on my birth certificate when I applied for a passport. I tracked him down through the scientific community. Wanted a bit of revenge initially, if I'm honest." She shrugged. "But he's changed." Her eyes glistened. "Oh Callie, if you'd seen his face when he found out I was his daughter. The light in his eyes."

Callie stopped and pulled her jacket hood off her head, straining to hear over the slapping of rain on the polyester. "Can you hear that?" She felt another flush of adrenaline. Another engine. Faint, but definitely mechanical. Friend or foe?

She ran to the start of the jetty and scanned the horizon. Certainly nothing visible out there that was bigger than the waves.

Laura stood beside her, eyes wide, mouth slightly open. "I think it's a helicopter."

Together they ran for the main house and the helipad. Laura was about to rush onto the open helipad when Callie grabbed her arm.

"Wait. Let's check who's coming first."

They circled towards the shore, keeping to the cover of brutalised palm trees and shredded native bushes, and peered out across the ocean towards the far-distant mainland, scanning left and right.

"Anything?" Callie said.

"No… not yet… wait! There!"

From the south-west, a small blob grew larger and eventually sprouted whirring blades. Callie breathed fast and shallow. She wanted to sob, she wanted to hide, she wanted to hope.

Larger and larger it came. Colours came with it. It wasn't black and it wasn't small. It was a big, long, bright chopper—blue and red and yellow.

As it hovered above the island in the rain and gusting wind, large letters along its side spelled the most beautiful word Callie had ever seen: RESCUE.

49

"**G**et on the ground! Get on the ground! Get on the ground!"

From the main house, Jack slammed open the door and raced towards Callie, half-skidding on the rain-slick steps. She and Laura had approached the chopper and a man in black now stood over them with some kind of big ugly gun while rain splashed in the puddles by their heads.

"Leave them alone!" Jack yelled as he ran.

He caught only the barest glimpse of the man's colleague approaching fast from the right. He shoved Jack to the ground, face first. A heavy boot ground into the centre of his back, his lip tore on the sand, he tasted blood. How could they get so close to survival and then be attacked?

"Who are you?" Callie demanded, feisty even while lying on her belly in wet sand and debris. "Identify yourselves!"

"Please don't hurt us." That was Laura, also face down, her voice shrill and breathy.

"Laura?" It was someone else, someone emerging from the chopper. Jack could see a set of feet and legs out of the corner of his eye. Not black-clad. Dark green? "Is that you, Laura?"

"Dave? What the hell is *happening*?"

"Let them go. That's Laura Jensen. She's the deputy director here."

The boot was lifted from Jack's back, but only slowly and after a slight delay. He heard the helicopter change note as it began to power down, and the rain now landed in sporadic clumps, batted by the slowing blades. The big ugly weapon stayed trained on him as he rose to his feet and stared down the taller of the two black-clad thugs. The man wore a bulletproof vest and his sleeve bore an embroidered insignia and a number—they were *official* thugs.

Jack was glad he'd started his camera rolling in the shoulder holster as the helicopter landed, hoped it was tough enough to have survived the face-plant, and made sure that, if it was still working, the man in black would be in its line of view. He was careful not to give any sign that there was a functioning camera on his chest. The camera was dark; his t-shirt was dark; hopefully it blended in. This kind of goon would not hesitate to confiscate it—and there was far too much infinitely precious footage on it to risk that. A whole cyclone of footage. Even a majestic eyewall.

Callie was upright now too and she was mad as hell. He even found it in his heart to feel a little sorry for these blokes.

Dave looked to be a paramedic in his dark blue-green uniform, red crosses on his shoulders. "They sent police with us, because of what Kevin said. Why didn't you answer our radio calls this morning?"

"What?" said Laura.

"They said you'd been under attack. We didn't know what we'd find."

Callie cut in, addressing the police, not the paramedic. "Why did you not identify yourselves?" She stood at her full magnificent height, eyes steely. Jack angled his shoulders—and his camera—slightly towards her.

The wider thug, nearest her, stood with his feet planted far apart, both hands on his weapon slung ready at his waist, and gave her a sardonic look. "We don't have to answer to you, ma'am. This is a full-scale terrorist situation."

"I think you'll find that under the laws of Queensland, you *do* have to identify yourself when a member of the public asks you to do so."

Did she know that, or was she bluffing? Either way, the cop shifted his weight, just slightly.

Jack turned to the taller thug, extended his hand forward for a handshake, and said, face hard, "Jack Metcalf." He paused half a beat. "Journalist." The thug's eyes flickered infinitesimally.

The thug did not shake hands.

<hr>

CALLIE WAS INORDINATELY PLEASED THAT JACK HAD JOINED her in resisting these idiots.

She could understand police needing to make sure of safety in a volatile situation, but she was confident these two storm troopers would have seen very quickly that she and Laura were not dangerous. They had made a much bigger show than necessary, simply because they enjoyed it. She'd met so many cops in her work that were good, dedicated men and women. The few power-hungry bullies among them raised her ire, every single time. Laura was trembling beside her, so Callie stepped slightly in front of her to greet with a handshake the paramedic called Dave, and then the second one stepping out of the chopper behind Dave, laden with medical gear, who turned out to be named Sara.

"We're very glad to see you. Kevin is in here." She indicated with an expansive hand gesture, as though they'd just arrived at her country estate. "Let's get out of this rain."

She flicked Jack a significant glance as she stalked past the storm troopers to the steps, and was pleased to look over her shoulder a moment later and see him following, one arm around Laura's waist in support as he followed with a calm and confident stride, measured just right to keep her moving steadily without hurrying her too much.

Paramedic Dave seemed to have worked out not to ask Laura anything just now. He approached the long table inside where Aaron seemed to be standing tall-and-angry guard behind their injured leader. He said, "Kevin, how are you mate?"

"I've been better," Kevin said in a jokey voice, grinned, and then coughed a deep, loose cough. "Think we might add a heart attack to the list after that ridiculous charade outside."

Good on you, Kevin. Half-dead, and you can still stand up to bullies.

While Sara began applying ECG electrodes to Kevin's chest, Dave kept the banter going. "Uh, sorry about that. But why didn't you answer us? We've been calling every hour on the hour since 4.00 am."

Kevin sighed, which only made him cough again.

Jack stepped in. "Because the marine radio we found yesterday was stolen in the night."

Sara jerked upright. "Stolen?" She looked out the windows front and back, nervously.

The posture of the two storm troopers had subtly changed, too.

"By our chef, Romeo," Callie said. "Although we didn't know it was him till he scarpered with it this morning."

Now it was Dave's turn to look up, just as he was about to pierce the back of Kevin's hand with a cannula. "Scarpered? How?"

Callie said, "His girlfriend turned up in a yacht."

"A dismasted yacht," Jack added.

"Dismasted and a whole lot more," Callie said. "'Seaworthy' would be rather a strong word to use for the *Celestial* right now."

Dave asked Kevin a couple of quiet medical questions, took his temperature, then glanced up again. "But why would he do that?"

Callie made full eye-contact with Jack for a long moment and raised one eyebrow.

"It's a long story," Jack said.

She said, "A long story full of confusion and misunderstanding."

Jack looked at one of the cops. "You need to find him and charge him with armed robbery." Callie inhaled sharply but managed to do it silently.

"Armed?" said Thing 1.

"He had a gun that belonged to one of the terrorists."

Thing 2 was pulling a notebook from one of the many pockets on his Inspector Gadget vest. "How'd he get that?"

Jack sighed. "Another long story."

Aaron spoke matter-of-factly. "The gun and radio were found where they'd been hidden in the water pump housing. We used the radio to call marine rescue at dinner time. During the night, Romeo stole both items. You should notify the coast guard that he was heading north. He will need to find a port where they can repair the yacht."

"So he used the gun to steal the radio?" Thing 2 squinted at his notebook like he didn't know what to write.

"No, he'd already stolen the radio. He used the gun to steal some"—Jack glanced at Kevin—"chemicals from the lab, which he thought he could sell as a weapon." He rubbed his face and shoved his hands in his pockets. "But it was just pepper spray."

Thing 2 looked like he *really* didn't know what to write.

Dave said to the storm troopers, "This one's ready to transport. You'll have to interview them later."

"The yacht is *Celestial*," Jack said. "They only left here about an hour ago. He's with a woman named Mary."

Thing 2 wrote something then.

"We can take one other person." Sara shifted her weight. "I'm sorry there's not room for all of you."

Aaron said, "When will you come back?"

"We can't come back." Dave's tone was no-nonsense. "Things are an absolute mess over on the mainland just now. It's been a pretty wild night. We'll be flying and refuelling all day just to tend to the injured."

Jack said, "So… how…"

"We'll tell Marine Rescue, and hopefully they'll send someone in the next couple of days. A chopper or a boat. Probably a boat if the sea is clear enough by then."

Callie's stomach fell to the floor and oozled through one of the cracks in the floorboards. Everyone but the storm troopers stared at Dave.

Couldn't they leave the cops to swim for it?

"Have you got water?" said Thing 1. "And food?"

"Yes, but…"

Aaron said, "The instigator of the terrorism was on this island. We're concerned his team will try to find him."

"Where is he now?" Thing 2 was peering at his notebook again.

"In the freezer." Aaron's wonderful clarity sometimes just ran into a brick wall.

Callie supplemented, "He's dead. He was stung by a jellyfish."

Jack said, "But his team wouldn't know that."

"And they might come looking for him," Callie said.

The storm troopers looked at each other.

Thing 1 said, "We'll tell Marine Rescue and see what they can organise. But there are hundreds of people needing help today. They have to triage the cases."

He didn't need to say: you are not a priority. Callie even had the grace to see that it was correct. Her group's danger was uncertain; others were in dire, immediate need.

Jack said, "Can you lend us a radio, at least?"

Sara looked at Dave. "There should be a spare in the chopper but it leaves us without a backup."

Dave looked at the floor a moment, then nodded at her. "Let's leave it with them, but we must get another before we go out again." He turned to the castaways. "Monitor it every hour on the hour in case there is a message for you."

Callie had a sudden thought. "Could you advise Marine Rescue of the names of the dead, please, once you're on the chopper?"

Dave frowned. "Why?"

Laura frowned at her, clearly mystified, but Callie ignored her. "People need to know." She turned to Thing 2. "Can I give you those names?" She listed them and he wrote them in his notebook.

He tapped the paper with his pen. "These other two?"

She nodded. "Gunshot victims. Shot by Silas. Also in the freezer. They will need to be retrieved when possible."

Sara said, "Now, which one of you is coming with us?"

The four lottery entrants looked at each other. Laura said, "Callie, you need to get that jellyfish sting seen to."

"I'm fine. You go with Kevin." She stepped close to Laura and spoke quietly. "Your father needs you."

KEVIN WAS STRAPPED INTO THE STRETCHER, LOOKING WORSE than before, not better, and the rotor blades were starting to turn.

Jack said, "Wait a minute! Please!" He turned and ran full pelt for the bunker, rummaged in his bag, and sprinted back to the helipad just as Sara was about to close the door. "Wait!"

He lurched into the narrow space beside the stretcher, banging his shin painfully on the edge, and held towards Kevin the photo frame from the lab. Kevin's parents, side-by-side and laughing, knee-deep in the ocean at Stanford Island, so long ago and far away.

Kevin saw what it was and his eyes opened wide. He reached for it, clutched it to his chest, and his face crumpled. He began to sob like a small child, eyes squeezed shut, mouth open wide beneath the oxygen mask. Jack leant close to be heard over the noise of the engine, and said, "This is not the end. You can come back from this, Kevin." He gripped the man's hand, and Kevin squeezed tight and looked into his eyes. "You *can* come back. Even from this."

50

"And then there were three," Callie said. They stood in the half-roofless dining room just inside the front door, listening to the rain and wind still battering and splattering, and looked at each other.

She said to Jack, "So. You decided to dob on Romeo after all?"

He shrugged and spoke mildly. "If you were in his position, which would you rather? Get caught by the Australian police and face relatively minor charges that might not even stick? Or try to sell something worthless to an angry arms dealer?"

"Oh."

Aaron half-hunched his shoulders and glanced around. "I feel like a sitting duck in this building. If they come, they'll come here first."

"What about a quick cuppa while we figure out our options?" Callie said.

They sat at the sheltered end of the table and she picked up a spare sticky ECG electrode left behind by the paramedics. It was squishy with gel under the adhesive and she pressed it from side to side. There was a metal button in the centre and she pressed that. *Boop-boop.*

Aaron stared at the electrode. "We've got the dinghy out there.

The tender from *Celestial*. If the motor still works we could try getting to Apostle."

Callie stopped pressing the electrode. "I asked Laura about that this morning. Because maybe there's more facilities there. There could be electricity if the damage isn't as bad as here. Internet, even."

"And…?" Jack said.

"Well, she said it might have flooded too, or blown away, and it's a long way to go for an uncertain result." She grimaced. "But what do you guys think?"

"Small boat, big seas." Jack stared across the lagoon to the white-capped water beyond.

Aaron said, "No EPIRB. No lifejackets."

Jack looked at him. "How confident are you that you can get us there?"

Aaron returned his gaze. "I've been there once. Someone else was driving."

Silence.

Jack shifted in his chair. "What if Silas told his team the weapon was a scam? Then they probably won't come at all."

Aaron did the slight shoulder hunch again. "Wouldn't rely on that."

Callie said, "He didn't strike me as the confiding kind." Pause. "Not if the information was humiliating. Humiliating for him, that is."

Jack said, "Why did you ask them to radio his name through? His team might be monitoring the emergency frequency."

"Well, I was hoping they would be. If they know he's dead they won't keep waiting to hear from him. They'll… act. Whatever that looks like. Either give up and go away, or come here to retrieve the toxin." She sucked her bottom lip then let it go with a slap. "Hope it wasn't a mistake. Hope it doesn't… trigger anything else."

Aaron gave her a long, considering look.

Jack nodded. "I guess if we're going to be stuck here for two or three days, it would be better if they came sooner than later. Get it over with. It's exhausting being on high alert."

Aaron said, "We need to work out a few hiding places. And we need to get out of this building."

Jack said, "Let's check the cottages. The first three still have roofs."

The third cottage proved to be in the best shape. Outer walls and a roof, even though the storm surge had been through it. Jack led the way carefully across the tilted, splintered, beachside timber decking that had torn loose in places and through the shattered sea-facing full-length windows. Inside, the rush-matted living room floor had disappeared under a thick layer of sand and debris. The lounge suite had been flung back to block the doorway to a ruined bedroom beyond where a bloated, swampy bed now lay at a drunken angle. A ludicrous quantity of coconuts, still in their husks, filled the short passageway to the front door to about hip height.

"Were they trying to make a run for it, do you think?" Callie said.

Aaron grabbed the first coconut and tossed it behind him, hard, towards where the front wall used to be.

Jack ducked the missile and stumbled to the side. "Let's keep a few. Something to eat if we're stuck here a while."

The blockage removed, Aaron wrenched the front door open and Callie disappeared through it. "See if I can find a broom tough enough to move that broken glass off the floor," she said over her shoulder.

Jack and Aaron retrieved the trolley from the main house and began transporting plastic drinking water tanks from the bunker. They moved fast, their conversation purely functional. Getting the trolley down the garbage-littered pathway was tough—the wheels barely helped and they had to use brute force to make headway.

Callie's continued absence made Jack uneasy. The storm was quietening more and more, and his ears constantly scanned for any sound that might be mechanical. Even a branch rubbing against guttering in too-even a rhythm put him on guard.

As they exited the cottage with the trolley to do another run, Callie was on the path, sweeping fast with a big commercial broom. Not sweeping clean, but sweeping more sand and leaves and garbage over the pavers. She looked up at their approach and leant on the broom handle, puffing. "The wheel tracks were really obvious. Like big arrows. 'Hey, look, bad guys! Here they are.'"

Jack looked at Aaron. "Let's leave the trolley here, then."

Aaron nodded. "That's all the water. We can carry everything else by hand."

Jack said, "Probably faster, anyway."

They brought cereal and bread and spreads, long-life cartons of milk and juice, plates and cups and cutlery, their personal bags from the bunker, and of course the precious computers and cameras.

The rain even stopped a while, and that's when they made a team dash with a single foam mattress each, lurching erratically into gusty winds.

They laid a tarp under each to stop the mattresses wicking too much water. The tarps were damp, but not as wet as the rush matting and layers of sand.

Then the three of them settled in to wait.

Callie sat on her lurid hibiscus-patterned mattress watching the ocean boil under a sulky grey sky as light rain spat at Stanford Island. She fought the urge to play with her phone. Stuck in a queue for takeaway? Play with her phone. Interviewee running late? Play with her phone. Couldn't sleep? Play with her phone.

But she had to save the remaining battery. It had already switched itself to low power mode.

She unlaced her shoes. They absolutely had to come off, despite her deep, dragging fear of being caught barefoot in this minefield of potential puncture wounds with bad guys in hot pursuit. The wet synthetics had been eroding the painful lesion across her foot where the jellyfish sting was still red-raw, and the shoes had to come off.

She eased the stung foot free first. The relief was magical. She took a moment to feel the full, glorious beauty of it.

And then the other one.

She sighed deeply.

She stretched her toes and wiggled them. Sand had gathered

between them and around the nails. A cleansing paddle in warm tropical seas would be nice. She glanced at the amount of rubbish on the beach before her and in the waves surging across it, and reconsidered.

She tried not to think about how sticky and salty her skin was, after a night in a gigantic washing machine. She tried not to think about how much she wanted a shower or a bath. She tried to be thankful instead that she'd managed to cram another change of clothes into her duffle bag, and it had survived, dry.

Aaron was propped on one elbow, writing in a notebook.

Jack was asleep, lying on his back like a pharaoh's mummy.

She drew pictures in the sand beside her bed with her fingernail.

She tried to get the sand out from under her fingernail.

She traced the outline of a red-and-yellow mattress hibiscus, up and along, round in a big curve.

Beep-beep beep-beep! It must be one minute to the hour. Thankfully, Jack was not reliant on his phone for the time but wore a good old-fashioned watch with various impressive dials, one of those chunky stainless steel things divers wore, and it had an alarm function.

He opened his eyes like someone in a movie, perfectly alert, neither drooling nor confused, sat up, picked up the radio, and pressed the On switch.

Aaron stopped writing and watched.

They didn't transmit; they didn't want to advertise their presence. They just listened.

There was no call for Stanford Island, Stanford Island, Stanford Island. Not that they'd really expected one yet, but there was always hope.

After three minutes, Jack turned it off and lay back down. Before it seemed humanly possible, his breathing became slow and deep.

Aaron looked at her and said, "There used to be some books in the alcove off the dining room." He resumed writing.

Callie considered the shoes that lay between her and a possible book. It would be worth it. She dragged them back on, wincing as the mini-serrations on the edge of the shoe's tongue rasped over her wounded foot again.

She grabbed Jack's blue rain jacket. Her fluoro orange one felt like just too much of a beacon for bad guys, today. She ran all the way despite her sprained ankle and bruised knee, feeling so much more vulnerable than earlier.

She crept into the main house and flailed around looking for the bookcase. There it was. The bottom three shelves were empty and sagging—their contents no doubt distributed around the room by wave or wind. But there were five paperbacks teetering on the top shelf, and they even seemed fairly dry. She grabbed all of them and headed back at a run, breathing hard from panic more than exertion.

Back in the cottage, Aaron was asleep, too. She eased off her shoes again as she fumbled through the books. One was a horror novel about a group of people trapped in a hotel in a storm while a nameless monster prowled. Um, maybe not today. Among the rest she found a historical romance set in the American Wild West. Yes, that would do.

She lay down to read and as she became absorbed in the fortunes of the flinty-jawed preacher Jed and his surprisingly feisty mail-order bride, Lulah, the tension left her body.

Beep-beep!

Something clung to Callie's neck and part of her chin. The book. One of the pages was adhering to her bottom lip.

She pulled it free, swallowed against the dryness in her throat and took two attempts to prop awkwardly on her elbow to watch Jack turn on the radio. "Is it time again already?"

He grinned. "You've been asleep for three hours."

Every hour, Jack hoped despite the probabilities. Every hour, there was no call.

Every hour, he could tell the sun had changed position, even though the heavy cloud cover diffused the light so completely that it cast no reliable shadows.

Every hour, he slept again.

By midday, he felt refreshed. He ate a piece of bread and Vegemite.

He took his drone outside and took a chance, grabbing some footage of the broken island.

Then he grabbed one of the books Callie had retrieved. A horror novel. Not his favourite—he mostly read space opera or adventure memoirs—but it helped to pass the time.

Aaron had finished writing and sketching in his notebook and picked up one of the other books. The cover was bright pink and featured a woman sitting on a garden swing.

At one o'clock, they turned on the radio to a burst of static. All three gathered close, kneeling on Jack's mattress to listen.

It was not a call for Stanford Island, but some other drama taking place on a yacht somewhere out there.

Jack was about to turn the radio off when Aaron stayed his hand. "Listen."

An Irish accent. It was the *Celestial*. Whether the Coast Guard had caught up with them or was rescuing them was uncertain from the tail end of the conversation they'd heard, but either way, it seemed that Romeo and Mary would now be safe.

They looked at each other with little smiles.

"He'll talk his way out of it, somehow," Jack said.

51

By the time dusk closed in, Callie had left Jed and Lulah to their happy ending, complete with impending baby. She was eating a peanut butter sandwich while she partnered Jack in a robust game of Snap, using a pack of actually-dry playing cards discovered at the top of the remains of the cottage wardrobe.

Aaron had declined to take part. He had finished the chick-lit book and was reading the horror novel by the light of his headlamp.

"Snap!" Callie grabbed the whole pile of cards. "I win!"

"It's just a game," Jack said, deadpan.

Callie laughed, looked outside, and startled when she realised just how late it was. She really needed another trip to the bathroom —which meant going all the way up to the main house to the only facility with running water. And she needed it before dark, please and thank you.

She fumbled for her sneakers in the gloom, pulling at them in a fluster, rasping over her wounded foot like a steel file, but her feet would not go in. Why would they not go in?

Jack said, "You've got them on the wrong feet."

She took a deep breath, centred herself, swapped the shoes.

"What's the rush?" he said.

"Loo break."

"Oh." He picked up Jed and Lulah from where Callie had discarded the book and started reading. She'd been kind of hoping he'd come with her to stand guard.

Stop being such a coward. She strode briskly down the debris-cluttered path, headlamp at the ready in the fading light, and counted her steps under her breath for something to do.

"Seventy-six!" She jumped with both feet onto the roofless concrete walkway down the side of the main house and tried not to breathe too fast.

In the bathroom, she glanced around and thought about how there would have been space for a shower stall, if only they'd bothered. What would she give for a shower, even a cold one?

Back outside again, she glanced left, towards the ocean, then stared at the walk-in freezer—their temporary morgue. It stood askew on its platform where it had been shoved by the wall of water that had swept across this highest point in the night. She thought of the people lying in there with the thawing loaves of bread, and the damage that could be caused by zealotry, greed, and revenge.

Next to the freezer, a thin metallic tube protruded from under the edge of the coolroom that had been their cyclone bunker. She peered at it, curious, then bent to pull it out. It must have washed there in the storm surge. She pulled and it kept coming—it was at least a couple of metres long—until it suddenly snagged on something. It was the handle of something. Could be handy. A handy handle. She tugged, and it jerked free.

She was holding a long-handled fish net of the type used by anglers, slightly tattered, but still serviceable. It might be the one staff had used to retrieve jellyfish from the lagoon.

She pictured the gun down at the lab, lying on the bottom of the deep jellyfish tank, and narrowed her eyes.

Jack lowered the book and his eyes locked with Aaron's. Definitely a mechanical noise. Both their headlamps snapped off.

"Let's get out of here," Aaron said.

"Where's Callie?"

Aaron was already halfway out the front door of the cottage, heading towards a hollowed den among a dense grove of trees about twenty metres away—a hiding place they'd chosen earlier in the day for just such a time as this. They didn't want to wait in the buildings in case someone searched.

Jack ran out after him but turned towards the main house. "We've got to find Callie."

"I know!" Aaron grabbed his arm and hauled him towards the refuge. "Get in here while we figure out what to do."

Jack peered through a gap in the vegetation. "There it is."

A helicopter. Approaching from the north west, just visible against the last dull glow of the dying day. It was flying without navigation lights. Police choppers sometimes did that when chasing crims, Jack knew. This would not be one of those times.

It arrived and hovered high above the helipad. A bright search-light split the darkness.

But it wasn't just looking for a safe landing pad. The chopper swept towards this side of the island, over the row of broken cottages. What if those aboard saw three mattresses in a row on the floor of Cottage 3 through the missing front wall?

It banked and came back, straight towards their haven.

"In close," Aaron said, and grabbed Jack around the neck.

They huddled together, as far in as they could get under the densest leaves. The smell was musty and dank, and salty from the seawater that had swept through overnight.

Jack muttered, "Please, God."

The helicopter continued its sweep across the broken island, over the remains of the utility buildings, towards the jetty and the lab.

"Why you still think there's a God after all we've seen, I don't know." Aaron's voice was harsh.

Jack's throat tightened. "We've got to find Callie before they hit the main house!"

***

Callie dived beneath a bench, breathing hard, as a searchlight from above blasted through the wide windows of the upper lab. Harsh shadows thrown by the window frames flickered across the opposite walls. Her hands on the fishing net trembled and something sharp pierced her right knee. The chopper noise softened slightly with distance—it must be out over the far end of the lagoon now. It grew louder again and she squeezed her eyes tight shut like a child hoping to be invisible, dreading the attack to come.

But it flew over her and on, in the direction of the main house. Within maybe twenty seconds, the sound changed key as the engine slowed.

She lunged through the door onto the outer deck where the huge box-jellyfish tank stood and fumbled with her headlamp, holding it extended in her left hand, out over the water, directing the beam down into the tank. Swirling tentacles caught and diffracted the light, but through them she glimpsed the wobbly dark outline of the pistol. She raised the fish net in her right hand, preparing to thrust it into the tank, but its long aluminium handle caught against the high outer wall. She jolted, then gasped as the torch tumbled down into the water through layers of jellyfish, its waterproof light throwing up, down, sideways, down, sideways.

It settled on the bottom, beaming straight up.

Where any casually-observant bad guy couldn't help but see it.

***

Jack had made it as far as the shelter of another big clump of crushed trees and debris about twenty metres from the main house, crouched low, Aaron hot on his heels, when a man stepped down from the pilot's side of the chopper. A stocky man dressed all in black. He was facing the main house, his back to them. The man switched on a dazzling handheld spotlight and directed it at the path. In the reflected light, Jack could see he was Dean, their pilot from the other day. Dean threw a look back over his shoulder and barked, "Hurry!"

A second man appeared, dressed in… white shorts and a bright pink polo shirt? A guy who failed Burglar School? Or maybe the guy who drove their golf cart at Eden Island…

The pair strode towards the main-house stairs. Jack leapt up to rush for the side walkway, desperate to get to Callie first.

He crashed down again with a huge weight on his back.

"No!" hissed Aaron, right in his ear. "She will have to hide. It's the only way."

The weight on Jack's back did not release. His face ground into a dank pile of shredded leaves.

He heard footsteps on floorboards, doors opening and closing, a swing door—that would be the one between the dining room and kitchen—fainter footsteps, disappearing. Very faint footsteps. Then a grinding noise of a sliding door—were they checking the walk-in freezer? Pause. Grinding noise again. Footsteps on concrete.

The weight on Jack's back eased.

"They're headed for the lab," Aaron said. "She must have hidden."

<hr>

THE GUN WAS IN THE NET.

The wayward headlamp was almost in it, too.

Heavy footsteps were crunching down the walkway outside, drawing inexorably closer. More than one pair.

Callie jammed the net against the side of the deep tank, then started pulling upwards, hand over hand, breathing slowly through her mouth, controlling the movement.

The footsteps stopped. Muttered imprecations about the door code followed. Bang! She jolted, but managed not to drop her payload. Bang! Bang! Bang! Were they trying to kick the door down? A clump of tentacles fell clear just as the net broke the water surface, but were any still tangled in her prize?

Her fingers closed oh-so-delicately on the strap of the headlamp. She shook it, then looped it over her wrist. She grabbed the pistol's trigger guard between thumb and forefinger and let the fish net sink back into the tank.

A tentacle clung to the gun's muzzle. She sluiced it gently through the water till the tentacle fell away.

Bang-bang-bang! Explosions this time, splintering metal.

Maybe fifteen metres distant, across the width of the outer deck on which she stood and the dry lab beyond, the front door of the lab flew open. Brilliant light beamed in. The light started a sweep.

She dived for the huge blue tarpaulin that lay bundled behind the big tank in a messy heap where she and Laura had left it this morning. Wriggling under it then pressing against the floor, she wondered again if stray tentacles might still be caught in it. The edge of the tarp was raised in a half-loop not far from her face, just enough to see a thin sliver at floor level—across the deck, through into the dry lab and all the way to the cupboards on the opposite wall. The headlamp, still lit, still looped on her left wrist, dug into her belly where she'd rolled on her arm to smother its beam.

The wet pistol was gripped in her right hand. Was it loaded? Would it even work, after a night in salt water?

Her body, under the tarp, was shielded by the bulk of the tank.

Her ankles lay open to the air. Outside the tarp.

Footsteps. Voices. At least two men. Feet entered her range of vision, distant across the lab, approaching the door to the lower lab. A pair of black shoes. A pair of bright sneakers.

"Stand back."

She flinched at another multi-explosion. Sparks. Were they shooting the lock that barred the lower lab?

Two sets of intruder feet disappeared down the stairs. Was that all of them or were there others? Callie lifted the edge of the tarp, oh-so-slowly, and peered. No one else in view.

She reached underneath her, found the switch on the headlamp and clicked it off at the same time as she gently hooked a foot into the ropes still dangling from the tarp and pulled—silently, slowly rearranging the tarp to fully cover her feet and her hiding place between the tank and the outer wall. Cheek on the floorboards, she could still see through the small curved gap between tarp and floor.

A muted, metallic crash in the lower lab.

Muffled voices.

Footsteps mounting the stairs from the lower lab.

Heavy footsteps around the upper lab, squeaking across the linoleum.

"What's out here?" Sneakers approaching across the deck. He was almost close enough to touch her. "Hey, Dean, wanna swim?"

"Get your hand out of it! That's the jellyfish tank, ya fool."

"Ugh!" Water droplets spattering the tarp. "Anything else worth stealing? There's a tarp here." A sneaker swinging towards her face. Nearly catching the edge of the tarp. Callie's grip on the gun tightened. "We could carry stuff in it. Those microscopes are worth thousands."

"Forget it. This is worth a lot more than any microscope. This is the big time." Black workboots strode for the shattered front door.

Sneakers turned and followed.

———

JACK STRUGGLED TO BREATHE UNDER A MASSIVE WEIGHT. Again. In a different clump of vegetation. Within sight of the lab.

"Those were gunshots," he gasped from compressed lungs. "She must be in the lab. We have to help her."

Aaron did not release his hold. "Why would she be in the lab?" he hissed.

"I don't know." But then he did know. "The gun."

Aaron cursed. "What's it doing in the lab?"

The beam of the spotlight stabbed out of the shattered lab door and swept across their hiding place. The two men from the helicopter followed it out, but then turned immediately towards the main house and the helipad. A small black case in the hand of Dean the pilot glinted in the reflected light. They strode toward the west.

The moment Aaron's weight on his back eased, Jack scrambled to his feet and ran for the lab.

He stepped over the splintered door, flicked on his torch with its weakened battery, and swept the room in its feeble light. He sensed rather than heard Aaron follow him.

"Callie? Please God, where is she?" He stumbled towards another smashed door, the one that led into the lower lab, then corrected. The outside deck. She'd have gone there for the gun.

He couldn't see her anywhere, not even sprawled on the floor.

With dread he approached the tank and shone his light into it. He exhaled. No body.

He turned. Across the lab, Aaron was shining his own torch into the lower lab, preparing to descend.

A small voice said, "Jack? Is that you?"

In the distance, the engine started—the most beautiful sound Callie had ever heard.

Its tune changed as the helicopter rose.

The sound faded.

She melted into a boneless mess, right there in the shattered lab, held tight in Jack's arms.

52

They hooded their torches for the walk back to their cottage, though the chopper was long gone. Once inside the cottage, so confrontingly open to the ocean, they sat in complete darkness for at least twenty minutes.

Finally, Jack turned his torch on. When he did, Aaron showed him a series of numbers and letters.

"The helicopter registration number," he said.

Jack nodded. "Definitely the one that took us to the outer reef on Monday."

"Are you sure?" Callie said.

"Our video will confirm it."

Jack wasn't sure whether to continue the hourly radio monitoring right through the night, since their rescuers surely wouldn't come in the dark and the radio battery might need to last a few days while more urgent rescue work took place on the mainland.

He ended up deciding he'd rather do it than not. The other two didn't seem to mind.

At the 5.00 am check, the cloud was breaking up and the sky behind it was turning from black to royal blue when a flash of static came over the speaker.

"Stanford Island, Stanford Island, Stanford Island, this is Police Rescue 1, Police Rescue 1, Police Rescue 1, do you copy?"

Callie and Aaron both crawled onto Jack's mattress and hunched beside him, their faces tense, as he pressed the transmit button. "Police Rescue 1, this is Stanford Island. Over."

"Stanford Island, we're nearly there. See you at the jetty in five minutes. Over."

"Police Rescue 1, we'll be ready! Thank you! Over and out."

In the dark, he could only see the whites of their eyes and their teeth gleaming, but when he reached out to his friends the group hug was automatic and long and very close.

SATURDAY

Callie had been disappointed so often she was afraid to trust it this time but as the lights approached, the vessel that nosed its way down the channel, past the broken pieces of the jetty and what seemed to be another hibiscus-covered mattress, was unmistakeable. A white twin-hulled launch, solid and capable looking, with the distinctive stripe of navy blue and white checks and in friendly blue letters that beautiful word: POLICE.

Aboard were two men in navy blue shorts and polo shirts with various colourful embroidered badges on them. As they drew closer she saw that the shorts also bore the same beautiful word: POLICE.

The sky in the east had a turquoise tint as she stood on the jetty in the warm breeze with her duffle bag in hand. Jack stood beside her, holding his own bag and her other hand.

One of the sailors steered towards a bent ladder that descended from the boards, while the other one got ready with a rope.

Aaron stepped forward and caught it neatly.

"G'day, mate," the man drawled with a big smile. "Wanna go home?"

JACK SAID, "I'M OUT OF BATTERY. IS THERE ANYTHING LEFT IN your phone?"

Callie fumbled in her bag. "I think so—not much, but a bit."

There was also a little power left in the night-vision camera, and he used that too since it was still pretty dark. As they pulled away down the channel, he swept the length and breadth of Stanford Island, panning up towards the battered main house on the promontory to the right. He also got some shots of the debris churning in their wake.

As he walked back into the cabin, Callie said to the police officers, "How did we get so lucky? They said it might be two or three days."

"Ah, well, I dropped in to visit Kevin yesterday when he came out of surgery." The captain threw them a glance, then returned to keeping a close eye on where he was going. "He was pretty insistent that we get out here asap and rescue you lot. *And* that we don't let the bad guys know we were coming."

"Is Kevin going to be okay?" Jack grabbed for a handle and plonked heavily onto a bench as they moved into the heaving swells of the open water.

"Yeah, he'll be right. Had some pretty good first aid, from what I can gather."

"And did he tell you…"

"He told us. We'll have to wait and see what happens about that."

The other police officer pulled out a large thermos flask and some mugs. "Who'd like a coffee?"

"Oh, wow," Callie said. Jack could see her pupils dilate from here.

The lid came off and the aroma came out and filled the space, and all three castaways sat forward on their benches.

The man laughed and poured out several cups. "Sorry, it's got sugar and milk in it already. Hope ya don't mind."

"Oh, wow," Callie said again.

Jack turned his camera from the scene inside the cabin towards the stern, where Stanford Island was shrinking into the distance, and above the Great Barrier Reef a golden sun was rising.

EPILOGUE

Callie sat at the desk in her Sydney bedroom next to the window with the "harbour glimpses" and the hinges that squeaked on rainy days, and ugly-cried as the final documentary she'd downloaded from Jack's link finished playing on her laptop screen.

Jack's skilful, nuanced editing—every cut timed to a perfect cadence—had put the final polish to the raw and beautiful story they had written together. It showed the glory and the fury of nature alongside the ugliness and tenderness of humanity.

She wished Jack could be sitting beside her at this moment, holding her hand, but he was a thousand kilometres away in Brisbane. When she got her breath back, she'd call him and tell him her reactions.

Who knew where their relationship might go from here? She'd rather be with Jack than pretty much anyone else she'd ever met, but they lived and worked so far apart. And the religious differences were not minor—he'd been right about that. She wanted a man who didn't put his God ahead of her needs and wishes. He wanted a woman he could pray with every day.

She sighed. They'd figure it out eventually. Probably. Maybe.

After their escape from Stanford, she and Jack had both been targets in a media firestorm. They had given a few interviews but, without discussing it with one another beforehand, both had remained circumspect when it came to laying any blame. Within twenty-four hours, a dissolving terrorist situation had lost out to the better visuals of widespread cyclone devastation, and the hard-news reporters had moved on.

Her email program dinged and she clicked, expecting something from Jack, but it was a program director from a television network in Finland. The hard-news cycle might have moved on, but the deeper dive of a documentary was a different thing with a longer lifespan. She'd already received quite a few emails from the same television networks that had bought *Poison Bay*—and a few that hadn't. The news was out about *Venom Reef*, and they all wanted it—from the cable nature channels to the big commercial networks.

Jack's buddy in the police service had proven invaluable for off-the-record background material. It couldn't go in the documentary, of course, but it could help lead them towards other information. They had also been careful not to prejudice any upcoming trials—an expanded version might be released later, when criminal justice had taken its full, ponderous course.

With the news of Silas's death, some of his accomplices had come out of the compost pile and some had vanished into thin air.

Dean the reef pilot had been arrested before he could leave the country, made vehement denials, and then faltered when a hard plastic case containing vials of anti-venom and pepper spray turned up in the safe in his home office. A copy of Jack's night-vision of him landing on Stanford Island in the dark had been delivered to police, combined with stills of him with Silas out at the reef and Aaron's note about the helicopter registration number. A police search also uncovered bomb-making materials in his shed—the same chemicals found in the wreckage of the ferry that had evacuated island guests and staff; everyone aboard had made it home alive, though some would take a while to heal from their physical and emotional injuries.

Silas had no time to cover his tracks before he died. An email trail pointed to some of his helpers—such as the man who'd driven their golf cart on Eden Island and whose careless fingerprints in the lab could not be explained by any prior visit. He was in a cohort linked to Australia's criminal underbelly or aspiring to join it.

The email trail also led to people like Baz and Nina, over-zealous eco-warriors who had been deceived about exactly what they were getting themselves into.

Romeo and Mary had also been charged, but with Kevin and Laura declining to give evidence against them it was possible the charges would fall over. Romeo's police career was undoubtedly over, but he'd find something else to do.

Kevin was out of hospital. He and Laura had been charged with conspiracy offences and released on bail. Callie had called Laura just this morning for the details. The rift that formed between Laura and her parents because of her reconnection with Kevin was beginning to heal; her parents had even travelled north to visit them both, and her lawyer-mother was working on the case. They would plead guilty to avoid a trial, but the agreed facts had to be negotiated.

Other friends were considering forming a consortium to buy Stanford Island. The devastated resort was likely to sell at a knock-down price again, so who knew what might be possible there?

"We'll face the music," Laura had said, "and do our time in jail if that's what it takes, and when we get out we'll rebuild whatever we can of Stanford Island. Even if we go back to the simple model Kevin's parents used back in the beginning. But with a cyclone-proof building on the highest point, this time!"

Callie had said, "It sounds like an amazing plan. Keep me posted."

She was smiling at the possibilities when her phone pinged. A text message. From Jack. She felt a rush of warmth as she tapped to open it.

> Just got an invitation to do another docco.
> Interested?

A big-grin emoji accompanied it.

Callie laughed and picked up the phone. Her fingers flew across the keypad.

Let me check my diary…

Thank you for joining me on the adventure to Venom Reef. *I loved writing it and researching it, especially a couple of days getting generous tips from scientific researchers (none of whom were terrorists) on the remote and gorgeous Heron Island, where the mutton birds really do sound like a wolf playing the kazoo… all night!*

For Book 3 in the Wild Crimes series, *Scorched Earth*, Callie and Jack will be heading deep into the Australian Outback where it's so hot and dry, people live underground. So, that should rule out cyclones at least…?

Would you like to explore the backstory to the Wild Crimes Mysteries? Subscribe to my updates at the link below to receive a **free ebook copy of the prequel** *Toxic Delusion*. Two perilous stories of the Australian outback. Two old friends heading towards a devastating reunion… if they can just survive the weekend.

belindapollard.com/subscribe

If you enjoyed *Venom Reef*, it would help me so much if you could leave a review wherever you bought it, or on social media, and/or tell your friends or book club.

Belinda Pollard

ALSO BY BELINDA POLLARD

AVAILABLE NOW IN EBOOK AND PAPERBACK

FICTION

Toxic Delusion: Wild Crimes Prequel

Poison Bay: Wild Crimes Mysteries #1

Verschollen in der Poison Bay (German translation)

Venom Reef: Wild Crimes Mysteries #2

LIGHT MEMOIR

Dogged Optimism: Lessons in Joy from a Disaster Prone Dog

SPIRITUAL

Meet the Real Jesus: Explore Eyewitness Accounts in 40 Bite-Sized Pieces

WRITING RESOURCES

Use the Power of Feedback to Write a Better Book

ABOUT THE AUTHOR

Belinda Pollard is an award-winning former journalist who loves mountain hiking despite bad knees and a fear of heights. She has been a professional writer and book editor for decades and was a contributor to the *Closer to God* series for many years.

The words "Poison Bay" on a New Zealand map triggered her journey to the sinister end of the bookshelf. Spooky and remote, it was a location just begging for a mystery.

Belinda writes the Wild Crimes mystery series, light memoir, Bible devotionals and resources for writers, and co-hosts the Gracewriters Podcast. Her writing prizes include a Varuna Fellowship.

Belinda lives in subtropical Brisbane, Australia where she wrangles a boisterous terrier and dreams of snow...

Subscribe at the link below to receive:

- news about Belinda Pollard's new books

- occasional short stories
- a free ebook copy of TOXIC DELUSION, prequel to the Wild Crimes series.

belindapollard.com/subscribe

Connect with Belinda Pollard on social media:

facebook.com/BelindaPollardAuthor

x.com/Belinda_Pollard

instagram.com/belinda_pollard

youtube.com/@Belinda_Pollard

ACKNOWLEDGMENTS

Dr Elizabeth Perkins and the team at Heron Island Research Station on the Great Barrier Reef were generous with insights into their research projects, supplying countless plot ideas. They also shared what life is like on an island, from daily practicalities to the emotional impact of remote living. Professor Norelle Daly and Dr David Wilson at James Cook University in Cairns introduced me to venom research, and showed me a beautiful array of deadly things… including some that glow in the dark!

To all these scientists, I do apologise for the times I have been "creative" with how research happens in this book; writers make stuff up, for plot purposes.

Professor Iain McCalman, author of *The Reef: A Passionate History*—whose eyes lit up as he answered my question, "What's on the reef that's worth killing for?"—started a chain reaction in my brain from which this book emerged. Thank you for being a creative ally to novelists!

I honour the skilled beta readers who critiqued an early draft of my manuscript to help me make it so much stronger. They are:

- Dawn Dicker, content strategist and writer.
- Debbie Young, author of two cosy mystery series: Sophie Sayers and Gemma Lamb.
- Donita Bundy, author of the Armour of Light urban fantasy series.
- Lorraine Page, professional editor and emerging author of fiction and non-fiction.
- Molly Greene, author of the Gen Delacourt mystery series.

Seeking a new editor for this book was a nerve-wracking process. April Bennett has been a gift, picking up sneaky typos, corralling commas, and suggesting manuscript solutions with intelligence, insight, warmth and humour.

To Marg and Al: thank you for generously opening your home so I could have a writing retreat close to the Reef.

I honour my mother, Barbara Pollard, who encouraged and assisted me throughout the entire research, writing and publication process; it's been very hard at times, Mum, and your assistance has been precious to me.

Finally, my heartfelt thanks to the Creator, whose vast and beautiful imagination resulted in this most extraordinary natural wonder that continues to take my breath away, as well as all the astounding creatures that live upon the Great Barrier Reef.

POISON BAY

Wild Crimes Mysteries Book 1
Second revised edition
Paperback: 978-0-6482672-9-4
Also in ebook and Large Print

"The Maori call this place Ata Whenua—Shadow Land."

Television reporter Callie Brown likes safe places with good coffee. But she joins friends from the past on a trek into New Zealand's most brutal wilderness, in the hope of healing a broken heart.

What she doesn't know is that someone wants them all dead.

Lost in every sense of the word, the hikers' primal instincts erupt. Surrounded by people who have harboured secrets for a decade, Callie must choose the right ally if she doesn't want to be the next to die...

"Taut suspense and lush descriptions." LITERARY INKLINGS
"Satisfyingly insightful." MARGARET NEWMAN
"By turns shocking, satisfying, tragic, and poignant, but ultimately life-affirming." DEBBIE YOUNG, *Sophie Sayers mysteries*
"So far this is my favourite fiction read of the year."
CLARE O'BEARA, *Amazon UK Top 500 Reviewer*

VARUNA FELLOWSHIP WINNER, IPPY SILVER MEDALLIST

Two perilous stories of the Australian outback.
Two old friends heading towards a devastating reunion… if they can just survive the weekend.

Television reporter Callie Brown is far from her Sydney apartment, armed only with silk taffeta and stilettos for a glitzy awards night on the edge of the desert. Her key assignment: to make her famous partner look good. Will she yield to his demands and ignore the desperation in the eyes of a stranger who reaches out for help? More than her relationship is at risk; in the ruthless world of the gemfields, all that glitters might just get you killed.

In the lush Daintree rainforest at the pointy end of Australia, Jack Metcalf is hiking solo, getting in touch with his spiritual side—and a few leeches. When a cry pierces the tropical night, a cascade of traumatic events is unleashed. He will have to think fast and act even faster if he wants to save lives… including his own.

This pocket-sized book introduces the Wild Crimes Mysteries: when bad things happen in beautiful places.

Download the ebook of TOXIC DELUSION for free
when you subscribe to Belinda Pollard's email list
at belindapollard.com/subscribe

DOGGED OPTIMISM: Lessons in Joy from a Disaster-Prone Dog

Paperback: 978-0-9942098-3-2

Also available in ebook and Large Print. *Foreword Bronze Award. NextGen Indie Finalist*

In this humorous and uplifting read, Belinda recounts how her scruffy Aussie terrier Killarney has helped her through the toughest of days – and taught her to make the most of life.

Killarney is not afraid of anything that sub-tropical Australia can throw at her: venomous creatures, cancer, very large dogs. She becomes Belinda's furry comforter and cheer squad through job loss, grief, and failed romance.

If you've ever loved a dog or needed a laugh, you'll be inspired by Killarney's motto: grab life by the throat and shake every last drop of joy out of it. Wrestle it, if you have to.

"Dogged Optimism is an accomplished, inspiring piece of writing that had me completely hooked from the first page to the unexpected and gratifying end." GILL PAVEY, *thebookreviewers.com*

"A delightful read." MARIANNE WHEELAGHAN, *The Blue Suitcase*

"Evocative, humorous tale." MOLLY GREENE, *The Gen Delacourt Mysteries*

"Will charm you with its window into life Down Under." DAWN DICKER, *Writer & Content Strategist*

"A heart-warming tale of one woman's special bond with her four-legged friend." TANYA ARNOLD, *Pupcake Queen*

FOREWORD BRONZE AWARD, NEXTGEN INDIE FINALIST